THE GOOD SAMARITAN

ALSO BY JOHN MARRS

The One

When You Disappeared

Welcome To Wherever You Are

THE GOOD SAMARITAN

JOHN MARRS

THOMAS & MERCER

This is a work of fiction. Names, characters, organizations, places, events, and incidents are either products of the author's imagination or are used fictitiously. Any resemblance to actual persons, living or dead, or actual events is purely coincidental.

Published by Thomas & Mercer, Seattle

This edition contains editorial revisions.

www.apub.com

ISBN-13: 9781503903364
ISBN-10: 1503903362

Cover design by Mark Swan

Printed in the United States of America

'Service to others is the rent you pay for your room here on earth.'

—Muhammad Ali

'While seeking revenge, dig two graves – one for yourself.'

—Douglas Horton

PROLOGUE

'Where are you?' My voice was calm and my tone measured as I spoke softly into the receiver.

'My taxi has just pulled up in the car park and I'm trying to give away my loose change.'

'Why?' I asked.

'Because I don't have any need for it.'

'I understand.' I rolled my eyes. It felt like a waste of time and it concerned me that it might be a delaying tactic. But I couldn't pressure him. 'You do what you feel is for the best, and remember,' I continued, 'I'm with you every step of the way.'

I heard him mumble something to the driver, then he exited the taxi, closing the door behind him. I assumed it was raining lightly, because every few seconds I heard the rubber wiper blades squeak as they arched across the windscreen before the cab pulled away.

'How are we doing?' I asked, purposefully using 'we' instead of 'I' to emphasise that we were in this together, if not side by side then certainly in spirit. It was not my choice of location and I wondered if, once he saw its magnitude, it might give him second thoughts. If that were the case, I'd have to accept his decision. It had taken time for me to get in the right headspace, but now that I was, I wanted him to see it through to the end. And I'd make sure to remind him why he was there and how far we had come.

He read my mind. 'Don't worry,' he said, 'I've not had a change of heart.'

I let out a sigh of relief.

'Really,' he continued, 'I'm in a good place and I'm ready for this. Now that I'm here, now that I can see what's before me, I know one hundred and ten per cent that it's the right thing to do.'

I believed him. I don't think he'd ever lied to me, because he'd never had a reason to. He'd told me many times that he was more honest with me than with anyone he had ever known, and I was proud to hear it.

'Can you see her yet?' I asked. 'She's driving a red Vauxhall Astra. Registration number V987—'

'. . . THG. Yes, she's just flashed her lights at me. It feels like we're in a spy film and you've arranged for me to pass her secret documents.' He gave a nervous laugh and I pretended to laugh back.

'OK, let me give her a call,' I said. 'Stay where you are for now. We don't want to scare her.'

My number was automatically withheld when I dialled her. She answered after seven rings, too many for my liking.

'Hi there,' I began softly. 'How are we doing?'

'I'm not sure,' she replied. Her voice lacked the confidence of his. I'd accompanied enough people in her situation to recognise a heightened state of anxiety. I'd have to tread carefully.

'It's good to hear you,' I said soothingly. 'Did your journey go well? Did you find the place okay?'

'I got here an hour ago, so I had a cup of tea in a café up the road.'

This was another red flag. She'd had time on her own to think.

'Is there anything you want to talk about before we start?' I asked.

She hesitated. 'I'm really sorry, but now I'm here I'm starting to think I might not be doing the right thing anymore,' she replied.

I gritted my teeth. I was not going to let it end like this. I needed to reaffirm her sense of purpose.

'It's about the baby, isn't it?' I asked gently.

'Yes.'

'You're worried that you're making a selfish decision.'

'Yes,' she said again, this time in a barely audible voice.

I sank back into my chair. 'That's perfectly understandable, but you need to realise this isn't you talking, it's your hormones. They're giving you a false sense of what might be possible; making you think that everything could be all right in the end if you just give it time. Listen to someone who has learned from experience. When that child is born, things are only going to get so much worse for you. They'll up your medication so that your life is even more of a blur than it is now. You won't be fit for purpose as a mother, and the chemicals you've put into your body already are going to have a knock-on effect on your baby. It will grow up exactly like you, with exactly the same pain and problems you have; it'll be history repeating itself. Do you really want to be responsible for all that? Unlike you, I can see things clearly and I know that is exactly what is going to happen. Your baby doesn't stand a chance in this world. And deep down you know that too, don't you?'

'You're right,' she spluttered, no longer trying to fight back her sobs.

I'd been bad cop, now I needed to be good cop again.

'You know, I've been thinking about you all night and day,' I continued. 'I know how far you've come since you found me all those weeks ago. I'm so proud of you for your courage and strength. You know that, don't you?'

'Yes,' she replied. She didn't sound as convinced as I'd hoped. It was time to step it up a gear.

'I've been thinking about your family, too. They're very lucky to have someone in their lives like you, someone who is so selfless and so courageous. These are rare traits and I know that at first, it's going to be difficult for everyone to understand, but in time they're going to realise you loved them so much that you put their needs above your own. You've told me on so many occasions that you're never going to be the wife your husband needs. But that's not *your* fault, it's *his* for putting you on a pedestal. *He* has done this to you. Just keep reminding yourself of why you came looking for me in the first place. Together, we explored every avenue before you decided this was the only route that made sense. You are moving on and allowing everyone else you love to do the same. And I admire that so much.'

I'd spent so long repeating the same message, week after week, conversation after conversation, slowly reinforcing the belief that there was only one way forward. He, however, had required less work. There was no middle ground with him. Things were either black or white and never grey. He told me once I was like a rope that had pulled him from the quicksand and then set him on the right path.

'You're right,' she sniffed. 'Thank you.'

'Okay then. Well, blow your nose, take a deep breath and we'll do this together. Start by opening the door and walking towards him.' I tried to imagine I was there with them. 'Now, can you carefully describe what you're seeing in front of you?'

'I think that's him waiting for me,' she said. 'He's smiling. And behind him the sun is trying to make its way through the clouds. It's cold, but not freezing.'

I heard the crunch of the gravel under her feet, the pitter-patter of January rain bouncing off the shoulders of her overcoat, and the squawking seagulls above. I could almost smell the salty sea air around them. I switched telephone line to his.

'Hi,' I began. 'She's coming towards you now, but she's a little more anxious than you are. You will look after her, won't you?'

'Of course,' he replied, more assured than I'd ever heard him.

As they came face-to-face for the first time, I imagined them smiling at one another. I opened up both phone lines and heard a muffled, scratching sound of fabric against fabric, as if they were embracing. I'd told her to wear a coat big enough to hide her baby bump. The last thing I needed was for it to spook him now that we were so close.

I felt my skin burning under my shirt and adrenaline coursing through the sixty thousand miles of veins in my body, edging me towards a kind of euphoria.

Bide your time. Keep a firm grip on yourself, because too much can still go wrong.

I pictured them standing there, two perfect strangers who hadn't needed to speak to communicate. They were united in a common purpose and I had brought them together. Their lives would be forever connected because of me. I didn't know whether to laugh or cry.

'Can you both hear me?' I asked them.

'Yes,' they replied in unison.

'If you're still comfortable with it, I'd like to stay with you for as long as possible. So, when you're ready, each take a deep breath, then take hold of each other's hand and start to walk. No matter how tough it gets or how heavy your legs might feel, hold on to each other for support. Don't turn around and don't stop. We can do this together.'

'Thank you,' he said. 'Thank you for understanding me. You've been incredible.'

'It's been my pleasure,' I replied. In the past when I'd reached this point, I'd been so much stronger. But he'd been too big a part of my life for this not to hurt. I balled my fists as our journey came to an end. Now it was their turn to continue the story.

I closed my eyes tightly. I inhaled and exhaled in time with their breaths as they made their way further and further from the car park. The gravel faded into grass and the rain fell more heavily. She began to weep, but I was convinced they were happy tears. I was sure he was clasping her hand in his just that little bit tighter, offering her the strength I so admired in him.

And then—

Nothing.

Nothing but the sound of their last breaths and the coastal wind howling through their phones as they fell five hundred and thirty feet into the water below. And as their bodies sank and their souls soared, I bit my bottom lip hard until I tasted blood. It was over.

I gave myself a few moments before reluctantly replacing the receiver in the cradle. I took a tissue from my desk drawer, blew my nose, uncurled my toes and thought about my anchor until calmness once again took control of my body.

I lifted my head briefly and glanced around the room to reassure myself that no one beyond the confines of my booth had heard me.

'Are you all right?' Mary's honeyed voice came from the side, making me jump. She shuffled from the kitchen to my desk, sensing something was wrong. The years had not been kind to her face.

'I'm fine,' I replied.

'Was it one of *those* calls?'

'Yes.'

'They didn't do it while you were talking to them, did they?'

I nodded and she patted my arm with her hand. My skin prickled, as it did when anyone touched me uninvited. Such gestures had never comforted me.

'I'm so sorry,' Mary continued. 'You hope that when they call us, all it'll take is a friendly voice and someone to listen and it'll put them off ending their lives for that little bit longer, don't you?'

'Yes,' I lied.

'And I know we're not supposed to talk them out of it or even offer an opinion, but it's hard when you just want people to see that life is worth living.'

'It certainly is,' I nodded. 'I wish everyone could see the beauty of the world through our eyes.'

It was a busy afternoon and there weren't enough volunteers to man the helplines, so Mary made her way back to her corner of the office. When the red light on my phone began flashing to indicate another call, I cleared my throat and answered it, as required, within five rings.

'Good afternoon,' I began, 'you've reached the End of the Line, this is Laura speaking. May I ask your name?'

PART ONE

LAURA

CHAPTER ONE

FOUR MONTHS AFTER DAVID

I heard their muffled chatter as I made my way up the staircase and towards the door.

Inside End of the Line's call room, I counted five heads, all sitting in their individual booths. Some propped themselves up on their elbows as they sat listening to callers through their headsets; others casually leaned back in their chairs with receivers held to their ears. One doodled triangles in a newspaper crossword grid.

I was early for my shift and waved cheerfully at Kevin and Zoe, who were listening to their respective callers. I pointed to the cake tin under my arm then towards the kitchen. Mary, the eldest of the volunteers at the charity, sat in a corner booth at the front, her knitting needles moving almost silently at full throttle as she spoke into a headset. Today's colour of wool was as grey as the hair on her head.

I made my way into the poor excuse for a kitchenette and placed my lunchbox with the remains of last night's pasta bake inside the fridge. I tossed away the mounting number of out-of-date plastic milk bottles and removed the lid from the cake tin so that everyone could help themselves to my freshly iced cupcakes. There were more than enough for the afternoon shifts to enjoy; any that remained could be shared by those on evenings and nights.

I opened the sash window to allow some fresh May air in and the stale second-floor funk out. Then, back inside the call room, I plucked my notebook from my bag and sought out my favoured booth at the back. Our desks hadn't been officially allocated to us, so we couldn't stake a claim on one over another. But there was an unspoken hierarchy that said those who'd worked there for longer should be allowed the spot they felt the most comfortable in. I opted for the most private spot, by the boarded-up Victorian fireplace. There, behind the partition, my soft, calming telephone voice couldn't be heard anywhere else in the room. Not that we ever admitted to listening in to each other's calls, but it's normal to be nosy once in a while.

For four and a half years I'd stared through the very same window across the rooftops of Northampton, and wondered who might be the first person I'd lift my receiver to today. The later – evening – shift was usually when things became more interesting. For the more vulnerable out there, once the darkness falls, so do their barriers. Night-time is their enemy, because with fewer visible distractions there's more opportunity to dwell on how hopeless their lives have become. It's when they reach out for somebody's hand.

We are supposed to treat every caller the same way, with kindness, respect and professionalism. Being listened to makes them feel valued, but it's unrealistic to think you can help – or even like – them all. Once they begin recounting their woes, there are some you take an instant dislike to and others you can see yourself in. Some you want to grab by the wrists, dig your fingernails in deeply until you draw blood and shake some sense into. Others you'll offer a non-judgemental shoulder to cry upon.

But when it comes down to it, almost every volunteer in that room is there for the same purpose – to be someone a caller can unload their problems onto.

And then there's me. I have my own agenda.

'You brought cupcakes!' said Kevin enthusiastically. He began to peel away the paper case from the sweet treat as he approached my desk.

'Remind me to get your shirt out of the car before I leave,' I replied.

'Careful now, or they'll start talking about us,' he said, and gave me a wink.

I pretended to laugh along with him. 'I've sewn the button back on the cuff and starched the collar.'

'Where would we be without you, Laura?'

'And don't forget it's your wedding anniversary at the weekend, so pick up a card and some flowers. And not those cheap petrol station ones. Order a bouquet online.'

'Will do.' He gave me a peck on the cheek and I rolled my eyes with false modesty. 'You're like the office mum,' he added.

I liked being thought of as the maternal type. To them, I was helpful, inoffensive and indispensable, and that suited me down to the ground. Because when you're not considered to be a threat, you can get away with much, much more.

CHAPTER TWO

The first thirty minutes of my four-hour shift were relatively quiet, so I flicked through a folder of photographs on my mobile . . . the ones my husband Tony didn't allow me to display in the house.

I removed the silver-plated fountain pen from my bag and opened my notebook. I use it to jot down basic details of each caller, including their name, a summary of their problems and a few questions to include if there is a lull in the conversation. The caller is always in control of the chat, or at least that's what I lead mine to believe.

End of the Line's mandate is clear and simple, and it is one of the many things that encouraged me to offer it my time. It believes that everyone has the right to live or die on his or her own terms. Provided it isn't under duress and doesn't hurt anyone else, we believe it's absolutely their decision to end their lives and we won't try to talk them out of it. In fact, during our training we are given the emotional tools to be there right up until their last breath, if that's what the caller requests. We listen, we don't act.

The red light on my landline flashed with urgency. Every time I answer a call I remember what my mentor, Mary, told me during my induction: 'You could be the last voice this person ever hears. Make them believe that you care.'

'Good afternoon, you've reached the End of the Line, this is Laura speaking,' I began in the same friendly manner I had countless times before. 'May I ask your name?'

I was greeted with silence, but that wasn't uncommon. Callers may go to the effort of dialling our number, but most don't plan what they're going to say once their call is answered. It's my duty to put them at ease and coax their worries out of them. Sometimes just hearing the calm in my voice is enough to take the edge off their fears.

'Take your time,' I assured the caller. 'I have as long as you need.'

'Things are really bad at the moment,' she eventually began. Her voice was deep – decades of high-tar cigarettes deep.

'Well, let's talk it through, shall we?' I offered. 'What would you like me to call you?'

She paused for long enough to think of a pseudonym. 'Carole,' she replied. It was impossible to tell her age through her smoke-damaged vocal cords.

'Okay, Carole,' I continued, writing her name down, 'when you say things are awful, what aspects of your life are causing you difficulty?'

'Money and my marriage,' she said. 'I was made redundant in March and I can't find work. My Jobseeker's Allowance barely covers the food bills, I'm four months behind on the council rent and my husband has a chronic lung condition that's slowly killing him.'

I'd liked to have asked how much her forty-a-day habit was helping his lungs but I stuck to the script. It's not that I'm anti-smoking – one of the many things my colleagues and family don't know about me is my penchant for a cigarette on the way home from a shift. But I'm always in control.

I made bullet-point notes on what she was telling me. What I really wanted to learn was just how close to the edge her circumstances were pushing her. Why was she calling us today and how far would she go to find a resolution? However, I couldn't bulldoze my way into her headspace; she needed encouraging.

'That does sound like a lot to be coping with at the moment, Carole,' I replied. 'It's times like this that test us the most, isn't it?'

'Yeah, but I'm pissed off with being tested. I need a way out.'

My interest flickered. 'In what way?'

I heard a flint wheel turn and a flame flicker to life as she sparked up a cigarette. 'I feel like a right bitch for saying this out loud . . .' She paused to inhale the smoke.

'I'm here to listen, not to judge you.'

'I've just reached breaking point. I can't carry on.' Carole's voice cracked before she burst into a deep, chesty cough.

'Start by telling me what you mean when you say you "need a way out".'

'I've been seeing another fella and I want to leave my husband, but I don't know how to do it.'

I rolled my eyes, and it was all I could do to stop myself from hanging up on her. We're allowed to end abusive, sexual or aggressive calls. Sadly, being as common as muck wasn't a good enough excuse.

Carole wasn't looking to end her life in the physical sense; she wanted to start a brand-new one without the baggage of the first. For a moment, I'd thought I might have struck gold, but answering a call at random from someone who's serious about wanting to die is like finding a pearl in an oyster. I get four, maybe five in a year – if I'm lucky – but this year had been exceptionally good so far. However, Carole was not that person.

I did what I was trained to do and let her cry and moan until there was nothing left to get off her chest. Eventually she hung up – and without a word of a thank you, I might add.

Then I waited patiently for the next call, because there is always a next call. Someone, somewhere in the country, is always having a worse time than you. The expectation, the thrill of picking up that telephone and never knowing what direction the conversation might take: the next call is everything.

I live for the next call.

CHAPTER THREE

'Hello?' I shouted as I pushed open the front door and pulled the key from the lock. 'Can someone give me a hand with the shopping, please?'

There was no answer, but that wasn't a guarantee the house was empty. The mention of shopping bags wasn't the best way to lure two children and a husband out of hiding to help, unless the bags came from H&M or Zara, or a sports shop.

I made three trips before they were all placed neatly across the wooden kitchen worktops. Each bag was below the wall cupboard or above the drawer where its contents were to be placed.

Bieber the cat, an ugly grey-and-white thing with a deep coat of soft fur and a hiss like a coiled cobra, belonged to my younger daughter Alice. He lay stretched by the bifold doors, basking in the sun's warming rays streaming through the glass. He turned his head to see who was disturbing his slumber and made some guttural rasp when he recognised me. I rasped back. I was the one who fed him and emptied his litter tray, but that wasn't enough to earn his respect and still he detested me.

When I was sure I was alone, I flicked the radio on. A DJ introduced an unfamiliar song, so I switched to a channel playing only music from the 1980s – the era of my childhood. Several callers to End of the Line had told me that my voice was like one of those late-night broadcasters on commercial stations who only ever play ballads. Apparently it was 'soothing'.

George Michael was admitting to kissing a fool before Madonna began urging me to dance for inspiration. Most of the time I didn't listen closely to the songs; background noise in an empty house was enough to stop me from visiting dark spaces in my head that it did me little good returning to.

With tins and packets placed inside the cupboards – the labels facing forward, and arranged in accordance of light colours to dark – I took a bag of frozen chicken breasts and stuffed them into a crammed fridge to defrost for tomorrow night. I unboxed a Victoria sponge, stuck my knife into a jar of jam and smeared some around the sides, then put a little more icing sugar on the top left-hand side than the right to make it look less perfect. I held up and examined a pair of jeans belonging to Zoe, one of my younger colleagues, who'd asked me to replace a broken zip. 'No problem,' I'd told her. 'Give me a couple of days.'

To the End of the Line team I was a superwoman, a devoted mum-of-three who could turn her hand to any task, from repairing a jacket pocket to reupholstering a chair. But I knew little about baking or sewing – that's what supermarkets and tailors were for. And no one I worked with needed to know that I outsourced my pastries and repairs.

A yawn caught me by surprise – it was only approaching four o'clock but it felt like much later in the day. The kids would have been let out of school by now, and Tony finished work in a couple of hours. So I poured myself a large glass of red wine while I had the opportunity and sank into the armchair next to the bifold doors overlooking the patio and garden. I gazed out across the lawn, beyond the beds of brightly coloured lupins and peonies, towards the wooden fence and the flat grassy playing fields.

When the first of the children arrived two years into our marriage, Tony often reminded me to make the most of my 'me' time where and when I could get it. Now they were older, I had too much 'me' time to fill, especially in this house, the one he'd made us move to. I'd been more than content in our last home, but Tony was insistent that once we made it onto the property ladder, we must keep climbing.

I inhaled the floral scent coming from a jasmine reed diffuser and glanced around the open-plan room. We'd knocked the kitchen, living and dining rooms into one large living space. I'd overseen the landscaping of the garden, the internal remodelling, the replastering and redecorating, and I knew every inch of the place like the back of my hand. Everything was just how Tony had envisaged it. Yet it felt alien to me.

'We'll only need to stay here a couple of years,' he'd explained. 'Once all the work is done and we can make a tidy profit, we can move on.'

But we hadn't moved on. It had been three years and I was still sitting in the same living area.

I finished my wine and gave a sly smile as I stepped on the cat's tail, causing him to spit and run. Upstairs, the bathroom door and the kids' bedroom doors were shut, so I made sure they were ajar. They knew there were no closed doors in my house.

I peered into Alice's room first. Her walls were still adorned with pink, sparkly paper and covered in posters of pop stars and TV personalities, like most nine-year-olds' rooms were. But she was growing up fast and I was already feeling the apron strings tugging as she began to pull away. It wouldn't be long before her thoughts became polluted with boys, make-up, and clothes that were tight in all the wrong places.

Effie's bedroom showed the difference in their ages. Pictures of YouTube and Instagram stars I didn't know the names of were affixed around a mirror and taped to her door in collages. She'd printed out photos of her friends, too, all of them featuring small gangs of overly made-up girls sucking their cheeks in so tightly they must've met in the centre of their mouths and pouting. Tummies were also held in, to make them look even skinnier than fourteen-year-old girls already are.

Effie's confidence had grown and she was aware she was beginning to catch the eyes of boys her own age, along with men who had no business looking at young girls. Once upon a time, they used to look at me like that. Now it was as if I didn't exist. I couldn't help but hate her a little for it. She was like a vampire, sucking the beauty and vibrancy from me and keeping it for herself.

She was also keeping secrets from me, so I had to learn about my daughter's private life by other means instead. I sat on her bed, switched on my mobile phone and clicked on the Facebook app. She still hadn't changed her login password so I checked her inbox. Most of the messages were from her friends. Occasionally boys' names appeared but the subjects were innocuous, with the exception of one.

She seemed keen on a boy called Matt, who was pictured behind the wheel of a small blue car that he'd obviously spent time and money trying to make look sporty. In another, he'd sent Effie his photo, lifting his T-shirt and revealing his bare belly. I remembered when Tony's stomach had been as flat and smooth as that. I'd watched him in his swimming shorts from the shallow end of the school pool, imagining how it might feel to run my fingertips across him. *Like velvet.* When he caught me staring, he grinned and I swiftly turned my head to hide my reddening face. But the way he looked at me . . . the way he tilted his head, the way his eyes widened, the way the corners of his lips unfurled when he smiled . . . I knew that if I remained patient, he'd approach me and eventually he'd be mine. I always get what I set my sights on.

Effie had matched Matt's picture like for like, only with her bra poking out from under her rolled-up T-shirt. I bristled.

The door to the third bedroom was the only one I left closed. One day I might venture in there, but not yet. I wasn't ready yet.

I changed from my skirt and blouse into a T-shirt and a pair of jeans. I'd only bought them recently and I was struggling to button them up. And when I finally managed it, I looked down in dismay at my paunchy stomach perched upon the waistband like a fat pigeon bowing the branch of a tree. My thrice-weekly hot yoga classes and two swims weren't doing to my figure what the posters on the gym wall promised. I wondered if there was any part of my body that Tony still found attractive. If there was, he'd never thought to mention it.

I glanced in the mirror at the prematurely ageing woman looking back at me. My dark roots were beginning to show through my highlights, and my once-prominent cheekbones appeared to have slipped down my face to create an avalanche of jowls. My light-brown eyes with their youthful shine didn't belong to this face.

I'd hoped the stress of ovarian cancer and chemotherapy had only damaged where people couldn't see, but I'd been kidding myself. I was dead on the inside and decaying on the outside. Even now, over a year later, the impact was still revealing itself through my face. It wouldn't be long before I'd be forced to ask one of the plastic school-gate mums for the number of their Botox and fillers clinic. The injections plus tooth veneers and the contact lenses for my nearsightedness meant there'd be very little left of the original me soon. Maybe Tony would prefer that.

I poured my third and fourth tablets of the day from the bottle of aspirin I kept in the bathroom cabinet, and swallowed them without water. Tony had no idea what the bottle actually contained – slimming tablets not approved for sale in the UK by the Medicines and Healthcare products Regulatory Agency. I'd ordered them from an online Eastern European pharmacy instead. They bound my fat and helped me lose weight quickly, but the side effects were crippling stomach cramps and oily diarrhoea. It was a small price to pay if it meant Tony might look at me again like he'd done that day in the swimming pool.

By the time I reached the bottom of the stairs the paperboy was cramming the local newspaper through the letterbox. I hurried my way through it, past the news and the property pull-outs until I found the pages I was searching for.

The hairs on my arms prickled into life when I saw Chantelle's face for the first time. She was close to how I'd pictured her – plain, gaunt, angular, with a scrunchie keeping her scraped-back hair in place. I tore out the page, made a mental note of the date and placed it inside my bag. Then I waited patiently with another glass of wine for the time to pass until the conversation of three people I barely knew returned.

CHAPTER FOUR

FOUR MONTHS, TWO WEEKS AFTER DAVID

I removed the Kindle from my bag and placed it on the desk in my booth.

I flicked through the library to choose from one of a dozen eBooks I'd downloaded but had yet to start reading. As a rule, novels bore me. The concentration it takes to remember what you've read and who is who as you swipe from one page to the next is arduous. I much prefer downloading a television programme and watching it on my phone instead. But Janine, our branch manager, frowned upon us doing that, one of many petty little dislikes she'd made us aware of since she'd taken charge seven months earlier.

I'd barely made it past the prologue of a psychological thriller before the first call of my evening arrived. I cleared my throat and slipped into character like an actor preparing to take to the stage.

So much can be won or lost in the first words a caller hears. Appear overenthusiastic and they'll think you're too upbeat to empathise with them. Sound too matter-of-fact and you risk appearing like an authoritarian about to berate them. I like to think I keep the right balance.

It was a teenage girl who spoke; she'd found herself pregnant and had no idea how to tell her parents. I listened sympathetically, asked my open-ended questions in all the correct places and quietly wondered how I'd react if Effie ever found herself in that kind of trouble. I'd insist on a termination, but she'd probably keep the baby just to be awkward. The girl on the phone cried a little. I pretended to care and by the end of our chat she decided she would test the family waters by telling an aunty she was close to of her predicament.

Next, it was my turn to get 'the masturbator'. Once a week, usually on a Thursday, he was compelled to call us and audibly pleasure himself. He wasn't bothered if it was a man or woman who answered, because by the time we answered, he wouldn't be far from climaxing. We were supposed to hang up as soon as we were aware of what he was doing, but tonight I was feeling generous, so I told him how horny it made me feel and let him complete the task in hand before wishing him a good evening.

After two immediate hang-ups, I was approaching the end of my shift and anticipating a gruelling hot yoga class. I contemplated ignoring the call at first as I didn't want to be late, but I picked up.

'I've not called somewhere like this before. I don't know where to begin,' a male voice began.

'Well, let's start with a name. What shall I call you?'

'Steven,' he replied. It came to him too quickly for it to be a pseudonym. I made a note of it.

I placed him in his twenties; he was softly spoken and his accent was local. He did little to disguise his nerves.

'It's nice to talk to you, Steven. Can I ask what made you decide to call us this evening?'

'I'm not sure. I – I feel like I haven't got . . . anyone. I don't think I want to be . . . *here* . . . anymore.'

He ticked box number one all by himself, which made my job a little easier. 'Well, it's great that you've called,' I said. I'd allow my instinct the usual five minutes to decide whether he was genuine or seeking attention. 'Tell me about the people who love and care about you. Who do you have in your life who falls into that category?'

He paused for a moment to think. 'Nobody really,' he replied and let out a deep breath. Saying it aloud was clearly a pivotal moment for him. 'I've got no one at all.'

'Do you have anyone you'd call a friend?'

'No.'

That was box number two ticked.

'I'm sure it's difficult when you are completely alone in the world.'

'It's shit.'

'Are you working at the moment? Are there any opportunities to build up personal relationships in your career?'

'Not really. Sometimes days can pass and I realise I haven't had a proper conversation in almost a week.'

Box number three ticked – the fewer people in his personal or working life the better. I was glad I'd answered his call after all.

'A week is a long time not to have a proper conversation with someone,' I replied, empathising with his situation and keeping him on point. 'Have you seen your doctor and told them how you're feeling?'

'Yes, and she put me on antidepressants.'

'And how have they worked for you?'

'It's been four months and I still don't feel there's anything to get up for in the morning. Sometimes I think I'd be better off just saving them all up and . . . you know . . .'

'Sometimes or often?'

'Often,' he whispered, so quietly I could barely hear him. It was like he was ashamed of his suicidal thoughts.

Box four usually took much longer than this to tick, which made my job a little easier. *I might have something to work with here*, I thought.

I scanned the room. Zoe was playing a game on her mobile phone while speaking into her headset; Sanjay's legs were jiggling up and down as he listened to a caller; and Mary was drinking something from a thermal flask that smelled like toxic soup. Nobody was paying me the slightest bit of attention in my corner.

Inside my bag, I fished for a second notebook, the one used solely for callers I might be able to help in my own unique way. Inside it, I kept detailed notes on everything they told me. Later, I'd bring them up again as conversation points to reinforce that I'd been listening and I understood. I wrote Steven's name on a fresh page and underlined it.

'You don't need to be embarrassed, Steven,' I replied. 'We've all thought about ending our lives at some time or another. Have you ever tried to do it before?'

'No. But I did plan it out once.'

'You planned it out once?' I was careful to mirror his language, making him aware I'd listened and of how seriously I took his admission. 'Can I ask what you had in mind?'

'I printed out my bank details and bills and left them in envelopes on my desk, along with the passwords for accounts and deeds to the flat for the police to find. I'd plotted out the route to a bridge in the countryside over the railway line, near the village of Kelney. Do you know it?'

'Yes, I do.'

'There's a gap where the railings have rusted so you can squeeze through to get to the tracks. I made it halfway down the bank and waited for ages for a train. I was just going to jump in front of it and that'd be it. But it took so long for one to arrive that I talked myself out of it.'

'I see. While you were waiting for that train, did you wonder how death might feel?'

'It won't feel like anything, because after death there is nothing.'

'Will it bring you peace?'

'My life hasn't, so I can only hope.'

Everything I'd asked, he'd already asked himself. He hadn't made his decision rashly.

I'd become increasingly frustrated by ditherers of late. There were too many callers who all-too-casually threw around suicidal threats, but when it came down to it they were too gutless to do anything about it.

So I needed to push and pull Steven to reinforce how serious he was. The 'fear-then-relief technique', that's what psychologists call it. I lowered my voice, held the phone closer to my mouth and launched into a well-rehearsed but selectively used speech.

'Perhaps, deep down, you aren't serious about ending your life,' I began. 'Maybe it's a cry for help? I get plenty of calls from people who tell me they want to die, but when it gets down to the nitty-gritty, all they're really doing is just feeling sorry for themselves. Are you one of those people, Steven? Are you just trapped in a cycle of self-pity? Are you so deep into it that you don't realise nothing is going to change unless you find the courage to do something about it yourself? Because if you don't take charge, for the rest of your life – maybe another forty, fifty years – the pain you're feeling right now, the pain that's so bad that it led you to call me, is only going to get worse. This – how you're feeling right now – is going to be it for you. Can you live like that, Steven? I know I couldn't.'

I'll only use those words if I come into contact with a potential candidate, and often my directness catches them unawares. They'll have called expecting me to be sympathetic towards them and perhaps reassure them everything's going to be okay in the end. But I'm not that person. I know from personal experience that everything isn't always okay in the end. Often, it'll get much worse than it is right now. And sometimes it's completely unbearable. But I can make it stop. They just have to trust me.

'I – I – I'm not a timewaster, honestly,' Steven stuttered, taken aback. 'It's something I've thought long and hard about and it's what I want, but if I can't do it, that must make me a coward, right?'

'No, Steven, you're not a coward. You called me today and that makes you courageous. Maybe you just chose the wrong day when you were waiting for that train. It happens to plenty of people. Just remember, we're here for you in whatever capacity you want us to be.'

'You mean to listen to me?'

He was fishing. I'd let him sniff around the bait before I withdrew it. 'If that's all you want from me, then yes.'

'What if . . . What if I need . . . What if I decide . . .' His voice went quiet and then faded away.

What Steven needed was someone to tell him death was the right choice. But first I needed to know for certain what he wanted from me. I'm not supposed to finish a sentence, even if I know what they're going to say, but I make exceptions for potential candidates.

'Are you calling to tell me you want to end your life and are looking for my support in doing it?'

'I . . . I suppose I am.'

Once a candidate thinks they understand me, I'll wrong-foot them by going back to how I was when I first answered their call. I trust no one until I know just how desperate they are.

'End of the Line is an impartial, non-judgemental space,' I began. 'We are here to listen to you. We won't try to talk you out of anything you decide to do, we just ask that you talk to us first and explore all your options before you take such a huge step. Do you understand that?'

'Yes,' Steven replied. A silence hung awkwardly between us. 'But . . .'

'But?' I repeated.

'But if I wanted to, you know, go ahead with it, would you . . . ?'

'Would I what, Steven? What would you like me to do?'

He became quiet again and I sensed his increasing anxiety. 'I'm sorry, I have to go,' he said before the line went dead.

I tapped my fingers on the desk and examined my fingernails. There was a slight chip in the burgundy varnish on my index finger. I'd need to make an appointment to get them repainted.

I wasn't worried about Steven calling back. Of course he would, and when he did seek me out again, he'd have shown me he'd put in the effort. You can't just contact End of the Line's number and reach me, as we have no direct lines. There are ninety-four of us, all volunteering for different shifts, and it's pot luck who you're put through to.

I remembered how David had kept calling back until he found me. Once we'd built up a rapport, I gave him my shift timetable so we could speak more regularly. We'd chat three or four times a week, and not just about our arrangement; sometimes we'd discuss world events, our days, or the countries we'd like to travel to.

And as he spoke, I'd close my eyes and imagine we were sitting on opposite sides of a table in a café abroad somewhere; we'd have spent the day sightseeing, and in the evening, we'd be making the most of the balmy Mediterranean weather and eating at a bistro, enjoying a fish supper, drinking Chianti and chatting like friends do. Then reality would reassert itself and I'd realise none of that could ever happen.

All these months later and I still longed to hear his voice again. I wondered if that feeling would ever completely pass. David had understood me as much as I'd understood him – but my presence in his life wasn't enough to encourage him to stay. I wasn't enough to make him choose life.

My stomach began to knot.

Remember your anchor, Laura. Remember your anchor.

I considered what Steven and I might accomplish. He'd made plans, he'd got his affairs in order, and he'd chosen and been to a location. All he needed was me. I had a good feeling about him.

I wanted to hear him die.

CHAPTER FIVE

I double-checked the time printed in the advert I'd torn from the local newspaper, and glanced at my watch. It was already ten minutes later than advertised. I hated tardiness.

My restless eyes fixed upon a group of young women who were also waiting for the doors to open. I patted the creases from my jacket to make myself more presentable. I needn't have bothered – by the look of them, I was the only one to have made any effort. And because I wasn't wearing running shoes or a hoodie, I stuck out like a sore thumb.

I looked towards my Mini and spotted a familiar figure further down the road. He was perched on a plastic bus-shelter seat with a bottle by his side.

'Nate . . .' I began as I approached him. The old backpack of Tony's that I'd given him was already so caked in filth that it was hard to spot the pale-blue colouring beneath. Tobacco, alcohol, urine, and the areas he chose to sleep rough in had all brewed together to create an unwelcoming odour. But I didn't comment on it as I hugged him tightly. It felt like wrapping my arms around a bag of bones.

'Hi, Laura,' he muttered, and offered a thin smile. 'What are you doing here?'

Normally it took a few minutes for him to register who I was through his boozy haze, but this morning he was lucid and relatively sober. There was just a year separating Nate and me, but every time I saw him, our age gap seemed to widen. His lank, greasy hair brushed his collar and there were holes in the front of his shoes that showed his socks. His inch-long beard was greying, and his eyes had darkened from a warm brown to a coal black. There was very little left in him that was alive.

'How are you?' I asked.

'Not so bad.' He gave a hard, hacking cough.

'You don't sound it. Do you still have that chest infection?'

'Yes.'

'I offered before to drive you to the walk-in centre to see a doctor. We can still go – this afternoon if you like?'

'No, no, it's fine,' he replied.

'Do you need some money?'

'Ha! I always need some money, Laura, but you've done enough for me already.'

I reached into my bag and pulled out all I had, a £10 note. I was embarrassed by such a poor offering. 'Please take this. Buy yourself some lunch.'

'You know how I'll spend it.' His eyes watched mine as I clocked his bottle of cider. His addiction was the only one I could overlook. His was present for a reason. His was there because of how he'd saved me.

'Just promise me you'll at least get yourself a sandwich.'

'Okay.'

'Promise me,' I repeated.

'I promise.'

When he smiled, I noted he'd lost another tooth from the bottom row; they were falling like pins in a bowling alley. Seeing Nate living and looking like this broke my heart, but having rejected my efforts of help in the past, there was little else I could do but watch him gradually disintegrate. I hoped it gave him a little comfort that someone in the world still cared for him.

Behind us, a plume of white and grey smoke from the volume of cigarettes being smoked ascended skywards. I made my way back towards the crowd as the previous party left through the double doors.

I hung behind. I didn't want to be so close to the front that I was asked who I was, but I didn't want to be so far towards the back that I missed what was being said about her. Slap bang in the middle of the crematorium would suffice.

By the time Chantelle Taylor's unvarnished pine coffin was carried inside by four suited undertakers and placed upon the plinth, the Adele song blaring through the speakers was approaching its second chorus. The coffin was adorned with flowers, most likely plastic, including one of those awful-looking wreaths with the word 'MUMMY' written in yellow carnations placed on top of the lid.

There were only thirty or so mourners in attendance and most were around Chantelle's age: single mothers in their early twenties wearing fake gold jewellery and with tattoos on their hands. If proof were ever needed I'd done the right thing in helping her to die, it was right there in the eyes of the walking dead.

I glanced at the flimsy black-and-white photocopy of an order of service with a photograph of Chantelle on the cover. She was holding a pint glass in a pub beer garden and her belly was swollen with pregnancy. I shook my head; even *in utero* her children hadn't stood a chance.

Doubtless it was them sitting at the front with a tearful older woman. She turned her head and dabbed at the over-applied mascara oozing down her face like an oil slick. They were too young to be here – both under four, I remembered Chantelle telling me. By the look of their grandmother, I decided they'd be better off under the care of the local authority. I made a mental note to tip off social services that drugs were being dealt from her premises. I had no idea if they were, but chances were a police search would find something to use against her. I'd be doing those kids a favour. Being a ward of court hadn't been a walk in the park, but it hadn't killed me either.

The minister read from his script and I recalled that when Chantelle first started phoning End of the Line, we'd discussed how she was trying to kick heroin for the sake of her unfortunate little ones. It was only with my help that she gradually began to realise that, in sobriety, happily-ever-afters weren't made for families like hers. I had her back on the stuff within a few weeks.

'How does it make you feel, knowing your children can't give you the high that drugs do?' I once asked her, a couple of weeks into our regular chats. I sensed by her tone that she was in a particularly dark place that day.

'Like a shit mum,' she said bleakly.

'I'm sure your children don't see you like that . . . They just love you for who you are. They aren't aware of the life you've given them. The mess they're in is all they know.'

'What do you mean by "mess"?'

'That their mum is dependent on drugs or drug substitutes; that she doesn't have enough money to give them food with proper nutrition; that when they're old enough to go to school they'll see that all their classmates have things you'll never afford. And I know you're the kind of person who'll feel dreadful for that, aren't you?'

'Of course.'

'Do you think they might grow up resenting you?'

'Yes, all the time.'

'Does it worry you that they might follow in your footsteps and end up addicts like you and their father, too? It can be hereditary, can't it?'

'I won't let them get into drugs.'

'I bet your mum said the same thing about you, but it's hard to tell people what to do, isn't it? It's no wonder you feel like you've let them down as a mum. What else do you worry about?'

'That they'll feel disappointed in me.'

'It's very easy to fall into bad habits when it comes to addiction, especially when you don't feel like there's a reason to stay on the wagon.'

'I thought I had a reason – for my kids . . . but I'm not strong enough.'

'And as you've already told me, you know they're probably already disappointed in you for the life you're giving them. And life away from heroin is hard, isn't it? Especially when you have nothing else. It must feel like life is never going to get any better than it is now.'

'What can I do to make it better for them?' she wept.

It was the question I'd been waiting for her to ask. And I knew that once I talked her back into her addiction, she'd reach the same decision I'd made for her. Everyone would be better off without Chantelle.

When her day of reckoning arrived, she'd purchased enough heroin from her violent, drug-dealing ex-boyfriend to do what was necessary. I closed my eyes and listened intently to the sounds of her feet shuffling along bare floorboards she couldn't afford to carpet, her curtains being drawn, the bedroom door quietly closing and her body stretching out upon her bed. I heard the flame from a cigarette lighter and imagined it heating up the metal spoon. I pictured the barrel of a syringe drawing up the dirty liquid and Chantelle tapping at her arms and legs, trying to raise a vein that hadn't already collapsed under the weight of her weak will.

'You'll find my kids when they're older and tell them I did this because I loved them, won't you?' she asked.

'Of course I will,' I lied. 'Just keep reminding yourself that you've explored every other avenue, but this is the only route that makes sense. You are moving on and allowing everyone else you love to do the same. And I admire that so much.'

Within moments, the needle had penetrated her skin and I listened with blissful satisfaction right until her final breath. That's the one sound that matters to me above all others . . . that one precious moment when someone breathes their last then slips away. People in pain like

Chantelle place themselves in my hands because I understand them better than anyone else in the world can. I know more about what they need than their brothers, sisters, parents, spouses, best friends or children. I understand them because I know what's best for them. If they place their trust in me, I'll reward them by going to the ends of the earth to help them. I'll alleviate their suffering. I'll bring all that is bad in their lives to an end. I will save them from themselves. *That is what I am: a saviour of lost souls.*

Twenty-two days after I saved Chantelle, she and I were finally in the same room together. A burgundy-velvet curtain encircled her coffin before she disappeared from view. And as her friends made their way back outside, I took Chantelle's order of service and placed it inside the black bag I carried with me to all the funerals I attended.

It was where I kept all the other orders. Chantelle's made fifteen in all. It was becoming quite the collection.

CHAPTER SIX

'Oh, Laura, this is as light as air,' began Kevin as he took a second mouthful of my Victoria sponge cake. I hadn't been able to resist leaving a slice on the desk of a man with high cholesterol.

I tried to divert my stare from his scruffy beard as he approached me in the office kitchenette. He was kidding himself if he thought it was distracting anyone from his rapidly receding hairline. He spat a crumb onto my skirt. I'd have to wash that tonight.

'Thank you,' I replied with false modesty. 'It's not as attractive as I'd have liked it, and the homemade jam got a bit gloopy.'

'I can't believe you make your own jam, too. You are like the perfect wife.'

'I try my best.' I silently thanked the supermarket and encouraged him towards another slice. There are many sides to me, but all they ever saw was one: the nurturer.

'I know why all that food you make for the fundraisers sells, literally, like hot cakes,' Zoe added. 'Seriously, though, you should think about entering one of those baking competitions on the telly. You'd storm it.'

She had lipstick on her front teeth again. What was wrong with people?

Fundraisers are my speciality. End of the Line is a registered charity and doesn't receive local or national government handouts. With branches in almost every county, they're all expected to be self-sufficient and responsible for paying their own running costs. Telephone lines, computer upgrades, software, stationery, rent, utilities and council tax, et cetera, all total around £80,000 a year. As treasurer, I'd been quite happy to lead the charge myself to find the money, until head office promoted Janine Thomson to manager. She didn't just tread on my toes, she danced all over them with the grace of an ostrich on hot coals.

I'd known at first sight when she started as a volunteer two years earlier that we were unlikely to become friends. Everything about her appearance offended me, like her squinty little eyes and her brows plucked into ridiculous curves resembling the McDonald's golden arches. Grey hairs crawled across her scalp like unsightly slugs, and she tried to plump up her paper-thin lips by colouring above and below them in a gaudy red. She was a clown in search of a circus.

Then, when she was given the manager's position above me after all the hard work I'd put in, my dislike turned to loathing. I hadn't even wanted the job, as it would have given me less time to man the phones, but it was the principle that mattered. It should have been offered to me on a plate.

Janine immediately became one of those women who needed you to know that she was in charge, even though we'd been running things successfully long before her interference.

But what annoyed me the most was that she demonstrated an unhealthy preoccupation with me. Sometimes as I sat in my booth listening to another troubled soul spilling their secrets, I'd catch her in her glass-walled office, her glasses perched on the tip of her nose, staring at me, straining to pick up on something I was saying that wasn't in the rule book. If only she knew just how far away from that book I could stray when the mood took me. And when Tony had accompanied me to a dinner to celebrate Mary's sixtieth birthday, Janine could barely take her eyes off him. I watched as she flirted and he humoured her. But deep down she must have known that she could never attract a man like my husband, or any man with a pulse and without cataracts, for that matter.

'Try some of Laura's cake,' Kevin suggested when Janine stepped into the kitchen to rinse her coffee mug. An awful orange handbag with the emblem of a Chinese dragon on the side – a self-portrait, I assumed – hung from her sloping shoulder. It was the only bag she appeared to own and it matched nothing in her limited wardrobe of drab, patterned rags. I believed her when she said the bag was one of a kind, because nobody else would want it.

'I don't know how you find the time to do so much,' she began. The others couldn't hear it but I recognised something accusatory in her tone. 'You volunteer here, you have a family and you still manage to give Mary Berry a run for her money. Quite the domestic goddess, aren't you?'

'I like to set a good example for my children and I'm very good at multitasking,' I replied through a narrow smile. 'If you need me to give you some tips, you have only to ask. Would you like a slice?'

'No thank you, I'm gluten intolerant.'

'Is that really a thing? Do you just wake up one morning and realise that after fifty-odd years you can't eat cake?'

'I'm forty-two.' She glared at me and I made an imaginary chalk mark on a board. Kevin and Zoe tried to hide their amusement.

'I'm not very good with ages,' I added.

Janine had soon learned that her job would be much more difficult without the thousands of pounds' worth of sponsorship and donations I alone brought in each year. I had no hesitation in going cap in hand to local companies or schmoozing at business leaders' events to get what I wanted, even if it meant being pawed at by overweight bald men who stank of whisky, cigars and desperation, and who assumed I found them attractive.

My hard work brought me praise and freed up Janine's time to spend on the gambling websites she visited when she thought nobody else was looking. She might have deleted them from the Internet browsing history, but I found them in the cookies section of her computer with the speed of one of those roulette balls she liked to bet on. I'd kept that knowledge, the screengrabs I'd taken and her account password to myself. For the time being, anyway.

The afternoon shift was often quiet. Desperate housewives and mums rang during the day when they were free of husbands and children. It was a time also favoured by prisoners, making use of our freephone number. Early mornings were mainly men on their way to work, commonly plagued by money worries and scared what bills might be lying on the doormat on their return home later. Most suicidal callers waited until the evening, when, alone, they had time to think.

That was the time David had favoured. More than seven months had passed since we had first come into contact, and almost five months since we'd spoken last. Sometimes I missed him so much that it physically hurt me.

I'd known from his very first call that he and I shared a connection. My intuition picks up on desperation in a voice, in the phrasing or the way a person articulates certain words. Instinct will tell me from that conversation if they're a candidate. And there's no feeling quite like when they come into my life.

David was a gentle, softly spoken but emotionally paralysed man who'd struggled to move forward after the violent death of his wife. She'd been killed at home following a break-in by three men while he was working nights. An oppressive cloud of guilt had since smothered the new life he hadn't chosen for himself. It became impossible for him to navigate it alone, which is why, one desperate evening, he picked up the phone and reached me.

There was something about David's sadness that mimicked mine and bonded us. He wasn't seeking sympathy or asking for someone to assure him that her death wasn't his fault, because he had plenty of people around him to do that. All he wanted was for someone to listen and really hear him – and there was no one better suited to understand loss than me.

We were kindred spirits, bound together by the atrocious actions of others. I had chosen to soldier on. He, however, was done. And as our conversations became more frequent and our emotional connection grew, I found myself wanting to keep him alive for selfish reasons. I needed our discourse, I needed to hear him speak and I needed him to need me. I veered away from my well-trodden path and threw myself into trying to help him see that if only he could fight that little bit harder and stretch his hand out that little bit further, his might reach mine and I could save him. My objective became to keep him with me, while his was to convince me that he was better off dead. I already had my anchor and I was willing to be his. But I was being selfish. I just didn't want to let him go. And eventually, although it broke my heart, I conceded defeat.

David's biggest challenge was that he didn't want to leave this life alone. So my biggest challenge became trying to find someone willing to end theirs with him.

Then suddenly *she* came along.

CHAPTER SEVEN

I was grateful the house had more than one bathroom when the side effects of my slimming tablets began making themselves known.

I found myself glued to the en-suite toilet for the best part of half an hour. Afterwards, with the smell of Febreze in the air but still with a cramping tummy, I examined the side profile of my torso in the mirror. There were definite signs it was becoming a little flatter, even in the last week. I ran my fingers across it and imagined they belonged to Tony. I could burn at least two hundred more calories that morning if I did the school run by foot rather than by car. If I kept making this kind of progress, he might really see me again.

I loaded the dishwasher with my breakfast dishes and saw Tony had used one of the good mugs for his coffee again, much to my irritation. Outside, it was warmer than the tubby weatherwoman on breakfast television had predicted, so I tied my hoodie around my waist and thought of how it didn't seem like five minutes ago when I'd taken Alice for her inaugural day in reception class. Week in, week out we'd make the same journey as I had with Effie, who'd eventually thought herself too cool to be with us so skipped a few feet ahead. Alice would hold my hand, singing the chorus of a song she'd heard on the radio over and over again, driving me mad with her love of repetition. I'd squeeze her fingers just hard enough to make her squeal and beg me to stop. Nowadays, neither wanted to hold Mummy's hand and that suited me. And by the time I arrived at the school gates, Alice was already in the distance running around the playground with her friends.

For a moment, I considered trying to engage in conversation with a few of the other mums as they took up their regular positions in the morning gossip circle. 'The Muffia', Tony had nicknamed them. But it would have been pointless, because there were never any vacancies in their superficial little clique. I'd see them on the gym floor like a pack of hyenas, their knowing glances tearing strips off any woman above a size ten. Then I'd watch them from the back row of a spin class and imagine them sweating out their skin fillers onto their white towels below. Afterwards, I'd be quietly amused as they devoured sugary smoothies and pastries in the café. They fascinated and repulsed me in equal measure.

My journey from school to my next destination took exactly twenty-two minutes, a time I used to smoke a cigarette and empty my head of all negatives. Because whenever I went to visit my anchor, I needed clarity. I wanted my thoughts and my heart to be as pure as his.

Before long, the Kingsthorpe Residential Care Home loomed ahead of me. It was a large rectangular building with wings sprouting from each side like branches from a tree. Broad, established oak trees flanked the brick-paved driveway that led up a slight incline towards the frosted-glass double doors of the entrance. It was surrounded by rolling landscaped gardens and a lake.

I smiled at the young receptionists and signed the visitors' book. I checked to see if Tony or the girls' signatures had been added since my last visit, but their names were absent. They were always absent. None of them knew I went four times a week.

I was buzzed into the communal area where I found Henry with a small group of his peers, all sitting separately and all preoccupied with different objects.

He sat almost motionless in his wheelchair and didn't acknowledge my presence. I'd come to expect that and it didn't matter. I could tell he knew I was there. Call it a mother's intuition.

My son's head had drooped to the right but his eyes remained transfixed on the television attached to the wall. I never really knew just how much he was taking in, but he appeared to be concentrating intently on a *Peppa Pig* cartoon. A thread of saliva, as faint as a spider's web, had fallen from the corner of his mouth, down his chin and onto the breast pocket of his T-shirt. I took a tissue from my bag and dabbed at it, then used my fingernail to gently prise small crumbs of breakfast from the other side of his mouth.

I slid my hand under the straps holding him firmly in his wheelchair to check they weren't too tight around his waist or shoulders. I'd yelled at a nurse once when I found the belts had left deep impressions in his skin. I hated that he might be in pain and unable to express it.

I stared into Henry's eyes; once upon a time they could light up a room, but now they seemed to be losing their shine. It hadn't been an immediate transformation but I was scared I was beginning to lose him. I had no one to share my observations with, because I was the only one who ever came to see him.

I ran my hand through his fine, mousy brown hair. It had been combed forward even though they knew I didn't think that style suited him. So I splashed some water from a plastic cup over my fingers and rearranged his fringe into a side parting. That seemed to be the favoured style with the boys his age at Alice's school.

Henry's sinewy arms and legs jutted out from beneath the clothes they'd dressed him in. He'd not put the weight back on that he'd lost when he developed pneumonia. I'd spent the best part of two weeks here sleeping by his side in an armchair, then again later, in hospital, when his lungs needed draining. It was just my son and me together and it was the longest period of time I'd been able to spend with him since before the ambulance arrived at our house to take him away from me.

I was the first to admit those early days with Henry hadn't been easy, from his weak immune system that rendered him susceptible to all manner of infections, to the screaming fits that lasted the best part of a day. Of course he was a lifelong commitment, but then what child isn't? But try as I might, I couldn't get Tony to accept him. Towards the end, he could barely even look at his son.

I knew I'd never walk Henry to school, watch him play with his friends, or be the mother of the groom at his wedding. We wouldn't share memories and I'd never really get to know what he was thinking. All the dreams and plans I'd made for him when I was pregnant had long since evaporated.

So I developed new hopes instead: I wanted to help him become the best version of himself that he could be. Even the smallest of achievements, like identifying shapes and colours, became massive and all-consuming. Gradually I learned to accept the now and not hang on to what might have been.

His mind would never grow older than one-year-old or become jaded. He'd never expect anything more from me than I had to give. To me, Henry was a perfect seven-year-old, just in his own individual way.

I'd desperately wanted to remain Henry's caregiver because he was part of me. And we were muddling along just fine until my cancer diagnosis ruined everything. The treatment required was urgent and rigorous and left me hospitalised. By the time I returned home weeks later, Henry had vanished. At first Tony claimed he was in respite care and would return when I was well enough to look after him. But when my strength came back, he gave me an ultimatum – our marriage and the girls, or Henry and me, on our own.

Everyone from Henry's doctors to his caseworkers assured me that it wouldn't resonate with him that he wasn't returning home again, but I knew my son. He thought that I'd given up and dumped him in the hands of people who'd never love him the way I did. And it killed me that he didn't know that it wasn't my fault – that it was my disease, not my lack of willingness, that had rendered me useless. The guilt almost swallowed me.

I took a little comfort that, here, Henry would be looked after properly. He had people to feed him, people to bathe him, people to dress him and people to take him outside in the garden or by the lake to breathe in the fresh air. He wanted for nothing and he didn't need me, but still I came. All I could do was brush the crumbs from his mouth and slick his hair into a parting. At least it was something.

I took hold of Henry's hand and placed my fingers on his wrist just to feel the rhythm of his pulse.

'I can feel his heartbeat inside me,' I'd said to Tony once, when I was pregnant.

'Don't be daft,' he'd replied. 'It's your own heart you can feel.'

He didn't understand that Henry's heart and mine were one and the same. And as long as I could feel his pulse, he would always be my anchor.

CHAPTER EIGHT

FOUR MONTHS,

THREE WEEKS AFTER DAVID

I scowled at the partially empty polystyrene coffee cup that had been left on my desk.

I hated it when other volunteers used my booth in my absence, especially when they didn't have the courtesy to clean up after themselves. As it was, the office was shabby, to say the least, what with its threadbare 1970s patterned carpet, faded white woodchip wallpaper, and nicotine-stained ceiling that no one had seen fit to repaint a decade after the indoor workplace smoking ban.

Like a graffiti artist's wall tag, I recognised the litterbug by the lipstick smeared around the cup's rim – Janine. I flicked it into a plastic bin, then squirted the desk with an antibacterial hand-sanitiser and wiped away all traces of her before answering my first call.

Based only on his nervous 'Hello', I knew immediately who was on the other End of the Line before he'd introduced himself. Some people never forget a face, but I never forget a voice, even when all that person has spoken is a solitary word. My eyes lit up.

'My name is Steven. You probably don't remember me, but I think you might be the lady I spoke to recently?' He was trying, but failing, to hide his fear.

'Yes, hello there, Steven, it was me you spoke to and, yes, I do remember you. How are things with you today?'

'Okay, thanks.'

'That sounds more positive than the last time. Has something in your circumstances changed?'

'Nothing much really, I guess.'

'Oh, I'm sorry to hear that.' I wasn't, of course. But I'd already concluded that if there had been significant improvements, he wouldn't be calling me a second time. 'But regardless, you're having a good day today at least?'

'I suppose so.'

'Well, sometimes after a good night's sleep, we just wake up in the morning feeling better about things.'

'It doesn't mean the bad stuff goes away though, does it?'

Arriving at that conclusion himself was one less seed I'd need to plant in his head.

'How do you think you can make this good day extend by another twenty-four hours?'

'I'm not sure.'

Something in the pause between my questions and his answers made me think this wasn't the conversation he wanted or expected. But it was *exactly* what I wanted, and I could almost hear his eyebrows knot as I appeared only to seek positive responses from him. He'd been hoping for a continuation of what we'd spoken about last time, when he'd wanted my support in ending his life but didn't have the backbone to ask.

If a potential candidate finds me a second time, I'll know they're serious. But I'll always gloss over aspects of our first conversation. I'll act like the part where I suggested they weren't serious about killing themselves didn't happen. I'll consult my notes and throw in the odd fact or phrase they mentioned last time, to reiterate that I'd listened. But that'll be it. It's the callers who find me intriguing enough to track me down for a third time who'll receive my undivided attention.

For the next ten minutes, our conversation was by the book. On the surface, I aimed to reinforce the positives in his life. But because he was in such a negative headspace, hearing his own pessimistic responses only served to highlight his isolation.

'Steven, I hope you don't mind me saying, but earlier you said you were okay, but you don't sound like you are.'

'I think I've just got in the habit of saying I am so that people don't worry about me.'

It was time to give him another hall pass to what he really wanted to discuss. 'This is a neutral place. You don't have to pretend to be feeling anything you're not with me. Is there anything you'd like to talk about in particular?'

'Um . . . the last time we spoke . . .'

'I remember . . .'

'I told you something.'

'You told me a lot of things.'

'About me thinking about killing myself . . .'

'Yes, you did.'

'You asked me if I was prepared to do it.'

'I don't recall those being the exact words I used, Steven. I think you may have misinterpreted what I was saying.'

'Oh.'

I was confusing him. 'What conclusions have you made regarding ending your life since last time?'

'I've given it a lot of thought. In fact, it's been the only thing on my mind and I can't make it stop. You're right – no matter what I do, nothing is going to change. All I'm going to feel like is this.'

He was quoting me, almost verbatim. This was another positive sign. 'And how do you think you can rid yourself of these feelings?'

'I don't know.'

'I think you do though, don't you? If you're being really honest with yourself.'

'Yes,' he whispered, 'I'm ready. I mean, I want to . . . I want to die . . .'

'Steven, I'm very sorry to interrupt, but I'm afraid I'm going to have to go now, as my shift is coming to an end. Unfortunately, I can't transfer you to one of my colleagues, but if you call back, I'm sure someone else would be happy to pick up where we've left off.'

It wasn't the end of my shift, I still had another hour left and I'd never end a call that abruptly with someone who wasn't a candidate.

'What? But—'

'Take care, David,' I continued, then hung up without giving him the chance to say goodbye. He'd call back another day. I was certain of it.

Wait, did I just call him David? I think I did. Bugger!

David had been on my mind a lot recently, and hearing Steven talk about his feelings of hopelessness reminded me of what David had confessed.

I'd offered to be there on the other end of the telephone for David when his time came. But he'd needed more than that.

'I don't want to go on my own,' he admitted. 'I need someone to be there with me. Someone who, like me, is afraid of doing it alone.'

I'd never had anyone make that request before. Flashbacks of miserable places I'd been to in my childhood began swirling through my head, and if circumstances had been different I might have given brief consideration to joining him. But I had a family, and Henry needed me. My anchor held me firm.

I had to think. Where on earth might I find someone willing to participate? It's not like I could advertise on Match.com – *Male, 39, good-looking, great sense of humour, seeks woman to join him in suicide pact.* So I returned to Internet message boards and forums I'd frequented in the early days, searching for potential candidates. But it's hard to trust and recruit someone when they're hiding behind an avatar.

Then as luck – or fate – would have it, *she* came into our lives. She was a young woman who was pregnant and with a severe case of prenatal depression. It gave her dark thoughts, and the longer the pregnancy continued, the more convinced she became that she would make a terrible mother. She thought her husband was having an affair, as he'd been making covert phone calls and sums of money had been vanishing from their joint account. He was spending longer at work than normal, and because she'd been feeling fat and deeply unattractive, she thought he was finding affection elsewhere. I didn't care if he was or wasn't a cheating bastard. It just suited my needs that she believed he was, as it made her more depressed.

Under different circumstances, I might've suggested she held out until after the birth before acting on her suicidal thoughts. But I needed someone malleable and open to suggestion and she fitted the bill perfectly.

I was also very aware that I needed her more than she needed me. So I treated her with kid gloves and used every trick in the book to fast-track the process. I upped my shifts to every other day and encouraged her to keep calling until it was me who answered; I suggested she stop taking the low dose of antidepressants her doctor had prescribed, in case it gave her a chemical optimism; I advised keeping a distance from her friends and philandering husband, and I directed her towards particular Internet suicide message boards I knew well, to see that she wasn't alone. After three weeks of intense conversations, research and manipulation, she was keen to meet David. And in the seven days before they were to meet, we'd only communicate through pay-as-you-go, untraceable mobile phones.

The one and only time they came face-to-face was the day they stepped off Birling Gap's cliff top in East Sussex together. They'd never spoken by phone, text or email. They had no idea what the other looked or sounded like or their reasons for dying, only that they shared a mutual destiny. They had trust in me and in each other – we were three friends all making the same leap of faith.

Listening to them on the phone as they took their final steps across the verge and towards the cliff edge, I'd never felt such pride, joy, happiness, anticipation and excitement all at once. But deep down, I was envious of her for sharing that precious moment. It clawed away inside me when I saw it on the local TV news. I wasn't able to bring myself to watch it and see her as a real person, so I turned the channel over. I had been instrumental in ending David's pain, but she took the glory.

I took a moment to close my eyes and imagine how it might've felt to hold David's hand and feel his warmth travel through me as we took that one last step together. I sensed the softness of his skin, the smell of cologne on his neck, his pulse beating in rhythm with mine – and all with such clarity, as if I were there.

'Laura!' Janine's irritated voice came from behind and startled me. My angry eyes opened wide. 'Your phone is ringing. Could you answer it, please?'

She pointed to the flashing red light.

'Of course,' I replied, and wondered how it might feel to take that phone and smash her across the face with it.

CHAPTER NINE

I scribbled on a piece of paper and slid it towards Sanjay's desk. Even from this angle, I could see his shirt buttons straining and clumps of dark hair poking out through the gaps.

The ever-incompetent Janine had messed up the rota and booked too many of us in, so the room contained more people than I was comfortable with.

Why are the police in Janine's office? I'd written.

'No idea,' Sanjay mouthed. He'd doused himself in a musky oud-based cologne, but it was doing little to mask his body odour. I glanced towards Mary, who was also on a call, and raised my eyebrows, but she shook her head.

I was supposed to be listening to a widowed pensioner complaining about her crippling loneliness. But I was far too preoccupied by the uniformed officers talking to Janine.

Their proximity made me feel uneasy – was this something to do with me? Had Steven reported me to the police? Had my instinct failed me and had I gone too far, too soon with him? I guessed the odds were that it might happen some time. And it would only take one person's accusation to ruin my reputation.

R U OK? Sanjay wrote back. I hated text talk when it wasn't written on a phone. And even then I wasn't comfortable with it.

Yes, just being nosy! I scribbled, and added a smiley face.

Quietly, I wanted to grab my bag and dash out of there. But I needed to know for definite if what was going on in Janine's office involved me.

My caller started droning on about her two estranged children while my eyes were fixed upon the two young officers drinking from mugs and tucking into more of my pastries. I leaned forward and craned my neck to try to pick up on their muffled conversation, but only a lip-reader could have translated it.

I felt a knot expand in my stomach to the size of a watermelon as I replayed my two conversations with Steven in my head. I was quite certain I'd never told him in actual words that I would support him in ending his life. I was too careful for that. So any accusations would be his word against mine.

British law had decriminalised suicide back in 1961, so it was no longer illegal to try to take your own life. However, encouraging or assisting someone else's suicide was a different matter and the police had a duty to investigate accusations. The maximum penalty, if found guilty, was fourteen years' imprisonment. Henry would never survive that long without me.

The more I glared at the officers, the more my initial panic made way for anger. What was I doing that was so wrong? I was only helping people, just as End of the Line was supposed to. Granted, I had an agenda, but I had my own boundaries, too: no children, teenagers or anyone with learning difficulties – everyone else of sound mind could make their own decisions, with my assistance of course. If society's moral compass weren't so screwed up, I'd have been rewarded for the lengths I'd gone to in order to help those in need. People are their own worst enemies when they try to plod along even if it means leading miserable, hopeless lives. It's up to me to save them from themselves.

But there'd be no point in trying to explain that to Janine or to the police; they'd only spin it into something negative to use against me. Social workers, counsellors, doctors . . . they'd all judged me in the past and they'd all been wrong. I wouldn't sit back and allow history to repeat itself.

As they left, I watched Sanjay wander into her office, and willed my caller to shut up before I followed him inside.

'They've found our number in another phone of someone who died,' Sanjay began.

'Who?' I asked.

'A young mum who overdosed on heroin.'

Ah, Chantelle.

I'd spoken to her God knows how many times leading up to her death, but her calls could never be traced back to me. Callers trust us because we protect their anonymity and we can't trace their numbers. There are no direct lines to us and we don't have extension numbers. Based on the dialling code of a landline or the GPS of a mobile, calls to End of the Line's national number are diverted to the caller's nearest branch. And whichever of us is free to answer will do so. If a branch's lines are all engaged, the call goes to one of four neighbouring counties. The police must have assumed that because Chantelle was local, we'd get her calls.

'How many deaths have been linked to us now?' Sanjay asked Janine.

'According to the records,' Janine began, leafing through a printed-out spreadsheet, 'this new case makes twenty-four in Northamptonshire in the last five years.'

I couldn't take credit for all of them, as much as I'd liked to have.

'Hmm, slightly higher than average, then,' said Sanjay.

Janine was being distracted by her computer's refusal to accept her password. 'Bloody thing,' she snapped.

'It's your initial and then surname and your chosen four-digit number,' Sanjay reminded her. I memorised the numbers she added to a list of notes entitled 'Passwords' on her iPad before she slipped it back into her ugly orange handbag.

'I don't understand what the police want,' I said. 'They know our job isn't to talk people out of dying or break their confidence. We're just here to listen.'

'Thank you, Laura. I am very aware of what we do,' replied Janine piously. 'They're investigating whether they can build a case against a drug dealer she was in a relationship with, and wanted to find out if she'd spoken to one of us about him. I reiterated, anything that's said in conversation is in the strictest confidence.'

Chantelle had spoken to me about him on many occasions. Had he not constantly eroded her self-confidence and plied her with heroin, our paths might never have crossed. I owed him my silence.

'How many times did she call?' asked Sanjay.

'Nineteen times in the weeks before she died,' Janine replied, and removed a packet of biscuits from her drawer, emblazoned with the words 'gluten- and dairy-free'. 'If she came through to this branch, someone must remember her. And they must know that we don't encourage callers to be reliant on talking to just one of us. A second volunteer might offer a different mindset that helps them more than another can.'

'Perhaps you might want to send a memo out reminding people of that?' I suggested.

Janine gave me another one of her withering glances, so I made my way back to my booth, willing a terminal illness upon her. Not a short one that developed quickly and snuffed her out within a couple of months, but a long, nasty one that ate the bitch alive.

It felt like it had been a close call. As a precautionary measure, I needed to protect myself, so I promised myself I'd take a step back from lining up any future candidates. But only after Steven and I finished our work together.

There are five rules I expect each candidate to follow if our relationship is to prove effective, and Steven would be no exception if he was to make that third, all-important call.

The first rule is that I am the one in control. Ultimately it will always be a candidate's decision whether they live or die, and there's nothing I can do about that. But I need to make them understand that without my help, their attempt to leave this world with minimal fuss will likely fail.

I'll throw statistics at them to prove my point, like how three-quarters of people who try to take their life end up botching it because they're ill-prepared. Mentally they might be ready, but if they think they can slice into any vein or hang from a tree and ta-da, that's it, game over, then they're wrong. Pain-free, romanticised suicides only ever happen in television dramas. When it's done incorrectly, an attempt can leave a person with crippling, life-changing injuries.

My second rule is that a candidate must trust me because I know best. I am a walking encyclopaedia when it comes to ways and means. I have *done* my research. I have *read up* on all feasible methods online, in public libraries and in medical reports. I have *attended* inquests of suicides and I have *learned* from the successes and failures of the dead.

I know how to jump from even a relatively low bridge or building and have the best possible chance of a fatal outcome – even a seven-storey plunge has a decent survival rate if you don't get it right. I know the most effective painkillers and benzodiazepines to combine, and which countries export them with no questions asked. I know which DIY shops sell the strongest, best-quality ropes and I know the angle they need to be knotted. I know how to fatally land in water from a great height, and what length of a barrel to hack from what make of shotgun to stretch from mouth to trigger finger. I even know the best saw blades to use to cut it. I know how to properly secure a pipe to a car exhaust. I know how to suffocate and self-strangulate and the local bodies of water where riptides and sea tides will sweep you away no matter how strong your anchor. I know all of this because *I am an expert.*

The third rule is that a candidate must agree to do it within five weeks of our arrangement. If they can't get their affairs in order by then, I'll know they're wavering and I'll cut them off. There will be no second chances. I don't like wasting my time.

Number four is that they must leave most of the nitty-gritty work to me. I will plan for every eventuality once we agree on a preferred method. I'll set to work tailoring a package, with attention to detail that is second to none. Time, location, cost of materials, where to purchase them from . . . there's nothing I won't have thought of. All they have to do is make sure they leave no mention of me or our relationship anywhere. Under no circumstances must they ever write down my name or that of End of the Line, not on a piece of paper or even in the notes section of their phone.

My fifth and final rule is that I demand just one thing in return for my efforts – transparency. I expect candidates to tell me everything there is to know about themselves before we part ways. I want to hear their most cherished memories, their darkest thoughts, their unreached goals, their biggest regrets, their dirtiest secrets, who they are leaving behind, who won't care and who they'll hurt the most. I want to know about their everyday lives and the lives they don't want their best friends to know about.

I liken it to putting livestock in the lushest pasture, feeding them the best grains and allowing them plenty of access to light and sun – do that and you will always have a better-tasting meat. For me, by really knowing what makes a candidate tick, their last breath will sound sweeter to me than any other sound in the world.

CHAPTER TEN

FIVE MONTHS AFTER DAVID

On my return from visiting Henry's residential care home, and before I started at End of the Line, I made a diversion to a coffee shop in town.

'Here or to go?' a disinterested young man behind the counter mumbled. His face was familiar but I couldn't place him.

I glanced at my watch – I was still too early to start my next shift. 'It's for here,' I replied. He filled a mug with a latte, then rolled his eyes when I asked for a spoon.

I chose a table in the middle of the busy room and sat with my eyelids tightly shut, listening carefully to the conversations of strangers gathered around their circular tables. If I concentrated hard enough, I could block out the rest of the noise in the café, like the cappuccino machine, dishwasher and even the radio, so that all I heard was the communication between customers.

It was the buzz I got from listening to snapshots of others' lives that had first drawn me to offer my time to End of the Line. I recalled how Alice, then four, was in the living room scribbling pictures of farmyard animals on sheets of paper spread across the coffee table. Effie was nine and doing her maths homework. I was on the sofa, supposed to be watching over them, but admittedly more interested in checking my messages on Internet suicide message boards. It used to be exciting knowing how much I was helping people by encouraging them to end their pain. And over time, I gained a reputation in certain dark corners of the web as the go-to girl for no-nonsense, detailed advice on the best and worst ways to do it, based on research I'd collated. I even gained a nickname, the 'Freer of Lost Souls'. It made me feel necessary.

But online posters were transient and anonymous. They were scattered far and wide and when they ceased leaving messages, I'd never know if it was because they'd carried out their threats to kill themselves or if they'd just changed their minds and stopped posting. Rarely would I learn of their outcome, and eventually it wasn't enough for me.

What message boards lacked was a human connection. Reading typed words was not the same as hearing pain in a person's voice. I needed to suck up their angst, their uneasiness, their desperation and their confusion. So when I read in the local paper that End of the Line had a shortage of volunteers, I wondered if I could take my skills and knowledge in an important new direction.

Curiosity made me call their number to learn first-hand how their advice differed from the frank and honest encouragement I gave online. I made up a story about feeling desperately lonely and that I was seriously contemplating taking my own life. Except there was no advice. Instead, the woman on the other End of the Line offered calm, caring words and the time and space to talk and break down my problems. Mary still has no idea that I was the one she'd answered the phone to.

There was something habit-forming about making that first call and hearing her awful, non-judgemental, anodyne response. So, over the next two weeks, I called again and again and got the same perspective from multiple Stepford volunteers. I tested these poor misguided souls under various guises, citing debt, rape, a cheating husband, childhood sex abuse and the horrors of war as reasons for my woes. I was curious as to how long they could maintain their saccharine-sweet words before their masks slipped and they told me what they really thought. But they never did. Not once.

And that was precisely why End of the Line needed me – someone who could offer their callers an alternative viewpoint, a truthful take on their predicaments. I would be willing to go that extra mile for the right candidates and, where necessary, offer them a gentle nudge over the finishing line.

A clock on the wall in the café chimed and I opened my eyes. I put my empty mug back on the counter and received a weak smile from the boy. I looked at his name badge. *Matt*, it read, and suddenly the penny dropped – I'd found his pictures on Effie's phone. He'd been encouraging her to send him photos of her semi-naked body.

My mood darkened as I walked towards the office. With my head bowed and my phone in my hand, I logged in to my daughter's Facebook account. This time her inbox contained a naked and aroused photograph of Matt he'd sent her – and by the look of the decor around him, it had been taken in the back of the coffee shop. I was furious at him, and just as angry at her for not deleting it. He was a seventeen-year-old man sending a fourteen-year-old child pornographic images.

If I reported him to the police, in all likelihood he'd receive a slap on the wrist. So I took matters into my own hands.

Nothing was confidential anymore when it came to young people and social media. So if Matt was so eager to share and be validated by the world, let's see what he thought when they started judging him by his less-than-impressive genitals. He'd been foolish enough to keep his face in the shot, so I screen-grabbed the picture and tweeted it using my anonymous account to the international chain of coffee outlets that employed him, stating his name and the branch where he worked and had taken the picture.

Then I logged on to the fake Facebook account I'd created to investigate candidates' profiles if they gave away enough of themselves. I posted Matt's picture to his own timeline for all to see, then to the timelines of anyone in his friends list who shared his surname. I posted it on the school's own Facebook page, plus all those set up by parents for each individual year group. Then I logged back into Effie's profile and posted it on her page. Finally, I changed her password so that she couldn't take the picture down.

By the time I reached the office, I was satisfied that it was going to be the End of the Line for Effie and that boy.

CHAPTER ELEVEN

The corridors leading away from the high-dependency unit at Northampton General Hospital were eerily quiet for mid-afternoon.

I'd just missed visiting hours, but that hadn't stopped me from turning up unannounced to check if there'd been any improvement in Nate's condition.

We'd been in this building many times over the years, for various conditions common to the homeless. Hepatitis B, bronchitis, infected foot calluses, gum abscesses and, more often than not, his early-stage cirrhosis of the liver stemming from frequent alcohol abuse. Now tuberculosis had poleaxed him, a direct result of the damage to his immune system caused by his HIV. Each disease was speeding up the progress of the other, leaving his body in constant turmoil.

His NHS records listed me as his emergency contact. Tony didn't understand my need to stand by Nate no matter what the predicament or self-inflicted ailment that was knocking nine bells out of him. My husband had urged me many times to 'do myself a favour' and wash my hands of him. But I could never do that.

The doors to his ward were locked to prevent the spread of infection, so I peered through the windows that stretched across three sections of the room, but still I couldn't locate him. Last time, he'd struggled to breathe, so – while he was heavily sedated – a noisy machine did the hard work for him. A plastic mask had been taped to his mouth and a pipe inserted into his throat, making his chest rise and fall. It had been heartbreaking to watch.

Living rough, he'd wear layer after layer of clothing. He'd told me it was easier to carry them on his back than risk leaving them somewhere and having them stolen. I remembered how emaciated and angular he'd looked in just a blue, paper-thin hospital gown, barely making a dent in the bedsheets. I'd remained by the side of his bed for the best part of a week, like I had when Henry battled pneumonia, and I wondered how much of my life I'd spent willing someone I loved to fight for their life.

I scanned the room again; perhaps I hadn't recognised Nate because the nurses had cleaned him up. He'd likely have been scrubbed and bathed, his beard trimmed and his hair cut short. He'd hate that. He hated any resemblance to the boy I'd shared a foster home with.

◆ ◆ ◆

Our foster mother, Sylvia Hughes, was the greatest manipulator I'd ever met. The only positive experience from my time spent living under her roof was learning how to convince the world you are one thing when, inside, you are someone altogether different.

She'd convinced everyone of importance that she was providing a safe haven for the dozens of foster children she'd welcomed over the years. But to those of us in her care, we were there to serve a purpose.

Even now I can remember the taste of fear that lodged in my throat and how my pace slowed when I turned the corner on the approach to her apartment block. When the weekend loomed, I'd dread returning to the tired, ten-storey, grey-concrete building. Being at another new school with no friends was still more appealing than being in Sylvia's company for a whole weekend.

I can remember every minute of that last weekend with Nate, right from the moment I walked up the staircase on a Friday afternoon, holding my breath as I turned the door handle. I crossed my fingers and hoped Nate would already be home, but the flat was silent.

Social services had us listed as living in the apartment next door. It was a pleasantly decorated place with two spare bedrooms packed with toys, and a kitchen with a fridge full of food. However, we were only rarely allowed inside, when social workers made appointments to check on our well-being. 'Hell-being', Nate had renamed it. The flat where we actually lived was very different.

I kicked a clear path through the old newspapers and bags of rubbish clogging up the corridor, and with a rumbling belly I opened the fridge door. But, as was often the case, all it contained was a broken light and an avalanche of freezer frost. Inside was a solitary frozen cheese and tomato pizza that I placed under the grill.

I cut it into symmetrical slices as the front door opened and Sylvia and Nate entered. My heart sank. By the dazed look on his face, I knew where she had taken him. Through half-closed eyes, he tried to pretend everything was okay by offering me an absent-minded smile that we both knew was disguising something else. At fourteen, Nate was on the cusp of manhood, but his height and slender frame gave him the appearance of a boy much younger. At thirteen, I too was small for my age. He stumbled into his bedroom and closed the door behind him.

'How was school?' asked Sylvia, and grabbed a slice from my hand, vacuuming it up like a snake swallowing a mouse. As her T-shirt rose up and exposed her belly, I noted it had fresh puncture wounds. She must have given up trying to locate a vein in her arms or legs that hadn't already collapsed. She relied on long-sleeved tops to mask the fact that she was a functioning heroin addict.

'It was okay, thanks,' I replied.

'Good girl,' Sylvia replied, then sparked up a joint and made her way to the living room. 'I'm going next door to chill.'

I waited to hear the sound of the television before tiptoeing to Nate's bedroom and quietly pushing the closed door ajar. I hated closed doors. He awoke with a start, throwing himself back against the wall like a cornered animal.

'It's okay, it's me,' I whispered. 'I've brought you pizza.'

'Thank you,' he croaked, his throat sore, and he calmed down.

We remained in silence, sharing the food from the plate as I tried hard not to acknowledge the bruises on his wrists and neck, or the dried crusts of blood inside his nostrils. I noticed the red spotting in the underwear he'd left lying in a heap on the floor, still inside his trousers. But I knew better than to ask what'd happened or who'd been responsible.

He slowly drifted into the safety of sleep to the sounds of the radio being played loudly next door, permeating the walls. I squirmed my way in front of him, protecting his skinny frame with my back. I moulded my body into his and pulled his arm over my chest.

'I love you, Nate,' I whispered, knowing that we were safer together than when we were apart.

◆ ◆ ◆

'Hello, Mrs Morris, isn't it?'

The past evaporated at Dr Khatri's voice. I hadn't heard him approach, and I recoiled when he tapped me on the shoulder. 'What brings you to High Dependency?'

'My friend Nate,' I said.

'Oh, right,' he replied, a puzzled expression on his face. 'I wasn't aware he'd been admitted.'

'You said last time he was here that he needs to make some serious changes to his circumstances or you were worried about his future. Well, I don't know what else I can do. I've begged him to start getting his CD4 cell count monitored, to stop drinking, and I've even offered him a room in my house to get clean. But he refuses.'

My lips began to tremble and I curled my toes and fingers to stop myself from crying. Dr Khatri nodded sympathetically, as if he understood my predicament and had seen it many times before.

'Unfortunately, that's about all you can do,' he replied with a kind smile. 'I can try to talk to him again if you'd like?'

'Yes, please.'

'Okay, leave it with me.' He smiled again before leaving me alone outside Nate's ward.

I left without seeing Nate, but hoped he could feel my presence.

CHAPTER TWELVE

FIVE MONTHS, ONE WEEK AFTER DAVID

There were thirty or so members of the Northants Women's Circle inside the function room of Great Houghton's village hall.

They queued at a table, on which was a tray of biscuits and an urn of hot water. They dropped teabags and spoonfuls of instant coffee and sugar into mismatched mugs. Most of them looked as if they were knocking on heaven's door, and they'd come to hear Mary and me discuss our voluntary work at End of the Line.

Janine had only sent me there with Mary out of spite. She was well aware that my comfort zone extended only as far as charming local businesses, applying for National Lottery grants and organising bake and jumble sales. It most definitely did not include this decrepit audience.

Mary had more in common with them than I did. Most old people made me feel uncomfortable, as if their years of wisdom and experience gave them the capacity to see right through me. Mary, however, was an exception. I could have been a serial killer working my way around the room and euthanising every last one of them, and she'd still find some good to see in me.

We sat side by side on two plastic chairs at the front of the hall. I fixed my gaze on her as she used brightly coloured cue cards to remind her of the subjects she wanted to address. Her voice was confident, like she was comfortable among her own kind, whereas I just wanted to be back in the office waiting for the next call.

It was more than five months since I'd helped David and I was craving a new challenge. Steven was supposed to have fitted the bill, but his all-important third call still hadn't come.

In an ideal world, I'll only ever take on one candidate at a time. But sometimes, like buses, two can come along at once and juggling them is exhausting. Like Brendan and Helena, two of my early candidates. He was a middle-aged man with late-stage prostate cancer. It was a Monday evening when he suffocated himself with a plastic bag and a gas canister. The next morning, Helena took an overdose of painkillers. She was a twenty-something having an affair with a married dad-of-two who had reneged on his promise to leave his wife for her. After I helped her see that her death would teach him a lesson, I made sure to hammer the point home by placing an obituary in the local paper on his behalf, using his full name and making sure to describe her as his 'beautiful girlfriend'.

As luck would have it, their funerals fell on the same day in neighbouring churches. I had walked from one to the other, and still got to the office in time for my afternoon shift.

'Do you need a lot of training or can you start answering calls straight away?' asked a woman in the front row. Her ankles were as thick as her calves. I wanted to tell her that there were many pointless bureaucratic hoops to jump through first, which taught you to go against your instinct and to listen rather than advise. But I didn't.

'Yes, there is a lot of training to be done to prepare you for what you might hear,' I replied. 'Some calls we get are quite hard, so we need to be ready for anything.'

After my first interview at End of the Line, I did my homework and read up on the answers expected in their psychometric and personality tests. I was asked my opinions on everything from abortions to what I'd tell a terminally ill friend who didn't want to continue treatment. All were designed to see how open-minded, liberal and non-judgemental I was. The truth is that I am judgemental, but I went against my real self because giving advice isn't listening. Only once did I slip up and say the words 'commit suicide'. 'Commit' is a word we never use, as it makes suicide sound like it's a crime, which it isn't.

I passed, and then came the training – one day a week for the best part of two months. I was quick to get the measure of my mentor Mary. Her adult son had long flown the nest and the country, leaving her with a husband who'd rather spend time on the golf course than with her. I sensed she was aimless and empty and in another life, I'd have fast-tracked her as a candidate.

She filled her days between now and death by offering a friendly ear to others. Her body was slimmer than mine but she hid it away under frumpy clothing and abided by the World War II slogan 'make do and mend'. I'd see her quietly green-eyeing the fashions I wore, and I'd make a point of telling her where I'd bought them and how much they cost.

Mary wore little make-up, ageing her further, and all the fillers in the world couldn't have ironed out the wrinkles in her face. She didn't even colour her short silver hair, as if she didn't see the point of making an effort anymore. When she was considering a question or was lost in thought, she'd move her jaw from left to right like she was easing her loose dentures back into place. I'd rather be dead than become Mary.

Together, we embarked on an exploration of hypothetical depths of despair to see how much I knew about the types of problems callers were experiencing. It wasn't in my nature to try to cheer someone up or tell them I knew how they felt, so that wasn't a habit I needed to break.

Despite her maturity, Mary was easily hoodwinked; that's the problem with those who only ever see the good in people. I found it easy to appear saddened as she recounted some of the horrors callers had told her. Secretly, I couldn't wait until she let go of my reins and I could experience their suffering first-hand.

When the time arrived, I had to stifle my excitement. Not every call came from someone with suicidal thoughts, but when my first one arrived, I had to clench my fists to stop myself from clapping like a sea lion. For the first of my eight probationary shifts, Mary wore an earpiece to listen in on my conversations. Occasionally she'd pass me a suggested line of questioning on a Post-it note, and once the call was over she'd debrief me and offer constructive feedback. Well, *she* found it constructive. I found it time-consuming nonsense. Finally, with the wool well and truly pulled over her eyes, she unscrewed my stabilisers and I was off on my own.

There were many guidelines to follow, and even now I obey them, by and large. I don't agree with them all but there's no point in trying to break the rules just for the sake of it. Remain below the radar and no one will ever see you for what you are. And just to be on the safe side, I took three, maybe even four months before I began playing by my own rules.

I didn't abandon the Internet message boards completely. I'd visit weekly and answer some questions, or continue talking to people I'd already started conversations with. But End of the Line gave me what the boards couldn't.

'What do you think about when you go home at night?' asked a woman at the back of the Northants Women's Circle meeting. 'Do you ever worry how the people you've spoken to are getting on?'

I never forget a voice and I recognised hers. She'd called me before, up to her eyes in credit card debt. She certainly hadn't spent all her money on her appearance.

'Some of them stay with you longer than others,' I replied, and thought of David. His and that of the woman I'd matched him with were the only funerals I hadn't been to. I hadn't even seen a photograph of them. Yet he still burned deeper inside me than anyone else.

CHAPTER THIRTEEN

I hated this house.

I glanced around the open-plan space that was full of barely used objects. A top-of-the-range fifty-two-inch television that was hardly ever turned on, an eight-seater dining room table and chairs that had yet to be eaten off, and two L-shaped sofas were rarely sat upon. Our £20,000 kitchen was adorned with branded, built-in appliances, Corian surfaces and Italian marble-tiled flooring. It was all less than a couple of years old, so beautiful, so box-fresh, but so hollow. The house had everything a family could need with the exception of love. In fact, try as I might, I couldn't remember the last time that all five of us had been under the same roof, together at the same time. The more hours I whiled away there, the darker the walls became and the more I resented the house for changing everything.

The sound of a sneeze broke the silence. That cat had been asleep and curled into a tight ball on the windowsill before waking himself up. I'd assumed it was only dogs that gave their owners enthusiastic welcomes when they returned home. But Bieber always dashed through the house at the sound of Tony's car crawling up the drive. As soon as the front door opened, he'd purr and rub his needy little head on Tony's ankles, and would be rewarded with more attention than my husband gave me. Tonight, Bieber would have to join me in waiting. I took my place at the breakfast bar, staring at the oven. I had to think for a moment to remember what I was even cooking.

I sent all three of them a group WhatsApp message to find out where they were, but no one replied. They must have gone somewhere without a phone or Wi-Fi signal. I'd left the mail neatly arranged on the kitchen counter and I assumed Tony had sifted through it, as it was no longer how I'd left it, in size order.

I turned on the radio to find my favoured 1980s music station. Whitney Houston was asking 'How Will I Know', the Eurythmics wanted to discover 'Who's That Girl?' and Carly Simon inquired 'Why'. They asked a lot of questions back then. All I wanted to know was where was my family?

When the six o'clock news began, I assumed Tony had already left the office and gone to the gym to knock the hell out of a punch bag. He was probably training for another of his white-collar boxing tournaments, where he and other like-minded office workers take each other on in the ring in organised, regulated matches. When things became strained between us, he'd spend more and more time there training. And while he'd told me in no uncertain terms not to attend his fights, I couldn't help myself, and stood in the shadows at the back of the Freemasons' Hall function room, increasingly aroused by each punch he threw and the damage inflicted on his opponent.

Alice was probably still at an after-school club and would be dropped off later by a friend's mum, while Effie might be crying on her friends' shoulders over Matt, who was likely blaming his public humiliation on her, for sending all and sundry his naked selfie. Or maybe Tony had taken the girls out for pizza without me. I wouldn't put it past him.

I'd grown accustomed to watching my family interact while I lurked on the sidelines like a bit-part character in my own local theatre production. I didn't blame the girls completely – Tony had taken it upon himself to organise birthday parties and trips out, and he spoiled them by making too much time to listen to every minute detail of their lives. That put immense pressure on me to keep up appearances and pretend to be interested in their stories, or else I'd look like an uninvolved mother. Only I wasn't as convincing as my husband.

The distance between Tony and me had expanded from a crack to the size of a chasm shortly before my cancer diagnosis. I wasn't even worthy of a peck on the cheek when he brushed past me on the stairs. I'd remind him how good he looked as he changed into his gym gear, then pretend not to be hurt when he didn't reciprocate with a compliment of his own. I'd even feign liking the sleeve of tattoos gradually expanding up his left arm from wrist to shoulder, when quietly I hated them.

For a man approaching his late thirties, Tony was in enviable shape. When his friends had visited our former house for summer barbecues and he wore a sleeveless top and cargo shorts, I'd watched their wives ogling him. Their husbands had 'dad bods' and beer bellies, and it was all the women could do to keep themselves from panting when they saw Tony. Once upon a time, I'd felt sorry for them, but now I was envious because at least their out-of-shape partners were present. Tony wasn't. He was far, far away.

I poured myself another glass from the bottle of Merlot from the online wine club he'd joined and never got around to cancelling, and asked myself if I'd been more in tune with Tony's feelings, might I have been able to pinpoint the exact moment he'd looked at me and decided I was no longer the woman he'd married?

The last time I'd instigated intimacy between us, the girls were playing with Henry in the garden and I'd followed Tony upstairs. He'd moved into the spare room weeks before, but I'd told myself it was only because the stress of setting up his own IT support business was giving him sleepless nights. Then, somewhere along the line, he had decided to make the temporary measure permanent, and without discussion.

I crept up on him as he changed out of his work suit and, before he could protest, I slipped my hand down the front of his trousers and wrapped my other arm around his waist.

'What are you doing?' he'd asked. He sounded irritated.

'I think you know what I'm doing,' I replied, and moved my hand inside his briefs and played with his balls.

'It was a rhetorical question,' he replied. I could feel him stirring but he tried to resist. He squirmed until I removed my hand. But I wasn't ready to give up, so I began unbuttoning my blouse. He used to find it sexy when I'd get naked while he was fully clothed. It would turn him on like nothing else.

'Laura, stop it. I told you, I don't have the time.'

'You never have time,' I sighed. 'Not for me, anyway.' Part of me hated myself for still desiring a physical relationship with someone who didn't want one with me. But I longed to connect with him.

'Maybe you should occupy more of your time with your children, and leave me the hell alone.'

'What's that supposed to mean?'

He didn't answer.

'Do you think I'm spending too long at End of the Line? I can cut down my hours, if that's what you want.'

'I don't care what you do.'

'You used to. We can't sort out whatever is happening between us if you don't try.'

'Some things are beyond sorting out.'

I felt sick. 'I don't understand why you're being like this. We've been married for almost sixteen years. Every couple has bumps in the road . . .'

'A bump? Is that what you've convinced yourself this is?' He lowered his voice to make sure the children couldn't hear him through the open window. Then he looked at me with a contempt I'd never seen in his eyes before.

'I know about you, Laura,' he growled. 'I know what you are and what you've done. *I know everything.*'

My eyes locked on to his and my legs felt as if they were about to give way. He couldn't have been referring to what I thought he was.

'What . . . what are you talking about?' I stammered.

'You tried to hide your old social services file from me, but I found it and read the whole fucking thing,' he snapped. 'You have lied to me right from the very beginning of our relationship, and then every step of the way since. About what happened when you went into care in that house with Nate . . . the lot. I have no idea who I'm married to.'

I took a step back and felt the bile rising from my stomach, up my throat and into my mouth. I tried to pretend his words hadn't just slashed me like broken glass.

'You don't have anything to say, do you?' he continued.

He was right, I didn't. I cursed myself; I knew it had been a huge mistake digging up the past. But once I had it written in black and white, I couldn't dispose of it, no matter how hurtful and inaccurate it was. Instead, I'd hidden the file, so I could reread it and torture myself over and over again. Only Tony had clearly stumbled across it, too. It explained why he'd become so distant with me, why sometimes when I looked at him with love, he looked at me with loathing.

Suddenly I was brought back to the present by the sound of a car engine outside. I craned my neck, hoping to see Tony's car. But it was the obese couple that lived next door. Tony was probably waiting until later, and for me to go to bed before he brought the girls home.

The oven timer chimed, so I slipped on my oven gloves and removed a large cooking pot. I pushed the lid to one side to remind myself it was a chicken casserole I'd made. I poured some into a bowl for me, and the rest I'd leave for the others to heat up if they were hungry. They'd probably ignore it though. The freezer was packed full of Tupperware meals I'd made for four, but that'd only been eaten by one.

CHAPTER FOURTEEN

FIVE MONTHS,

TWO WEEKS AFTER DAVID

'If you can't see yourself getting any better, what's the best outcome you could hope for?' I asked Steven.

Like all my questions, it was delivered in a caring, measured manner. But it was a loaded one. I focused on the second hand of the clock on the wall, measuring the time of his response. Twenty-four seconds elapsed before he spoke again.

'That one morning I just don't wake up.'

'You don't want to wake up,' I reiterated. 'I understand.' And I did. The same thought had crossed my own mind over the years, more times than I cared to admit. Only, I possessed the strength to soldier on.

'Aren't you going to ask me what I have to live for?' he said.

'Would you like me to? Would you listen to me if I came up with some reasons?'

'No, probably not.'

'Then I won't patronise you. When you've thought long and hard about bringing your life to an end like you have, I don't have the right to tell you you're wrong, and that's not what End of the Line is here for. I'm not going to try to pull you out of a hole; I'm in that hole with you. Have you considered how you might do it? In our first conversation, you mentioned ending your life by standing in front of a train.'

'I've changed my mind.'

'What are your thoughts now?'

'Hanging.'

My eyes lit up. Almost sixty per cent of suicidal men end their lives by strangulation, but I'd yet to come across one. The prospect immediately excited me. My tally to date was eight overdoses on illegal or prescription drugs, three jumpers and four who'd bled to death.

I took a moment to compose myself. 'Where would you do it?'

'In my bedroom. I live in a house with a vaulted ceiling and wooden beams. I've tested them by doing pull-ups so I know they can take my weight. Honestly, it's the perfect place.' His voice was animated, like a child trying to impress a parent.

I was pleased to hear from Steven now he'd finally found me again, although he took a little longer than I'd expected. He seemed more serious than ever about wanting to die, as if he'd taken the time between calls to really consider how he might go about it.

The door to the office opened and Zoe entered. She gave me one of her lipstick-on-her-teeth smiles and a thumbs-up, then took a seat a couple of desks away from mine and unpacked her bag. It was a satchel I hadn't seen before. If there was any doubt she was a lesbian, she'd just answered it. I moved the receiver closer to my mouth and chose my words carefully so she didn't overhear me.

'Why would you choose . . . those means . . . over any other process?'

'Because I reckon it's quick and it's easy and not much can go wrong.'

I shook my head. This was precisely why people like Steven needed people like me. He was naive. Only if his method was meticulous and well researched would it be 'quick and easy'. There was so much he hadn't taken into account. If he chose a drop hanging, he'd instantly fall unconscious and death would soon follow. Now *that* would be 'quick and easy'.

But chances were the beams in an old house weren't high enough for that, so Steven's drop would likely be just a few feet. If he got it wrong, he could suffer a long and drawn-out death. I had so much to teach him.

'I've bought some rope and I've been practising my knots by watching YouTube clips,' he offered.

'I don't think it will be as easy as that.'

'Why not?'

I glanced over towards Zoe. She was engrossed in a Snapchat conversation, sending silly pictures of herself with rabbit ears and a dog's snout to some equally juvenile-minded fool.

'Because there are a lot of complications involved in your method, if that's what you choose,' I whispered. 'But we can work through that another time if it's the direction you decide to take.'

'So you'll help me?'

'As I've explained to you before, it's not my job to try to talk you out of anything or into my way of thinking. I'm just here to listen.'

'What if . . . ?' His voice trailed off.

I waited for him to finish his sentence, but he didn't. 'David?' I asked. 'Are you still there?'

'David?'

'Sorry, I meant Steven.' I pinched my arm hard. 'You were saying, "what if"?'

'What if you were with me when I did it?'

My stomach somersaulted like it did each and every time someone asked me that question.

'If you need someone to be with you, then I'm happy to listen and keep you company.'

'I don't mean on the phone.'

His question caught me off guard and I wasn't sure if I understood him correctly. He was hesitant before he spoke again.

'What if I asked you to be with me, Laura, here in my house, when I hanged myself? Would you come?'

CHAPTER FIFTEEN

I slept through my alarm and no one had thought to wake me up, so the house was silent and empty by the time I left my bed.

I passed the spare room that Tony had taken as his own and wondered if I'd ever feel his breath against my neck again as he slept. My arm brushed against the staircase wall and left a black mark on my white dressing gown. I cursed the wall and threw the gown into the washing machine. And as I waited for the thirty-minute cycle to finish, I sat at the breakfast bar in my pyjamas, tucking into two strawberry yoghurts that Effie loved but were soon to go out of date. The machine's drum tossed my dressing gown around in all directions. It resembled how the inside of my head had felt since Steven's last phone call.

His request for me to be there for him in person as he died was all I could think about. For the last thirty-six hours, every time I tried to process one thought, another would come crashing down upon it, and they generally involved him.

Often, people don't like to die alone. Many I'd assisted had shown their gratitude by asking to share their final moments with me on the other end of the telephone. A minority had been too self-centred to think about my needs, and I'd only learned of their deaths through notices in the local newspaper. But no one, not even David, had asked me to be there in person when they died. Until Steven.

What if I asked you to be with me, Laura, here in my house, when I hanged myself? Would you come? His question still echoed inside me.

At the time, I'd blinked hard and shaken my head, taken aback by his offer. I'd attempted to retain my calm, professional veneer.

'I don't think that would be appropriate,' I replied.

'Sorry, I'm just . . . scared that I might get it wrong.' He sounded disappointed in me.

'I understand that, and I'd probably feel the same way if it were me. But I can be with you by phone for as long as you want.'

'I need you here, to tell me if I'm messing something up and reassure me it's all going to be all right. And to be there for me . . . you know . . . at the end.'

'Are you having second thoughts?'

'No, no, I'm not. But it's just that you, like, *get* me. You aren't like those therapists and counsellors who try to tell me how much I have to live for, or dose me up on a cocktail of drugs so I can't think straight anymore. You properly care.'

'I do.' I was flattered he saw that in me.

'Would you at least think about it?'

'I can't, Steven. I'm sorry, but you're asking me to do something that's illegal and completely unethical. I could get into so much trouble.'

An awkward silence surrounded us, neither knowing what to say next.

'You're right and I'm sorry, I shouldn't have asked,' he replied. 'I won't do it again.'

'That's okay.'

'I should go now,' he said and hung up.

I'd remained rigid with the receiver clamped to my ear as the end-of-call tone sounded. The rational side of me bristled at his invitation.

I was annoyed with him for putting me in such a difficult position. But I felt excited, too – and that made me anxious.

'Is everything all right, Laura?' asked Sanjay. 'You're away with the fairies.'

Bugger off and leave me alone, was what I wanted to say. I needed space to process Steven's request.

'Yes, I've just had a difficult conversation,' I replied. 'Rape, you know.'

'Do you need a time-out in the appointment room to talk about it?'

'No, I'll be fine. But thank you.'

I gave him a half-hearted smile and hurried from my booth to the bathroom. I splashed cold water on my face, then patted it with a paper towel. I stared at my reflection in the mirror as I reapplied my lipstick and foundation.

Of course you can't do it! Why would he think you might? You're a mother, for God's sake. He has nothing to lose, whereas your children and husband need you. You have no idea who he really is when he's away from the phone. He could be a lunatic. You'd never be so stupid as to say yes.

Suddenly the washing machine beeped to inform me the spin cycle had finished. I put my damp dressing gown in the tumble dryer and shoved a cinnamon bagel in the toaster.

I'd made the right decision to refuse. Being present for Steven's death was a ridiculous, dangerous idea.

CHAPTER SIXTEEN

'I'm afraid I can't find any record of him being here,' the nurse began, scanning through Nate's case notes on his computer. 'Are you absolutely sure you've got the right hospital?'

'Of course I'm bloody sure! Do I look like I'm stupid? I was here two weeks ago when he was in the high-dependency unit. Look again.'

He checked once more, but when his response came in the form of an apologetic shrug, I wanted to launch myself across the desk at him.

I'd arrived at the ward where Nate was being treated to find he was no longer there. Naturally I feared the worst and hurried towards the reception desk. My relief that my friend wasn't dead was replaced with frustration that he'd clearly discharged himself.

My nose ran, and angry, burning tears poured down my cheeks as I dashed back to my car. I sat in the driver's seat, slipping from present to past as memories of that final weekend under the care of our foster mother came to mind.

I recalled that whatever liquid anaesthetic Sylvia had given Nate to drink with his breakfast turned out to be much more powerful than the usual dose.

'It'll make you relax for longer,' she'd advised as she passed him a brown glass bottle and told him to drink its contents in one gulp. Nate obliged and screwed up his face at the bitter taste. The one occasion he'd spat out something similar without her noticing, he'd ended up in more physical pain than he'd ever imagined. Sylvia was looking out for his best interests, he told me, as if to put me at ease. Neither of us believed it. Within moments, the liquid had the desired effect and his limbs drooped loosely from their sockets as if he had no strength left in them. Nate barely acknowledged Saturday morning's visitor when he arrived to take him away soon after.

Hours later, he'd been returned and was moving restlessly in his sleep. I remained with him in his bedroom because I wanted the first face he saw when he awoke to belong to someone who loved him.

As I patiently waited, I played with his toy cars and built dream homes with large windows and gardens out of his Lego – presents that Wednesday night's visitor brought before Nate disappeared with him for hours at a time. I loathed dolls and plastic ponies and the sorts of toys girls were supposed to prefer. I also despised the clothes Sylvia put me in. That weekend I didn't understand why she'd insisted I wore a pretty skirt with white daisies around the hem and a too-tight T-shirt that cut into my underarms and overemphasised the slight curves of my chest.

By early evening, Nate had awoken and we'd made the most of the empty living room. I absent-mindedly pulled out specks of foam stuffing from the arms of the sofa as we tried to guess what was being shown on the side of the television screen that had been smashed. We loved to watch travel programmes and imagine we were anywhere in the world but in that flat. However, when Sylvia eventually appeared at the door, she wasn't alone. The atmosphere instantly darkened.

'Say hello to my friends, don't be rude,' Sylvia began in an everything-is-fine tone. Sensing our trepidation but needing us to be on best behaviour, she shot us a glare, but neither Nate nor I responded. The three men behind her transfixed us.

The strangers stared at us and smiled with their mouths, but not their eyes. Nobody in my immediate world, with the exception of Nate, ever smiled with their eyes. And as time marched on, I'd noticed the light behind his eyes was gradually dimming. It made me sad. I had made him my anchor, but other forces were dragging him along the seabed, further and further away. I felt him pulling at me.

I glared at the unwelcome guests; two were dark-skinned, with salt and pepper beards and baggy clothing. The other was white, slim, clean-cut, with dark, swept-back hair and a flawless complexion. I remember I'd never seen such shiny shoes.

'Nate, my friends want to know if you'd like to go for a drive with them in their car?' Sylvia continued. 'You like your cars, don't you? You're always playing with them.'

Nate eyed them suspiciously, knowing what their plans for him really meant.

'And Laura, my other friend wants to take you shopping,' she added. 'I told you she was a pretty little thing,' she said to the smart man. 'Stand up and show him your skirt.'

'But the shops are all shut now,' I replied meekly and remained seated. I looked to Nate, who clambered stiffly to his feet, clearly still in pain from earlier.

'No, leave her alone, just take me,' he said.

Sylvia scowled. 'What did you just say?'

'I'll go, but leave Laura alone.'

'Who are you to tell me what's best for her?' Sylvia yelled. 'I feed and clothe you and put a roof over your heads and now she's old enough to start paying her way.'

'No!' shouted Nate.

I hadn't witnessed my friend this angry before. My eyes brimmed; I didn't want to go with the stranger. I wanted to stay there with Nate. He would protect me like he'd promised until we were old enough to run away together.

Suddenly Sylvia surged across the room faster than I'd ever seen her move, and reached out to grab my arm. Nate pushed himself into her path. It fuelled her fury and she clipped him hard around the side of the head with the back of her hand, shoving him backwards onto the sofa.

The three men stood in silence, watching, as again Nate rose to his feet to come between Sylvia and me. She craned her neck in the direction of the men. 'If you want him, then help me,' she barked. But before they could assist, Nate drew his arm back and gave the hardest punch his young arms would allow. His fist collided with Sylvia's temple and she lost her balance, toppling sideways and hitting her head on the fireplace mantelpiece. She landed on the floor, but before she could move again, Nate lifted a ceramic ashtray above his head and brought it down upon her forehead.

The men hurried out of the flat and back into the dusk. Nate and I remained motionless, staring at Sylvia; ash and cigarette butts littered her cheeks and neck. Her last breath was swift and sudden, not laboured. And I felt no pity or remorse for having played a part in it.

When it was clear to us she wouldn't be moving again, we hurried to our rooms, threw our only clean clothes into bin bags along with our toothbrushes, a bar of soap and a towel. Then we ran. Even huddling together that first night in the cold, dark woodland of Delapré Abbey, we felt safer than we ever had with Sylvia. But it was only to last another day before we were approached by two policewomen.

When questioned at the police station, we told the truth about how we'd hurt our foster mother and how she had treated us, but they didn't believe us. I was dismissed as an impressionable child caught under the spell of an older boy, and no matter how vigorously I tried to convince them Nate was trying to protect me, he faced the full force of the law.

On the advice of a solicitor who didn't care about his young, damaged charge, Nate pleaded guilty to Sylvia's manslaughter and was sent away to a young offender institution. Then, as he came of age, he was transferred to an adult prison, and by the time he was released back into society in his mid-twenties, the deterioration in him was already in full swing. Meanwhile I'd moved on to other foster homes, eventually finding a new anchor in Tony. Nate found his in alcohol.

I left the hospital car park and drove to the places where I'd found Nate in the past: bus stops, the food recycling bins behind supermarkets, a day centre, park benches, and a row of derelict houses ready for demolition. All I needed was a glimpse of him to reassure myself that he was okay. But he was keeping himself well hidden.

CHAPTER SEVENTEEN

Mary wrapped both of her wrinkled hands around a mug of chamomile tea and closed her watery eyes.

Her incessant sniffs as she tried to choke back another sob were getting on my nerves. I wanted to slap her around the face and tell her to get a grip. Instead, I gritted my teeth and placed my hand on hers and hoped that liver spots weren't contagious.

We were sitting together on the sofa in the appointment room at End of the Line. It was a rarely used ground-floor space designated for visitors who preferred to talk to a volunteer face-to-face rather than anonymously by phone. Our surroundings were every bit as miserable as the lives of the visitors who came here to spread their doom and gloom. Faded reproduction watercolours hung on the walls above a white plastic rack containing dog-eared advice leaflets. A padlocked door linked our building to the derelict offices next door.

A barely visible green light attached to the security camera above us remained static, indicating our conversation wasn't being recorded. Had Mary been a client and not the least threatening sap you could ever meet, one of our colleagues upstairs would be monitoring and recording our chat.

'He was determined to end his life,' Mary whimpered. 'I asked every open-ended question I could think of to find something or someone to make it worth living, but he was adamant.'

'You know it's not your job to make them feel better about themselves or to change their outlook on life,' I replied. 'The last thing they want to hear is your disapproval. They're often frightened to die by themselves and want their last moments to feel as normal as possible, though.'

'I could hear him preparing himself in his bedroom and he sounded just so . . . normal . . . but then hearing someone taking an overdose and slowly dying . . . I'll never get used to that.'

'We've all been there, so we do feel for you,' I said. It was a lie. I didn't feel sympathy and, if anything, I was angry she'd got to that call before me. Death had fallen into the lap of an ungrateful old woman who hadn't deserved it.

The extent of distress a volunteer feels after a particularly harrowing call is graded from one to five. And when Janine spotted the emotional state Mary had wound herself up into, she called a level four. The rules strongly suggested that Mary didn't complete her shift and instead debriefed with one of her peers. As I was the only one not on a call, the job fell to lucky old me.

'Towards the end, I'm sorry to say this, but I thought about hanging up on him,' Mary admitted. I wanted to slap her again, this time hard enough to send her dentures flying across the room. To not hear his final breath would've been like waiting for hours at a concert and leaving just as the singer came on stage. 'He started making this horrible, guttural rasping sound and I think he might have vomited. I wouldn't be surprised if he choked to death. What a horrible way to leave the world.'

That would have been a new one, even for a veteran like me. Now, quietly, I was grateful Janine had asked me to debrief Mary. It meant I'd made her relive the pain of that call all over again.

◆ ◆ ◆

'I'm so sorry, I really am.'

I had no doubt that when Steven called back later that week and offered me his apology, it was heartfelt.

'It's fine,' I replied.

'No, it's not. I shouldn't have put you in that position and I don't know what I was thinking. I've felt shitty about it for the last few days and I really need you to know I understand I was wrong.'

'Honestly, Steven, I'm not here to judge you, I'm here to listen to everything you have to say to me.'

'Who listens to you when *you* need to talk?'

I paused. Once upon a time it was Nate, then Tony, and most recently David. Now the only ear I had was Henry's. 'I have friends and colleagues,' I replied.

'Do you have a family?'

We were discouraged from answering personal questions in case our answers made us sound self-satisfied. But we weren't supposed to lie about it either, just downplay it. 'Yes, I do,' I replied.

'I'm trying to imagine what you're like in the real world.'

'Why's that?'

'I was just building up a mental picture of you. I imagine you looking a bit like an older Jennifer Lawrence. No offence.'

'None taken,' I chuckled and felt my cheeks blush. 'Even the "older" part is flattering. But alas, I'm not in her league.'

'Do you have kids?'

'Yes. Do you?'

'No.'

'Is being a father something you have ever considered?'

'I didn't have a dad, so I wouldn't know how to be one. I'd just fuck it up.'

'Nature and instinct have ways of leading us into parenthood.' I read that once in a magazine lying on a table in a therapist's waiting room. I didn't believe it, but I copied it into the back of my notebook in case it came in useful.

'There was someone once, I guess, who I considered having a family with,' Steven said.

'Would you like to tell me about her?'

'She was sweet and kind and I thought that she really loved me, but suddenly she disappeared from my life.'

'I'm sorry to hear that.'

I was happy to hear it, actually. Because the more open and vulnerable Steven made himself to me, the more I believed he was genuine. I'd tried catching him out by asking him to repeat stories he'd told me before and listening carefully for contradictions. But each time, they remained almost word for word identical.

It didn't mean he wasn't being dishonest, though. If somebody like me can portray an image of a person I'm not, there's nothing to prevent anyone else doing the same thing. And frustratingly, I didn't know enough about him to check up on him. Could I trust him like I'd trusted David?

With every conversation, Steven reminded me more and more of the friend I'd lost. However, this time I wasn't going to allow myself to become so emotionally involved. The mistake I'd made with David was that I'd allowed him to get to me. I'd hoped that when he stepped over the cliff top and the tide swept his body away, that would be the end of our relationship and I could move on. But even now I heard his voice in the wind as it swayed the branches of the trees; it was inside the music I played to cover the silence and now it came through the telephone line in Steven's voice. Perhaps Steven had been destined to find me and make me his offer. Maybe by being present as he hanged himself, I could actually free myself of David.

I glanced at Mary, across the room. Her eyes were still puffy as she slipped on her well-worn coat and picked up her bag, ready to return to an empty nest with a husband who hadn't seen her properly in years.

For the briefest of moments, I could see myself becoming like her, surrounded by people but so desperately alone, too set in her ways to take a risk. It scared me to death.

She couldn't cope with hearing a person die, but I could. I also knew I could deal with watching it happen, too. So I made a decision and hoped I wouldn't live to regret it.

'I'll do it.'

'I'm sorry?' replied Steven.

I whispered into the receiver, 'If you are serious about wanting to end your life, then I will be with you in person when you do it.'

CHAPTER EIGHTEEN

SIX MONTHS AFTER DAVID

'Why don't you tell me what brought you to where you are today?' I asked Steven over the phone.

I gingerly took a sip from my steaming mug of peppermint tea and sank my hips down into the chair, making notes in the book I kept hidden in my bag. I listened quietly as Steven filled in the blanks of his story.

He hadn't been a victim of physical or sexual abuse, he was addiction-free and he wasn't in debt – the most common reasons for suicidal thoughts. Instead he was, like a quarter of the British population at some time, suffering from depression. It had begun in his teenage years with occasional depressive chapters. Gradually those episodes became a series until they took control of his life, affecting his studies, ruining his exam results and leading to a career of unfulfilling jobs. When he found me, he'd been struggling for two years with psychotic depression that had led to hallucinations and paranoia.

To give Steven credit, he hadn't just given in and accepted his fate; he'd battled against his own brain with therapies and an alphabet's worth of drugs. Some had brought him temporary relief but made his world a blurred, false reality. And none of the professionals he consulted could help him see how the next twenty-eight years of his life would be any better than the first. He was taking up space in this world and offering nothing in return.

'What do you get out of our arrangement?' asked Steven suddenly. 'You're going to all this trouble to help me, and in return all you're asking is for me to tell you about myself. Is there nothing else I can do for you?'

I was touched by his thoughtfulness. Nobody, not even David, had asked me that.

'No, there's nothing,' I replied. 'Your faith is all I need.'

'Can I ask if you've done this for anyone else?' he asked.

'Yes, there have been others.'

'Can you tell me more about them?'

'Would you like the next person I choose to know about you?'

'No, not really.'

'Then you have to respect their privacy.' I hesitated before continuing. 'I help different people in different ways. This life is difficult to negotiate alone. Some people fall by the wayside and need help in finding their way back onto the right road. Others want to stay off the road completely, and that's where I come in.'

'You called me David before. Was he someone like me?'

My skin prickled as if it had been brushed by stinging nettles. 'Yes, I did help David. You remind me of him a little, which is why I might have said his name in error.'

I took a cursory glance around the room at the rest of the team. Two of them were gossiping by a boiling kettle in the kitchen, one was on a call, and Janine was in her office staring hard at her computer. The glass in a picture frame behind her reflected the image of a moving roulette wheel on her screen. Her expression told me it wasn't moving in her favour.

'Now, let's get back to what we were talking about earlier,' I continued, and detailed where the noose should sit on his neck. 'If you don't do it correctly, your instinct isn't going to be to just remain there until you pass out, you're going to claw at that rope and try to stop yourself from being strangled. You'll be in a huge amount of pain and it'll take five minutes to lose consciousness and a further twenty to die.'

Hearing him scribbling notes satisfied me. I was quietly making a to-do list of my own, reminding myself to search his house after his death to ensure he'd left no evidence linking us. No stray notes screwed up and tossed into a bin, and my name not written on a pad anywhere. I'd also need to take the contract-free pay-as-you-go mobile I'd asked him to buy to call me once I'd agreed to help him. And I didn't need the police sniffing around his actual phone and finding End of the Line's number on there again like they had with Chantelle.

'Can I ask you for something before . . . *it* happens?' he asked.

'Of course.'

'I feel almost embarrassed saying this, but could you . . . hug . . . me? We don't need to talk or anything and it's not some kind of sexual thing, it's just that I can't remember the last time I felt anyone's arms around me.'

My mouth opened and then wavered ever so slightly. 'Yes,' I replied, trying to gain control of any sign of emotion. But I knew exactly how he felt.

CHAPTER NINETEEN

SEVEN MONTHS AFTER DAVID

I woke from a dream with a sudden jolt, confused but aware I'd just yelled the word 'no!'.

I sat bolt upright in my darkened bedroom and turned to Tony for reassurance, momentarily forgetting he no longer slept in our bed. I used some breathing techniques cribbed from my yoga classes and thought about Henry's beautiful smile until I felt calm again.

Since I'd agreed to be present for Steven's death, it was nigh-on impossible for me to enjoy more than a couple of hours of sleep at a time without waking up and thinking of him. I attempted to tire myself out in the early evenings by signing up for Zumba and body-pump gym classes, but all they did were make my endorphins skyrocket, leaving me wide awake into the early hours.

I began to think about the five rules I gave my candidates and what amendments I'd created specifically for Steven. After all, this was the first time I'd ever been invited to the scene to supervise a person taking their own life. While I trusted him as much as I could trust anyone in his position, I'd need to protect my safety and ensure I knew where I was going and in good time. I told him that at no point must anyone join us. Also, everything in his house would need to be exactly where he said it was. If I had the slightest inkling something was out of sorts, I would leave.

The alarm clock read 4.27 a.m. I couldn't shift my anxiety and needed comfort from my husband. So I padded quietly along the landing, passing the girls' ajar bedroom doors where it was too dark for me to see inside. The curtains in Tony's room remained open, however, and an orange streetlight cast a tangerine glow against the wallpaper. It was as I moved to slip silently between his sheets that I realised his bed was how I'd left it that morning, unused and with four decorative cushions propped upright by the pillows. He had not returned home.

I moved both hands in front of my mouth as if in prayer. Where was Tony? And more importantly, who was he with?

Entering the kitchen, I poured myself a glass of water from the dispenser in the fridge, and tried to repress my unease. I unplugged my phone from the charger and checked to see if he'd texted me or left a voicemail after I'd gone to bed. But there was nothing.

I looked at the suicide message boards on my tablet, because reading people's misery and answering questions often helped to relax me. But not this morning.

Eventually I gave up, defeated, and headed upstairs to change my clothing before leaving the house.

◆ ◆ ◆

The wind hit my face like a sharp slap before circling my head and blowing my ponytail in all manner of directions. I'd learned from last time how cold it could get up here even in August, so I'd brought a pair of patterned gloves and a matching scarf with me. I stood firm behind the safety railings, two hundred feet above the car park below.

The Hartley Hotel had been a blot on Northampton town centre's landscape for as long as I could remember; a grotesque twenty-five-storey building that was only possible to ignore if you walked with your eyes closed. I made my way unnoticed through the mahogany-clad lobby towards the clunky lifts and up to the top floor. There was a musty stairwell to climb, illuminated by a green emergency exit sign, before I reached the door to the roof.

It was my fifth candidate, Eleanor, who'd told me about it. She'd lifted her feet from the asphalt where I was standing now, clambered over the railings and dropped to the ground below. Now I'd occasionally use the location to check if I was still needed in this world. I'd lean forward against the rusty railings, and if the metal bars were to bend and snap, it'd be fate deciding my time was up, not me. If I remained where I was, it meant God still had a plan for me to rid the world of the terminally unhappy.

There were some occasions, especially after Henry was taken away from me, when it wouldn't have taken much for me to have leaned a little too far until gravity won out. Eleanor had allowed me to hear her final gasp of breath before she died on impact. The only thing to prevent me from doing the same was my anchor, and the knowledge there'd be nobody to hear my final exhalation. What a waste that would be.

Ever since I was a little girl, I've thought the most beautiful sound in the world is a person's last breath. It's a singularly unique noise that marks the transition from this life into the next. To have spent time working with a candidate, encouraging and reinforcing their decision to die and then to be rewarded with their final breath is intoxicating. It's something that can never be replicated. The first time I heard it, it came from my mother's lips.

The inherited cancer gene that came close to killing me years later took her life when she was just thirty-two and I was eleven. For days, it had been just her and my dad alone in their bedroom, with twice-daily visits from Macmillan nurses.

Dad wanted to keep the inevitable away from me and my younger sisters, Sara and Karen, for as long as possible. So we'd been uprooted and landed on the Ronson family's welcome mat further up the road. But every so often I'd sneak back home to visit Mum, even though she was asleep much of the time. On her final day, I hid in the living room of the bungalow and waited until Dad was in the bathroom before I crawled under their bed. That way I could be close to Mum without having to look at her skeletal frame and sunken face.

Her body barely made a dip in the mattress above me, but I traced where her outline might be with my fingers. Her breath was becoming heavy and laboured, then suddenly she gave out a thick gasp like she was being suffocated before there was silence. I heard Dad flush the toilet just as Mum exhaled one last time. It was a long, drawn-out and delicate breath that I imagined being as soft as cotton wool. I felt it inside me, like something lighting up my spine and making each of my nerve endings tingle. I thought that if I could push my lips out as far as I could and breathe in, I might capture that last breath and hold it inside me forever.

But our shared moment was all too brief, because when my father returned and discovered she was dead, he fell to his knees and sobbed with guilt for allowing her to die alone. I didn't admit I was there and remained motionless until he left to call for help.

Without his soulmate by his side, Dad didn't know how to function as a father or a human being. Even his body seemed to shrink under the pressure of grief. It wasn't enough for him to see her image live on in his three daughters. And over the following year, as his depression escalated, I took on Mum's role around the house, washing dishes and clothes, cleaning bathrooms and reading the girls their bedtime stories.

By day, Dad rarely washed, changed his clothes or left the house. At night, I'd lie in my bed listening to him aimlessly pace or watch the television way into the early hours until he finally fell asleep.

Sometimes, when the bungalow was quiet and I was alone, I'd close my eyes and remember the sound of Mum's last breath, and it brought us closer than two people could ever be. How I longed to hear something like it again.

Gradually, a divide opened up between my younger sisters and me, because while I attended school during the day, they got to spend time at home with their remaining parent. And then for a while, it was as if they were accomplishing what I couldn't by lifting him out of his dark place with their imaginary tea parties and garden picnics.

'What are you doing, Daddy?' I asked him one Saturday afternoon. He was in the kitchen, crushing something on a breadboard with the back of a spoon.

'Would you like to help me?' He smiled warmly and passed me a rolling pin. I'll never forget that smile, because it radiated from his eyes, too. It was the first time I'd seen it since Mum died. 'I need you to turn these tablets into a powder, put them in that jug and then stir it really well.'

He gave me a handful of pills. I was too buoyed up by his need for me to ask the purpose of what we were doing. When I finished, he popped more tablets from another blister pack, like the one he kept by the side of his bed to help him sleep, and we turned them into powder, too.

Quietly, we worked together, me with the rolling pin and him with a spoon, neither of us saying a word but me sensing everything in our world was about to change for the better. I was being rewarded for my patience; my dad was coming back to me. When we ran out of tablets, we brushed the small powdery mound into a jug. He added a pint and a half of semi-skimmed milk, heaped in tablespoons of sugar and squirted some strawberry-flavoured milkshake syrup inside.

'Girls, come and get your milk,' he shouted, and Karen and Sara skipped in from the garden to join us, squishing their bottoms on the same wooden seat at the kitchen table. He poured out three glasses and I pushed my empty glass towards him.

'You're a big girl now,' he told me. 'Why don't you get some cola instead?'

'This tastes funny,' complained Sara, but Dad ignored her and grinned at me. I liked being in on the joke even if I didn't understand the punchline.

'Can we go and play in the garden now?' Karen asked, draining her glass.

'Why don't we all go and lie down for a nap?' he replied.

'But I'm not sleepy,' Sara replied.

'Well, let's play a game. We'll all keep our eyes closed for half an hour and if we don't fall asleep then we can go to the park for ice creams instead.'

My two excited siblings skipped towards Dad's room and jumped on the mattress as he and I followed. But as I was about to enter, he stretched his arm across the door.

'It's just us today, sweetheart.' He leaned forward and kissed me on the forehead. 'You're stronger than us. Once you find your anchor, never let go of it. No matter what.'

Before I could ask what he meant, he gently closed the door and turned the lock. I didn't know what was going to happen in that room, but I had a strong sense that I needed to hear it. So I remained with my ear pressed to the door, straining to decipher their muffled chat. Eventually I slumped to the floor with my back to it, waiting for the thirty-minute deadline to pass. I hated closed doors, because closed doors meant secrets and I didn't like being kept out of secrets.

Gradually their conversation petered out into silence as they drifted into sleep. I guessed that we wouldn't be going to the park and crossed my arms in an exaggerated sulk. I was ready to walk away when I felt my body tingle. A few moments later and it happened again. Then a longer time passed before I felt it once more. It was the same warm feeling I'd had on hearing Mum's last breath.

Only then did I understand what a wonderful gift my father had given me. He'd loved me with such intensity that he wanted our family to live on inside me, the strongest member of our unit. No matter where I was or what I did with the rest of my life, his act had allowed me to hold them all inside me where they would never have to suffer loss or pain.

I padded around the house for days, waiting patiently in case I was wrong and they reappeared from Dad's bedroom. Sometimes I made the most of having the television to myself, and sat watching dramas and Children's BBC. But it all came to an abrupt end when my English teacher appeared at the front door to ask why I'd been absent from school for the best part of a week.

Later, when the police cars and ambulances arrived, I was kept behind a closed living room door as a policewoman in uniform held my hand and told me everything would be all right. She was lying. She couldn't have known that.

I glanced out of the window at the neighbours huddling together on their driveways, puzzled as to what terrible thing had happened in their street that required so many flashing blue lights. Some held each other tightly when black plastic bags containing my family were stretchered out.

'That poor little lass!' I heard one exclaim as I was led out, too. The only person not to feel sorry for me was me.

In the following weeks and months, people in authority kept asking me how I was feeling, if I understood what had happened, whether I wanted to talk about it or if I needed anything. I didn't tell anyone about capturing my family's last breaths because they wouldn't understand, nor would they comprehend that thanks to my dad it would become my purpose to help and carry other lost souls inside me when and wherever I came across them.

Six years of foster homes then group homes – some good and some not so good – didn't do any lasting damage to me in the end.

Sylvia taught me how to hide in plain sight, and Nate showed me the value of finding an anchor that keeps you in place despite the storms engulfing you.

The sharpness of the wind around the hotel roof made my eyes water, but I was feeling empowered and leaned further over the railings, balancing on my tiptoes. It might only take a rogue gust to tip me over the edge. But fate hadn't intervened and it wasn't my time. I still had work to do. Steven needed me, as would others.

Early this evening he would call me for the last time and we'd run through my plan. There might not be anyone to hear me when I breathed my last, but I'd ensure there was somebody who cared enough to be there for his.

CHAPTER TWENTY

SEVEN MONTHS, ONE WEEK AFTER DAVID

The interior of my Mini was almost silent but for the hum of the engine and the vehicles I passed. I maintained a speed a little below the legal limit of 30 mph so that a road camera wouldn't catch me.

Occasionally the clipped accent voicing my satnav broke the quiet, but I was anxious that nothing else would remove me from the calm, collected headspace I needed to maintain on the approach to Steven's house.

Before I left home, I'd texted the girls to tell them I was going to be at the office a little later than planned, but they must have run out of phone credit as I hadn't heard back from them. I picked a coat to wear with deep pockets on the inside and outside. These I stuffed with gloves, a battery-operated torch, a packet of wet wipes and a steak knife, just to be on the safe side. And as each half-mile counted down to my arrival, my heart pounded faster and faster.

I'd called Steven's recently purchased disposable phone from the office at six o'clock, as agreed, to get his address, and immediately I'd typed the postcode into an app that offered me an aerial view of the road and another taken from street level. It was as he described. Then I'd visited a property website to view photos posted online the last time the house was up for sale. It was a potentially attractive house but quite shabby. However, Steven had warned me that since purchasing it, his worsening depression meant his interest in keeping it maintained had waned. I looked at the floor plan and his bedroom was where he'd told me.

I'd spent the week preparing myself for the moment I was to meet with him in person for the first and last time. It would be nerve-wracking and thrilling to watch as he slipped a rope around his neck using the method I'd suggested, then stepped off the chair and let gravity and nature take its course. His death would be better than anything I had ever imagined I'd get out of joining End of the Line.

I'd prepared myself for what to expect during and after Steven's death by surfing Internet images of the lifeless, contorted bodies of people who'd chosen the same route. Each one differed from the next. I looked closely at grooves made by ligatures around throats; bloody, crimson-frothed nostrils and mouths; elongated necks; prominent eyes with dilated pupils; swollen tongues and clenched hands. I watched videos that foreign terrorists had uploaded of public hangings, slow suffocations and strangulations. But no pictures, footage or descriptive text could prepare me for the final expression on Steven's face. And, of course, his last breath.

It felt like an age, but I'd only been behind the wheel for twenty minutes when I arrived on the outskirts of a village. KENTON – PLEASE DRIVE CAREFULLY, a sign read. I followed the satnav's directions towards clumps of houses set back from the road.

'You have reached your destination,' the satnav voice said, so I pulled over, turned off the engine and remained for a moment, staring at house number 11 just a little further ahead and to the right of me. My fingers involuntarily wrapped around the arc of the steering wheel to prevent me from sinking so deeply into my seat that I could never climb out.

I looked closely at Steven's house. Some of the slate roof tiles were askew or needed replacing and the white paint on the window frames was flaking. The garden was overgrown and a wooden gate had fallen from its hinges and was propped up against an unkempt hedge. A porch on the right-hand side had a pitched roof and a front door you couldn't see from the road.

I glanced at my watch: it was 7.50 p.m. and I was due inside in ten minutes. Now that I was here and the place was in view, my fear rose, causing my legs to tremble like they were trying to keep up with the ever-increasing beat of my heart. Try as I might, I couldn't keep them still. Dusk was enveloping the village and it gave my mission a more sinister feel.

'Calm yourself, Laura,' I spoke out loud. 'Remain in control and think of your anchor.'

But not even Henry could help me now.

I remained where I was for the time being until I was sure I hadn't been seen. I wasn't naive to the risks of what I was doing. A tiny, rational portion of my brain held on to my initial suspicions about Steven's motives in having me there. And that part urged me to sit outside his house a little bit longer to confirm this wasn't some kind of sick joke. If it was, Steven's storytelling put mine to shame.

I craved a cigarette and began to nibble the skin around my fingernails as I questioned what I was doing there. Nobody was twisting my arm to go inside; if I just turned over the ignition and drove away, I'd be safe at home within minutes. That's what a sensible, cautious person would do. That's what Mary would have done. But she was weak, and I was not like her and would never be. And the lure of what was going to happen under that roof was all too powerful for me to ignore. I *had* to go inside.

I slipped on my brown leather gloves so as not to leave fingerprints on anything I touched, and walked cautiously up a gravel path, passing windows with drawn curtains. I looked up at the only illuminated window, on the first floor, where Steven had said he'd be waiting.

The door was ajar and I pushed it open, then took a deep breath and stepped over the threshold. I fished out my torch and directed the beam towards various closed doors. The only pieces of furniture in the porch and hallway were a small table with some dried flowers in a vase and a wooden chair. Propping the front door open with the chair, in case I needed to beat a hasty retreat, I slid my hand into my pocket and gripped the handle of the knife.

As agreed, Steven would meet me in his bedroom. I climbed the stairs, one at a time, each of them creaking as if to announce my arrival. On the landing, I paused to take another breath, then made my way towards the only door with a faint light shining under it.

'Steven?' I whispered from beneath the architrave. I scoured the dimly lit room but he was nowhere to be seen. In fact, the room was empty – there was no bed, no wardrobe, no chest of drawers. Just a wallpapered, almost bare room with a lamp on the floor. I looked up and the vaulted ceiling had beams like Steven had described, and I saw the rope attached. It moved ever so slightly from the draught of the open door. Alarm bells sounded in my head.

This is all wrong. Where is he? This wasn't what we agreed. Get out of here!

Fear crawled from the small of my back, up my spine and towards my shoulders, wrapping itself around my neck like a snake and squeezing my throat. I wanted to run away so badly but I was too frightened to move. Suddenly something caught my eye. I paused to squint at it until it came into focus, and my stomach fell.

'Oh, Jesus,' I whispered, and clasped the knife even more tightly. Instead of finding a man I'd promised to help in the last moments of his life, I was confronted by something shocking in the patterns of the wallpaper. I realised I wasn't looking at wallpaper at all. It was hundreds of photographs of me.

Me walking up the steps and into the office. Me in my street. Me driving. Me on a spin bike at the gym. Me pushing a trolley around the supermarket. Me through the kitchen window. Me sitting in the coffee shop in town. Me entering the Hartley Hotel car park. From what I could see, every picture appeared to be different; Steven must have been following me for weeks.

It got worse, because I wasn't the only focus of the lens. Tony had been caught boxing at the gym and going to his office. There were also my children on their way to school. Me watching Alice in the playground with her friends. Effie in the passenger seat of a boy's car. Henry in the residential home's community lounge as I combed his hair. To take some of the photographs, Steven must have been standing just a couple of feet behind me and I hadn't known.

Instinct and fear made me grab at them, yanking them down by the fistful, cramming them into my pockets or throwing them to the floor as if doing that would be enough to wake me from the nightmare. But there were too many to dispose of. And if Steven had gone to all this trouble to scare me, what else might he be capable of?

'Don't you like your picture being taken?'

I spun around quickly in the direction of Steven's voice, which seemed to come out of nowhere. A figure was standing in the doorway, the darkness of the hall masking his face. He stepped forward two paces so I could see him more clearly, and I moved backwards. His hands were by his side and I now could make out the intensity of his stare.

'I've gone to a lot of effort,' he continued, his speech firm and confident, much more so than I'd ever heard him by phone. 'I spent weeks following you and your family around. The least you can do is appreciate them.'

I took another step back into the bedroom, but realised that in doing so, he was cornering me. I struggled to breathe. It was like someone was choking me.

'What . . . what do you want from me?' I eventually stammered.

'I want you to tell me why you manipulate vulnerable people and what you get out of it,' he responded. 'And none of that wanting to "help people who've fallen by the road" bullshit.'

He moved towards me, so I tugged the knife from my pocket and held it in front of me. The dim light in the room kept catching the silver blade as my hand shook. I could see Steven's face more clearly now. It wasn't as menacing as he sounded, but his body language terrified me.

He laughed mockingly as he looked at the knife. 'You are many things, Laura Morris, but you don't have the guts to actually kill anyone with your own bare hands. You do it from behind a telephone or a keyboard. Me, however . . . well, I'm an unknown quantity, aren't I? You don't know what I'm capable of.'

'Don't come any closer,' I said. My groin suddenly felt warm and I realised I was wetting myself, but I couldn't stop. 'Let me go. Please.'

'You think saying please is going to help you out of this? You aren't going anywhere, Laura. You see that rope? It's not me who's going to be hanging from the beams tonight. It's you.'

I stretched my arm out further, waving the knife at him. Only he edged closer to me, so he was just a couple of feet away. I stepped backwards again until I reached the wall.

'Go on then, Laura, do your best. I've got nothing to lose because you have taken everything I had away from me already.'

It felt like someone had pressed pause on the moment; neither of us showing our hand or making the next move. Then suddenly Steven went to grab my wrist, his fingers digging in until they felt like they were going to break the bone. I yelled as he pulled me around and twisted my other arm behind my back and pushed me towards the rope.

I struggled to break free, but he held me tighter and my fingers began to lose their grip on the knife until it fell to the floor.

'Don't worry, Laura. It's not going to take long. The noose has been tied in exactly the way you told me to do it, at exactly the right height for a swift death.'

'Please, Steven,' I begged. 'Whatever I've done to you, I'm sorry.'

'It's too late for that.'

'I have children . . . I'm a mother . . .'

'And they'd be better off without you.'

He grabbed the rope with his other hand and started to put it over my head. So I seized the opportunity to elbow him in the groin and kick his shin hard. The shock made him loosen his grip on my arm, just enough for me to shake completely free. I bent down, grabbed the knife, turned in his direction and thrust it blindly in front of me. It only stopped when I felt his hand grasp my wrist again and the knife went no further. But as I went to hit him with my free hand, he suddenly dropped to his knees. He looked up at me and then down at his stomach. My knife was embedded in him.

I froze – I had just stabbed the man I'd come to watch die. And while none of it had played out like it was supposed to, I had no desire to remain there any longer or even hear his last breath. Because what if he wasn't alone? What if there were others waiting in the house? I needed to protect myself.

While Steven remained kneeling on the floor, groaning and clearly in pain, I bent over and, before he could prevent me, yanked the knife from his stomach. He screamed and fell to his side, shouting something but I couldn't make out the words.

Then with all the strength I could muster, I ran from the room and along the landing. But without the torch lighting my way, in my panic I misjudged the first step on the staircase and hit the ridge of the second. I fell forward, head and body first, and my cheekbone smacked the base of the banister. Then I tumbled in a sideways motion, catching my forehead against the handrail as my body crumpled in a U-shape and came to a halt close to the bottom. Lying still, dazed and confused as to what had just happened, I only pulled myself together when I heard groaning and Steven dragging himself across the floorboards upstairs.

With all my remaining strength, I pulled myself to my feet with both hands gripping the handrail, and moved as quickly as I could towards the front door. Stumbling back into my car, I locked the doors and forced my key into the ignition. The wheels spun as I pulled away as fast as the Mini would allow.

RYAN

CHAPTER ONE

Drumming my fingers against the steering wheel in time with the beat of a song playing on the radio and singing at the top of my voice, I was pretty pleased I could still remember all the words to Justin Timberlake's 'SexyBack' more than a decade after it played the night I met Charlotte at the student union bar.

She'd been dancing to it with a group of her friends when I saw her, then sparked up a drunken conversation. Lately, when she was going through one of her funks, I could still make her smile by dancing around the bedroom naked, miming along to the song, the irony being that bringing sexy back was pretty much the exact opposite of what I was doing.

I remembered her admitting on one of our first dates that she had a crush on Justin from his *NSYNC days. And after a few Jägerbombs, she confessed how, when she was a girl, she'd scribble out the face of his then-girlfriend Britney Spears in her mum's gossip mags and pretend that she was dating him. I hoped her teenage self wouldn't be too disappointed she was now Mrs Ryan Smith and not Mrs Timberlake.

I stopped the car at a red light and my eyes wandered uphill to Northampton's skyline of new-build offices and high-rise flats. I'd been born and raised here and remembered how once, when it had felt so small and claustrophobic, I couldn't wait to break out on my own. It only took a couple of terms at the University of Sunderland before I understood that once you strip away a town's facade, they're all the same underneath.

Charlotte's willingness to laugh at the less cool aspects of herself was rare among the type of girls I'd hung out with back then. So was the way she looked. With her delicate features, chestnut curls, sky-blue stare and the androgynous clothes she wore, I knew early on that she was something special. Eleven years later and I was still right.

It was in our final year at uni when we decided to try to make it in London after graduation. We were fresh-faced, bursting with enthusiasm, and nothing could stop us from conquering the capital. Once we got there, the reality was that we were two anonymous little fish in a ginormous polluted pond. We shared a ridiculously overpriced flat above a Chinese takeaway, lived an hour's commute from all the cool places we wanted to hang out at and barely had any spare cash to live the city life we'd imagined. But it served its purpose, and after a year of training it got me on the career ladder and we sucked it up without complaint.

Once we were married and had decided the time was right to start a family, I was adamant I didn't want to do it in London. I landed a job back home before Charlotte did – she wasn't so convinced it was the right place for us to be. However, she gave it a chance and started work as a graphic designer at an agency not far from the flat we bought together.

The traffic lights turned to green, and as January's night began to fall I drove past Becket's Park, just about making out the colourful moored canal boats in the marina. I couldn't stop myself from grinning when I passed the Barratt maternity unit building, because in a little over two months, Charlotte and I would be waiting for a bed there. It hadn't been easy: a combination of her polycystic ovaries and my low sperm count meant we'd had to rely on NHS-funded IVF to conceive. But on our second cycle, bingo! We were expectant parents.

I couldn't wait to be in that hospital to meet my kid for the first time. And to be honest, I was even a little bit envious of Charlotte and what her body was able to achieve, while mine couldn't even finish its part without my helping hand and a fertility expert's syringe.

I soon changed my mind. Some women take to pregnancy like a duck to water, but after the first month, Charlotte really struggled. Morning, afternoon and evening sickness sapped all her energy levels and she was constantly feeling crappy. It became so bad that she was forced to take a leave of absence from the job she enjoyed. She spent much of her day mooching around the flat, and never too far away from a toilet bowl. But as we approached the final part of our third trimester, she turned a corner.

I glanced at the time as I continued on my way home – I reckoned I'd have half an hour to shower and spruce myself up before we headed to her favourite Thai restaurant to celebrate our fourth wedding anniversary. And it was there that I planned to give her the surprise of her life. I patted my jacket pocket just to reassure myself that the gift-wrapped box was still inside. I couldn't wait to see the look on her face when she opened it.

Charlotte's car wasn't in its space in front of the flat when I drove in through the gates and pulled up onto the driveway, so I called her mobile to see where she was. It went straight to voicemail. I'd spoken to her at lunchtime while she was running errands, and hearing her voice sounding so chirpy had given me butterflies. 'I love you, Ry,' she'd said before she hung up, the first time I'd heard her say that in weeks. It felt like the tightest and warmest of hugs.

I climbed two flights of stairs and opened our front door to the overpowering scent of cinnamon and spices. She'd always been fond of air-freshener plug-ins, but now that she was pregnant our home smelled like Christmas all year round. She'd also had a thorough tidy-up. There were no dishes draining by the sink; tea towels were neatly folded on the worktop; the bathroom reeked of bleach; dried toothpaste had been rinsed from the electric toothbrushes and magazines were neatly arranged on the coffee table. *She's nesting*, I thought, and smiled.

I phoned her again when I climbed out of the shower, but when she didn't answer I began to feel a little uneasy. If she'd gone into an early labour, I was sure I'd have been told by now. I checked my phone again after drying my hair and trimming my stubble and then, just to be on the safe side, I called the maternity unit. I also called her friends, but when they hadn't heard from her either, something inside me tightened and turned, like the wringing of a wet dishcloth.

Suddenly the front door buzzed.

Thank Christ for that, I thought, and hurried to it.

'Have you forgotten your keys?' I began as I opened it, only to be confronted by a stony-faced man and woman.

'Mr Smith?' he began.

'Yes. And you are . . . ?'

'My name is DS Mortimer and this is my colleague, PC Coghill. May we come in, please?'

CHAPTER TWO

ONE DAY AFTER CHARLOTTE

My distraught parents sat either side of me, asking the questions I couldn't bring myself to.

They'd rushed to the flat with my brother Johnny within half an hour of the police turning up at my door. It was uncharted territory for everyone in the room. Mum and Dad had no idea what to say to me to soften the blow. The best the police could do was offer me their condolences and reassurances that an investigation had already begun to find out what had happened to my wife.

All they could tell me was that Charlotte's body had been found at the foot of some cliffs in East Sussex. A witness had spotted her in the company of someone else and they'd fallen together. They'd yet to identify the other body, as it had been swept away by the sea. Charlotte had landed on rocks.

'Why would someone want to murder my wife?' I eventually asked.

The officers glanced at each other, and DS Mortimer looked like he wanted to say something, then thought better of it.

'I really don't know. I'm sorry, Mr Smith.'

Before leaving us to grieve alone, they explained that their colleagues investigating the case would visit the following day.

The case. Charlotte had gone from being my wife and the mother of my unborn child to *the case* in under an hour.

The trauma of losing Charlotte overpowered everything. It was too much for me to take in all at once. For the rest of the night and the early hours of the next morning, the four of us concentrated on trying to comprehend that we'd never see her again, while aching at the loss of my baby.

Two fresh police officers appeared the next day to learn more about Charlotte. DS O'Connor was a chubby man, forty-something, with broken red capillaries across his nose and cheeks, and awkward body language that suggested he'd rather be anywhere than in my company. I shared his sentiment. DS Carmichael was considerably younger, with a sympathetic smile and red hair scraped up into a tight bun. I imagined that in an interrogation scenario, she'd be the good cop.

They suggested it would not be in my best interests to identify Charlotte's body, based on the height from which she'd fallen and the position in which she'd landed. I took that to mean head first. She'd been airlifted by helicopter back up to the clifftops, but it was clear she was long dead. I felt selfish for being relieved that I didn't have to see her in that state.

'Do you know why my wife died yet?' I asked.

'We don't know the exact circumstances of what happened yesterday,' said DS Carmichael. 'So we're working from eyewitness accounts.'

'Who was the person who abducted her?'

DS O'Connor shifted uncomfortably in his seat. 'Again, we can't answer that yet until his body is washed up or retrieved from the sea. We're hoping it'll turn up soon.'

'So it was a man?'

'We believe so.'

'It doesn't make any sense,' I continued. 'Why would he kidnap Charlotte and drive all the way down there to kill her? Surely it must be someone we know, or she'd never have got in her car with him. And why isn't this flat being treated as a crime scene? Shouldn't you be looking for evidence?'

Mum clasped my arm tightly. Johnny, two years younger than my thirty-one years but always the more pragmatic of us, looked like he wanted me to guess what he was thinking. DS O'Connor glanced at all of them and then at me, but nobody said a word.

'What am I missing here?' I asked.

'This isn't going to be easy for you to hear, Ryan, but from our initial investigation, it appears Charlotte was a willing participant in what happened yesterday.'

'Don't be stupid,' I replied. 'Of course she wasn't. She was taken against her will, or that man coerced her into going there for some reason—'

DS Carmichael interrupted. 'Ryan, two separate eyewitnesses saw them walking towards the edge of the cliff together. Neither Charlotte nor the man appeared distressed. They were both holding mobile phones to their ears when they climbed over a fence and then stepped off the edge. Unfortunately, the car park CCTV cameras weren't in operation, so we can't back their statements up yet.'

'Then the witnesses are wrong,' I replied adamantly. 'Charlotte had been a little down lately, I admit that, but she was getting better and she wouldn't just kill herself. We tried so hard for a baby and we only had a couple of months left to go. She wouldn't end her life, or our child's. She had no reason to.'

'They were walking hand in hand,' said DS Carmichael softly.

'What?'

'The witnesses say Charlotte and the man were holding hands when they died.'

My world suddenly ground to a very sharp halt. I opened my mouth to argue with her, but by the look of everyone else in the room, they believed her. I couldn't lift my hand up to my eyes quickly enough to quell my tears. Dad pulled me into his shoulder and I sensed he was trying to stop himself from crying, too.

'What do you think the relationship was between this man and Charlotte?' Johnny asked.

'It's another question we can't yet answer,' DS O'Connor replied. 'Our investigation is still in its early days.'

'So you do think they were in some kind of relationship?'

'Only because something brought them to that place at the same time, for what we believe was the same purpose.'

'To die,' I said. It wasn't a question. They nodded their heads while I shook mine.

'No, I'm not buying it. Charlotte wouldn't do this to herself or to us. It makes no sense to me, but you believe it because you don't know her. Mum, do you think she was having an affair or suicidal?'

'I don't know what to think anymore.' She looked down at the table.

'The evidence so far seems to point to the fact her death was voluntary, Ryan,' my dad added. 'But let's not worry about that for the moment.'

'Then what should I be worrying about?' I asked with a raised voice. No one could answer.

I couldn't listen to the police or my family any longer. I stormed out of the living room and into our bedroom, slamming the door behind me so hard that I heard the wedding photos hanging in the hallway juddering.

I wanted so badly to call Charlotte and have her answer, telling me it'd been some huge fuck-up and that she was fine. How could I even start to get my head around not hearing her voice again?

CHAPTER THREE

THREE DAYS AFTER CHARLOTTE

So much of what you believe – or what you have convinced yourself to be true – can be flipped on its head quicker than you can ever imagine.

I was desperate to believe that what had happened to Charlotte had been the result of foul play, that she'd been murdered by this unidentified stranger – not that she'd willingly gone with him and jumped to her death.

After another restless night, I turned on my iPad and went online to look up the location where she'd died. Birling Gap, in East Sussex, was part of the Seven Sisters coastline, with panoramic views of the English Channel. Charlotte had been found at the base of a five-hundred-foot cliff drop that was notorious for its erosion.

That makes much more sense! She and this man didn't take their own lives; the ground simply gave way beneath their feet.

Surely if they'd travelled that far to die, they'd have driven a few miles further down the coast to Beachy Head. That was a suicide spot, not Birling Gap.

'Dad, I think I know what happened to Charlotte . . .' I began hurriedly as I marched towards the kitchen. My parents, Johnny and DS

Carmichael were sitting around the table with an open laptop in front of them. I was surprised to see the police there on a Sunday morning.

'Sit down, Ry,' urged Johnny, and I obliged.

'The cliffs, they've been known to collapse,' I continued. 'What happened to Charlotte was an accident.'

'I have something to show you and it won't be easy to watch,' DS Carmichael began gingerly.

'Please, Ryan, sit down, just for a minute,' Mum urged.

DS Carmichael pressed play. Footage had been retrieved from a dashboard camera a driver had failed to turn off when he'd parked for a clifftop dog walk. He'd returned to find his bumper scratched. It was only when he reviewed the recording that he noticed what else it had taped.

I held my breath as I watched Charlotte leave her car. Compared to a lot of expectant mums, her baby belly was relatively small, and she was disguising it that day with an overcoat. Her phone was clasped to her ear as she walked across the car park. A male figure came into view. He had his hand to his ear, too, like he was also on the phone. I recoiled as they embraced. I wanted to shut my eyes, but I couldn't tear them away from the screen. Then they held hands and walked slowly but deliberately across the car park and towards the safety railings that prevented visitors from going too close to the edge.

He was the first to climb over them, before holding his hand out to help her until they were side by side. Then, with their phones still clutched to their ears, they began their walk towards the horizon. My stomach sank when they suddenly fell over the edge and out of view. Mum's hand covered her mouth and Dad looked away from the screen.

It was absolute proof that Charlotte hadn't been abducted, she hadn't slipped in an awful accident and the ground beneath her feet hadn't crumbled. No longer could I tell myself the eyewitness statements were mistaken.

We all remained in silence for I don't know how long. I could feel everyone's eyes drilling through me, waiting for a reaction, for me to say something, anything. But I didn't have a reaction to give.

Instead, I tried to imagine what had been going through Charlotte's head in her final moments. Was she scared? Did she die straight away or was she in pain? Was she thinking about me, or had she put me out of her mind? Why did she do it? Had she learned there was something medically wrong with the baby and felt she had no choice but to end both their lives? Had this man, this unidentified stranger, been a part of her life for a long time, skulking about in the shadows, hiding behind my back? Had he made her pregnant? Who was on the other end of the phone as they walked to their deaths? Just how shit must our life together have been for her to take herself away from it in such a brutal, catastrophic way?

Among all the confusion there was only one thing I was certain of: I didn't know my wife as well as I thought. I grabbed my jacket and keys and left the flat without saying a word.

I made my way by foot towards Becket's Park, where I'd spent many a school holiday and weekend as a kid playing football and cricket with my mates. More recently, it had become a place where Charlotte and I took long Saturday-afternoon strolls, throwing bread to the ducks and geese in the lakes and buying Gallone's ice cream from the van near the children's play park.

I used to think one day it would be me there, catching my kid at the bottom of the slide, or hovering under the metal rungs of the climbing frame in case they got scared. Not now though.

I sat on a bench, staring at a Sunday-league football match being played on one of the pitches, but I wasn't taking in much around me. I absent-mindedly turned my wedding ring around my finger in a clockwise motion until I became aware of a lump in my jacket pocket. I remembered what it was and removed the small box that I'd gift-wrapped with a bow. I'd been going to give it to Charlotte the night of our anniversary. Inside was the key to a house she had no idea I'd bought.

That morning before work I'd exchanged contracts and picked up the keys to a house she'd fallen in love with. It was in Kenton, a village on the outskirts of town, and the house had been empty for years. She'd seen it many times when we'd borrowed Oscar, my parents' dog, and taken him for walks around villages as we considered where we'd like to move to when we outgrew the flat.

I vaguely remembered visiting the house a few times as a kid. And although it was now a bit rundown, Charlotte had seen its potential and fallen in love with it.

Keeping its purchase a secret from my wife had been as hard as hell, and I'd had to sneak around behind her back to deal with conveyancers, my estate agent, the mortgage broker and bank. I'd even had legal letters sent to my parents' house. God knows how people having an affair manage to keep secrets.

I held the key so tightly in my palm that it made a deep impression in my skin. And I wondered if I'd told Charlotte a day earlier we were set to complete on our forever home, might it have saved her? I'd never know.

CHAPTER FOUR

SIX DAYS AFTER CHARLOTTE

My love for Charlotte was fast being swallowed by hate.

Days ago, I'd wanted to lock myself in our bedroom and never leave. Everything about the room was her, from the Laura Ashley floral wallpaper to the scent of her perfumes that lingered on the matching curtains and pillows. I knew those smells would eventually fade, so I'd immersed myself in them while I could. But now they only made me feel sick.

I needed an explanation as to why she'd do this to me, so I ransacked the flat, searching everywhere to see if she'd left a suicide note. The police had taken her electronic devices, so I searched notebooks, bins, coat pockets, and inside books, cupboards and drawers, but I drew a blank.

I needed to be in a safe place, far away from the woman who, with one selfish act, had destroyed me. So I went back to the house where I was raised. Being at Mum and Dad's brought it home how much I'd taken for granted as a kid. My only worries then were fitting in homework around playing FIFA '99 on the Nintendo 64, and how long Johnny and I could stay out before Mum called us in for our tea. I longed for those days again. I no longer liked being an adult. This adult, anyway.

Mum and Dad were handling me with kid gloves. They never accused me of neglecting my wife or asked how I could have let her slip through my fingers. They left that to my own conscience and to Charlotte's parents, Barbara and Patrick. They'd taken early retirement and moved to a large white villa on the slopes of Alicante's hillsides, but were away on a Mediterranean cruise when the police tracked them down. They'd flown home from Turkey on the next available flight.

Instantly – and understandably, I guess – once we came face-to-face in my parents' living room, they needed someone to direct their frustration at. I became their whipping boy.

'You told me she was getting better!' Barbara snapped, making no effort to disguise her bitterness towards me. 'You lived with her, couldn't you see she was getting worse?'

'She said she was feeling better.'

'Why didn't you talk to her doctor and explain she needed a higher dose of antidepressants?'

'She was limited to what she could take because she was pregnant.'

Barbara shook her head, refusing to accept my answers. The whites of Patrick's eyes were bloodshot and the sockets dark. 'I don't understand any of this,' he muttered. 'All I know is that you promised me you'd look after my little girl, and you failed.'

'I know and I am so sorry . . .' My voice trailed off.

I recalled months earlier, when Charlotte and I should have been at our happiest, and how a sort of darkness had descended within weeks of her becoming pregnant. I put it down to the morning sickness at first. It wasn't just at breakfast when she was ill, it was often after lunch and dinner, too. Sometimes she couldn't even keep a slice of dry toast down.

But when that eventually passed, I thought things would start getting better and that she'd share my enthusiasm as a parent-to-be. Instead, she remained in her funk.

The NHS website explained prenatal depression was pretty common. Her symptoms matched those listed – she felt down a lot of the time, she was generally apathetic, she was tearful, she couldn't sleep and she was often agitated.

I suggested mentioning it to her midwife at her next appointment, but Charlotte insisted on managing her mood swings herself and shunned medication. I tried to lift her spirits by changing our diets, cutting out all processed food and replacing them with more mother-and-baby-friendly foods packed with antioxidants. It didn't work; in fact, it just got worse.

The slightest little thing seemed to upset her, even watching the news. Each terrorist attack, war or natural disaster had her hooked to the screen, like she couldn't get enough of the rolling headlines and fretting about what it might mean to our baby.

'What kind of world am I bringing my child into?' she once asked. 'One where people are burned alive in cages or thrown from buildings because of their religion or sexuality?'

'Well, firstly, it's *our* baby, so the responsibility isn't just on *your* shoulders,' I replied. 'It's our job to keep him or her safe and to look after each other.'

'What if I can't even carry it properly? Look at me, I'm barely even showing.'

'The scans say everything is perfectly all right.'

'Every morning I wake up with this horrible feeling and I can't stop crying. That glowing pregnancy period all mums talk about? Mine just makes me ache.'

I brushed away a tear rolling down her cheek. 'Think for a moment about the millions and millions of people to whom nothing horrible has ever happened . . . those who've never been blown up on a bus or washed away by a tsunami. Who's to say we're not going to be one of *those* families?'

It wasn't the first time we'd had that conversation and it wouldn't be the last. And each time it cropped up, Charlotte nodded in agreement as if she believed my reassurances. Looking back, I should have known she was just trying to shut me up. She didn't think I understood her and I guess she was right. I could have done more. I *should* have done more.

Charlotte's parents continued firing questions at me that I couldn't answer. As each one came, I felt more and more like a failure as a husband. However, it pissed me off that they were pretending Charlotte's depression came as news to them. They'd seen how bad it had become on their last visit home, yet they didn't think it was serious enough to leave the balmy Spanish climes. They accepted no responsibility; apparently it was all my doing.

I remembered that later, when Charlotte's bad days were still outweighing the good, I went from feeling concerned to scared for her. After much persuasion, she began cognitive behavioural therapy. Three sessions later she dismissed her therapist as 'a dick' and never returned. Finally, when she'd hit rock bottom, she gave in and agreed to her doctor's suggestion of a low dosage of antidepressants.

That's when the Charlotte of old gradually began to emerge like a butterfly waking from hibernation. She started leaving the flat again, she smiled without being prompted and she'd disappear to our bedroom to chat for ages on the phone. Shortly before Christmas, she replanted the window box with spring bulbs and chose colours and fabrics for the nursery while I decorated it. She also spent time on online message boards where she said she was talking to other women who understood what she'd been going through. She was engaging in the world she'd shied away from.

She suggested we book our first holiday abroad as a three instead of a two; we mulled over which of our friends would make suitable godparents and wondered if we'd ever find a house like the one she loved in Kenton. Only now could I see that none of this mattered to her; it was all a brilliant disguise. She'd no longer wanted any of it. She no longer wanted us.

The morning she died, she'd told me she loved me. How could she say that to me and then throw it all away hours later?

CHAPTER FIVE

EIGHT DAYS AFTER CHARLOTTE

With the exception of two grandparents whom we'd lost to cancer when I was a kid, I'd been lucky to have reached my early thirties and remained relatively unscarred by death. Now I wondered if the Grim Reaper had simply been biding his time until he could make the maximum fucking impact on my life.

I was learning what many other people my age already knew, that grief is the worst place in the world to be trapped in. In fact, it's a kind of sub-world that you believe only you inhabit. You aren't alone, of course, because those you're close to share your pain. But it's not really their pain, is it? It's yours. And it's a million times worse for you than it is for anyone else. Sometimes I thought that if I stretched out my arm, I could physically touch it.

While grief had me caught like a rabbit in headlights, I was also floating in a kind of limbo waiting for the police to release Charlotte's body into my custody. Without it there couldn't be a funeral. I didn't understand what the delay was, because the mystery wasn't how she died, it was why. But an autopsy needed to be carried out regardless.

Until that was completed, I had no choice but to fill my days by going for aimless walks around the park with my parents' dog, or staring at the television watching endless quizzes, soaps and reality shows until, before I knew it, a whole evening had passed and I hadn't registered a single thing I'd watched.

One morning I awoke before six and found myself driving to Northampton railway station. I bought a ticket from a machine and caught a rush-hour train to London Euston, and then took the Hammersmith and City line to Shepherd's Bush Market in the west of the city. By 9 a.m., I was sitting at a plastic table in a bustling McDonald's staring through the window at a second-floor flat above a row of shops along a noisy high street.

Inside the filthy pea-shingled exterior was an equally shabby home, the first one Charlotte and I had rented in the capital as twenty-one-year-old university graduates. I recalled black and blue patches of mould crawling up and fanning out across the bathroom walls, and how we'd take it in turns to scrub them with a fungicidal liquid. The glass in the windows was so thin that the frames rattled when a bus or lorry drove past. And the boiler was so unpredictable that in winter, we'd sometimes turn on the oven and keep the door open just to stay warm. But the rent was cheap and the landlord had only asked for two weeks' deposit.

The material things didn't matter back then. In fact, nothing had mattered to Charlotte as long as we were happy. And we were happy. Weren't we? Or had I read her wrongly? Because now I was doubting everything. Every grin in a photograph, each text message with a kiss at the end . . . was it all just pretend?

Maybe even back then depression had been lying dormant under Charlotte's skin. Perhaps she'd always had it inside her, but she'd been better able to mask it. Then when pregnancy and her hormones shook everything up, the illness broke through the surface and leaked like a foul-smelling gas.

Whatever its cause, whatever its reason, it didn't really matter. It had killed her and now it felt like it was threatening to spread through me. If I wasn't crying, I was numb. If I wasn't numb, I was suffocating. If I wasn't suffocating, I was crying. And so on and so on. A never-ending circle of shittery.

I took a sip from a cup of milky tea and pushed my McMuffin and hash browns around my plate with a plastic fork. I couldn't finish more than a couple of bites from either.

My reflection in the window caught me by surprise. My short, dirty-blond hair was flat and without product, and my cheeks were gaunt. I was pale and my eyes vacant. At five-foot-ten I was neither tall nor short, but I felt myself shrinking by the day. Despite our two-year age difference and his glasses and beard, Johnny and I had been the spitting image of each other. Now, if you put us next to each other, you wouldn't know we were brothers.

A staff member brushed my shoulder with his arm as he passed, and I recoiled so sharply that he glared at me for my overreaction. 'Chill, blud,' he muttered.

So many people had tried to console me with hugs that I could no longer stand physical contact. Being touched by anyone, no matter how emotionally close we were, felt like acid burning holes into my skin.

I dumped the half-eaten food on my tray in a bin and loitered by a bus stop, unsure where to go next.

'Borough Market,' I suddenly blurted out, and ran my finger up and down a bus timetable fixed to a lamp post.

With little money to spend on activities, and surviving on cheap microwaveable meals, Charlotte and I had made sure to hold enough money back each week in the house kitty to treat ourselves to fresh produce at the market every Saturday morning. Then we'd stretch it out to make an organic lunch and dinner, our only healthy meals of the week. We were broke, but we were content. Well, at least I had been.

I hopped on the red Routemaster bus and made for the back row of seats on the top deck. That's where Charlotte and I would sit. I imagined she was by my side and, for a moment, I felt loved again.

I looked at my phone to check the time. I'd kept it on silent and saw I'd missed seven calls – three from my mum's mobile and four from Dad's. In addition, there were a handful of text messages from familiar names.

Once the news of Charlotte's death broke within our friendship groups, they all wanted to know what had happened, and it was horrible explaining to them that I wasn't really sure but it appeared Charlotte had ended her life. I might as well have said, 'It was so fucking awful being married to me that she'd rather die.' They'd try to analyse what she'd done, searching for reasons, but they were never going to get their answers. If I had a pound for everyone who said 'I just don't understand it' or 'She had everything to live for . . .', I'd have had enough money to pay for her funeral in cash.

Her friends fell into two camps, each connected to the other by a common loss. On one side were the people racked with guilt for not recognising or reacting to how much pain Charlotte was in. Without fail, they wanted me to know how responsible they felt for letting her slip between the cracks. They pitied me and my loss, and in return I hated them for it.

Then to the others, I was an object of suspicion: a convenient get-out clause for their own failings. Blaming me was much easier than blaming themselves or Charlotte.

The bus reached Southwark Street and I got off and stood on the opposite side of London Bridge, staring at the glass roof and art-deco-style green metal arched beams of Borough Market Hall. I pictured myself crossing the road with Charlotte's arm linked through mine, two hessian grocery bags in our hands and inhaling delicious food aromas wafting from all the stalls. Then we'd wander from trader to trader, choosing vegetables and meats and bickering over whose turn it was to cook. This used to be Charlotte's and my playground, but those days were gone and there was no point in me going any further inside. There was no point to anything anymore.

CHAPTER SIX

TWELVE DAYS AFTER CHARLOTTE

He was a boy. He *was* a boy. The baby Charlotte and I were expecting was going to be a boy.

Throughout her pregnancy, we were adamant we didn't want to know its sex. We'd just felt so lucky that while some couples struggled for years to conceive, IVF had succeeded for us on our second attempt. So we didn't care if it was a boy or a girl. But after her death, and while I tortured myself trying to imagine how our family might have looked, there was a gap in my mental picture. I needed to know if I'd have been standing on the sidelines cheering him on in a rugby match, or being the proud dad watching her playing netball.

The desire to know became an obsession that dominated everything. A day after I called DS Carmichael, she phoned back.

'According to the coroner's preliminary findings, Charlotte was expecting a boy,' she said.

'Thank you,' I muttered, and hung up before she could try to console me.

Now I was picturing him in my head. His name would have been Daniel, like we'd decided. He had my dark-blond colouring and

Charlotte's clear blue eyes. He had dimples in his cheeks like mine, but a smile that could melt a polar icecap like his mother. He had my athletic build and her speed. I imagined teaching him how to sail, like my dad had with my brother and me at Pitsford Reservoir. Or maybe he'd be more creative and I'd teach him how to play the piano. I shook my head, and he disappeared into a thousand tiny fragments just as quickly as he'd arrived.

I was alone in my parents' house for the first time since I'd temporarily moved back in. Mum had returned to work at the shoe shop in town, and Dad had gone back to the printworks. Johnny was at the bank playing God with who could have mortgages, while I remained in quicksand, clutching a flimsy branch for dear life and waiting for it to snap. All around me, other people's lives were beginning to restart and edge forward. Not quite back to how they were before Charlotte, but they were in gear and moving in the right direction, at least.

I walked to the local corner shop to buy some cheap lager. People are right when they say alcohol takes the edge off things; too much of it, though, can distort your reality. I wanted just enough to get me through a particularly tough day. Mrs Verma served me from behind the counter with a sympathetic smile, but I was grateful she stopped short of asking me how I was. I was sick of that question.

It must have been the end of the school day because I kept passing mums and dads holding their kids' hands on the way home from the nearby primary school. I wanted to yell at them, 'You don't know how lucky you are!' because if I had Daniel's hand to hold on to, I'd never let go of it.

My thoughts gravitated again towards Charlotte. I couldn't fathom why, when she knew how much I wanted to be a dad, she would rip the opportunity away from me so cruelly? She had murdered my longed-for boy. If she really, truly hadn't wanted to live anymore and was convinced dying was the only option, maybe I could have understood if she'd done it *after* Daniel was born. I'd still have been gutted but he'd have given me the strength to carry on. Now she'd murdered my son, I had no reason to carry on.

I carried my six-pack home in a plastic bag and chose to drink it in the back garden. Conifers, large green and red bushes, and six feet of wooden fencing ensured privacy from the neighbours, not that I'd have cared if they'd seen me boozing away the afternoon. I didn't bother to pull the canvas cover from the patio furniture and flopped onto a chair, sinking two cans and watching dragonflies skim the pond. My parents' dog kept me company, but the buzz of the third drink on an empty stomach was starting to cloud my brain. Instead of mellowing me out, my thoughts were becoming more sombre.

I started thinking about my son again, questioning if he'd picked up on the chemical imbalance in Charlotte while he was still in the womb. I speculated how much pain he'd felt when she'd jumped. Months ago, I'd read that at just twenty weeks an unborn baby can feel pain more intensely than an adult. Did he notice the difference in gravity in those few seconds as she fell through the air? I'd been told Charlotte's traumatic head injuries had probably killed her instantly. Had Daniel died immediately, too? Or was he trapped inside her, in pain and slowly being starved of oxygen? It was almost too unbearable to think about, yet I couldn't stop. I began to cry for him.

The compressed gas in the fourth can hissed then effervesced when I pulled back the ring pull. I took a long swig but vomited it up almost immediately across the lap of my jeans and the lawn. I brushed Oscar's head away when he came to investigate the smell, and I remained there on all fours, heaving until every last drop was out of my pathetic body and dissolving into the grass.

'I hate you, Charlotte,' I mumbled. 'I fucking hate you for what you did to us.'

CHAPTER SEVEN

THREE WEEKS AFTER CHARLOTTE

'Denial. Anger. Bargaining. Depression. Acceptance.'

My eyes skimmed the website Johnny had emailed me a link to. He was trying to be helpful and make me realise everything I was feeling was typical, but instead it pissed me off. I didn't need anyone to tell me how to feel. According to the experts the site quoted, those were the five stages of grief. But I was struggling to make it past anger. It advised that the angrier you get, the more ownership you take of that emotion and the faster it'll disappear. Then you'll be ready to move on to the next stage.

Bullshit to that. I don't want to move on. I know where I am, I'm angry because I'm grieving the loss of my son, and I loathe his mother who killed him. If I forgave her and accepted what happened, then where the hell would I be? I'm better off where I am now because this has become the familiar. And the unfamiliar scares me.

My bitterness was that sharp I was struggling to even speak Charlotte's name. And I'd not even started trying to come to terms with the affair she'd been having with another man that led to their suicide pact. I was festering, and with no one but a ghost to blame I directed my anger towards my parents, her parents, our friends, the police investigating her case and a God I'd stopped believing in.

'We can't find any proof that Charlotte and that man were friends or in any kind of relationship before their deaths,' DS O'Connor informed me. 'So that might come as a relief.'

'Oh yes, it's a huge relief.' I made no attempt to disguise my sarcasm.

He took a sip from his mug of tea and glanced at my parents as if he expected us to be grateful for that small mercy. I hoped I was making him feel uncomfortable, because he could only retain eye contact with me for the briefest of moments. I remained poker-faced. It made no difference to me now whether Charlotte had been screwing that one man she died with or half of Northamptonshire.

We were sitting around the table in my parents' dining room as DS O'Connor updated us. I thought I could smell booze on him; Dutch courage before facing the angry widower, I suppose.

Widower. Shit, that's me. I'm a widower. From husband to widower in a heartbeat.

'So how did they know each other?' my father asked.

'We're still looking into it,' he replied.

'You don't know?' I said. 'It's your job to find this out and you are still "looking into it"? You've had almost three weeks. How much longer do you need?'

'Let him continue, son.' Dad gave the detective an apologetic look.

'As you know, we've gone through Charlotte's mobile phone and landline records and there's not a single call registered to any numbers that aren't explainable. We've also checked her email addresses and Skype calls, and again there's nothing. She doesn't seem to have FaceTimed, communicated on Internet message boards or via any other social media with anyone matching his description. We have spoken to her friends and nobody recalls her ever talking about another man. For all intents and purposes, they were complete strangers until the afternoon they met. The only thing of interest that shows up in her phone records is a number for End of the Line.'

'What's that?' Dad asked.

'It's a helpline for people with emotional problems. Charlotte had made multiple calls over the last few weeks to a central number which diverts to the nearest branch.'

'Why?'

'We don't know.'

'How many are multiple calls?'

'Almost a hundred.'

'Jesus,' I replied, and puffed out a breath. I really didn't know my wife at all.

'Then a week before her death, they suddenly stop.'

'That doesn't make sense,' my mum said, and looked at me as if to ask how I could have not known about this when I'd lived with the woman.

'The afternoon she died,' I said, 'she was walking towards the clifftops because she'd made up her mind to die with that man. Her hand looked like it was held to her ear. If she died with that phone, then how come it was found after she died in her car? And who was she calling?'

DS O'Connor gave a limp shrug. 'She must have had two mobiles. The other man also looked like he was on a call.'

'To End of the Line?'

'Unless we can identify him or find his phone, we have no way of knowing.'

'So let's find out who they were speaking to at the helpline in the run-up to her death,' Dad suggested. Johnny leaned against the sideboard and nodded his agreement.

'It's not as easy as that, I'm afraid.' DS O'Connor pinched the top of his nose and closed his eyes. Maybe the buzz from the alcohol was wearing off. 'End of the Line guarantees complete anonymity to its callers. They cannot see or trace anyone. They're under no legal obligation to report a person who's suicidal. Even if someone's about to do what Charlotte did while speaking to them, they don't have to call 999. Plus, she could've spoken to any of their volunteers across five counties. That's several hundred people and we don't have the resources to work on that. I'm sorry to say, if circumstances were different and Charlotte had been . . . unlawfully killed . . . then things would be different.'

'But because it's a suicide, it's not taken as seriously,' I suggested.

'Honestly, Ryan, we are taking this very seriously. But the difference is there's no reason for us to think a crime has been committed here. And unless whoever spoke to Charlotte and the other man comes forward, we'll probably never know their reasons or learn the nature of their relationship.'

'What about a moral obligation?' asked Johnny. 'Surely if they know why you want to talk to them, they'll be willing to help us understand what happened?'

'Then it's up to them to volunteer that information.'

As the conversation continued and more roadblocks were thrown in our way, I became increasingly frustrated. It was like being behind the wheel of my own car but having someone drive it remotely.

'There is something else,' DS O'Connor added. 'We've been approached by a news agency. We have a verbal agreement that they don't normally report on suicides, but this is different as it was seemingly a pact between two strangers. They've had a tip-off and they believe it's in the public interest to report on it.'

'Tell them we don't want to talk,' I snapped. 'It's bad enough that our friends know, let alone the rest of the world.'

'It might work in our favour though. It could help put names forward as to who the stranger might be.'

'No,' I replied adamantly, and slammed my hand down on the table.

'Okay.' DS O'Connor sighed and took a quick gulp of his tea. 'I will pass your message on.' He stood up to leave. 'But we have no control over what they can and cannot write about. So you should prepare yourself, as there might be some interest in this story.'

He wasn't wrong. Two days later and it had made the front of our weekly newspaper, page leads in four tabloids and a column in two broadsheets. Journalists raided Facebook for photographs of Charlotte and spoke to former workmates and acquaintances she had barely known. Stories were illustrated by tasteless graphics of the clifftop and the trajectory of their fall.

When journalists left me voicemail messages and texts urging me to talk to them, I turned off my phone. I could barely speak to the people around me, let alone strangers.

CHAPTER EIGHT

TWO MONTHS AFTER CHARLOTTE

I didn't care about attending Charlotte's funeral.

I didn't need to say goodbye to her. I didn't want to remember her fondly and I didn't want to pay her my last respects. She deserved nothing from me. The only reason I agreed to attend the church ceremony and short journey to the crematorium was because I'd been guilt-tripped into it by my parents. If Charlotte didn't want to celebrate her life, then why should I?

I was so muggy from swallowing two of Mum's sleeping tablets and hungover from another beer binge the night before that I couldn't focus on who was standing at the lectern, scrambling to find positive things to say about a woman who murdered her baby.

My eyes wandered around the church, which was decorated with vases of daffodils and posters advertising forthcoming Easter celebrations. But once they snapped towards the coffin as four pallbearers carried Charlotte in, they never left it. I ignored the order of service and didn't join in with the hymns. I didn't even bow my head in prayer.

Dad and Johnny flanked me and kept me steady for the moments when I was required to stand; and later they apologised to anyone who tried to converse with me as they guided me back towards the funeral car. I cared so little that I didn't even try to avoid the reporters at the church gates, trying to engage anyone who made eye contact with them.

Once Charlotte's body was released to me, I'd left it to my in-laws to organise her farewell. Choosing a funeral director, picking which clothes she would wear to go into the flames, what objects to throw into her coffin, what music should play as she was brought into the church, how many cars were required . . . She was their daughter so she was their problem. I told them through a third party that they could also keep her wedding ring. I had no use for my own, let alone hers. Everything it signified was a lie. Charlotte had thought so little of me, and now the feeling was mutual. I just wanted it all to be over.

I did, however, want to go to the coroner's court later that same week for Charlotte's inquest. I allowed Johnny and my mum to accompany me. We sat two rows behind Charlotte's parents, but neither family looked at each other, not even the briefest glance.

I didn't know why I'd wanted to attend. Perhaps I didn't think I'd suffered enough and needed to know how much more pain I could endure before I completely cracked.

I listened carefully as witness and character statements were read aloud, and I watched as the dashboard footage taken at the clifftop was shown. Eventually, the senior coroner, a plump, middle-aged woman with a soft face and sympathetic eyes, ruled the medical cause of her death as 'multiple injuries'.

'No shit,' I mumbled to myself. I think Johnny might have heard me.

'Before I record a verdict of suicide, I have to be positive of two things beyond a reasonable doubt,' she continued. 'That Mrs Smith caused the act which led to her death and that she did so with the intention of killing herself. I have to be sure on both accounts this is what happened – and I am. Mrs Smith went to the top of Birling Gap with an as-yet-unidentified man, then tragically died when she impacted with the rocks below. Therefore, in these circumstances, I record a conclusion of suicide.'

So there it was: in the space of three days, my wife had been cremated and it was on public record for all the world to see that she had killed herself. Perhaps now I could move on.

After eight weeks of living at my parents' house, I felt a prevailing urge to be back inside my flat again. I needed to surround myself with familiar objects to help me feel like something close to my old self. I couldn't allow Charlotte's ghost to bully me out of my own home.

As I unlocked the front door, I hovered nervously in the doorway. There were faint traces of the air fresheners she preferred. Her raincoat hung shapelessly on a coat hook. We grinned under an arch made of roses in a wedding photograph gathering dust in its frame.

I'd spent almost a third of my life as an 'us' and suddenly I had to accept being an 'I' again. It hit me that the former life I'd loved so much was irrecoverable and I'd never be able to copy it with anyone else. Once the tears began, I couldn't shut them off.

I wasn't ready to return to our bedroom, so I chose to sleep in the box room. It was the only part of the flat that we hadn't got around to decorating in our time there. We'd just about managed to wedge a single mattress and the tiniest of Ikea bedside cabinets inside. But it suited me fine for now. Next door was the nursery. I wasn't ready to face that yet. While it remained as it was, in neutral shades of yellow and with soft toys scattered about, I could pretend Daniel was sleeping there. I didn't want to let him go.

Days later, I printed out Charlotte's mobile phone records. I'd believed DS O'Connor when he'd told us how frequently she'd called End of the Line, but I still wanted to see it with my own eyes. I scanned each column and most of the calls had been made in the morning or early afternoons when I was at work. Occasionally, she'd called evenings and weekends when we were both at home. I remembered her wandering into other rooms claiming to be catching up with friends, but now I knew that just metres away from me, she was actually telling a stranger that she wanted to die.

Some calls lasted seconds, others continued for more than an hour. For a moment, I let my anger dilute into pity.

Why couldn't you tell me how much pain you were in?

I thought about Charlotte's car and how, at some point, I'd have to sell it. In fact, there were a lot of things I needed to organise as my new normality began. But packing away her clothes, sifting through her documents, changing the name on the utility bills, closing her bank account, et cetera, would all have to wait.

And so would my job for now. The thought of walking into that perpetually cold lobby as if everything in my life was exactly the same as the last time I'd been there filled me with dread. My sympathetic doctor signed me off for another month, but he wouldn't let me leave the surgery until he'd given me a handful of leaflets about coping with loss and the telephone numbers of grief counselling organisations. I scanned the advice given in one when I reached my car. 'Try going away for a weekend somewhere that's brand new to you, or take a long walk. Perhaps you might think about getting a pet.' I laughed out loud.

Yes, doctor, I'm going to replace my dead wife with a hamster. Marvellous idea.

Johnny and the lads I played Sunday-league football with took turns to visit the flat and keep me occupied, but despite their best efforts, they rarely got much conversation from me. Johnny also insisted on dragging me out to our local pub, The Abington, and did his best to re-engage me with a world outside my cloudy little bubble. But I didn't care for it. There was little I cared for anymore.

'Mum and Dad are worried about you,' Johnny began earnestly one evening. The bar was quiet and he was perched on the edge of a threadbare sofa, glancing at the floor and absent-mindedly fiddling with the drawstrings on his hoodie. 'They're scared you might . . . you know . . . do the same as Charlotte.'

'What, kill myself for no reason? Hurl myself off a cliff and smash my head on rocks so my face is completely unrecognisable?'

I knew my reply was uncalled for. I'd be lying if I said the thought hadn't crossed my mind. But it had only been fleeting. 'What about you?' I asked. 'What do you think?'

'I told them you're not that selfish, that you know it'd destroy them if you did something like that.' I nodded slowly. 'It'd destroy me too,' he added, and looked up at me with a deep concern in his eyes.

Johnny and I were close, but we'd rarely speak about matters of the heart. However, since Charlotte had died, he'd been my rock. He'd seen me at my very worst and at my most desperate. He'd sat with me as I cried my eyes out, he'd wiped drunken vomit from my face, and he'd used up all his holiday to spend time with me and offer me his strength.

'If you hurt yourself, I'd never forgive myself, Ry,' he continued. 'Watching you go through hell has really affected me too. I need you to promise me that you won't do anything daft.'

'I promise.'

'Good. And tell me you'll think about what Dad suggested, like grief counselling or getting some medication from the doctor.'

'Okay, I will.' I had no intention of doing either. I only agreed to get him off my back. 'I need a piss. You get another round in,' I said, and patted him on the shoulder as I left the table.

As I made my way through the lounge area, I spotted a noticeboard covered with business cards for taxi firms and flyers for pub quizzes and a beer festival. Among them was a leaflet for End of the Line. I removed the pin and slipped it into my pocket. Later, after Johnny dropped me off at the flat, I stared at the leaflet in my hand. *We listen, not judge*, it said in blue writing.

The only way I could understand what the helpline had offered Charlotte that I couldn't was to call them. Tentatively, I reached for my phone and dialled. Within five rings it was answered.

'Good evening, you've reached the End of the Line helpline, this is Kevin speaking. May I ask your name?'

I had no idea what to say to him.

'Take all the time you need,' Kevin continued after a short silence.

'Ryan,' I said. 'My name is Ryan.'

'Hi there, Ryan, and how are you feeling this evening?'

I don't know if it was actually Kevin's voice or the four pints of real ale floating through my bloodstream, but he sounded so warm and compassionate. I wondered why he'd chosen to stay up until late in the night to talk to people he didn't know. Maybe, like me, there was a huge gap in his life.

'I'm okay,' I replied.

'That's good to hear. Is there a reason that brought you to call us tonight?'

'My wife . . .' I began, but I struggled to complete the sentence.

'Your wife,' he repeated. 'Did something happen to your wife?'

'She . . . died. A couple of months ago.'

'I'm sorry to hear that, Ryan. Would you like to tell me about her?'

I racked my brains to think up any reason other than suicide as to how she might've died, as I didn't want him to judge me. But the alcohol slowed me down and I couldn't think of one that quickly. So I told him the truth and how I swung from missing Charlotte with every fibre of my being to never wanting to think about her again.

'That's completely natural to go through a wide range of emotions,' Kevin explained. 'Do you want to talk me through some of what you've been feeling?'

I sat on the floor of my living room, telling a stranger things even my family didn't know about how I felt. And while he didn't offer any miracle solutions, at least he didn't suggest I took a long walk or bought a pet. Instead, our conversation gave me more of an insight into why Charlotte might have found End of the Line's volunteers easy to talk to.

But it had yet to explain why she'd needed to call them more than a hundred times.

CHAPTER NINE

FOUR MONTHS AFTER CHARLOTTE

The police eventually returned Charlotte's mobile phone, iPad and laptop after the inquest. They were contained in clear, sealed plastic bags with evidence and case numbers written on stickers with a black marker pen. That's all she was to people who didn't know her: a case identified by two letters and seven digits.

Her electronics had been thoroughly examined by a digital forensic team, but nothing of note or concern had been discovered. And, frustratingly, there was still no link to the man she'd died with. Despite the media attention their story had generated, he'd yet to be identified by the public and his body still hadn't washed ashore.

I'd never had any reason to check up on Charlotte, but she'd left me with so many unanswered questions, she owed me explanations. It was eight o'clock in the evening when I began with her phone and relived our text conversations. I didn't like that the police had probably read through our private moments, even the mundane crap about whose turn it was to get the car serviced. I hadn't realised how much I'd missed seeing her name appear on my phone.

As Charlotte's pregnancy progressed, the number of calls she'd made to friends fell steeply but her emails and texts rose. I guess it was easier to hide her sadness behind the written word than to disguise the emptiness in her voice.

I scrolled through her Facebook timeline, and in her last few months she hadn't posted a single thing. Most mums-to-be can't wait to talk about what stage of pregnancy they're at or their cravings or to complain about how fat they're feeling. But I'd been the only one of us to give our friends status updates or share photographs. Charlotte had gone from an active poster to a lurker.

I leafed through the saved documents on her laptop, but they all dated back to her pre-pregnancy design work. Her music library was full of the cheesy pop she loved so much and there was nothing suspicious about either her browser history or her favourites bar. Most of her emails had been deleted, and then deleted from the deleted folder. Her cookies were also cleared. Just as I feared, there was nothing new to learn about my wife.

I was surprised – and disappointed – that there were no photographs of us at all on her phone or her iPad. I'd teased her about how trigger-happy she was when it came to her camera phone; it didn't matter where we were – in the kitchen, on holiday by a pool, or in the aisle of a supermarket, the girl loved a picture. I flicked though several folders on her devices, but she'd erased every image she'd ever taken of us. It was like our relationship was so hideous to her that she needed to wipe away any trace of it. Even four months after her death, she was still finding new ways to hurt me.

As midnight approached, I knew from experience that if I continued down this road any further tonight, I'd wind myself up further and further and wouldn't be able to sleep. But as I was about to put the iPad away, I lost grip of it. My fingers slid across the onscreen keyboard as I scrambled to stop it falling to the floor.

As I picked it up, I suddenly became aware of two calculator apps – the standard operating-system version and another. Who needed two calculators? I clicked on the unfamiliar one and four numbers had already been inputted – 1301. I recognised them immediately: it was the date Charlotte died; a date she had been working towards.

I pressed the equals key but nothing happened. I followed it with the plus, the minus and divide keys, but it wasn't until I pressed the percentage symbol that an entirely new screen popped up. It was a home screen that burst into a hive of activity as various folders of photographs, documents and notes sprang to life and covered the screen. She'd downloaded an app that allowed her to hide what I was never meant to find.

I took the tablet to my bedroom and propped myself up on the bed. The first documents folder contained dozens of screengrabs she'd taken from a variety of websites, and pages of links to other sites. All of them related to suicide.

Images included illustrations of where best to sever an arm to effectively bleed to death, and documents featured the best combination of tablets needed for a successful overdose. There were hyperlinks as to where they could be purchased online and from which country.

Charlotte had also favourited a link to a message board called The Final Push, which suggested 'suicide hotspots' around the country. There were multistorey car parks without safety railings or netting, accessible bridges, railway lines with broken fencing, and stretches of water with powerful undertows that would drag you under in seconds. There were photos, street maps, written instructions of how to find them, postcodes for satnavs, and Ordnance Survey map coordinates. Everything had been thought about in minute detail, and Charlotte hadn't only read them, she'd bookmarked them, too.

I couldn't tear my eyes away from the screen, saddened by the desperation of people who were at their wits' end and sickened at the enthusiasm of others encouraging them to die. As far as I could see, nobody had inserted a link or a telephone number to End of the Line. Nobody had suggested maybe death wasn't the right way to go about things or urged them to talk to someone.

There were threads from teens who'd had enough of living their too-few years and victims of terminal illnesses and mental health problems. Some came from elderly people so scared of a long, drawn-out death that they wanted to go on their own terms. Loneliness, abuse, depression, war, bullying, sexuality, eating disorders . . . the list of reasons to die was endless.

I scoured the pages for names that might indicate Charlotte was a member of these boards but I couldn't find any proof she'd posted. Maybe she'd just lurked there like she had on Facebook.

A thread on another message board caught my eye, made just days ago. The subject heading was 'Need someone 2 Talk 2 As I Die'. The poster had almost three hundred messages numbered under her avatar. She'd chosen a photo of a young Angelina Jolie and the screen-name GrlInterrupted.

So guys, I've decided where and when to do it (pills arrived on Wednesday from Trinidad and I've booked into a hotel in Birmingham). Also decided that even though I came in alone, I don't want to go alone. Anyone here want to be on the other end of the phone as it happens? I need company.

Among the many congratulatory replies, nobody in her online support network had the guts to blur the lines between fantasy and reality and take her up on her request. But they were quick to recommend other screen-names who might help.

Whereabouts are you hon? asked someone by the name of R.I.P.

Leicester, UK, she replied.

U know Chloe4 who used to post here? She was a Brit. She used to talk about a woman over there who'd helped friends of hers once and who was now helping her. It must've worked as we never heard from Chloe4 again, and we were pretty tight.'

What do you mean by 'help'?

She tells people what to do, what not to do, she knows the risks, suggests what to say in notes, etc. Chloe4 called the woman the 'Freer of Lost Souls'.

Does she post here?

No, she's pro. She keeps it on the downlow cos she works for a suicide helpline called End of the Line or something like that. Lol. Someone recommended her to Chloe4.

I let out a deep breath I didn't know I'd been holding, prised my eyes away from the screen and glanced outside. The darkness was making way for a rising sun. An occasional car headlight illuminated the road as commuters began their new day.

I'd spent months searching for something – anything – to explain why Charlotte had ended her life and why it was with a complete stranger. Now something told me that if the 'Freer of Lost Souls' actually existed, she would have an answer for me.

CHAPTER TEN

FOUR MONTHS, ONE WEEK AFTER CHARLOTTE

It was like banging my head against a brick wall.

It had taken effort, skill and organisation and where was I? Nowhere. Try as I might, I was no closer to finding out whether the Freer of Lost Souls was a real person or the figment of a morally bankrupt website's imagination. However, the one thing searching for her had given me was purpose.

The day after first reading the post about her, I did a keyword search on the same message board and four others. Her nickname was buried within hundreds of other posts but she'd definitely been mentioned a couple of dozen times, although not as often in recent years. Like every decent urban myth, nobody could actually verify her existence. I guessed if she was that good at what she did, the proof of her successes were lying six feet under, not boasting about her online.

I still struggled to comprehend that someone who worked for a helpline might have an ulterior motive. I don't know why though – until a day earlier, I hadn't realised message forums existed to encourage suicidal people to die. If she was real, I'd hunt her down and lure her out from beneath the rock where she was hiding.

I set up camp on the dining room table and created a profile for my own message board account. When R.I.P. ignored my direct message, I turned to GrlInterrupted instead.

Hi, sorry to bother you, I typed, *I just wondered if you had any luck trying to find the woman from End of the Line that R.I.P told you about? The Freer of Lost Souls?*

I paced the flat as I waited for an alert to say she'd replied. Within the hour, she had.

No, sorry, bro. R.I.P didn't know anything more about her. Even called the branches myself but kept getting different folk. Like finding a needle in a haystack, eh? Not sure what I'd have said anyway – 'hi, which one of you bitches wants to listen to me die?' Lolz.

I replied with a 'lolz' of my own but nothing about this amused me.

I needed air and caffeine so I swapped the flat for a nearby parade of shops. I used to be a regular at the café most Sunday mornings, and I'd return home with a bag of muffins, cinnamon swirls and hot drinks for Charlotte and me. It was the first time I'd gone back since she'd died and it felt peculiar ordering for one.

I asked for a double cappuccino and, as the coffee machine spluttered to life, a wave of guilt washed over me in a sliding door moment. I wondered how different my life might be if only I'd been a better, more attentive husband. A man who wasn't so insistent that his way was the right way. *That* Ryan would have realised earlier just how serious Charlotte's depression was, and listened to her instead of trying to cure her. Now Charlotte would be standing with him in the queue, one hand clutching her purse and the other clasping the handle of Daniel's pram. I shook my head and the alternate universe melted away like a snowflake.

I took my drink back to the flat, trying to guesstimate how long it might take to prove or disprove the Freer of Lost Souls' existence. The only way would be to call, and to keep calling the helpline until I tracked her down. The odds were against me. Northamptonshire had ninety-four part-time volunteers, Leicestershire eighty-six, Warwickshire fifty-eight and Bedfordshire sixty. Give or take a few who might have come and gone since the last tally was published in its annual report, I had about a one-in-three-hundred chance of finding her.

I couldn't think of a way to cut corners and speed up the process. And that was assuming the person I was looking for really was a *her*. It could very easily have been male. Either way, they'd need to be convinced I was for real.

I devised a backstory for myself. I'd claim depression was ruining my life and that I didn't see any purpose in continuing. I'd tell them not only had I contemplated suicide but I'd almost gone ahead with it; however, something had held me back. I needed someone to help me take those extra few steps forward because I couldn't do it alone.

To make it work, I needed to be organised. I opened up a blank Excel spreadsheet on Charlotte's laptop to make a note of the name of each End of the Line volunteer who answered. I'd add the time of the call and a brief outline of their responses to what I told them. Some likely shared the same Christian name, so I'd type adjectives like 'old', 'young', 'nasal', 'regional' or 'foreign accent' to separate them.

I'd give them my middle name, Steven, and I'd adjust my sleep pattern to cover all their shifts. The task ahead of me was Herculean. But the quicker I cracked on, the quicker I'd know for sure if I was hunting for a real person or a ghost in the machine. I even got hold of a Dictaphone, and with a little bit of gadgetry bought online, I could plug it into my phone and record all my calls in case it was her.

Each day, I spoke to as many different volunteers as I could. My conversations continued for as long as necessary until I could either include them on my spreadsheet as a 'yes', a 'maybe' or a probable 'no'. Patterns began to emerge of who worked when, how frequently, and which days of the week I could find them.

A little over a fortnight later and my spreadsheet went on for pages, packed full of names, dates, times and descriptions. But there had been no obvious 'yeses'.

I felt shitty for abusing End of the Line's resources by calling so often and for pulling the wool over their eyes, especially as they seemed like good people. They didn't try to talk Steven out of wanting to end his life; instead, they listened, helped him explore what he was feeling and let him find his own way forward. Without exception, every voice was coming from a place of goodness. I had to keep reminding myself that so was I.

There were times when I found their kindness so warm and heartfelt that my guard slipped and Ryan came out. Then it was me admitting to feelings of hopelessness and me who was struggling.

I began painting mental pictures of what the Freer of Lost Souls might look like. She was in her late fifties, a spinster with pale skin that was beginning to loosen and hang from her cheeks and neck. There'd be deep lines etched across her forehead and her shoulders would be hunched from the weight of the guilt she carried but refused to acknowledge. On the surface, her eyes would seem charitable but if you stared into them deeply enough, you'd catch a glimmer of the woman inside – a dark, cold soul who thrived on the pain of others. She was like Judi Dench in that film *Notes on a Scandal.* Only even more devious.

Whoever she was, the Freer came to dominate my days, my nights, my waking thoughts and my unconscious dreams. While she had given me a function, I'd also made her an obsession that was delaying my healing. But I knew that if I threw in the towel now without completing what I'd set out to do, I'd forever wonder if she actually existed.

Of course I didn't tell my family or friends what I was up to because they'd think I was mad. But judging by the number of frustrated voicemails and texts they left, complaining that my phone was permanently engaged, they had an idea something was up. So I started joining them just often enough for drinks at the pub, a family dinner at home or a get-together at a restaurant to convince them that over four and a half months after Charlotte's suicide, I was on the road to recovery.

In part, it was true. I was on a road. And, eventually, it led to the woman I was looking for.

CHAPTER ELEVEN

FOUR MONTHS, TWO WEEKS AFTER CHARLOTTE

Eighty-two people. That's how many I'd lied to and misled before I found the person nicknamed the Freer of Lost Souls.

'Good evening, you've reached the End of the Line, this is Laura speaking. May I ask your name?' she began.

I pressed record on my Dictaphone like I did with each call, and with the earpiece in place I slipped quickly and easily into my alter ego, Steven, like a comfortable pair of slippers. I trotted out the same reply I'd given the last eighty-one times. 'I've not called somewhere like this before. I don't know where to begin.'

'Well, let's start with a name. What shall I call you?'

Like most of the other volunteers, there was something reassuring about her voice. She was well-spoken, her tone friendly and soothing. I could imagine her reading a bedtime story on children's television.

'Steven,' I replied.

'It's nice to talk to you, Steven,' she continued. 'Can I ask what made you decide to call us this evening?'

'I'm not sure. I – I feel like I haven't got . . . anyone. I don't think I want to be . . . *here* . . . anymore.' I'd read the script so many times recently that I knew it off by heart. I knew where to sound choked and where to pause for dramatic effect. If an Oscar were ever awarded for Best Dramatic Role via the Telephone, I'd be a dead cert to win.

'Well, it's great that you've called,' she said. 'Tell me about the people who love and care about you. Who do you have in your life who falls into that category?'

I pretended to think for a moment. 'Nobody really.' I exaggerated a deep sigh. 'I've got no one at all.'

She asked if I had friends I could turn to and sympathised when I said I had none. Her responses were textbook. My fingers slid quietly across the laptop keyboard, adding her to my spreadsheet. Laura wasn't an unusual name but she was the first volunteer that I'd come across with it. Already I could tell she was a glass-half-full kind of woman.

Unlikely, I typed.

'Have you seen your doctor and told them how you're feeling?'

'Yes, and she put me on antidepressants.'

'And how have they worked for you?'

'It's been four months and I still don't feel there's anything to get up for in the morning. Sometimes I think I'd be better off just saving them all up and . . . you know . . .'

'Sometimes or often?'

Again, I hesitated. 'Often,' I whispered.

Our conversation wasn't going any further than the last eighty-one times with her predecessors. I heard a faint rustling and guessed she was new and consulting a manual. If nothing else, I'd be good practice for her. I stifled a yawn and started to look at the football results on the BBC Sport website.

'You don't need to be embarrassed, Steven. We've all thought about ending our lives at some time or another. Have you ever tried to do it before?'

Hold up, did she just say 'we've all'?

None of the other eighty-one helpline staff admitted that. Maybe she just wanted me to believe that she really did understand me.

'No,' I replied, as if I were ashamed. 'But I did plan it out once.'

'You planned it out once?'

I followed the advice I'd read online and told her about making it easier for those I'd leave behind by getting my affairs in order before I died. I looked at a page of notes I'd made and brought up the railway track near Kelney that could be reached through a broken fence. She listened quietly as my imagination did the talking.

'Perhaps, deep down, you aren't serious about ending your life,' she said. It was less of a question and more of a statement. And then something in her voice switched from warm and comfortable to accusatory.

'Maybe it's a cry for help?' she continued. 'I get plenty of calls from people who tell me they want to die, but when it gets down to the nitty-gritty, all they're really doing is just feeling sorry for themselves. Are you one of those people, Steven? Are you just trapped in a cycle of self-pity? Are you so deep into it that you don't realise nothing is going to change unless you find the courage to do something about it yourself? Because if you don't take charge, for the rest of your life – maybe another forty, fifty years – the pain you're feeling right now, the pain that's so bad that it led you to call me, is only going to get worse. This – how you are feeling right now – is going to be it for you. Can you live like that, Steven? I know I couldn't.'

I knew in that moment I'd found her.

None of the others had even come close to talking to me like this. I should have been excited, but in all my preparations I'd stupidly not considered where to go if I ever reached this stage. I'd assumed I could wing it but I was wrong. Instead, I became tongue-tied.

'I – I – I'm not a timewaster, honestly,' I stuttered. 'It's something I've thought long and hard about and it's what I want, but if I can't do it, that must make me a coward, right?'

'No, Steven, you're not a coward,' she continued. 'You called me today and that makes you courageous. Maybe you just chose the wrong day when you were waiting for that train. It happens to plenty of people.' Now her tone had returned to calming.

Am I just imagining all this?

I could almost picture her smile as she spoke, like butter wouldn't melt in her mouth. 'Just remember, we're here for you in whatever capacity you want us to be.'

'You mean to listen to me?'

I held my breath as I waited for her reply. She'd basically just agreed with me that I had nothing to live for and now she was telling me I had courage. I wasn't sure who was the cat, who was the mouse and who was toying with whom.

'If that's all you want from me, then yes.'

'What if . . . What if I need . . . What if I decide . . .' My voice trailed off. How on earth could I put it into words without scaring her off?

'Are you calling to tell me you want to end your life and are looking for my support in doing it?'

She'd done it for me. Butterflies rose en masse in my stomach and took flight. *Oh fuck! This is it! What the hell do I say next?*

'I . . . I suppose I am.' I grimaced as the words fell clumsily from my mouth. And again her tone switched, as if she were lecturing me.

'End of the Line is an impartial, non-judgemental place,' she continued. 'We are here to listen to you. We won't try to talk you out of anything you decide to do, we just ask that you talk to us first and explore all your options before you take such a huge step. Do you understand that?'

'Yes,' I said. I racked my brain for how to respond. The best I could manage was a meek 'But . . .'

'But?' she repeated.

She had me on the back foot and she relished it. 'But if I wanted to, you know, go ahead with it, would you . . . ?'

'Would I what, Steven? What would you like me to do?'

My mouth went dry and I fell silent again.

What is wrong with you, Ryan? Come on! You have her! Just say something!

But I was stumped. I needed time to think. 'I'm sorry, I have to go,' I said, before hanging up.

'Fuck!' I yelled at the top of my voice, then grabbed a mug from the table and hurled it at the wall. It smashed into pieces and sent a framed print crashing to the floor.

I remained with my head in my hands, taking sharp breaths. Laura wasn't like any of the other volunteers I'd spoken to. She was *the one*. She was the Freer of Lost Souls and her ability to switch personalities in a heartbeat scared the hell out of me. She hadn't just come out and said, 'I will help you kill yourself,' but she'd pretty much told me that I was going to remain living in this hell unless I did something drastic.

I rewound the Dictaphone and listened to the whole conversation again. She'd taken complete control of the call and I was angry at myself for losing grip of my own plan. Instead of playing it cool I'd panicked, then hung up on her. My instinct was to call her again straight away, but I held back. If I did it immediately, I might look indecisive or an attention-seeker. She had to think I was almost sure I wanted to die – 'almost' being the operative word – because turning that into a certainty would give her a challenge and I bet that's what she enjoyed. I'd pretend to spend the next few days mulling it over before I called End of the Line to try and find her again.

What to do until then? I had to put my time to good use. There was a chance Laura had given me a false name, but it was all I had to go on. I googled 'Laura' and 'End of the Line', but all that came up was the author of a book about historic steam trains. I refined my search with the words 'charity' and 'suicide' and it took me to the website of a local newspaper, the *Chronicle & Echo*.

The headline £300 RAISED IN CHARITY BAKE SALE ran above a photo of three women and a girl standing behind a table full of baked goods. The story was dated around a year ago. *Almost £300 has been raised for helpline End of the Line by staff baking cakes*, it said. *The helpline, which has been running for eight years, made the money with a stall at the Racecourse Town Show. A spokesman said: 'We are self-funded and this cash will really help with our escalating running costs.' Pictured above (from left to right): Zoe Parker, Mary Barnett, Effie Morris and Laura Morris.*

Laura Morris. I boosted the size of the picture on my screen and stared at the woman on the right. She was actually quite normal-looking, not at all like the dowdy frump I'd pictured her as. She was attractive, even. She wore a smart blouse and pleated skirt, her hair was slicked back and tied into a ponytail and her smile revealed perfectly positioned teeth. There was something familiar about her daughter Effie's face and name. I looked her up on Facebook and it clicked when I saw a clearer image of her face.

I typed *Laura Morris* into the search engine along with *End of the Line* and one more story appeared. CHARITY FUNDRAISER WINS TOP AWARD. The photo featured the same woman. A man in a wheelchair was presenting a silver shield to her for single-handedly raising £50,000 for the charity in a year, the largest sum of any of their branches.

I've worked here for a few years now so I know first-hand the good work the charity does, Laura was quoted as saying. *It's taken a lot of hard work to raise the money, from jumble and bake sales to sponsorship, and I'd like to thank my husband Tony's business for its help with sponsorship, too.*

So she was married. I wondered how calculating a person had to be to pull the wool over her husband's eyes. Or maybe he was like-minded. Perhaps he knew what she did and turned a blind eye to it.

There was always a chance this was a gargantuan fuck-up and my hunch was wrong. I was about to close the lid of the laptop when the last line of the story caught my eye.

When asked what advice Laura would give to anyone thinking of calling End of the Line, she replied, 'We're here for you in whatever capacity you want us to be.'

It was exactly the same line she'd used on me when I'd told her I wanted to die. I googled the phrase and it wasn't something she'd taken from End of the Line's website or anywhere else and just repeated. It was her own. This had to be the same woman I'd spoken to.

I smiled to myself, as I knew exactly how I was going to get to Laura.

CHAPTER TWELVE

I sat in the driver's seat of my car a few metres away from End of the Line's offices.

I was parked on double yellow lines, and every forty minutes or so I'd spot the same sour-faced traffic warden in my rear-view mirror patrolling the avenue. Each time she made her way in my direction, checking car registrations with the electronic device in her hand, I'd start the engine and drive around the block. Then I'd park in the exact same spot once she'd gone.

I'd learned Laura Morris was volunteering that day when she'd answered on my third call to the helpline. I wondered what the odds were on that happening so soon. But I didn't want to talk to her today. I'd immediately hung up, grabbed my coat, keys and phone, and hurried to their office to wait for her to emerge.

I'd been there for much of the morning when a handful of people entered within minutes of each other. I assumed a new shift must be about to start. Soon after, Laura left. Her head tilted up towards the cloudless sky to gauge the May bank holiday weather, then she walked down the handful of concrete steps and passed my car. I compared her face to the online newspaper story I'd printed out, and I was as sure as I could be that it was the same woman. Seeing her in the flesh after the weeks of effort I'd put in to track her down and unmask her made me giddy. I clenched my fists and took a deep breath.

She wore white running shoes and a waterproof jacket and carried a handbag-sized folded umbrella, so I assumed she wasn't driving. I grabbed some loose change from the ashtray in case I needed to follow her onto a bus, opened the car door and, no longer caring about traffic wardens, began my pursuit. I held back for a moment when she looked behind her, then she opened her bag, pulled out a cigarette and lit it.

I'd watched enough telly cop dramas to know to keep a safe distance. Chances were Laura wouldn't know she was being followed, but I couldn't take the risk. If I could see her, then she could see me. I slipped my headphones over my ears so that if she turned around, I'd just be a man listening to music.

She kept a steady pace and while she wasn't a power-walker, she moved with purpose. I followed her for about thirty minutes before we entered a housing estate. It was a moderately affluent area with long front gardens, neatly trimmed hedges and lawns, and rows of flowers.

One house stood out from the rest like a silver penny among coppers. And Laura was making her way up its driveway. The walls had been rendered and painted a creamy white and the window frames weren't like the neighbours' houses – brown, plastic and diamond-leaded. They were modern, dark grey frames and the glass was slightly tinted. Instead of a grassy lawn there was block paving and enough room for two more cars to park next to the yellow Mini Cooper already there. Under a window were some carefully arranged terracotta plant pots. Although stylishly tied together, the house and garden didn't fit in with the surroundings.

Laura unlocked a double front door and, as she crossed the threshold, I briefly registered the walls and their unusual colour, patchy with dark grey and black streaks. I waited for her to close the door behind her before returning to my car, satisfied.

I headed back the next morning at seven, desperately needing to know more about a typical day in her life. With lukewarm coffee in a flask, I parked on the opposite side of the road and waited.

I must have missed her husband, as the only car parked on the drive was the Mini, which by its garish colour I doubted was his. When Laura finally left an hour and a half later, a pink rucksack was strapped to her back and she set off on foot.

She strolled briskly and I stuck to the other side of the road, dodging behind trees and cars, taking pictures of her en route with my camera phone. She paused outside Westfield Junior School's gates and concentrated on a group of girls and boys running around and laughing together. She waved to one, but her smile faded when the girl didn't see her. Laura briefly became distracted by some of the other mums standing by the gate, and she looked as if she might want to join them in conversation. Instead, she turned and walked away as if she were afraid to take the risk.

Her journey continued and more photos followed, until finally she approached the driveway to a large white building split into several wings that I was familiar with. *What is she doing here?* I wondered.

It was Kingsthorpe Residential Care Home, where my Granddad Pete had been moved after a stroke left him paralysed down the right-hand side of his body. He was barely able to move or talk. Mum and Dad visited him twice a week; Johnny and I less so, especially after Charlotte's death. I'd been too busy thinking of myself to remember him.

The receptionist appeared to be familiar with Laura Morris, because she buzzed her in through the doors without asking to see any ID. Then Laura wandered along a corridor before veering out of sight.

I remained outside, shuffling from foot to foot, unsure of how to play it. Would I be pushing my luck if I followed her inside? Maybe, but I had to chance it.

'Hi, I've come to see Pete Spencer,' I told the young woman behind the desk, and gave her my brightest smile.

'What relation to Mr Spencer are you?' she asked, stony-faced.

'I'm his grandson. I haven't been for a while.' She looked at me as if to say, *I know. Shame on you.*

At her request, I passed her my driver's licence as identification and she handed me a visitor's lanyard to wear around my neck. Granddad's room was located in a separate wing, to the right of the corridor, along with other physically impaired patients. But Laura had turned to the left. I glanced around to make sure nobody was watching me before I walked down the same corridor she'd taken. It wasn't long before I found her.

She was sitting in a lounge area, holding the hand of a boy strapped into a wheelchair who was laughing along to a book she was reading him. Her eyes only flitted between the book and his smile, like if she looked elsewhere, he might vanish into thin air. Only a mum could look at her own child with so much love. She stroked his hand and laughed with him.

I was taken aback, trying to reconcile the woman before me with the one who, just days earlier, had suggested I should kill myself. I watched them for a couple more minutes, but felt intrusive. I had to remind myself that having a child with special needs didn't change who she was or what she did to vulnerable people.

I left as silently as I'd arrived, and decided to visit Granddad while I was there. I knocked on the door to his room and entered. While his eyes were closed, I took in his appearance. He was nothing like the bulky, soundly framed builder I recalled as a kid. I remembered being nine and playing in our garden with Johnny, both of us watching Granddad Pete make his way up and down a ladder with a hod resting on his shoulder, retiling the roof. He gave us each a piggyback up to the very top, where we straddled the ridge and waved to the passing cars and buses on the road below. Then Mum came back from work and screamed blue murder until he carried us down again.

Two decades had passed, and an adult lifetime of smoking two packs of high-tar cigarettes a day had likely brought on his series of strokes and turned him into the shadow of a man before me.

Photos of my late Granny Elsie and Mum and Dad were arranged on floating shelves surrounding his bed; Johnny and me as kids were on his wall, and in a large silver frame was a photo of Charlotte and me from our wedding day. It caught me off guard.

'Hi, Granddad, it's Ryan,' I said quietly, and took hold of his hand. His skin felt paper-thin and his purple veins stood out like speedbumps on a road. 'I'm sorry I haven't come for a while.'

His eyelids slowly unfurled and I watched as his milky grey eyes focused on where and who the voice was coming from. Sections of his brain controlling his speech and movement had been irrevocably damaged by the final, massive stroke, but he still recognised his eldest grandson. The left side of his mouth rose ever so slightly as he tried to smile. His index finger brushed against mine.

'Lot,' he muttered. I frowned.

'What's that?' I asked gently.

'Lot,' he repeated and looked ahead of him. 'Lot. Cha. Cha.' He was looking at my wedding photo.

'Lot cha,' I repeated. 'You mean Charlotte?' His finger touched mine again. 'Mum told you?' I'd never actually asked if she had. He indicated yes.

'Things have been a bit shit lately,' I admitted. And before I could stop myself, I was talking at a million miles an hour, telling him about Charlotte's death, how I thought she'd been coerced into killing herself and how I'd found the woman responsible. I just needed to get it off my chest.

'I'm scared, Granddad,' I continued. 'I'm scared of how far I might take it with that woman. I wish you could tell me what to do.'

He stared at me with such intensity, like he was willing his brain to allow his mouth a complete sentence. His cheeks and forehead turned crimson as he opened his lips and a rasp came out.

'It's okay,' I replied. I'd been selfish to dump all this on him.

'Eye,' he muttered. 'Eye, fa.' He was imploring me to understand him.

'Eye, eye, fa,' I repeated, before understanding what he meant. 'An eye for an eye,' I said, and his finger pressed against mine.

His head nodded ever-so-slightly.

'Thank you,' I replied, and clasped his hand tightly in both of mine.

CHAPTER THIRTEEN

FOUR MONTHS, THREE WEEKS AFTER CHARLOTTE

I held out for a few more days before I called End of the Line again.

I'd returned from a lunchtime pint at The Abington with Johnny and Dad, still maintaining the appearance of a man on the slow road to recovery. They seemed relieved when I told them I was returning to my job soon. I'd only been there for nine months before Charlotte died and I'd been off for almost five months, so I gave my boss, Bruce Atkinson, a date when I wanted to return and he said he'd set the wheels in motion. It would be a gradual return rather than anything immediate.

But today my priority was Laura. A torrential summer downpour had soaked me to the skin, so as soon as I arrived back at the flat I stripped off my wet clothes, hung them over the shower rail to dry and couldn't wait to get started. Fortune was on my side, and I tracked her down within a couple of hours.

'My name is Steven. You probably don't remember me but I think you might be the lady I spoke to recently?'

'Yes, hello there, Steven, it was me you spoke to and, yes, I do remember you. How are things with you today?'

'Okay, thanks.'

'That sounds more positive than last time. Has something in your circumstances changed?'

'Nothing much really, I guess.' The biggest change was now I knew a lot more about who was on the other end of the phone.

'Oh, I'm sorry to hear that. But regardless, you're having a good day today at least?'

'I suppose so.'

'Well, sometimes after a good night's sleep, we just wake up in the morning feeling better about things.'

'It doesn't mean the bad stuff goes away though, does it?'

It was like our first conversation had never happened. She was laying on the positivity thickly and I wondered if there was any way she could be on to me. Maybe this is what she did – she played with people to find out how serious they were about wanting to die. They say the best way to drive a dog mad is to stroke it then smack it so it never knows where it stands. Was I her dog?

We danced around each other like a scorpion circling a rattlesnake, neither of us striking. Finally, when I refused to offer any positive answers to the questions she asked, she took the bait.

'Steven, I hope you don't mind me saying, but earlier you said you were okay, but you don't sound like you are.'

'I think I've just got in the habit of saying I am so that people don't worry about me.'

'This is a neutral place. You don't have to pretend to be anything you're not with me. Is there anything you'd like to talk about in particular?'

'Um . . . the last time we spoke . . .'

'I remember . . .'

'I told you something.'

'You told me a lot of things.'

'About me thinking about killing myself . . .'

'Yes, you did.'

'You asked me if I was prepared to do it.'

'I don't recall those being the exact words I used, Steven. I think you may have misinterpreted what I was saying.'

That threw me. 'Oh.'

'What conclusions have you made regarding ending your life since last time?'

I flicked through my notebook but couldn't find the page where I'd written what she'd said before. I had to bluff it.

'I've given it a lot of thought. In fact, it's been the only thing on my mind and I can't make it stop. You're right – no matter what I do, nothing is going to change. All I'm going to feel like is this.'

'And how do you think you can you rid yourself of these feelings?'

I couldn't go in with all guns blazing. She had to think she was in control. 'I don't know.'

'I think you do though, don't you? If you're being really honest with yourself.'

'Yes,' I whispered. 'I'm ready. I mean, I want to . . . I want to die . . .'

'Steven, I'm very sorry to interrupt but I'm afraid I'm going to have to go now, as my shift is coming to an end. Unfortunately, I can't transfer you to one of my colleagues, but if you call back, I'm sure someone else would be happy to pick up where we've left off.'

'What? But—'

'Take care, David,' she continued.

The phone went dead and I sat rigid in the armchair listening to the rain lashing against the balcony window. I ran my hands through my hair trying to suss out whether Laura, our conversations, what I thought she'd encouraged Charlotte to do – everything, in fact – was actually all in my head. Had a combination of grief, booze and a lack of sleep meant that, first time around, I'd only been hearing what I wanted to hear? Or had she seen straight through Steven and found Ryan?

No, she couldn't have. It was far more likely that she was testing me to see how genuine I was and how far she could push me.

And who the hell was David?

For the rest of the week, I continued to park close to Laura Morris's home at various times of the day to watch or follow her. Nothing about surveillance was fun. A heatwave decided to kick in that very week, so to avoid heatstroke I'd either wind down the windows or give myself frequent blasts from the air conditioner. The nearest public toilets had long since closed, so I was forced to empty my bladder in an alleyway instead. My eyes were sore from constantly straining to look at the wing and rear-view mirrors.

When Laura was in view, I'd snap as many pictures as I could of every mundane task. She went nowhere without me following close behind and learning the minute details of her everyday life.

Sometimes, when she was at home, my eyes followed her darkened figure through the tinted windows as she moved from room to room. I could just about make her out through the gaps in her open blinds and in the kitchen, where she'd sit, mostly alone. Once, as evening fell and before she closed the blinds, I stood close to her kitchen window and watched as she spoke to someone out of view. I wondered who else was there that I didn't know about.

I checked the electoral register, and she shared the space with her husband Tony and three unnamed children under the age of sixteen. I already knew the boy wasn't there anymore, and another I assumed was the Effie pictured in the newspaper and who I'd found on Facebook. That left one more.

Tony wasn't hard to find, as Laura had mentioned him in her newspaper interview. He owned an IT support business and was easy to recognise because the name of his company – and his photograph – was plastered across the side of an Audi saloon.

I'd only just pulled up outside his place of work in an industrial estate when I spotted him leaving his office. I trailed him just like I followed his wife, only by car this time, taking photos as we were held at red lights and then from the other side of the street as he made his way into a gym. Then, once he changed into his vest and shorts, I sat in reception pretending to surf the Internet on my phone when I was actually taking pictures through the glass wall of him knocking the hell out of a punch bag.

Next it was Effie's turn to be the focus of my attention, and by the end of the week I knew exactly how I was going to take away everything that Laura had stolen from me.

CHAPTER FOURTEEN

FIVE MONTHS,

TWO WEEKS AFTER CHARLOTTE

Laura appeared to recognise my voice instantly.

She sounded relieved I'd called a third time, almost grateful, as if I'd proven something to her.

I hit the record button on my Dictaphone, and once again she began our conversation playing by the book. She hadn't got away with what she'd been doing by being sloppy. And this time, I'd already rehearsed in my head everything I thought she might ask, so there'd be no more surprises and I wouldn't need to hang up like I had the first time. I'd even written down some fake background history about Steven to throw into the conversation. She had to believe he was desperate, naive and vulnerable enough to manipulate.

'If you can't see yourself getting any better, what's the best outcome you could hope for?' she asked some time into our exchange.

I paused as long as I dared for dramatic effect. 'That one morning I just don't wake up.'

'You don't want to wake up. I understand.'

'Aren't you going to ask me what I have to live for?'

'Would you like me to? Would you listen to me if I came up with some reasons?'

'No, probably not.'

'In our first conversation, you mentioned ending your life by standing in front of a train,' she reminded me.

'I've changed my mind.'

'What are your thoughts now?'

'Hanging.'

I'd done a little Internet research and learned it was the most popular way men choose to kill themselves. She wanted to see just how much thought I'd given to it, why I'd chosen it, where it might happen and how I'd do it. I sensed my answers were irritating her.

'There are a lot of complications involved in . . . your method, if that's what you choose,' she snapped, and then quickly gathered herself. 'But we can work through that another time if it's the direction you decide to take.'

With that one sentence, I knew I had her. If there'd been even the slightest inkling of doubt in my mind, she'd just erased it.

The balance of power between us had shifted. She'd lapped up everything I'd told her and had stopped trying to help me find the positives in my life. Whatever test she'd spent weeks putting me through, I'd just passed.

'So you'll help me?' I asked.

'As I've explained to you before, it's not my job to try to talk you out of anything or into my way of thinking. I'm just here to listen.'

'What if . . .' My voice trailed off. This wasn't part of my plan, not yet. My heart was pounding quickly and I debated whether to take the risk and ask her point-blank. My mouth opened, but I hesitated.

'David?' she asked. 'Are you still there?'

'David?' I replied.

'Sorry, I meant Steven. You were saying, "what if"?'

Fuck it. Just say it. 'What if you were with me when I did it?'

'If you need someone to be with you, then I'm happy to listen and keep you company.'

'I don't mean on the phone.'

I'd caught her completely off guard. She knew exactly what I meant, yet she wanted me to spell it out for her.

'What if I asked you to be with me, Laura, here in my house, when I hanged myself? Would you come?'

There was complete silence before she answered. All either of us heard was the sound of each other's nervous breaths.

'I – I . . . don't think that would be appropriate,' she stuttered.

I had to think on my feet and justify my offer.

'I need you here to tell me if I'm messing something up and reassure me it's all going to be all right. And to be there for me . . . you know . . . at the end.'

'Are you having second thoughts?'

'No, no, I'm not. But it's just that you, like, *get* me.' I continued to appeal to her ego by insisting she had been more helpful to me in three conversations than months of counselling. 'Would you at least think about it?' I finished.

'I can't, Steven. I'm sorry but you're asking me to do something that's illegal and completely unethical. I could get into so much trouble.'

'You're right and I'm sorry, I shouldn't have asked,' I replied. 'I won't do it again.'

I was grinning from ear to ear as I ended the call on my terms. My plans for Laura all hinged on her saying yes. Now all I had to do was wait.

CHAPTER FIFTEEN

Laura was anxious, I could sense it. From the moment she answered the phone and I identified myself, something in her voice told me she was trying hard to keep her emotions under control. But she wasn't that good an actress.

I sensed she didn't want me to know how pleased she was to hear from me again, and I wondered if Charlotte had been fooled by the same veiled enthusiasm.

The flat had been feeling claustrophobic and, when the walls threatened to close in on me, I grabbed my phone and my notebook and headed to Becket's Park instead. I was watching ducks fight over a crust of bread in the smallest of the park's three lakes when I reached Laura again. I'd allowed a few days to pass after asking if she'd be with me in person when I died. I'd wanted my request to sink in and for her to mull it over – then, fingers crossed, agree.

I began with a fake apology for putting her in a difficult position.

'Honestly, Steven, I'm not here to judge you. I'm here to listen to everything you have to say to me.'

Her breath was more uneven than normal and her tone forcibly controlled. It was as if she wanted to tell me something but was battling with herself over whether she should. We chatted some more and I began asking her questions about herself. I deliberately flattered her by saying I imagined she looked like that actress from *The Hunger Games* films. Of course I knew exactly what Laura looked like, because I'd been so close to her so often. But when she asked if I'd thought of having children, she caught me by surprise.

'There was someone once, I guess, who I considered having a family with,' I replied. 'She was sweet and kind and I thought that she really loved me, but suddenly she disappeared from my life.'

I hoped that the more vulnerable I made myself, the more she'd recognise weakness and want to take me up on my offer. Another quarter of an hour of small talk passed before she couldn't hold herself back any longer.

'I'll do it,' she said suddenly. 'If you're serious about wanting to end your life, then I'll be with you in person when you do it.' She was whispering, probably scared of being overheard.

I tried to sound appreciative, when really I was both ecstatic and disgusted by her enthusiasm. She went on to explain that she only worked with people whom she felt she knew inside and out. So she expected me to be open with her about every aspect of my life. She would provide me with her work rota and I was to call and check in with her at set times and at least three times a week. Only then would we set a date for my death.

'I will be on your side from the beginning to the end of this process, but this is a business relationship,' she added. 'We both have our parts to play, Steven. Yours is to tell me who you are and mine is to ensure your transition is a smooth one.'

The first test had been about persistence and convincing her I was ready to die. The second was to make her believe one hundred per cent that Steven was real. And if there was even the tiniest crumb of doubt, I knew she would spot it.

I had to be on the top of my game to knock Laura from the top of hers.

CHAPTER SIXTEEN

SIX MONTHS AFTER CHARLOTTE

'The knot needs to go high and behind your neck so it pulls tighter as more pressure's applied,' Laura explained. Her tone was quiet and sometimes I had to strain to hear her. 'When you practise it, make sure that when the rope's tied to the beam, it doesn't slip. It's so important to remember that.'

She had given me five weeks until the day of my self-execution. By week two, she'd begun detailing the practicalities of how I should hang myself. I lay on the bed with the phone clamped to my ear, my knees pointed upwards like two pyramids and my notebook resting on my thighs. Sometimes I'd draw stickmen doodles. Today, I was hanging them from stickmen gallows. As long as she heard the sound of rustling or my voice repeating her words, she seemed happy.

Next, she advised me to test the rope's strength and to use padding so it didn't dig into my neck and make it bleed. She explained where exactly I should put the knot and what type to use. She seemed to want to make sure my death was clean and, if possible, pain-free.

I couldn't work out why someone so eager to watch me die cared whether I was hurting as I swung from the beams. Surely it made no difference to her?

I closed my eyes as she spoke and tried to imagine her hunched over the desk in her office, whispering to me down the receiver, getting a kick out of giving me instructions on how to end it all, while surrounded by a room full of people who didn't have a clue what she was up to.

There'd been times when we'd spoken about more mundane things. In fact, death and how I was going to achieve it made up less than a quarter of our conversations. She wanted to know details about my life, from my relationships with my parents and Johnny, to my favourite meals, films, the songs I wanted played at my funeral, ex-girlfriends . . . You name it, she asked it. I believed she was genuinely interested in what I had to say. It was as if she wanted to harvest everything she could in our time together so she'd have the perfect picture of who would be dying in front of her.

At times, I even wondered if I'd got it wrong about her, and perhaps Laura was just a bored housewife with a fantasy, seeing how far she could take it before she or I gave up and admitted it was all make-believe. However, as the weeks went on and the day of my 'suicide' approached, she gave no indication she was ready to quit.

Creating the persona of a man preparing to take his own life was a lot tougher than I imagined. It became all-consuming and I had to make a note of every lie I told her. My notebook was a biography of a man who didn't exist.

'Can I ask you a question?' I began during another conversation.

'Yes, of course,' Laura replied.

'Can you tell me something about you? It doesn't have to be too personal or anything.'

She paused before answering. 'Why?'

'Because I want to know more about the person who cares enough about people like me to help them.'

'What would you like to know?'

I knew where she lived, the place where she worked. I'd seen her family. I'd followed her around her favourite shops. I'd watched her read a book to her disabled son. She seemed like a perfectly normal woman. But I didn't have the first clue about why she did what she did.

'Can I ask if you've done this for anyone else? Have there been more people like me?'

'Yes, there have been.'

'Can you tell me more about them?'

'Would you like the next person I choose to know about you?'

'No, not really.'

'Then you have to respect their privacy.'

We were on our twelfth conversation so I was familiar enough with the slight nuances of her tone to know when she was leaving her comfort zone. But with not long left to go, I gambled that she was too invested in me to be put off by my familiarity. Instead, she explained how everyone was different, so with each person she took a different approach. It was as if she tailor-made suicide packages for them. Not that I ever heard her use the word 'suicide'. She seemed to deliberately shy away from saying it out loud.

'This life is difficult to negotiate alone,' she continued. 'Some people fall by the wayside and need help in finding their way back onto the right road. Others want to stay off the road completely and that's where I come in.'

I thought of Charlotte and how if only Laura had encouraged her to stay on the road for a little longer, I'd be watching my four-month-old baby son playing with soft toys on the floor right now. I wouldn't be planning to take down the woman who destroyed his mother and his own life.

'Have you ever thought afterwards that you might have got it wrong with someone? Have you helped them and thought later that maybe they should have just held on for that bit longer?'

'No,' she replied without a pause. 'Everyone who comes to me is a volunteer, like you are. I don't seek people out, they seek me. I have never – and will never – regret anything I do.'

I had a feeling Laura would soon be changing her mind.

CHAPTER SEVENTEEN

SEVEN MONTHS, ONE WEEK AFTER CHARLOTTE

Steven's day of reckoning had arrived.

It was early afternoon when I trampled across the overgrown lawn to face the house I'd bought as a surprise for my wife.

An estate agent's white-and-blue 'Sold' board was still hammered into the ground, so I yanked it out and threw it behind some bushes. Paint was flaking from the original window frames. Patches of cement between the brickwork were cracked and needed repointing. Some of the grey slate tiles were off-kilter and would need replacing or straightening before the roof leaked. The seven months of neglect I'd shown, on top of the four and a half years it had already been empty, meant two-feet-high thistles and stinging nettles in the borders met with the dandelions hiding the gravel path.

My parents had given me a £30,000 loan to put down as a deposit, and a mortgage took care of the rest. Charlotte and I had some savings to pay for the urgent repairs and the rest I'd thought we'd do in due course. It was a win/win situation – my dad loved his DIY, and with nothing left to alter in his own house, he was itching for a new project to sink his teeth into. He was set to save us a fortune in workmen's bills.

But the house that had promised so much was never given the chance to deliver, because Charlotte killed herself the day I got the keys. Since then, I hadn't been able to face even driving past it, let alone going inside.

'Are you thinking of buying it?' asked a woman with a headscarf and a tiny rat-like dog on a pink lead as she walked past.

I shook my head. 'No.'

'That's a shame,' she continued before shuffling off. 'It'd make a lovely family home again.' Her casual observation choked me. I'm sure it would, one day. But not tonight. Tonight I needed it to deal with Laura Morris.

Back at the car, I removed a rope, a lightbulb, three cardboard folders stuffed with photographs of her and her family, and two rolls of tape, and carried them to the front door. Hesitantly I unlocked it and pushed it open. I'd already paid to have the electricity turned back on, so I flicked the light switch and the hallway slowly illuminated. A few pieces of old furniture and ornaments thick with dust had been left behind by the previous occupant, but the place was largely bare.

I set to work covering every available inch of the bedroom wall with pictures until there was no space left. I screwed in a low-watt lightbulb so she wouldn't spot them immediately and, step by step, memorised which stairs creaked and how to avoid them. Then I spent twenty minutes tying and retying the noose until it was exactly how she expected it to be, before hanging it from the wooden beams. What I had planned for Laura she deserved, I had no doubt about that. But I wasn't going to kill her. I wanted her to admit what she'd done to Charlotte and then terrify her by making her think she wouldn't be leaving that room alive. I would let her go – but I wanted her to know that her actions had consequences. Maybe then she would stop.

I sat on the floor of the bedroom and at our prearranged time she called the pay-as-you-go mobile phone I'd bought, to find out where I lived.

'There's definitely not going to be anyone who might just turn up unexpectedly?' she asked. For the first time since I'd unmasked the Freer of Lost Souls, I sensed real fear.

'No – nobody,' I replied in my usual pensive tone.

'And you'll remember to keep the front door open and the lights on?'

'Yes. Don't you trust me?'

'Of course I do. But you are a human being and, by design, human beings let you down. I need to be as sure as I possibly can that you have listened to everything I've told you, so that there are no surprises or complications. Now, run me through the procedure again.'

'You'll get here for eight p.m. sharp. If you see anything suspicious or you're not comfortable, you'll drive away. I will be on my own, in my bedroom, which is the second on the left at the top of the landing. The rope will be affixed to the beams and the knot will be padded and tied correctly as you've told me. You'll then watch as I climb on a chair and take one step off it. When you're sure I'm dead, you'll leave.'

'Good. And Steven, I know I haven't said this to you before, but thank you for asking me to be there with you. I have enjoyed talking to you these last couple of months. If you have any doubts, just keep reminding yourself why you came looking for me in the first place. Together, we explored every avenue before you decided this is the only route that makes sense. You are moving on and allowing everyone else you love to do the same. And I admire that so much.'

'Thank you,' I replied. Her speech sounded rehearsed and I wondered if Charlotte had heard these exact same words.

It was just before eight o'clock and getting dark when I saw her from where I was standing behind the overgrown conifers in the front garden. She couldn't see me. I held my breath and watched as her car pulled over to the kerb. My eyes were drawn to her fingers as they gripped the steering wheel. She waited, unsure whether to follow her heart and enter the house ahead, or listen to her head and get out of there. She turned around a handful of times in as many seconds to examine the house from every angle her position would allow.

She's here. She's actually here. Laura Morris is here because she wants to watch me die.

I clenched my fists as I willed her to go inside. After looking around one last time, she opened the door I'd left ajar, then returned seconds later to prop it open with a chair. My stomach was in knots, as if I desperately needed the toilet.

I gave her time to make her way up the stairs to our meeting place before I followed, careful to avoid the noisy steps. I watched from the darkness of the corridor as she frantically pulled at the photographs on the wall. I moved silently into the room and when I spoke, she spun around, her eyes wide at the sound of my voice. I stepped forward and she retreated.

'What . . . what do you want from me?' she asked, in a tone I'd never heard her speak in before. She didn't even try to disguise her fear.

I moved towards her again to intimidate her further, telling her I wanted to know why she did what she did to vulnerable people. She responded by pulling out what looked like a kitchen knife from her coat pocket, waving it weakly in front of her. She didn't have the balls to use it, and I told her so.

Suddenly came the unmistakeable smell of urine and I realised she had pissed herself in her panic. Guilt briefly hit me, before I remembered what she had driven Charlotte to do and why she was here – to watch me die. I edged closer to her.

'You see that rope?' I asked. Of course she had. 'It's not me who's going to be hanging from the beams tonight. It's you.'

For a moment, her shaking hand and that knife were the only things in the room to move until I broke the deadlock. I reached over to grab her wrist, then spun her around and got her in an armlock. As she howled in pain, the knife fell to the floor and I frogmarched her across the room towards the rope.

I planned to tie it around her neck, then once she begged for her life and was at the most pitiful and apologetic a person could ever be, I'd let her go. Tomorrow, I'd hand over the recordings of our phone conversations to her manager at End of the Line and let them and the police deal with her.

Only I hadn't thought about how I would get the rope over her neck. As I released my grip on her arm, she took advantage of my hesitancy and elbowed me in the balls and kicked me hard in the shinbone. It was an automatic reaction for me to ease my grip on her, but that gave her the opportunity to free herself, pick up the knife from the floor and plunge it into my stomach.

It was a lucky shot – for her, anyway. I felt the pressure of the blade at first but not the pain; that only came after I put my hand on the wound and felt blood dripping down the waistband of my jeans. I felt a small whoosh of air when Laura bent down and pulled the knife out of me, and as I fell to my side I heard her footsteps disappear through the house, then a loud crash of something heavy on the staircase like she'd fallen. I paused to listen, hoping to God she hadn't broken her neck, and then panicked over what I'd do with her dead body. Suddenly she began moving again, and I heard her leave the house and a car pull away.

I lay in the room, alone, surrounded by pictures of her on the wall and those she'd torn down and left strewn across the floor.

We had underestimated each other, and she had beaten me. For now, anyway.

PART TWO

CHAPTER ONE

LAURA

I inhaled deeply to get the scent of sandalwood emerging from the bubble bath, and inched my body a little further down until the warm soapy water covered my breasts, stopping just short of my chin.

Seven vanilla-scented candles were arranged around the bath top, and every now and again the silence of the room was interrupted by a sharp crackle of the burning wick and wax.

I began my mindfulness exercises and focused on how the water felt against my skin, how my toes felt as I raised my feet and they came into contact with the bubbles on the surface, and the pressure of the tub against my back. I focused on my breathing and allowed it to become slower and deeper, letting my tummy rise and fall instead of my back and shoulders. Then, as I was at my most relaxed, I pushed my bum forward, opened my mouth, slipped my head underwater and took the biggest gulp of water I could until it flooded my lungs.

My brain's immediate reaction was to force myself to the surface and cough the water out, but I fought hard against it and remained underneath, thrashing about like a fish caught in a net. I felt the muscles around my larynx contract and let the countdown begin on the remaining oxygen in my blood. My eyes stung but remained open, and I could make out the blurred blue of the towels on the radiator. It took all my strength but I held myself down a little longer until I couldn't take the burning anymore. Light-headed, I pulled myself up and leaned over the side of the bath, violently vomiting water and bile onto the tiled bathroom floor. I was sure I'd remained underwater a little longer than last time.

I pulled myself together and made my way to the bathroom mirror, wiping the steam from it with a flannel. I stared at my reflection. Six weeks after the night of my confrontation with Steven and my fall down his stairs, my black eyes, split lip, grazed ear, and bruised cheeks, neck and arms were healing too quickly for my liking. I applied my make-up sparingly, so any scabs were still noticeable, and I pinched hard at my bruises so they retained their colour.

I was ready to return to work a hero.

◆ ◆ ◆

Inventing my assault soon after I escaped from Steven's house might have been a desperate, spur-of-the-moment decision, but it was a bloody good one. It had given me an alibi and brought me closer to my husband.

At first, I didn't even try to process that I'd just stabbed a man. I was in shock and needed to get back home where it was safe and familiar. My arms and head were already starting to feel the pain of falling down the stairs, but I tried to put it out of my mind as I sped along the road. Then cold shivers ran across my shoulders, and down through my arms and legs until there was no part of my body that didn't feel like ice. How had I been so stupid as not to have considered that I was being set up? Steven had known so much about me, and God knows how long he'd been following me.

I didn't notice the red traffic lights until another car blew its horn long and hard. I slammed on my brakes and skidded across the junction as the driver swerved to avoid me and mounted the pavement. I didn't wait to see their reaction or apologise; instead, I drove even faster.

I took a sharp left onto a side road and came to a halt in front of a row of tired-looking terraced houses, desperately trying to regulate my panting breath and tell myself that everything was going to be okay.

But it's not, is it? warned my inner voice. *You've just stabbed a man. What if he's dead? That makes you a killer.*

It wasn't that I might have been responsible for a man's death that concerned me. It was that if I'd killed him, there would be evidence in the house that could link the two of us. I'd begun tearing down photographs of myself from the walls until his sudden appearance had stopped me in my tracks. Many had remained.

Suddenly it struck me – the only way out of this was to become the victim, not the perpetrator.

Night had fallen by the time I left my car outside End of the Line, then I hurried along the streets, thinking clearly for just long enough to make sure there were no CCTV cameras above me. I made my way towards the Racecourse, a 120-acre rectangular park with only the occasional streetlight. Once in a darkened, secluded spot, I stared at the time on my phone and remained motionless, waiting for five minutes to pass. A sharp, searing pain burned my face like acid and my ear was ringing. I wanted to collapse to the ground in tears from the pain.

'Don't give in to it,' I muttered under my breath, and gritted my teeth. Then, when five minutes had passed, I took a deep breath and ran back into the open on paths by busy roads, past shops and lamp posts with mounted cameras.

'I've been attacked!' I sobbed to the duty officer at Campbell Square Police Station. I didn't need to encourage my body to tremble, and he could see by my bleeding face and hand that I'd been through the mill.

He called for a colleague, and a young woman in uniform ushered me towards a chair.

'Are you in need of any urgent treatment?' she asked gently.

I shook my head. 'No, he didn't . . . rape . . . me. I escaped before he did that.'

She led me into an interview room at the back of the station and the next two hours of my life went by in a blur. It was as if I had allowed someone else to control my body, my brain and my conversation. I became a spectator listening to myself conjure up lie after lie.

I explained how I'd been walking home from End of the Line through the park when I was pushed to the ground from behind. It was too dark to see his face when he rolled me over and kept hitting me in the face and then grabbed me hard by the shoulders and arms. I saw a knife in his hand, but somehow I'd managed to knee him in the groin, disable him and flee.

While officers were dispatched to the scene, the crime was recorded and my statement and photographs of my injuries were taken. I was hesitant when they asked me to remove my clothes for processing, especially as I'd be forced to wear an unflattering forensic suit.

I was now the victim of a crime. And should I ever be linked to what happened in the house, I'd have an alibi as to where I was. If that failed, I'd tell them Steven was a caller I'd grown fond of and who'd lured me to his home with desperate threats to kill himself. While it was unprofessional of me, I was concerned for his well-being. Then I'd tell them he attacked me and his death was self-defence. I had all my bases covered.

But the hours spent inside the station also had another purpose, as it brought Tony to me. In the early hours and following a call from the duty officer, my worried husband appeared. The moment his eyes fell upon his injured, vulnerable wife, over a year's worth of animosity melted away.

'Are you okay?' he asked, and placed his arm around my shoulders, instinctively kissing my crown. His lips were as soft as raspberries but I recoiled, as any physical contact hurt following my fall down the stairs. 'What happened?'

I mustered up the right amount of effort to burst into tears again, and placed my nose against his neck, breathing him in deeply. There was a faint scent of the previous day's aftershave and moisturiser left on his skin. The police officer explained to Tony what had happened to me.

'Can you take me home, please?' I begged.

We left with a crime number and orders to see my GP the following day if my injuries worsened. Within a quarter of an hour, Tony's car was pulling into our drive.

'Do the girls know what happened?' I asked.

'No, I didn't want to wake them and worry them. I left Effie a note in case she woke up and said I'd explain it to her in the morning. Where's your car? It's not on the drive.'

'I left it at the office,' I said.

'Why were you walking home when you're doing night shifts?' he asked as if he was frustrated with me, but fell short of telling me off.

'Are you saying this is my fault?'

'No, no, that's not what I meant. Let's get you inside.'

Tony helped me from the car and put his arm around my waist, gently assisting me up the driveway until we crossed the threshold. His touch felt magical. Tony's eyes were diverted to the walls and he stared at each of them before looking at me. I knew what he was thinking.

'I just want to sleep,' I said quietly, and turned away.

He helped me upstairs where I changed into my pyjamas and crawled into bed.

'Will you stay with me tonight?' I asked.

Tony looked at me awkwardly. 'Laura . . .' he began.

'Just for tonight,' I said. 'I'm scared and I need you to make me feel safe.'

He nodded, and I pulled the duvet from his side of the bed to invite him in. He turned on the bedside lamp but sank into an armchair in the corner of the room instead. It was progress; at least we'd be sleeping in the same room. Despite my physical pain, knowing he was in touching distance helped me to drift off into a satisfactory sleep.

By the time I awoke late in the morning, Tony had left me to face the day on my own. He texted to say he'd walked to End of the Line to pick up my car and it was parked on the driveway and that he'd return at teatime. That left me alone for seven hours. Only I wasn't alone, because Steven was ever-present in my thoughts. Was he still alive and in that house, slowly bleeding to death, or had he died moments after I'd plunged my knife into his stomach? I had to know the truth.

I took the car, drove to his village and slowly approached the house. Locking the car doors, I tried to steady my shaking hands. There was no police presence or tape sealing off the area. The front door that I'd propped open with a chair had been closed and the light in the front bedroom had been switched off, so something had happened after I'd left. Suddenly the door opened and a man appeared. He was much older than Steven. I watched as he picked up a pair of garden shears and began hacking away at a hedge. If Steven's body had been in that house, he'd have been discovered by now. There was no doubt in my mind that Steven was still alive.

But that in itself brought more problems. Where was he?

I was constantly on edge in the weeks that followed. Every couple of hours, I'd cautiously peek through the bedroom window blinds, first scanning each parked car, then each bush and neighbour's window, looking for a person or a shadow. I kept the curtains closed and, every morning and night, I'd check every window lock.

The radio remained unplugged, the slightest creak of a floorboard or the sound of the cat stirring would startle me. When Tony wasn't with me, sometimes I'd lock myself away from the world, turn on the burglar alarm and hide in the bedroom. I only left the house for doctors' appointments, and it was Tony who drove me to them.

The mornings melted into afternoons and the days into weeks. All the time, I tortured myself by allowing Steven to dominate everything, waiting for him to make another appearance. He was in the food I ate, the wine I drank to get me to sleep, the face of every stranger who passed the house. That's what scared me the most: that he knew so much about me, yet all I knew about him was his appearance.

The freedom I took for granted had been taken away from me. My actions had also placed Henry in harm's way, as Steven knew where he lived. I was scared to visit him again and risk putting him in danger. I called the care home every day, and they'd hold the phone to his ear so he could hear Mummy's voice, but it wasn't even close to being the same.

Without my anchor, I was adrift and lacked purpose. One morning as I bathed, I wondered how it might have felt if I – instead of Charlotte – had been with David the day he'd stepped off the cliff. What had it been like for him to drown in the sea?

I held my head under the water and tried to imagine what it must have felt like to have had no control over anything: over the temperature of the water, the current dragging him deeper and further away from shore and the pain his body felt from the impact. I inhaled water through my nose and mouth and it hurt so badly and so quickly that I pulled myself out. But it felt like the only control I'd had over my life since before that night in his house. And unless I took charge of myself again, that was how it would remain.

This is not who you are. You're a survivor. You need to pull yourself together.

I began thinking about all the people who were suffering without me to guide them. I thought about how Tony, the girls and Henry were coping as I hid from the world, and how Steven was winning.

I couldn't let that happen any longer. I climbed out of the bath, took some deep breaths and felt the warmth of the sun on my face through the window. It was time for Laura's return.

◆ ◆ ◆

On the morning of my first day back at End of the Line, I took one last, lingering look at myself in the hallway mirror, adjusting my blouse and tweaking tendrils of hair to ensure they framed my face correctly. I'd chosen my wardrobe carefully: a smart pantsuit that said 'survivor' not 'victim'.

Despite it being only thirty minutes to the office by foot, I took the car, emphasising to everyone – but without saying as such – my lingering fear of walking alone. I gathered myself when I arrived and opened the office door to Janine.

'It's nice to see you again,' she began, and offered me a lukewarm handshake.

'Thank you,' I replied, as those colleagues not on the phone made their way towards me. As twitchy as each hug and peck on the cheek made me feel, I accepted them. I reassured them I was doing better and better by the day, and handling what had happened as best I could.

I hadn't been allowed to go back to the charity immediately. Our job takes so much emotional strength that we all need to be at the top of our game to do our callers justice. But I'd persuaded the powers that be that what hadn't killed me that night had made me stronger. And eventually, like when I'd returned from my cancer treatment, I'd been allowed to sit with Mary and listen in on her calls to help re-acclimatise myself to End of the Line's environment.

Within a month I was back up to speed, and I began with three shifts a week. My confidence had returned – if Steven wanted me, I was ready for him. I'd brought myself out of hiding and hoped I could lure him out into the open. He had put so much effort into unmasking me, it was my turn to do the same to him.

I was living for his next call.

CHAPTER TWO

RYAN

It felt peculiar not speaking to Laura any more.

The time on the car stereo read 7.40 a.m., and at this time a few months ago I'd be putting together some notes ready for our conversation later in the day. Three times a week, 'Steven' had called her and I'd talk about his life in detail like she'd asked me to. There were some elements I'd made up and scribbled inside a notebook or typed into my phone as and when I thought of them. But when I spoke of his feelings of despair and hopelessness, they were more my words than his. I'd spent more time opening up to Laura than I had to my family and friends. It was like Stockholm syndrome, only I'd developed a psychological alliance with someone who wasn't even holding me captive.

I was her project and she was mine; she wanted me dead and I wanted to stop her from ruining other people's lives. And while I'd never let myself forget she had an evil streak in her a mile wide, I came close to understanding what my wife had seen in her. Laura was easy to talk to and we'd given each other a purpose of sorts. We'd developed a fucked-up, co-dependent relationship based on my lies and her sickness. Marriages have been built and survived on less.

But now there was nothing between us but silence. It was as if someone else in my life I'd relied on had died.

I parked in my allocated spot at work, grabbed my bag and an armful of folders from the back of the car, and made my way into the building. One folder slipped through my fingers and fell to the floor. I felt a twinge in my stomach as I went to pick it up. Having spent so long away from my job, and mostly in the company of my family or a handful of friends, I had to get used to being surrounded by a lot of people. But as the months passed, it gradually became easier.

My parents and Johnny were relieved that I'd turned a corner. I'd begun meeting friends for nights out, I was planning on rejoining my Sunday-league football team and I'd started going to the gym again. To them, I was returning to my old self. But they had no idea I'd buried the man they knew alongside Charlotte.

I walked the corridors with a fixed grin and nodded hello to familiar faces as I headed for my pigeonhole. Inside was a note from Bruce Atkinson requesting a catch-up before my working day began.

'Sit, sit,' he ushered, and pointed to the empty chair in front of the desk in his office.

'Is there a problem?' I asked.

'No, no, not at all, Ryan,' he replied. 'I just wanted to check how things have been since your return. You're in, what, your third month now?'

'Fourth, but yes, it's going well, I think. It's nice to be back . . . It takes my mind off things.'

'Yes, um, I'm sure after, um, what . . . happened with . . . your, um . . . wife . . . well, yes, I'm sure it has.' Ebony in Human Resources must have told him to check up on me, because this conversation was way too awkward for him to have instigated off his own bat. But a little part of me was amused watching him squirm.

'And how is everyone treating you?' Bruce continued.

'Again, good, good.'

He nodded his head, relieved that I wasn't carrying with me any problems for him to deal with. He blew his nose into a cloth handkerchief. 'Just so long as you know that if, you know . . . um . . . if you need more time to . . . um . . . or if there's anything I can do to help, then you only have to ask.'

'Thank you,' I replied, and quietly shook my head as he led me out of his office. He'd be the last person I'd ask for help.

I made my way along the corridor knowing he wasn't alone in not having the first clue what to say to me. If it was cancer or a heart condition that had killed Charlotte, people might have related to me better, because many people have lost someone to one of those illnesses. But when it's an invisible problem like mental health or suicide, people aren't sure how to talk about it. They'd rather say nothing than end up saying something insensitive, stupid or becoming tongue-tied. It made for a lonelier life for me, though.

I again felt a pinch in my stomach where the skin was still healing from the knife wound. It wasn't enough to make me wince, but I was aware of it all the same. I'd delayed my return to work by two weeks by telling them I needed a hernia operation, not the fact I'd been stabbed and left for dead. It would explain the scar the blade left if anyone ever noticed it.

I recalled how when Laura had fled the house that night, I'd remained bent double on the floor feeling like my whole body was on fire from the burning pain of the open wound.

Soon after I heard her drive away, I knew I needed to seek help. I couldn't phone for an ambulance and I contemplated calling my parents, but I'd have too much explaining to do. I had no choice but to deal with it myself.

Each step I took, down the stairs, along the path and towards my car, was agonising, and once inside I held a handkerchief to the wound to stem the bleeding. The journey to Northampton General Hospital's accident and emergency department took fifteen minutes but felt hours longer. And after dumping the car in a disabled space and dragging myself through the entrance and to the reception desk, a nurse saw me clutching my belly and a circle of blood on my shirt and whisked me straight into a cubicle.

The rest of the night was a blur. I was probed by doctors assessing and stabilising me. They checked my circulation, gave me an oxygen mask, an IV and an X-ray, and cleaned me up. While I'd lost blood, it wasn't enough to require a transfusion, and thankfully the blade hadn't penetrated any vital organs or the stomach itself, so only stitches were required. When they asked for next of kin, I claimed to be estranged from them.

The following morning, a woman in a white medical jacket and smart suit introduced herself as a psychiatric nurse and quietly questioned me on how I came to be injured. I told her it was the result of a botched attempt at ripping up some rotting floorboards but she didn't seem convinced.

'It's our policy to report wounds that we judge to be suspicious to the police,' she replied.

'No, don't do that,' I replied, feeling the panic rising inside me. 'It was an honest mistake. I'm clumsy and wanted to save some money instead of calling professionals in. Seriously, send someone around to my house to see the mess I've made of it if you don't believe me.'

I hoped she wouldn't call my bluff. She went on to ask me all kinds of questions, to see if I had mental health issues and the wound was self-inflicted. Eventually she left and another nurse said I could be discharged later that day, as long as I had antibiotics and someone to escort me home.

When I saw Johnny speaking to the psychiatric nurse shortly before collecting me, she knew I'd been lying about my 'estranged' family. Now I'd have to start lying to him, too.

'So you stabbed yourself doing some DIY to the house,' he began sternly as he drove my car. 'Since when have you done home improvements?'

'I thought I'd give it a go. Maybe not the best idea, eh?' I gave a forced laugh.

'At eight o'clock in the evening, you tried to repair some floorboards with a knife. On your own.' He was trying to pick holes in my story.

'It was a spur-of-the-moment thing and I know I should've left it for Dad to do. You haven't told him about this, have you?'

'If I had, he'd be here right now with me. I don't like keeping secrets from him or Mum.'

'I'm sorry. I'm an idiot.'

'Yeah, you are.' He hesitated before he spoke again, like he was choosing his words carefully. 'Tell me you didn't do this on purpose. And that despite all the crap that's happened to you, you're strong enough to keep fighting. Don't let what happened to Charlotte define you or swallow you up. You're better than that.'

'Of course I didn't,' I replied. When he failed to reply, I knew he didn't believe me.

We spent the rest of the journey in an awkward silence, my hand pressed on the padding over my sutures.

At this point, I knew I should have called it quits. I'd got what I wanted, in that I'd scared the hell out of Laura Morris. And she'd been lucky to escape before I'd finished what I'd planned, even leaving me for dead. So, it would have been the time to approach her boss at End of the Line, tell them my story and play them my recordings. Then I could vanish from Laura's life, knowing she wouldn't be harming anyone else who called in need of a sympathetic ear.

But a week or so recuperating at home gave me time to dwell on what had happened. Yes, I'd quite obviously terrified her, but now it wasn't enough just to take her job away from her. People like Laura are slaves to their compulsions. They do what they want to and they don't give a damn about who gets hurt. I'd bet my life's savings the Freer of Lost Souls would be back trawling Internet message boards searching for more potential victims within days of being sacked.

Taking her down had brought out something unexpected in me, some joyous, vindictive feeling. I needed to find another way to get at her.

Laura had taken away the person I loved the most, and she needed to know how that felt. I opened the Facebook app on my phone. I vowed to get to her in another way.

And now I was back at work and in a routine again, I had the means at my disposal to begin.

CHAPTER THREE

LAURA

I examined my reflection in all three mirrors in the unattended changing rooms.

Standing there in my bra and knickers, I turned to my left and was pleased to see how flat my stomach had become. I rubbed my fingers up and down it, and tried to pinch excess weight from my sides but there was very little left. The stress diet had been much more effective than the amphetamines in my slimming tablets.

One after the other, I slipped on each of the five dresses I'd picked from the shop's rails, and was over the moon that I could now comfortably fit into a size eight. I removed the pliers from my pocket, snapped the security label from the one I favoured and wrapped the dress in a bag, then placed it in my handbag. I handed the unwanted ones to the clueless shop assistant who'd now appeared, thanked her and left.

I walked along the second floor of the shopping centre, down an escalator, across the ground floor and then back up the stairs, before returning down the escalator again. All the time, I kept checking the reflection in the shop windows and glass doors to ensure no one was following me. Reassured I was alone, I began to relax and made my way back to the car. I'd waited twenty minutes in Abington Street for a place to park, because being in an open space was wiser than a multistorey car park where it's easy to hide between vehicles. I would never allow Steven to corner me in an enclosed space again.

Whenever I visited the town centre, I kept an eye out for Nate. Sometimes he'd hung around outside the office in the hope he'd catch me; other times I'd go and find him in his regular haunts near the bus station. But since he'd discharged himself from hospital, I hadn't seen hide nor hair of him, and I began to fear the worst.

I forced myself to think about something happier, and smiled for a moment as I drove, pleased with my new outfit. The dress was going to say everything I needed it to. It was sensible but not too mumsy, and revealed just enough of my legs and toned arms to convince me that Tony would notice the effort I'd made for a meeting with Effie's head of year.

Since my 'attack', Tony had shown more interest in my well-being than for as long as I could remember. He'd been seeing me as I wanted him to see me – a vulnerable woman who still needed the security he'd given me when we first met as teenagers. If only I'd thought about falsifying an attack a couple of years earlier, maybe I'd have no gap to bridge at all. Still, what was done was done, and although he hadn't returned to our bedroom yet, it would only be a matter of time.

For the first couple of weeks, he'd arranged for the girls to stay with his parents so they weren't scared by my injuries. Then he'd spent time alone with them to give me space to heal, mentally and physically.

However, I was surprised he hadn't mentioned us going together to the school. The email reminder they'd sent had arrived in my account – the first time they'd contacted me. But Tony had said nothing about it. Maybe he didn't want to put any undue pressure on me after what I'd been through.

Alice was an easy child to look after, obedient and eager to please. However, Effie was, by all accounts, proving to be a handful at school. Again, I only found out through emailed summaries of meetings Tony had attended with her teachers, none of which I'd been invited to.

Tony had insisted she be transferred to St Giles Upper School for reasons never fully explained to me. At the time, I'd been preoccupied with my cancer treatment, so I left it to his best judgement. However, her grades had slipped dramatically over the last few months. She'd dropped from solid As to Cs and Ds, and apparently her attitude had deteriorated, too. She'd grown more argumentative and moodier with teachers. She was no longer participating in after-school activities like hockey or drama, and she'd become distant from the friends she'd made.

That surprised me the most, as she'd always been such a popular girl in her last school. Ever since she was little, I was forever telling her 'no' when she asked to invite her friends around for tea. Then I did the same with Alice. Children brought with them sticky fingers on walls, head lice, snot, scabs on legs, repetition, neediness, smells, noise, relentless never-ending questions, chaos, stomach bugs, clutter, broken ornaments and unflushed toilets. So, I encouraged the girls to spend time at their friends' houses instead.

Either my attack had affected Effie more than I thought, or something else was wrong and neither Tony nor her teachers could get to the bottom of the problem. I was being kept on the sidelines of my own daughter's life. It was frustrating, to say the least. I knew Tony was doing what he thought best by shielding me, but she needed her mother right now. My presence at that meeting would show Tony I was strong enough to co-parent again. Maybe then he might fall back in love with me.

On my arrival at home, I went through my usual routine of spending the first ten minutes waiting outside in the car, my eyes flitting from window to window, looking for any warning signs like sudden changes of light or shadows between the blinds. Steven knew where I lived, and the thought of him being inside my home, waiting for me, made me nauseous.

I could just about see the figure of a tightly balled-up cat asleep on the windowsill. Bieber had grown useful of late, if for no other reason than his impeccable hearing and loud meow that warned me of any sudden noises or movements outside.

Once inside, I turned off the burglar alarm, locked the door and took the bread knife from the drawer in the hall table, then silently padded from room to room. I looked behind doors, drawn curtains, wardrobes and under beds. Only when I was sure I was alone could I relax.

◆ ◆ ◆

Tony's face was a picture when he spotted me across the school reception area. It creased with surprise before he regained his composure. The effort I'd made to look my best hadn't gone unnoticed.

'What are you doing here?' he asked, approaching me. He sounded irritated, which confused me.

'What do you think?' I replied. 'Do you like my dress? I got it especially for tonight.' I pulled my stomach in and gave him a twirl.

'I don't care about your dress,' he barked. 'We had an agreement. You don't come to anything like this, I do.'

'But it's time I started. She's my daughter, Tony. There's something going on with Effie that you've been hiding from me and, as her mother, I deserve to know.'

'Really?' he replied. 'You honestly think that? You think either of the girls actually need you?'

I took a step back, willing myself not to get upset. 'Why are you being so horrible? I thought that since what happened to me, we'd become closer. We were feeling more like a family again and now you're treating me like I'm not welcome.'

'Laura, we have been through this a dozen times.' Tony sounded exasperated. 'You and I . . . we are never going to happen. Our family isn't what you've convinced yourself it is.'

My heart felt like it wanted to pound its way out of my chest and I clenched my fists. 'No,' I replied. 'I don't accept that.'

'This isn't the time or the place to be discussing this. Please go home. We'll talk about it properly later.'

He turned his back on me and began to walk away. The gulf between us widened with every footstep. But no matter what Tony hurled at me or how much he tried to hurt me, I still loved him. And when it came to our daughter, I was determined to prove him wrong.

Ahead, a door with the name of the school's head teacher opened and a man with more hair sprouting from his ears than his head looked at us.

'Mr Morris and, oh . . .'

'I don't think we've met before. I'm Effie's mother, Laura,' I said, finishing his sentence for him.

The head looked at Tony, puzzled. Tony closed his eyes and nodded, begrudgingly.

'Come in,' the head continued, and we followed him into his office, where two large windows overlooked a cricket pitch and a match in progress. Another teacher stood with his back to us watching the game.

I started talking before we'd even been offered seats. 'I've been reading Effie's reports and I'm not happy,' I said firmly. 'I need to know why my daughter's grades have fallen so badly. You're responsible for her education, so as far as I can see, this is down to you.'

'Let me introduce you to Effie's head of year,' he replied. 'Mrs Morris, this is Ryan Smith.'

'It's nice to meet you,' he began as he turned around. I recognised Steven's voice immediately, then his face. The bottom instantly fell from my world.

'Please believe me when I say that, as her teacher, I want only the best for your daughter, too.'

CHAPTER FOUR

RYAN

My pulse raced like the throbbing engine of a sports car the moment I heard Laura's muffled voice in the corridor from where I was standing in Bruce Atkinson's office.

She was talking to her husband, and whatever they were discussing sounded as if it was riling him.

As Effie's form tutor and English teacher, I'd met Mr Morris on a couple of occasions to discuss Effie's poor marks, weak midterm exam results and distracting behaviour. He'd been listed in school records as the first and only point of contact in all email and telephone communications. There'd been a note attached, strictly forbidding us from contacting her mother except in extreme circumstances. However, none of the other teachers I had asked knew why. I removed the note and reinstated Laura's email address.

A couple of times I'd slipped Effie's mum into the conversation just to test the waters, but Mr Morris didn't acknowledge her. I assumed she played a limited role in her daughter's academic life. However, since I'd begun blind-copying Laura into those emails, I'd made sure she was up to speed, and I had a feeling it wouldn't be long before she crawled out of the woodwork.

I watched her in the reflection on Bruce's window as she strolled in confidently. She was a very different woman from the one I'd confronted in my house. Then, she'd been dumbstruck, before lurching from wall to wall, tearing down images of herself and her family, thinking I was going to kill her. Now she was at ease, hair curled and make-up perfectly applied. In our telephone conversations, her voice had been reassuring and calm. At the house, it had been shaky and tearful, but today it was forceful and accusatory.

It took just one introductory sentence and the split-second sight of me to pull the rug from under her feet. After a long separation, Steven and Laura had been reunited.

It had taken a lot of time and effort to engineer our meeting, and I'd needed an unwitting Effie's help to do it. The moment I saw her photograph in the local newspaper with her mum I'd thought I recognised her, but I cross-checked it with her Facebook profile just to be sure. She was a student at my school. And as I prepared to return to work for the new term, the pregnancy of English teacher Mrs Simmons was a stroke of luck for me. It meant I wouldn't just be Effie's teacher, but her head of year and form tutor, too.

I started work again during the school holidays, getting to grips with the syllabus and helping out at some of the extracurricular sports tournaments. I'd insisted on light activity at first, blaming my inability to do anything too strenuous on my fake hernia operation. When school began again in September, I was ready to return full-time.

My colleagues gave me the low-down on which pupils made up Year 10's hierarchy, and Effie's name came up time and time again. She was, by all accounts, a very intelligent young woman, but she had a bossy streak. From the first week she transferred to our school, she'd built a clique around her. Social media was her favourite tool, and if she didn't like someone, she'd rally the troops to make her victim's online presence hell. When it all became too much for one of her classmates, he'd taken to cutting his arms and legs with a craft knife. He'd since moved schools. However, Effie had been smart enough to avoid being caught. The apple really hadn't fallen far from the tree.

I was mindful of the fact she was only fourteen years old and there was a chance she could grow into a better person. But for now, she was exactly what I needed her to be. Bullies like her are always more insecure than the people they attack, so it'd only take a light touch to push her from her pedestal. In my nine years of teaching, I'd learned popularity and intelligence were the only things that mattered to girls like her. Take those away and she'd have nothing.

I started by grading her English essays and tests a little lower than Mrs Simmons had. At first it was an A– instead of an A. Next time, it had slipped to a B+, until by the end of my first month with her, she was averaging Cs. Each time I handed the class their marked papers, I took a moment to watch her scowl as she hid the disappointing bright-red grade on the top left-hand corner of her page from those around her. After the second month, she snapped.

'Why do you keep giving me bad marks, sir?' she demanded after waiting until the rest of the class had moved on to their next lesson.

'I don't think you're understanding what I want in your answers,' I replied.

'Mrs Simmons never graded me like this.'

'I'm not Mrs Simmons.'

'She said English was one of my top subjects.'

'Your grades tell me otherwise.'

Her face dropped, and the first of several crocodile tears pooled in the corner of her eyes. I remained stony-faced. She had to learn that reaction wouldn't work on me, otherwise I wouldn't gain her respect. Instead, I pointed out that some of her reasoning was valid but next time she needed to back up her theories with evidence in the text. Only, when each 'next time' arrived, her grades remained the same, or lower.

She could only look on, bewildered, as her classmates maintained their marks. I was slowly chipping away at her confidence.

Her essays became longer and longer as she attempted to read between the lines and cover every single point she thought I might be looking for. I marked her down for rambling. One report on *Of Mice and Men* was so obviously cut and pasted from the Internet that I called her out on it in front of the rest of the class. I swallowed my smile as her face turned scarlet. She'd been expected to take her GCSE in English literature a year early. But when I gave her my predicted grade, she decided against it.

I'd hoped Effie would eventually start questioning her abilities in other subjects, too, but it happened faster than I'd expected. Underneath her bravado, she was much more sensitive than I'd given her credit for. Her standard of work across the board was sinking. Her history, geography, and philosophy and ethics teachers told me her essays were vague and her coursework lacked cohesion. It was as if she were second-guessing everything she wrote, even in subjects like maths, for which there could often only be one definitive answer.

And without her intelligence to lord over her classmates, she did what all bullies do and found another way to seek attention, by playing up and distracting everyone else. One evening after the final school bell rang, I asked her to stay behind and she joined me in my office.

'I'm not going to lie, I'm concerned about you, Effie,' I began, and handed her a mug of coffee. She tried to hide her surprise that I was treating her like an adult. 'Is there something you want to talk to me about?'

'To you?' she scoffed. Her default setting of arrogance remained. I had more work to do.

'Is everything okay at home?'

'Yes.'

'Is all good with your parents?'

She paused before she nodded.

'What about here at school? I know the other girls haven't been kind to you lately. Is that what's bothering you? Are you being picked on?'

She shot me a glance. 'What do you mean?'

'Are they teasing you about your grades and your – how do I put this properly – your appearance?'

'My appearance? What are you on about, sir?'

'Oh, sorry, I'm speaking out of turn. It's none of my business. I just wanted to make sure none of it was getting to you. You're a normal size for a girl your age, so please don't listen to what people who claim they're your friends say about you behind your back.'

Anger spread across her face. 'Who's been talking about my weight?'

I feigned irritation at myself. 'Oh, Christ, look, I'm not good at this kind of thing. The other teachers said I shouldn't say anything to you and should let the girls get it out of their system.'

'The other teachers? You're all talking about me? And what girls?'

'It's not for me to name names, but I reprimanded some of them when I heard them being nasty about you in the corridor. I don't like people who laugh about others behind their backs. You're not overweight and you're not stupid.'

She perched on the edge of her seat and sucked in her cheeks. 'How many? Who?'

'It doesn't really matter.'

'Bitches . . .' she huffed, folding her arms and sinking back into her chair. 'I bet it was Britney and Morgan.'

'Ignore those two,' I replied. 'You don't need people like them in your life. Or Melissa or Ruby.'

'Them as well? Will you tell me if you hear anything else?'

'I don't know . . .'

'Please, Mr Smith.'

'Okay, but I won't be naming any more names.'

She muttered a thank you under her breath and left. And later, when she'd been excluded for a week for starting a fight with Britney and giving Morgan a nosebleed, I couldn't help but feel smug. I watched from the sidelines as Effie's clique shrank and she became more and more isolated from her classmates. I'd send her father regular progress reports, but began secretly including Laura in the emails, too.

I'd set a date with her father when I'd met him in November to see him again four weeks later to discuss how Effie was doing. I could only hope the emails Laura had been receiving would spur her into action. But I'd also need to up the ante with her daughter.

I organised regular one-to-one private meetings with Effie each Monday and Friday after school in my office, listening to her as she complained about the teachers and girls who 'had it in' for her. Sometimes I'd add fuel to the fire by lying to her about what I'd heard other teachers saying about her in the staffroom.

Less than three months into our time together, and she was thinking of me as a confidant. And as the weeks progressed, I sensed she felt it was becoming something more.

It began with the opening of an extra button on her shirt for our meetings, then a little more lip gloss to make her pout shine. When I stood with my back to her, pouring hot water into our mugs, I saw her checking out my arse in the reflection of the window. When I turned, she averted her gaze.

I saw our closeness as an opportunity to learn more about her home situation.

'Why don't you ever talk about your mum?' I asked. 'You mention your sister and your dad, but never her.'

'I'm not allowed to.'

'Why?'

'She's . . . she's not like other mums.'

'In what way?'

'I heard about what happened to your wife.' The sudden change in direction took me aback.

'What did you hear?' I asked.

'That she . . . you know . . . killed herself.'

'Uh-huh,' I nodded.

'Do you miss her?'

'Of course.'

'Have you got a new girlfriend?'

'No.'

'Are you looking for one?'

'Not at the moment, no. But eventually, maybe, yes.'

'Why did she do it?'

'I don't think I'll ever really know. People are complicated and we don't always understand why they do what they do, even when we think we know them.'

'My mum's like that. "An unpredictable, destructive force," my dad says.'

'Are you close to her?'

She laughed.

'Did I say something funny?'

'No.'

'Then why did you laugh?'

'Why did you ask?' She ran her fingers through her hair and entwined several strands around one of them. 'You ask a lot of questions, Ryan.'

I raised my eyebrows.

'Sorry, I mean Mr Smith.'

'It's my job to ask questions. To help you.'

'I bet you don't spend this much time with the other students asking them questions.'

'They don't worry me as much as you do.'

'So you worry about me?' She tilted her head, and the sun coming in through the window illuminated her strawberry-blonde hair and her grey eyes. Suddenly, beyond all her bluster, I saw her as the child she was. My heart sank at what Laura had reduced me to doing.

'All my students worry me,' I replied.

'Okay.' She nodded, then picked up her schoolbag and made her way towards the door. But she didn't leave without turning around to smile at me.

By the time my second meeting with her dad came around, I had Effie exactly where I wanted her. And when I heard Laura outside the office, it was all I could do to stop myself from dropping an imaginary mic and yelling 'Boom!'

On realising who I was, Laura tried her best not to react. Her face froze, as if she'd become trapped in ice, but it was her eyes that gave her away. As adrenaline made her heart race to get oxygen to her muscles, her brain was working in overdrive. I couldn't see any of this, but her pupils gave her away. They'd dilated to allow the maximum amount of light in at the back of her eyes to make her aware of everything that was going on around her.

It was a classic fight-or-flight reaction. Although with her husband next to her, she could do neither.

CHAPTER FIVE

LAURA

It took every ounce of my inner strength to prevent my body from reacting in any way to Ryan as he took a seat next to my husband.

I begged my face not to redden or my hands to start shaking. I didn't want to show any signs of weakness. Inside, I couldn't stop my pulse from breaking new speed records. I knew my eyes were open wide but I couldn't take them off him, not even for a second.

Maybe I was wrong; maybe I was imagining this. Perhaps my brain was playing tricks on me again, like all those so-called experts told me it did. Perhaps I was only seeing and hearing what I wanted to hear. I stared at him so intently my eyes hurt.

'How are Effie's grades?' Tony began. 'Have they seen any improvement?'

'I'm afraid there's not been much difference on that front,' Ryan replied. 'She's maintaining steady Cs in English and art, but in history, sociology and geography, her marks are quite erratic.'

Yes, it *was* Steven. I was one hundred per cent sure of that. Steven, Ryan, Steven . . . it didn't matter what he called himself. It was still *him*.

Four months after I should have witnessed his body swinging from the rafters of his bedroom, there he was, smiling at Tony as if he didn't have a care in the world. This was not a coincidence, I was certain of that. He'd been lying low, biding his time and waiting for the right moment. Now I understood why I'd suddenly started receiving school emails about Effie. Ryan had wanted me here and I'd handed myself to him on a plate. It was the second time I'd let down my guard and he'd taken advantage.

He'd convinced Tony he had a genuine interest in Effie's well-being. But both he and I knew he was playing a game. What was it? And why involve my daughter?

Now I could see him in daylight and not the gloom of his bedroom, he was an unassuming, boy-next-door type. His eyes were a deep brown but the whites that surrounded them were pinkish, like he wasn't getting enough sleep. His dark-blond temples were flecked with grey and his skin was pale. It was as if he'd remained boyish well into his twenties but now circumstances had forced him into adulthood and his body was only just starting to catch up.

Half of me wanted to claw at Ryan's face with my nails like an animal, while the other half wanted to run a mile and pretend none of this was happening. Instead, I remained glued to my chair, unable to move an inch.

'It's like she no longer cares how she does,' Ryan continued. 'How have you found her behaviour at home, Mr Morris?' The concern in his voice sounded staged and it didn't match his expression. It was as if he were trying his best not to laugh.

Tony used words like 'quiet' and 'insular' to describe Effie, but to my ears it was like he was talking about another girl. It wasn't the daughter I knew, the girl I had loved as best I could. Had I allowed too much distance to come between us?

Suddenly Ryan turned to me. Chills ran through me. 'Have you considered there might be other issues that Effie might be facing, Mrs Morris?'

I opened my mouth but little came out, so I cleared my dry throat. 'Such as?'

'I don't know, I'm not a therapist, but there can be many psychological issues that influence the way a teenage girl behaves these days. She's mentioned to me the other girls in her class have bullied her because of her weight.'

'Her weight?' Tony replied defensively. 'She's not fat!'

'No, I'm not saying for one minute that she is. But if she thinks she might be, and if she hears it enough from other girls, then it might influence her thinking. Eating disorders and self-confidence problems are so common, and more than one in three teenage girls suffer from anxiety and mental health issues.' I watched as Ryan's fists clenched ever-so-slightly and he shifted his eyes towards mine. 'There's a reason they call depression a silent killer.'

I didn't know what he was insinuating, but whatever it was between us, it was definitely personal.

'My daughter isn't an anorexic nor is she depressed,' Tony replied.

'Hormones and chemical changes in their brains can give them feelings of inadequacy, loss of interest in their surroundings, their work and their friends,' Ryan continued like he was reading from a book. 'They become trapped in cycles of self-pity. It's my job as her teacher to make you aware of this and to be there for her in whatever capacity she wants me to be.'

'Cycles of self-pity'? 'Whatever capacity she wants me . . .'? He's using my own words from our conversations against me!

'Look, I might be wrong,' he added. 'All I'm saying is that when it comes to people, no matter how much you think you know them, you can never predict what goes on in their heads, even your own kids. They can be influenced to do things they shouldn't by the unlikeliest of people. People who kids think they can trust can talk them into actions that have a catastrophic effect on their future. Do you know what I mean, Mrs Morris?'

I didn't, but I knew he was directing his words at me. He'd said something to Effie, but what?

'And you think that she's susceptible to this kind of manipulation?' Tony asked.

'You might be surprised at what Effie is capable of.'

'Like what?' I asked.

Ryan was talking in riddles and waiting for me to figure out what he meant.

'I don't know,' he replied. 'All I can tell you is that when I left her at lunchtime, she wasn't herself. She seemed quite distressed, but she wouldn't tell me what it was about. I made her promise to talk to you, Mrs Morris, when she got home.'

The meeting drew to a close and Mr Atkinson saw us out of his office and back to the reception area. Suddenly Tony's phone began to ring and he glanced at the number. 'Sorry, could you excuse me for a moment?' he asked, leaving Ryan and me alone for the first time. My stomach churned and I wanted to be sick.

'What do you want from me?' I asked quietly. 'What have you said to my daughter?'

Ryan's grin disappeared and he leaned in to whisper in my ear.

'If I were you, I'd go home and check on Effie as soon as you can. Because I'd hate to think what she might have done after I finished with her this afternoon.'

CHAPTER SIX

RYAN

Even when I wasn't looking at Laura, I could feel her staring at me. Effie had shared the same deep, penetrating gaze.

Effie's eyes had been fixed on me while I monitored a lunchtime detention before I was to meet with her parents. Her gym teacher had given it to Effie for threatening another girl. Six other students from Years 10 and 11 joined her for various other offences. I wondered if Effie had deliberately caused trouble because she knew it was my turn to take detention.

They kept their heads down, using the opportunity to begin their homework. Effie, however, didn't even try to pretend to read the textbook she held. She was focused on me at my desk. Her number of friends had dwindled over the past few months. I'd devoted more attention to her, always treating her like an adult and listening to her complaints. I knew exactly where she thought our relationship was going. I could have nipped it in the bud at any point, but that wasn't part of the plan.

Finally, their hour of punishment complete, the others hurried from the classroom. But Effie deliberately took her time packing her bag and putting on her coat. Then she waited until we were alone before she made her way to the window. She fiddled absent-mindedly with a bauble on the class Christmas tree.

'It's raining outside,' she began.

'I can see.'

'I've got free study periods all afternoon and was going to go home but I don't have an umbrella.'

'And?'

'And I'm going to get soaked if I can't get a lift home.'

'A bit of rain isn't going to kill you.'

'But if I catch a cold, I could have an asthma attack and that could kill me.'

'I'm sure you'll be fine.'

'Could you give me a lift, sir? You haven't got a lesson for another hour and a half, have you?'

'Are you memorising my timetable, Effie?'

'No, sir, I was just showing an interest like you do in me. So you have plenty of time to take me home and come back for it.'

'Offering a student a ride is against the school rules.'

'I won't tell anyone.'

'That doesn't matter.'

'Honestly, I won't. I promise.'

'Effie, there are boundaries that we need to maintain. You're my student and I'm your teacher.'

'Is that all I am to you, sir?'

I paused for a moment; I needed to think. I'd put a lot of time and effort into getting to this place, but now I'd arrived, I was second-guessing myself. *What would Laura do?* I asked myself. Laura would do whatever was necessary to get what she wanted. And that meant I had to do the same.

'Meet me on the corner of Simpson Avenue and Talbot Road in ten minutes,' I replied apprehensively. 'There's a bus shelter there. I'll pick you up.'

Effie brushed my arm with her hand as she passed me, trying hard to hide her grin. I had to remind myself that this was a girl who'd bullied her classmates and got away with it. She was a manipulative little bitch, someone who was used to getting what she wanted, only she was too naive to realise she wasn't in control of this situation.

She was exactly where I told her to be when my car pulled over to the side of the road. I checked all around me to make sure that no one had spotted us. As she climbed inside, I noted she'd put eyeliner on to frame her eyes and she'd made her lips more inviting with pink gloss. Her hair glistened from the drizzle outside and she ran her fingers through it.

'Hurry up and put your seatbelt on,' I urged. 'We need to go.'

'It's stuck,' she replied, and struggled to fit it into the latch. I grabbed it and she held on to my finger while I slotted it inside.

'Who's that?' she asked, pointing to a screensaver picture on my phone. It was recharging in the centre console.

'It's my brother Johnny,' I replied.

'He's fit. You look alike.'

I watched from the corner of my eye as she tapped her foot to the music coming from the radio. She looked puzzled when we eventually pulled up a few doors away from her home.

'I thought we could go to yours for while?' she asked, her head tilted slightly to one side.

'You know I have to get back.'

'Then, another time?' She placed her hand just above my knee.

'Effie . . .' I began.

'Shhh,' she replied, and her hand made its way further up my thigh and stopped centimetres from my groin.

'Effie, I'm your teacher.'

'Not here, you're not.'

'I am. Here, at school, everywhere.'

'I'm not going to tell anyone.'

She twisted her body and moved her face towards mine. I felt her warm breath on my neck and ear. I could smell her sweet perfume. She paused as our eyes locked.

'There's something I need you to know first,' I said.

'What's that?'

'I need you to know I would never go near you in a million years. If you really believe that I'm interested in you, Effie, you're more stupid than your grades would suggest.'

She paused, then scowled, trying to make sense of what she'd just heard. Her head moved backwards and her hand left my leg.

'What?'

'You heard me correctly. I'm not attracted to you, Effie. You're an attention-seeking, immature little girl who picks on others and makes their lives hell. Now you know how they felt to be belittled and rejected. If you think I could be attracted to someone like you, then you're an idiot. Now get out of my car.'

Her face crumpled, and for a moment I hated myself for what I'd just told a kid. I'd never hurt anyone like I'd just hurt Effie. But it had been a horrible necessity. She threw open the car door and ran out into the rain, along the street and out of sight.

Four hours later and it was her mother's turn to know how it felt to be played. She had manipulated my wife for her own gain, and I had done the same to her daughter. As my Granddad Pete had advised, an eye for an eye.

CHAPTER SEVEN

LAURA

'Where's Effie?' I asked Tony. 'Right now, where is she?'

I'd left Ryan and found my husband at the double doors of the entrance, returning his phone to his jacket pocket.

The panic created by Ryan's warning was rising from deep inside my gut, up my chest and into my throat, almost strangling my words. The last time I'd felt like this, I was standing in his house with a knife in my hand, facing a man who was about to kill me. Now the same man had found a way to make me feel like that all over again, only this time he was threatening my daughter's safety to frighten me.

'Effie's at home,' Tony replied.

'Are you sure?'

'Yes.'

'Is she alone?'

'No, she's babysitting Alice.' He sounded hesitant.

'I want to see her.'

Tony shook his head. 'We talked about this, Laura, I don't think it's a good idea.'

'She's my daughter,' I said through gritted teeth. 'They are both my daughters. I need to see them tonight.'

'We agreed that you wouldn't visit the girls until they were old enough to make their own decisions.' I glared at him as fragments of an argument from long ago flashed through my head. 'Do you remember?' he asked.

'Yes, of course I do,' I replied, but in truth, a fog was descending from nowhere and everything was becoming muddled. 'But I need to go home and make sure they're okay. Please, Tony, just take me home.'

Acknowledging my angst, he took my hand in his and spoke softly. 'Laura, none of us have lived at home with you for almost two years now, have we? We live elsewhere, you know that. You remember why we moved out, don't you?'

I yanked my hand away and vaguely recalled my husband driving me home from hospital after the operation to remove my cancer, and the house feeling stark and silent. I could see myself drifting along the corridor from bedroom to bedroom searching for the children, and Tony informing me they wouldn't be coming home for a while. But I couldn't remember why. In fact, the only thing I knew for sure was that most nights since I'd cooked us all a meal, when no one turned up to eat it I'd put it into a freezer drawer until there was no room left. Then I'd toss them away and start from scratch again.

My temples began to flutter in rhythm with my erratic heartbeat. But in all the confusion I had to remain focused. I had to see my daughter. I had to know that Effie was okay.

'How much longer must I wait before I can see them?' My voice was growing louder. 'Five minutes with them, that's all I'm asking for. Just to put my mind at ease.'

Tony frowned, and scanned the area as a bell sounded to mark the end of the day and pupils hurried towards the doors to leave. 'Laura, you need to calm down before you start drawing attention to yourself.'

'Let them look, I don't care.'

He marched me towards an empty room off the corridor. Pupils' drawings and paintings were pinned to the walls. It reminded me of how much I enjoyed painting with Alice; she had a natural aptitude for it. Or was it Effie? I couldn't be sure. Everything was becoming too confusing.

'Call it instinct or mother's intuition, but I know when my baby's in trouble,' I continued, 'and look what's been happening since you kept me away from her. Are you trying to tell me that it's a coincidence her education is falling to pieces?'

'And are you not going to take any responsibility for this? Do you need me to spell it out why they're not with you anymore?'

I did, because I couldn't make the pieces fit together. An image of myself lying in a hospital bed, then one of Henry in the residential care home came to mind. But I didn't know if I was imagining it or if it had actually happened, and something told me it would do me no favours to ask. One memory was crystal clear, though.

'If you don't let me see the girls this afternoon, then first thing tomorrow morning I'll take the documents I have to the police that prove what we did to get the business up and running.' His face paled. 'I have every account number, statement and transaction stored at home. Don't make me do that, Tony.'

Deep breaths, Laura, deep breaths. Think of your anchor; he will calm you down.

'Something I can't explain is telling me that we need to leave here and find Effie,' I continued. 'You heard her teacher. What if Effie's problems are a lot worse than you think? How would you live with yourself if she's done something silly?'

'Okay,' he said reluctantly. 'We'll take my car.'

I don't know if it was the threat I'd made or that he finally recognised my fear, but I got my way.

As we hurried across the car park I wondered who Tony was texting and why he was trying to hide it from me. I reasoned it must have been Effie and he didn't want me to see her number.

'Can you call her?' I asked. And when he dialled from inside his car I made a mental note of the digits as they flashed across the stereo screen. There was no answer. He tried the landline, but that wasn't picked up either.

'Why isn't she answering?' I said anxiously. 'What's happened to her?'

'You need to get a hold of yourself,' Tony replied firmly. 'You already know what the last memory the children have of you is. They don't need to see you on their doorstep screaming like a mad woman.'

Again, I didn't understand what he was referring to, but now wasn't the time for questions. I was too busy trying not to yell at him to hurry up when he slowed for every amber light. He had no sense of urgency as he stuck to the suburban speed limits while we drove through the streets on the other side of town from the home where we'd all once lived together.

Eventually we pulled into the cul-de-sac of a new-build housing estate. He parked on the driveway of a contemporary home I'd never seen before with a landscaped front garden, large windows and closed curtains. Two lights were on upstairs. I steeled myself as he unlocked the door.

'Effie?' he shouted and I followed him upstairs. 'Effie!' he yelled again. He opened a bedroom, and the curtains were closed even though it was only late afternoon. In the dim light, we both stopped in our tracks and stared at our daughter – her eyes firmly shut, body motionless and her arm dangling limply over the side of the bed with her fingers pointing to the floor.

I rushed towards her, throwing her duvet back, grabbing her by the shoulders and shaking her. Her eyes shot open and she screamed before she recognised me.

'Mum! What the fuck?' she began as she ripped a pair of headphones from her ears and sat bolt upright. I kept my hand over my mouth while Tony remained where he was. 'What are you doing here?' Effie asked, confused by my unexpected appearance.

'We were so worried about you,' I replied. Her eyes were red, much more so than if she'd just been asleep.

'What's going on?' a young voice came from behind us. I turned to look at Alice, still in her school uniform and with her bag draped over her shoulder. A broad grin spread across her face.

New memories were starting to come and go, this time of me walking a much younger Alice to school hand in hand; then more recently, me doing the school run alone. I could see myself standing at the gates, waiting to catch a glimpse of her from afar as she played with her friends, hoping she might spot me. Hoping that she hadn't started to forget what I looked like or how I sounded. I couldn't remember my mother's face or her voice anymore.

'Mummy?' she squealed. 'Are you back?' She ran towards me and wrapped herself tightly around my legs and waist. I began to cry happy tears as I held her tightly. 'Come and see my bedroom,' Alice said and reached for my hand. I looked at Tony before I took it. He nodded hesitantly and I followed her out of the room and onto the landing. Her hand felt soft and small and I didn't realise how unappreciative of it I'd been when I'd rejected it so frequently in the past.

As we walked a short distance, another open door caught my attention. The coat I'd bought Tony the last birthday we'd spent together lay across his bed next to a gaudy orange cushion. But as I got closer, I realised it wasn't a cushion, it was a handbag.

An orange handbag.

Janine's orange handbag.

Janine's orange handbag with its Chinese dragon design was on my husband's bed.

CHAPTER EIGHT
RYAN

I clenched my fists. A soft glow of light came from a crack under the front door to my flat.

When I'd pulled up in the car park moments earlier, I was still on a high from coming face-to-face with Laura again. But I had a feeling that whatever lay beyond the threshold was about to bring me back down to earth with a bang. I hesitated, then slowly turned the handle. It was unlocked. I'd not had a fight since my schooldays and I couldn't imagine a punch from me would do much damage to whoever was inside.

I moved silently into the hallway and grabbed the heavy glass orb that was on the table. Then I inched my way towards the living room, where I could hear a rustling sound and drawers being opened and closed. I edged closer until I could get a better view of what I was up against.

'Jesus!' I yelled.

Johnny spun around, every bit as surprised as me.

'You scared the shit out of me,' I said. 'What are you doing here? How did you get in?'

'I still have my key.' His voice was deadpan.

It was only then that I noticed the doors to the sideboard were open, along with the bureau where I kept my bills and paperwork. Scattered across the top were photographs of Laura's family that I'd taped to the walls of the house and the rope I'd fashioned into a noose.

Days after my first confrontation with Laura in the house and with my stab wound still aching, I'd been back to rid the place of any traces of that night, including wiping the floorboards clean of my blood. I'd dumped everything in a black recycling bin. Only now, four months later, did I remember that I hadn't put the bin out to be collected; I'd left it in the back garden where it had remained ever since.

'Are you going through my stuff?' I asked. He ignored my question.

'Whose house were you parked outside for hours on Wednesday night?'

'What, are you following me now?'

'That's neither here nor there. It's what you were doing outside that house that matters to me.'

My first reaction was to feel shame at being caught. Every so often, I'd drive slowly past Laura's home, occasionally parking by the side of the road, wondering what she was doing inside. Sometimes I'd stay for five minutes; other times, hours passed before I'd noticed. But it wasn't as if I had anywhere else to be.

My second reaction was to fly off the handle.

'You're snooping around my home?' I asked in a raised voice.

'Damn right I am. Who's this woman and why are there literally hundreds of photographs of her? And what about the rope? That night you stabbed yourself, you were planning to kill yourself, weren't you? What was the noose for? A back-up plan in case the knife failed?'

My rage threatened to boil over. 'Get out, Johnny, or you and I are going to really fall out.'

'Not until you tell me the truth.'

'Johnny, I said get out!'

'And I said no. I'm not leaving until you tell me what this is all about.'

His stubbornness left me incensed. I went to grab his arm, but he moved it away quickly and shoved me hard in the chest. His swiftness took me by surprise and I lost my balance and sprawled across the armchair, making my healing wound ache. I rose to my feet and launched myself at him a second time, only he was more solid than I remembered. He grabbed my collar and pushed me backwards until I was pinned to the wall and his face was inches from mine, his forearm under my chin.

'Get this through your thick fucking head!' he shouted. 'I am your brother, but I am not leaving this flat until you tell me what you've done.'

I breathed hard and fast, trying to conjure up alternative reasons to explain my behaviour, but I couldn't think of anything fast enough. Then as quick as a heartbeat, everything came to a head – losing Charlotte, discovering what Laura had done, tracking her down, the stabbing, what I'd done to Effie and our face-to-face confrontation earlier in the day. Every emotion under the sun came to a head and there was nothing I could do to stop them from gushing out of me. My body grew heavy and Johnny's arms weren't strong enough to stop me from collapsing to my knees. He joined me there and didn't say a word as I cried like a baby.

Later that night, we sat at opposite ends of the dining room table, four empty bottles of beer between us. I was unable to look him in the eye while he digested everything I told him, from the moments I was proud of to those I felt a secret shame for. I was honest with him about everything. Johnny didn't interrupt me; his face didn't move. Only when he was sure I'd finished did he reply.

'What's your endgame, Ry?'

'What do you mean?'

'What's the point to all of this? Where's it going to lead? What do you want to get out of it?'

'I want to make Laura understand what she's done – that she can't play God with people's lives.'

'And you think scaring her and screwing with her daughter's head is going to achieve that?'

'Yes . . . No . . . I'm not sure. I don't know. But what else am I supposed to do? Do nothing and let the same thing happen to the next Charlotte?'

'Do you understand what you did to that teenage girl – your *pupil* – is just as bad as what her mother did to Charlotte?'

'It's not the same thing because I've not tried to talk anyone into killing themselves.'

'How do you know that when Laura and her husband got home they didn't find their daughter had hurt herself?'

'Because I know the kind of girl Effie is. A few hurt feelings, a bruised ego, that's all. She'll get over it.'

'Listen to yourself, bro. If you're being really honest with yourself, you have no idea of the lasting damage you've done to her. You chose to bring her into this. She's just a pawn in the game you're playing with her mum. And the worst thing is, you don't care.'

I shook my head. 'You haven't met Effie. You don't know what she was like before I started this.'

'And you know what? I don't care. Because she is a *teenage girl*. This is what teenage girls are like. What you did to her is so, so wrong, and on so many levels. You should feel ashamed of yourself.'

I felt my face turn red. I rubbed my scratchy eyes with the palms of my hands. When I stared at Johnny, for a moment I recognised the man I could have been had I never found Charlotte's hidden files and read about the Freer of Lost Souls. Once, my younger brother and I had looked so much alike. Now when I looked at him, a much older, darker version of me was reflected in his eyes. I knew that everything he was saying to me was true, but I didn't want to admit it.

'So if you have all the answers, you tell me what I should've done, then,' I said.

'I'd have gone to the police with the recordings of your phone conversations and told them what I think Laura did.'

'What I *think*? You mean what I *know*. But I don't have enough evidence, Johnny. She'd walk free.'

'She told you she'd encouraged others to die.'

'But she didn't give me any names, did she? She didn't mention Charlotte. She could just claim she was playing along with some fantasy we had going. And what proof do I have that she was ever at the house or stabbed me?'

'Then I'd have made an appointment with whoever is in charge of End of the Line and alerted them to her. Even if they can't do anything about it, at least Laura will be on their radar. But I wouldn't tell them everything, like the Effie stuff, or they'll think you're a danger.'

'And what about you? Do you think I'm a danger?'

He closed his eyes and took a deep breath. 'I think you've reacted to Charlotte's death in a way that's putting yourself at risk. What you did to that girl . . . how you led her on . . . it's the first time I have ever been ashamed of you. Now it's time to stop blaming Laura for your actions and start taking some of the responsibility. Neither she nor Charlotte have put you where you are right now. You have. Charlotte chose to die and you chose to respond to it in a way a rational person wouldn't have.'

He prised the tops from two more bottles of beer and slid one towards me.

'Obsessing about this woman has become your whole life, hasn't it?' he continued. I nodded. 'When did you last read a book or watch a series on Netflix? Have you got your washing machine repaired yet? When did you last go to the house? That hammer's been on the sideboard for months waiting for you to put that picture back up on the wall. You need to start getting on with real life. You're never going to move on if you don't.'

'How do I even start moving on?'

'Begin by drawing a line under things tonight. And then we'll take it from there, you and me.'

For the first time since the police had turned up at the flat to tell me of Charlotte's death, I felt the knot in my stomach loosen a little. Not much, but enough to help me breathe.

CHAPTER NINE

LAURA

It was all too much for me to take in at once. I didn't know how to even begin processing the day's events.

Ryan and Janine. Both hidden enemies conspiring to tear me to pieces, and both completely independent of one another. I sat cloaked in the darkness of the house that I now understood to be empty of my family. It had been like that for almost two years, according to Tony. Subconsciously my brain had refused to accept that he and the girls had left, and I'd convinced myself we might be living separate lives but at least we were all under the same roof. Now I knew the truth of the situation and I felt desperately lonely. I kept forcing myself to think about Henry but he still couldn't anchor me. The more tired I became, the more confused I was about what was real and what I'd imagined.

There were two things I could be sure of, however. Ryan wasn't just toying with me anymore; he was also toying with my daughter. And I couldn't let that continue.

Janine was doing exactly the same thing, but in her own twisted little way. She'd been playing a behind-the-scenes role in my life that I hadn't been aware of. Her affair with my husband explained the constant disdain she showed me, why she watched me from her office and took every opportunity to belittle me in front of the other volunteers. Now, like a cuckoo, she'd made a home in my nest, but instead of ousting my eggs to make room for her own, she was ensuring there was no room left for me when I returned. She was the reason why Tony and the girls weren't upstairs in their bedrooms right now, not me.

What has Tony told her about me? What does she know that she has no right to? What can't I remember that made everyone leave me?

I stepped into the back garden for another cigarette. I'd given up monitoring how many I'd smoked since I'd returned from Tony's. I replayed certain moments in my head, like when we were hurrying through the school car park and he was discreetly trying to text someone. He must have been asking Janine to leave the house because I was coming. I bet she left her bag there on purpose for me to see. Or perhaps she was hiding somewhere in a different room, laughing at me. While I was worrying about our daughter's safety, Tony had known all along that Janine had been there with Effie.

I couldn't tell him why I feared for my girl and he couldn't tell me why I had no reason to. He was too afraid to admit the truth about what had been going on behind my back.

How could you, Tony? How could you do this to us?

For much of my life I'd been a survivor, but it was only now I realised that somewhere along the line, the role of victim had taken precedence. I desperately needed the strong, confident Laura I used to know to take charge. I inhaled one last long drag from my cigarette and then stamped on it. Ryan and Janine, Janine and Ryan. They didn't have the first clue who they'd taken on.

But who should I target first? My heart told me Janine, my head told me Ryan. Yes, it had to be Ryan because I knew the least about him and he was the biggest threat to my stability. He'd met with my husband, targeted my daughter, knew where I lived and visited my son. Now it was my turn to discover who the enemy was and to make him suffer like he had me. And I knew who to ask first.

◆ ◆ ◆

I gazed across the playground, searching for Alice before the school bell sounded the start of her new day.

In these daily snapshots of her life each weekday morning, I'd see just how tall she was becoming, that her hair was getting longer and her body more agile. She was growing up, five minutes every morning at a time. I couldn't recall what her last memory of me was, but from what Tony had suggested, it hadn't been a good one. Once my enemies were out of the way, the rest of the pieces would all fit into place and I'd be walking her to school every day again.

Suddenly, Alice spotted me and her face lit up. I let out a sigh of relief. She still loved me. She began to run towards me just as the school bell sounded. 'It's okay,' I mouthed, and pointed towards the door, telling her to go inside. 'I'll see you soon.' She waved and skipped into the building and out of sight.

I saw Kate Griffiths before she turned her head and noticed me, not that she had the faintest clue who I was. She'd either gone to bed wearing a full face of make-up or she'd set her alarm for the crack of dawn, because no parent looked like that on the school run without a lot of preparation.

I'd see her most days at the school gates with her son but hadn't realised until she passed Tony and me as we left Effie's school that she also had a child there. I noted that she wore a sticker with her name handwritten across it and the words 'Parent–Teacher Association' underneath.

'Hello,' I began as she opened the door to her SUV. She turned sharply and gave me a cursory glance up and down. 'I'm Laura. My daughter's in the same class as your son.' I lied about the last part.

'Oh, of course,' she replied, but her fake smile couldn't disguise her lack of interest.

'I saw you at St Giles Upper School last night. I didn't realise you had a child there too.'

'That's nice,' she replied, but offered nothing by way of conversation. I was a dark cloud in her blue sky and she couldn't wait for the wind to blow me away. By the unnatural smoothness of her skin, I guessed she'd had more fillers injected into her than cream in a choux pastry.

'How's your daughter getting on in Year Ten?'

'Very well, thank you. She's going to be taking some of her GCSEs early. How about your . . .' She couldn't finish her sentence so I did it for her.

'My Effie? She's getting along well. She transferred there coming up for two years ago now.'

'It's a good school with amazing OFSTED reports,' Kate replied. 'I'm sorry, I don't mean to be rude but I've really got to dash . . .'

She tried to climb into her car but I ignored how desperate she was to nip our communication in the bud.

'We've been lucky that Effie's teacher Mr Smith has taken such a shine to her,' I said. 'I met him recently for the first time. Is he new to the school? I don't recall seeing him before.'

'He's been there about a year and a half now, if memory serves, and he recently became acting head of Year Ten. But before that, he took some personal time off after that whole sorry business with his wife.'

'His wife?'

This is why I'd chosen to speak to Kate. I'd recognised her type immediately. I'd seen it so many times before in mothers who became overly involved in their children's school lives. They have their fingers in many pies to make up for the fact they have little else going on in their own world. And the one thing they love more than listening to gossip is being the first to spread it to others.

'Did you not read about it?' Kate continued. 'It was quite horrible. Suicide. She jumped off a cliff. Can you believe it? What an awful way to go.'

I dug my fingernails into my palms.

No, it can't be her. Not Charlotte. Not David's Charlotte.

'How sad,' I replied.

'That's not the worst of it. She was two months away from having a baby, and she killed herself with a man she was having an affair with. From what everyone's been saying, it was some kind of Romeo and Juliet suicide pact.'

I shook my head sympathetically and stopped myself from setting the record straight. There was no affair with David. Charlotte was simply someone I'd shaped to help David finish what he'd started. I'd barely given Charlotte a second thought since it happened – maybe I was even a little envious of her, playing such an intimate role in David's final moments. I hadn't even bothered attending her funeral. Clearly, I'd underestimated the impact of her death.

So that's what Ryan had meant when he told me in the house I'd taken everything away from him already. Now that I knew what was motivating him, I could use it to my advantage.

'Well, I won't hold you up,' I added, smiling. I began to walk away.

'It's nice to meet you,' Kate called out, but I knew that if she saw me tomorrow, she wouldn't have the first clue who I was.

CHAPTER TEN

RYAN

'Thank you for agreeing to meet with me,' I began. I slipped off my blazer and folded it across the arm of the sofa.

'Can I get you a tea, coffee or a glass of water?' she asked as she opened a window to let the stuffiness out. I assumed the room wasn't used very often.

'Water would be great, thanks.'

It was the first appointment before the new year I could get with End of the Line's manager Janine Thomson. When she left the room on the ground floor of their building, I glanced around at the sparsely decorated walls and noted two security cameras attached to ceiling corners. Tiny green lights flashed intermittently and I assumed we were being watched. The woodchip wallpaper could do with a fresh lick of white paint, and the two past-their-prime sofas opposite each other needed replacing. A box of tissues had been left on a coffee table. I wondered what was behind the padlocked door.

Janine returned and placed my drink on the coffee table.

'You mentioned in our telephone conversation you wanted to talk about one of our volunteers, Laura?' she asked. She took out a notebook and pen from a bright-orange handbag. Her voice didn't have the same soothing quality as Laura's. It was more efficient.

'She's definitely not volunteering today?' I asked.

'No, she's not due in until Friday.'

'Okay, I think – well, I know – that Laura is encouraging some of your callers to end their lives.'

The look Janine gave me was precisely why I hadn't been to see her earlier and had taken matters into my own hands instead. My throat felt dry, so I reached for my glass and took a big gulp, then perched on the edge of the sofa and began to recount everything that had happened, from Charlotte's suicide right up to the moment when Laura turned up at the house. It had been much easier spilling my guts to my brother than a stranger. Plus, now I was forced to self-edit, or risk incriminating myself. I admitted to following Laura, but not her family, and I kept quiet about her stabbing me and how I'd used Effie for my own means. Janine took notes up until I finished talking.

'Right,' she said. 'That's quite an accusation, Mr Smith.'

'I know how it must sound – how *I* must sound – but Laura needs to be stopped.'

'Do you mind me asking – after your wife passed away, did you undergo any grief counselling?'

'No. Why?'

'It's just that sometimes grief can manifest itself in many different ways, and especially when someone we love has chosen to end their life. We start blaming ourselves or start misdirecting our anger towards others—'

'I'm going to stop you right there,' I said firmly. 'I know exactly what grief has done. It's torn me apart, but I haven't lost my sanity. I spent weeks talking with this woman and I heard how persuasive she was when she thought I was at my lowest ebb. So I know for a fact that she's a danger to vulnerable people calling you.'

'Do you have any evidence of what you've told me?'

I removed my Dictaphone and was about to press play when she stopped me.

I followed her eyes as she looked at me then at one of the security cameras. She removed a pair of in-ear headphones from her bag, plugged them into the recorder and played excerpts from some of our many phone conversations.

I watched her face as she listened, stony-faced but absorbing every one of Laura's manipulative words. After five minutes, she pressed stop and removed her headphones.

'You need to know that Laura's a very popular member of the team and a big fundraiser for us,' Janine said. 'If it wasn't for her, we'd be struggling to stay open.'

I felt deflated. She didn't care. I shook my head, grabbed the recording device and stood up to leave. 'So you're willing to overlook what she's done because she brings in money? I knew this would be a waste of time.'

'Ryan, wait,' Janine replied and rose to her feet. She looked up towards the security cameras again, lowered her voice and then spoke quietly into my ear.

CHAPTER ELEVEN

LAURA

I picked up a photograph of him on his wedding day. It was positioned so that he could see it from whatever angle he lay at.

He was a much better-looking groom than his wife was a bride. Judging by the age of the wedding car parked behind them and the style of dress she and her bridesmaids wore, the black-and-white picture in the rose-gold frame was probably close to six decades old. It had faded a little, but the love between them as they held each other's gaze for an eternity was still crystal clear. Now as Ryan's grandfather lay asleep in the bed behind me, he bore little resemblance to the stocky, grinning man that the camera had captured so long ago.

A day earlier, I'd sifted through dozens of photographs of faculty members on Effie's school website until I found a picture of Ryan. He'd taken photos of my son and me in the lounge area of Henry's home without me even noticing, but how had he gained entrance? I showed Ryan's image on my phone to two of the brainless receptionists, and one immediately recognised him.

'That's Peter Spencer's grandson, isn't it?' she began. 'I think he's called Robert or Ryan or Richard or something.'

Neither enquired as to why I wanted to know, and after thanking them, I headed towards Henry's wing, then took a diversion towards the geriatric care unit, walking along sticky, lino-clad flooring and through bleach-scented air until I reached another reception desk. I claimed to a nurse with a foreign accent that Mr Spencer was my uncle. She didn't ask me for identification and pointed me towards Room 23. I made a mental note to complain to the management about the lackadaisical security later.

Moments later, I loomed over a vulnerable old man, too poorly and weak to protect himself. All it might take was a firmly held pillow over his face to free him of the prison his body held him in. He might not be suicidal but I'd be giving him just as much mercy as I did my candidates.

I glanced around his sparsely decorated room and flicked through the clothes hanging in his wardrobe, stopping at his one solitary suit. I assumed it would only be worn again when they lowered him into the ground. Photos on the shelves were of what I guessed were his children and grandkids. Then I spotted one of Ryan on his wedding day, and Charlotte by his side in an off-the-shoulder, white lace dress. It was already a dated look. I picked it up to get my first proper look at her. She was more attractive than her voice had suggested; she was slimmer and taller than me. Even if she hadn't stepped from a clifftop, their marriage wouldn't have survived. She was too far out of his league to have stayed for long.

If Ryan had been allowed a peek into his future, I wondered if he'd still have married her, knowing what she'd do to him. I know I'd have still married Tony, despite everything that followed.

Our wedding had been a small affair, at a church in the village of Weedon, near to where he'd grown up. We were young, both only in our early twenties at the time, but I'd never been more sure of anything in my life.

The purpose of a wedding isn't just to commit to each other, it's also to bring two families together. Only I wasn't able to deliver my side of the bargain. Tony's ushers had to direct guests towards both sides of the aisle, so it wouldn't look weighted in favour of the groom. His mother tried to fill my mum's shoes by helping me to get ready in the morning. And when I held his father's arm as he walked me up the aisle, it brought home to me just how alone I was.

All day, when I should have been grinning from ear to ear, I just wanted it to end. It was a constant reminder I had nobody but my new husband. At the reception, when distant members of his family asked where my mother and father were, I'd have to keep telling them my parents were dead. I'd been forced to explain the same thing to everyone, from the wedding-dress shop owner to the florist, the driver of my car, and the restaurant manager arranging the top-table seating plan.

I had no relative to run my plans past, and my bridesmaids were girls I worked with who I barely knew but who were too embarrassed to decline when I asked them. Everything about my wedding was a compromise.

The best I could do to feel my parents' presence was to wear my mum's engagement ring and offer Tony my dad's watch. I was close to tears when he accepted. I didn't tell him I'd actually bought them at an antiques shop in the nearby village of Olney. I wanted a sense of nostalgia, even if it was someone else's nostalgia, not mine.

A silver watch lay unclasped and stretched out across Ryan's grandfather's bedside table. The inscription on the back read: *To our son on his wedding day.*

How sweet, I thought. Back then I'm sure it had cost his parents a small fortune. I slipped it into my pocket, along with the batteries from his TV remote control.

I left the room, then paused. I turned around and went back inside, closing the door quietly behind me.

I listened carefully to the old man's lungs as they struggled to take in air. His breath was wheezy and crackly, too weak for asthma and more likely to be emphysema. The poor bastard really was going to be better off dead.

◆ ◆ ◆

The call came out of the blue, but it couldn't have been more welcome. I stubbed out my cigarette on the footpath when a number I recognised flashed across my phone.

'Oh, my darling!' I began, and closed my eyes, thrilled and relieved to hear from Effie. It had been a week since I'd surprised her at their new house. I'd since texted the number I'd memorised from the display on Tony's dashboard and given her mine, hoping she'd want to open the lines of communication between us, which might, in turn, encourage Tony to do the same.

'How are you?'

'I'm okay,' she replied hesitantly.

'Are you sure about that? You don't sound it.'

'Could we . . . Would you . . . like to meet up?'

'Oh, of course, I would love to. When?'

An hour and a half later we sat side by side on a leather sofa inside a coffee shop. She'd chosen a Starbucks in a retail park on the outskirts of town because she didn't want us to be seen by her dad or his friends, she explained. We sipped hot chocolates topped with whipped cream and sprinkles as I listened intently to my daughter filling me in on the time I'd missed from her life. She explained how some of her friends had turned against her when her Facebook account was hacked and her ex-boyfriend Matt was humiliated. Then her grades had slipped and she'd found herself alone and without any confidence in her own intelligence. It was Ryan Smith I really wanted to know about, but I couldn't just shoehorn him into the conversation.

'Are there any subjects you like?' I asked. 'What was it you used to be good at? Chemistry, wasn't it?'

'English and biology. And now I get shit marks in English and I hate biology because we're expected to dissect animals. Baby pigs . . . It's gross.' She screwed up her face.

To begin with, Effie struggled to maintain eye contact with me and I understood that while I was her mother, I was also a stranger. I still struggled to remember what had torn us apart, and as frustrating as it was, it didn't seem appropriate to ask her and risk opening old wounds. Today was about moving forward and getting her back on side, to show my husband what he was missing without me. When her eyes finally reached mine and remained there, I could see so much of myself in them.

It gradually dawned on me, as Effie spoke, that I'd never really heard what she had to say before. I'd listened, but all too often I'd dismissed her words and feelings as those of a child. Now, with her fifteenth birthday approaching, she was a young woman, and it was time I treated her like one.

Several times she opened her mouth as if to ask me something, before having a change of heart and closing it again.

'I don't want to pry, but is there something else you want to talk to me about?' I coaxed.

She shook her head and looked across the car park at the shoppers loading their vehicles with bulging bags or strapping toddlers into buggies. She pursed her lips and looked so sad.

'I've messed everything up, Mum,' she said, before her face crumpled and she began to cry.

I couldn't have asked for anything better. I moved my chair closer to hers and draped my arm around her shoulders for comfort.

'I got this new teacher, and at first I thought he hated me because he kept giving me rubbish grades,' she continued.

'Is this Mr Smith?' I asked.

She nodded. 'He seemed like he really cared and gave me lots of attention after school. And then we started getting . . . closer.'

'How close?' I asked. Our reunion was turning out to be even more rewarding than I could have anticipated. While I hoped Ryan Smith hadn't hurt or abused Effie, would it be the worst thing in the world for my case if he'd stepped over the line a little?

'I didn't have many friends left and he was really lovely to me and I started to get feelings for him and I thought he had them for me too. But when I told him, he was so horrible.'

So that's what he'd done to her. He'd led the silly girl on. Now I had something to work with.

'Darling, did something physical happen between you?'

'No. And I know it was wrong, but I wanted it to. He turned me down and called me nasty and stupid. I feel like such an idiot. I can't even look at him anymore without wanting to be sick. I hate him.'

'He seemed so nice. I bet he's having a laugh about you in the staffroom over this.'

Fear spread across my daughter's face. 'You think he's told the other teachers?'

'Men of his age love attention from pretty girls like you. They boast about it to their friends. And you know how rumours spread in schools – maybe that's how he gets his kicks, leading girls on so he can humiliate them and boast about it. I just hope none of the students know.'

Effie held her head in her hands and began to cry again. I rubbed her shoulders but didn't encourage her to stop. I was torn between wanting to be the mother that Effie needed and demanding my revenge on Ryan. Effie potentially had all the ammunition I required, but I had to talk her around to my way of thinking first.

'Does anyone else know about your feelings towards Mr Smith?' I continued.

'No, I didn't tell anyone.'

'Were you seen together?'

'I guess so. I had meetings with him twice a week.'

'But it's not like you were spending time with him when there was no one else around?'

'We were always alone in the room behind his classroom.'

I wanted everything in the world to stop moving so that nothing could distract me from savouring her every word. This was how I was going to destroy Ryan: mother and daughter together, working towards a common goal.

'You were alone every time?' I repeated. 'You're sure of this?'

'Yes.'

'And did he give this kind of attention to any of the other girls?'

'No. He'd wait until everyone had left.'

'And how close were you, physically, when you were alone together?'

'A couple of metres apart.'

'Okay.' I must have looked disappointed because she added hastily, 'But sometimes he'd get a lot closer.' I'd always been able to tell when she was exaggerating.

'Did he ever ask you about your family?'

'A little – he asked about you and Dad.'

'And what did you tell him?'

'Nothing, really.'

'Did he say why he wanted to know about us?'

'He said he was trying to understand if I had problems at home that might explain my falling grades. But it was him who started it all by marking me down all the time. He told me he didn't want to worry you both, so it was best I didn't mention he'd been asking about you.'

'So he encouraged you to keep secrets from us?' I shook my head, folded my arms and let out an exaggerated puff of air. 'That's a fairly typical approach.'

'To what?'

'To grooming a child.'

'What, like a paedophile?'

I nodded. 'Part of my role at End of the Line involves talking to young people who've been through this, only by the time they reach me it's often gone much, much further. These poor children. Oh, Effie, the stories I could tell you.'

'But wouldn't he have done something when I made a move on him in his car?'

'You've been in his car?'

'Yes, he gave me a lift home and I thought it was leading to something else. Then he started telling me how disgusting I was.'

'Maybe he got cold feet; maybe he was playing mind games with you. It's hard to know how these people think.'

'I should tell Dad, shouldn't I? He'll know what to do.'

'No, I don't think we should do that just yet. You know how overprotective he is over you and he might do something rash. Leave this to me – I'll sort it out. But I need to know how far you want me to take this.'

She paused for a moment, then looked at me with a steely determination I'd not seen in her before. 'I want him to feel as shit as he made me feel.'

'Okay. But I'm going to need your help to make sure he never grooms or humiliates any girl ever again.'

'Thanks, Mum,' she replied, and I held her close to my chest and stroked her hair. It felt surprisingly good to have my elder daughter back.

I glanced around the coffee shop and lowered my voice. 'You know an accusation like this could ruin a teacher's career, don't you?'

She nodded, and gave me a smile that told me she was on board with anything I might suggest.

'Good girl,' I replied. 'Good girl.'

CHAPTER TWELVE

RYAN

'Someone's been in Granddad's room,' Johnny began on the phone. He sounded perplexed and anxious.

'What do you mean?'

'I don't want to freak you out, but you know that wedding photo of you and Charlotte on the shelf? Charlotte's face has been scribbled out with a pen. I only noticed it as I was leaving.'

'Are you sure?'

'Of course I am. I took it with me when he fell asleep so he wouldn't see it. Who would do something like that?'

'Laura,' I exhaled. 'Fuck.'

'What? You think it was her?'

'It could *only* be her.'

I fell silent. She must have somehow discovered Granddad was staying at the same facility as her son. And during their many conversations, Charlotte had clearly told Laura she'd scribbled out Britney Spears's face from pictures with Charlotte's crush Justin Timberlake. Laura was giving me a clear warning that, like me, she could do her homework.

I didn't want to believe she was responsible, because that meant she was stepping out from the shadows and telling me she wasn't afraid anymore, while I'd promised Johnny I'd let her go.

'Jesus Christ, Ryan! If it is her then you've got to do something about this, Ry, before it goes any further,' Johnny replied sternly. 'If she's as fucked up as you say she is, she could have done anything to Granddad when she was alone with him.'

'I know, I know,' I replied. 'I'm so sorry.'

He hung up, and I held the phone to my chest and regretted taking pictures of her disabled son in the care home where my granddad also lived.

'Shit, shit, shit,' I said aloud, and dropped the phone onto the sofa. I was at a loss as to how to respond. Maybe now I'd made Laura's boss aware of what she was capable of, I'd just need to remain patient and wait for Laura to mess up. However, until that happened, if Laura was gunning for me, I'd need to be prepared.

CHAPTER THIRTEEN

LAURA

'Hello, my dear, are you back in the land of the living?'

Mary gave me one of her all-encompassing hugs, the kind where she thrust her body into yours and which made you want to change your clothes immediately.

'Yes, it was a particularly nasty tummy bug. The girls had it too,' I lied.

Following my confrontation at Effie's school with Ryan, and the discovery that Janine was screwing my husband, I'd bought some time away from the office by faking the norovirus. I hadn't yet mustered up the strength to confront Janine without wanting to pour a kettle of boiling water over her head..

'Taking a few days off gave me time to whip up a batch of these.'

I eased the lid from a cake tin crammed with the contents of three boxes of clotted cream shortbread I'd bought a day earlier. 'Don't worry, I wasn't contagious when I made them,' I joked as Mary's wrinkled hand dipped inside. I took a moment to glance around the rest of the office. Full of enthusiasm and always with other people's best interests above their own, my colleagues were genuine, good people. But they were also incredibly blind. None of them could see what was right under their noses. None of them knew who I really was.

'Don't get too comfortable,' Kevin warned as I made my way to my desk. 'Janine's put you down for a one-to-one drop-in, in about half an hour.'

I rolled my eyes. Janine knew I wasn't comfortable with face-to-face callers, yet the spiteful cow had still appointed me one. Now I'd have to go and see her, and make up an excuse as to why I couldn't do it.

'She's not in,' continued Kevin, pre-empting my response. 'She's taken a couple of days off. She said she's going away with her new fella.'

I stopped in my tracks.

'New fella?' I repeated, almost spitting out the words.

'Yes, she's been seeing some bloke for a while now. It sounds pretty serious from what she's been telling Zoe.'

'Well, it just goes to prove there's someone for everyone. Even someone with Janine's unique appearance.'

I stepped into her office to fume alone. I wanted to put Tony and Janine and their grubby little liaison to the back of my mind, but it was easier said than done. Instead I was picturing them, arms entwined, walking along a beachfront. I could see them enjoying a picnic in the countryside, kissing under the sun. I could imagine him holding his jacket over their heads to keep them dry in a sudden downpour. Everything he should have been doing with me, he was doing with her.

I flicked through the appointments book and questioned how – of all the people my handsome husband could have replaced me with – he'd chosen that thing. That frumpy, weasel-faced shit of a woman, cuddling up to my Tony and playing mother to my children. It beggared belief.

I'd thought that he and I had grown closer after my attack, and now I was even starting to build a relationship with Effie and Alice again. We should have been on the same page, with the aim of us all living together under one roof. And in time, maybe Tony might have even accepted Henry back into our lives. All five of us, like it was supposed to be. Not them with her; not them with *Janine.*

It had been my plan to deal with Ryan first and then Janine, but as my rage rose like lava bubbling at the rim of a volcano, they now shared equal billing.

I took a deep, calming breath, but the smell of Janine's cheap supermarket perfume lingered in the air and caught the back of my throat, making me cough. I found the name of my drop-in caller in the appointments book and paused when I spotted Janine's diary peeking out from an open desk drawer. I made sure I wasn't being watched as I flicked from page to page. Today she'd scheduled the start of a long weekend. She'd written 'Iceland' with three exclamation marks; the 'i' was lower case and a heart used instead of a dot. Tony was aware I'd always wanted to see the Northern Lights but he'd refused to go with me because he hated the cold. Now he'd taken Janine there. I hoped the lights were so bright they blinded her.

Tony and I had taken many long-weekend city breaks. His parents looked after the kids and we'd spend Friday to Sunday in cities like Bruges and Barcelona. I hated that he was replicating our life with Janine.

I skipped back a few pages and noted she'd scribbled something out. She'd pressed pretty heavily on the page because it left an impression on the next. What was she trying to hide? Curious, I held the paper up to the strip light and the name became clear.

4.15 p.m., Ryan Smith, it read.

I glared at the name for a time, allowing my brain to absorb it and what it meant. I blinked hard and looked again and his name was still there. The only two people on my hit list were working together.

A knock on the door made me jump out of my skin, and I covered the diary with a ring binder.

'Laura, your appointment is here.' Zoe smiled. 'I'll start monitoring the cameras.'

Downstairs, a man with a pinched face and the stench of stale tobacco began grumbling about how dreadful his life had been since his wife walked out on him. Knowing we were being watched, I nodded at the appropriate times and gave enough sympathetic smiles where suitable. Even when he told me he thought he'd be better off dead than alone, I didn't bite. I didn't need a candidate right now. All I could think about was Janine and Ryan meeting under this roof and in this room. Not knowing what they had discussed was killing me.

Later, when the client left, seemingly satisfied that someone in the world now understood his woes, I went back upstairs and thanked Zoe for keeping an eye on me from the camera room. I waited for her to return to her desk, then went into the room and closed the door. She hadn't logged out from the computer, so I accessed a file containing saved footage of past drop-in callers. Each clip was labelled with their name, date, the interviewer and the camera monitor. However, none of the MPEGs had Ryan's name attached. I folded my arms, frustrated. Then I clicked the mouse on the trash can symbol. Among the deleted Word documents was a file titled 'R.S.'

'Ryan Smith,' I said out loud.

With no other names attached to it, I assumed Janine had recorded it herself then deleted it, but forgotten to empty the virtual rubbish bin.

I slipped on the headphones and pressed play. Eventually, Ryan entered the room followed by Janine. He drummed his fingers against his leg and tapped his foot on the floor nervously while he waited for her to return with a glass. This was a very different Ryan from the smug one taunting me at Effie's school.

I listened intently as he told Janine about his wife Charlotte's death and how he'd read online about the Freer of Lost Souls, and he recalled the effort he'd put into discovering if I were real. Then he recounted in detail our many conversations – how I'd encouraged him to die and how I'd accepted his invitation to watch as it happened. My heart raced.

I kept staring at Janine's face, but it remained emotionless despite the accusations.

Listening to Ryan talk in-depth about the loss he'd felt after his wife's death humanised him a little. Until that moment, he'd been an unpredictable force bent on tormenting me. But watching this video, he became a real person, a man who'd suffered; who was fractured and lonely. He was nothing like the formidable opponent I'd spent months hiding from in my house.

It made me want to break him even more.

Suddenly he handed her what looked like a Dictaphone. She glanced at the camera, then pulled out headphones from her bag and spent the next five minutes listening without saying a word. I hunched forward, literally on the edge of my seat, wondering what the hell was on that recording. Finally, she spoke.

'You need to know that Laura is a popular member of the team and a big fundraiser for us,' she said. 'If it wasn't for her, we'd be struggling to stay open.'

Janine's appreciation of my hard work wasn't the response I'd expected, as she'd never shown me anything close to gratitude before. And I began to feel a little relieved when a frustrated Ryan stood up to leave. It was his word against mine – a stranger wracked with grief and desperate to find someone other than himself to blame for his wife's death, versus me, a people person, a woman whose middle name was charity. Janine might not have liked me, but at least I had her support.

I began to slip the headphones from my ears, but continued to watch the screen as Ryan made his way towards the door. Suddenly, Janine stood up and stopped him. She looked straight into the video camera and whispered into his ear. I couldn't make out what she was saying, so I replayed it. Again, it was too muffled. Only when I turned up the volume to maximum could I understand a few words.

'I believe . . . saying,' she told him. '. . . suspicions . . . number of suicidal calls . . . higher . . . other branches . . . I promise . . . me a little time . . . kicked out of here . . . police investigation. This place . . . I'll take it away from her . . .'

I slumped in my seat, watching both figures leave the room until eventually the computer screen turned black.

Oh, Janine, why did you have to say that?

Everyone was too busy on calls to spot me rifling through her drawers, filing cabinet and the cupboard behind her desk, frantically searching for that damning Dictaphone. But it was nowhere to be found.

I gave up for now and deleted the video file – permanently this time – and it felt like a light switch in my head had just been flicked on. Now I could see everything much more clearly: the present and the future. I didn't need to compartmentalise Ryan and Janine. I could use them to cancel each other out. Two birds, and me holding the stone.

CHAPTER FOURTEEN

RYAN

My mum and dad sat on the opposite side of the kitchen table to me, their expressions serious, like when I was a kid and they were about to tell me off.

When they began talking, I knew they had rehearsed beforehand by the way they took it in turns – a sentence each, like a couple of breakfast TV presenters reading from a teleprompter. They'd even printed off their bank statements and highlighted their outgoings to prove their point.

'We just can't afford it any longer,' Mum continued, and took a sip from a glass of Prosecco. 'If we keep going like this, we'll have to cash in our pensions to keep paying for it.'

I nodded. 'You're right and I'm sorry. I didn't think about it. You should have said something sooner.'

They'd asked me to their home to discuss the two mortgages I had in my name. While I was paying for the flat, they'd been stepping in to pay for the empty house. A teacher's income wasn't a bottomless pit of money, and neither were their savings.

'I appreciate why you're reluctant to let either of them go,' Dad said, 'but you're going to need to make a decision soon. You can't keep both.'

I briefly weighed up the pros and cons of each home. I no longer had any love for the flat since Charlotte died. So making my home in a place she hadn't set foot in would be the sensible choice.

'I'll sell the flat.'

'Are you sure?' Mum asked. 'Do you want more time to think about it?'

'No, I need to start moving forward and in new directions.'

These were the buzzwords I'd picked up from the self-help websites Johnny kept emailing me links to. Over the Christmas period, curiosity got the better of me and I'd opened them, but it was only recently that their words were starting to resonate. Then I'd made it my New Year's resolution to start afresh.

When Johnny had confronted me at the flat and asked me what my endgame with Laura was, I didn't really have an answer. For months I'd thought of very little else except how I could make her life as miserable as mine. Since my brother had pointed out my actions were on a par with hers, I realised the attention I'd focused on Laura was a delaying tactic to stop myself from getting on with the rest of my life.

I'd told End of the Line's manager about Laura and she'd believed me. Now it was up to Janine to bring Laura down with the evidence I'd given her. I wondered when she might get in touch to update me.

Laura and I were over. I hoped that her defacing Charlotte's photo in Granddad Pete's bedroom was just a parting shot.

'One of Johnny's old school mates is an estate agent at Corner Stones,' I said. 'I'll ask him to give me a valuation and then I'll put it on the market.'

Mum placed her hand on mine.

'I know it's not easy, but you're doing the right thing.'

She was right, of course, as parents often are. But there was one more 'right thing' I needed to do before I could put all this behind me.

◆ ◆ ◆

Effie had kept a low profile in school since I'd given her a lift home and turned down her advances. There'd been no detentions and no class disruptions. But come the first term of the new year, she still couldn't bring herself to look me in the eye. She chose to shrink behind her desk, as if she hoped the ground might swallow her up.

I gradually began increasing her grades until they were around the mark they had been before I'd interfered. But each time I looked at Effie, I saw a girl that I'd broken, and I felt as guilty as hell about it.

'Effie, have you got a minute?'

She looked startled when I asked her to stay behind as the bell rang for lunch.

Her hand fumbled in her pocket and she looked all around me but not at me. What I'd done to her was unforgivable.

'About what happened that afternoon,' I began. 'It was completely inappropriate and I want to apologise.'

Her eyes lifted from the floor.

'I shouldn't have given you a lift. I shouldn't have said the things I did and I – well, we both took things too far. I'm your teacher and I should have known better. I blame myself for giving you the wrong signals. I won't put either of us in that position again, I promise.'

She nodded.

'Have you told anyone else?'

'No.'

'So we can keep it between ourselves?'

She nodded.

'Have you noticed your grades have improved?'

'Is that your way of shutting me up, Mr Smith? Giving me better marks so I'll keep quiet about what you did?'

I didn't reply.

'Thought so. Can I go now?'

'Yes.'

As Effie hurried from the room, I thought I could now start putting everything behind me and think about the future, just like the self-help websites told me to. It was time to start my life again, only without Charlotte or Laura.

CHAPTER FIFTEEN

LAURA

The estate agent was already parked outside the block of flats in a car emblazoned with his firm's colourful logo when I arrived dead on time.

With his brown chinos, white jacket and red hair he resembled a raspberry ice cream. He greeted me with a smile.

'How are things, darlin'? Nice to meet you. I'm Andy Webber.'

He was overfamiliar, behaviour that never sat comfortably with me. I didn't like his silly topknot or beard either.

'I'm wonderful, thank you,' I replied, and threw my bag over my shoulder. It weighed a ton.

'So it's number 7 you want to take a shufti around, right?' I didn't know what a 'shufti' was but I nodded anyway. 'Cool, well, let me lead the way.'

Not so long ago, the flats before me had been council offices. A dreadful gas explosion had razed them to the ground and taken a dozen staff with it. Eventually, the building was rebuilt as apartments. Andy glossed over its history and blathered on about the flat's potential and how many viewings he'd had since it'd been put on the market a few days earlier. We took the lift up three floors, but I wasn't really listening to him. I just had a burning desire to spend a few moments in the place that Ryan called home.

My opponent wasn't the only one who could do his research. I'd got the ball rolling with a written request to read the public coroner's report, which listed Charlotte's address. Curious to see where she'd called me from, I'd discovered on a property app that the flat was for sale. I made an appointment to view it, and after a brief meeting and handover with Effie before school, I was on my way. I'd already established with the estate agent that the vendor would not be in.

'As you can see, it's been recently redecorated,' Andy explained. 'The living and dining area is spacious and the kitchen has been refitted. It's a perfect place for a single Pringle if this is the kind of gaff you're looking for.'

It was hard to see any of that. All I saw was a cage with windows looking out onto a world Charlotte hadn't wanted to be a part of anymore. No wonder she'd felt depressed and that it would only get worse once she had the baby.

I wandered around from room to room, mentally redecorating the place. Currently, it had come straight from the pages of an Ikea catalogue. Everything – from the cheap fireplace framing an electric coal-effect fire to the furniture – said first-time buyer, no idea.

'Can I take a look at the bedrooms?' I asked.

'Sure,' the estate agent replied, and began to lead the way.

'It's quite a pokey flat. I'm sure I can find them on my own.'

He shrugged, and remained in the kitchen while I opened the door to a tiny little box room, with just enough space for a mattress and a bedside cabinet. The duvet was pulled back and the pillows had head-shaped impressions in them – I guessed Ryan was now using it as his room. The next bedroom was a nursery. It smelled stale, like the door hadn't been opened for some time. A mobile with drawings of zoo animals hung from the ceiling over a wooden cot. Everything in the room was either white or yellow: hedging their bets over the sex,

I assumed. Knowing how weak its mother was and how devious its father could be made me even more confident I'd given the child a lucky escape.

The master bedroom was dimly lit, so I opened the curtains and began to poke around. Against one wall was the flat's only piece of non-flatpack furniture, an antique dressing table with three rectangular mirrors. I wondered how many times Charlotte had looked at herself through their differing perspectives and failed to see what her husband had seen in her.

There were photos of her and Ryan inside mismatched frames on the dressing table, together with a few bottles of perfume. Taped to one mirror was the printout of a baby scan. Beneath it was a jewellery box containing rings and bracelets, all costume, of course.

I opened the wardrobe door and skimmed, hanger by hanger, her high-street-label clothes, her maternity wear outnumbering her pre-pregnancy clothing. Hidden at the back was a wedding dress – the simple, inexpensive lace gown I'd seen her wearing in the photo in Ryan's grandfather's room. It was covered in a clear plastic garment bag to prevent it from decaying like its owner.

'Perfect,' I muttered, pulling out a pair of yellow rubber gloves from my jacket pocket and slipping them over my hands. Then I reached into my bag to remove what was making it so heavy.

'Everything all right in there?' Andy's voice came from behind the door. I quietly closed the wardrobe so he couldn't see what I'd done, put the gloves back in my pocket and made my way back into the living room, nudging the dial of a thermostat on the wall up to full.

'I think it's a little too pedestrian for my needs,' I said, and a look crossed his face that said I'd just wasted his time.

I was following him towards the front door when something on the top of a bureau caught my eye. Without him noticing, I grabbed it and slipped it inside my bag, smiling to myself.

CHAPTER SIXTEEN

RYAN

It was impossible not to notice the heat or the smell as soon as I opened the door to the flat.

I'd spent Friday evening at Johnny's house with a Thai takeout and a pay-per-view boxing match. And after a few beers, I'd slept over. It felt good to get away from the flat for a night. Much of the following day was spent with my dad at the house, making lists and prioritising the work that needed to be done, room by room. For the first time in a long while, I'd begun to allow a little optimism into my life and not allowed Laura Morris to dominate my thoughts.

But on my return home, it was boiling hot and reeked of something foul. I checked the fridge to see what had gone out of date so quickly, but the smell wasn't coming from there. I figured someone viewing the flat must have caught their arm against the thermostat and accidentally turned it up, as I'd done it myself many a time. But that didn't explain the odour.

It smelled the strongest in Charlotte's and my bedroom. I looked under the bed, the dressing table and behind the curtain for the corpse of a dead mouse or rat. Charlotte had warned me that rats can climb up through the toilet bowl, even in a third-floor flat, though I hadn't believed her until now. But as I edged closer to the wardrobe, I realised something inside it was causing the stench. I put my hand over my mouth as I opened the door.

'Jesus!' I yelled, and stumbled backwards. Charlotte's wedding dress had been moved to the front, stripped from its polythene cover and the stomach area covered in blood.

At the foot of the dress was the small, pinky-white foetus of a dead piglet, also with blood on it. I kept approaching it, then stepping away, unsure of what to do and trying to process what the hell had happened during the thirty-six hours I'd been absent. Then, suddenly it hit me: Laura had been there. It was the only explanation. She'd been inside my bedroom, and not only was she mocking my dead wife but she was mocking my dead child, too. Furious, I held my breath and grabbed the stinking piglet using a tea towel, picked up my car keys, dropped the body into a recycling bin outside and made for my car.

Andy, the estate agent, was sitting in his office at his desk and facing the door when I stormed in, disturbing his quiet Saturday afternoon.

'All right, mate,' he began, 'how—'

But I wasn't interested in polite conversation.

'Who have you shown around the flat in the last two days?'

'Is something wrong?'

I raised my voice. '*Who*, Andy?'

His two female colleagues turned to stare at me. He nervously scrolled through his phone, checking his diary.

'A young couple with a baby, two gay lads and then some bird. Is everything all right?'

I really didn't want the woman to be Laura. Life would be so much easier if it wasn't her.

'What was her name?' I asked.

'Charlotte Smith. Same surname as you.'

Andy opened his mouth and began to say something else, but I was already out of the front door before I could hear a word.

My car's alloy wheels scraped against the kerb as I pulled up sharply outside Laura's house fifteen minutes later.

I threw open the car door, and a vehicle I hadn't spotted behind me jammed on its brakes and stopped just short of knocking me down. I didn't even turn to apologise as they blasted their horn at me. Instead, I ran across the road and up Laura's driveway. The window blinds were partially closed as always, but it didn't mean she wasn't in. I banged with both fists on the door and peered through the glass, but everything appeared dark inside despite it being daylight.

'Open this fucking door!' I yelled, then crouched to repeat my demand through the letterbox. 'I know what you did, you sick bitch!' There was no response. In all my life, I had never been angrier than I was in that moment.

My eyes scanned the front of the house to find a way through to the back, and I pulled on a gate but it was locked and too steep to climb. Suddenly, I had an idea. Laura's house backed on to playing fields. I'd played many a Sunday-league game there in the past. I ran along the street and into a cul-de-sac until I found an alleyway that took me to the grassy fields and then the rear of Laura's property.

The renovation work made it stand out from the others and easy to spot. It was larger from behind. A modern, double extension turned it into an L-shape and there were dormer windows where the roof sloped, suggesting they'd renovated the attic to create a third floor.

Behind low bushes and a waist-high wooden fence, I could see a trampoline with a torn, patchy net hanging from the side, on a knee-high lawn. Everything in her garden was overgrown and unkempt. It looked like it belonged to a different house. A gap in the hedgerow allowed me to clamber over the fence and into her garden.

I made my way towards the kitchen window first. No lights were on inside so I got up close to the tinted glass and peered in. The work surfaces and sink were clean and clutter-free. The cupboards were dark grey, and the walls close to black. I put my hand above my eyes to minimise the reflection and squinted, before realising the walls hadn't been painted like that; they looked like they'd been damaged by smoke. I stared into another window inside what looked like a pantry, and it was exactly the same. What had happened in there?

Puzzled, I headed for a set of bifold doors and looked inside. The dining room ceiling was also smoke-damaged, and in the living room, the television and furniture still appeared to have bubble wrap and price labels affixed to them . . .

'Shit!' I shouted.

My heart almost beat out of my chest when I saw Laura. She was perched on the edge of a sofa, watching me as she held a mobile phone at eye level. Then she gave me a wide smile before her face began to contort. It was scrunched up, and she placed her finger on the tip of her nose and pushed it upwards. I tried to make sense of what she was doing, but the woman was clearly insane.

She remained on the sofa and I could just about make out a noise coming from her. I edged closer to the glass until I was millimetres away from it. Finally, I realised what she was doing.

She was making the face and sound of a pig grunting.

Insane or sane, I no longer cared. All that mattered was finding an object heavy enough in her garden to smash my way through the doors. I was going to kill her.

CHAPTER SEVENTEEN

LAURA

I'd expected Ryan to appear at my house once he discovered who the last person was to view his flat.

Judging by his fiery expression and the way he was trying to break my windows, he hadn't appreciated the porcine present I'd left him inside his wardrobe.

First thing in the morning, Effie had removed the pig foetus from her science lab's freezer and passed it to me in my car outside the school. She didn't question why I wanted it or ask what was on the memory stick I pressed into the palm of her hand. I gave her strict instructions as to exactly what she must do with it.

Later, and alone in Ryan's bedroom, I'd swiftly removed the now semi-defrosted piglet and beaker of 'blood' I'd whipped up from water, sugar, red food-colouring and cocoa powder. I poured the contents onto Charlotte's wedding dress and the piglet, then quickly shut the door.

Of the many approaches I could have taken to antagonise Ryan, I knew this would cut straight to the core. I had to make him understand that whatever he was plotting next, from here on in, I would always be one step ahead of him. I didn't care how far I needed to go, how dirty I had to play or who I used to get there, he would never beat me.

I'd watched from behind the blinds as my scruffy nemesis, dressed in his running shoes, jeans and a Nirvana T-shirt, darted up the drive, searching for a way to gain entrance to my house. I predicted he'd try the rear next, and as I positioned myself in the living room, I poured myself a glass of Chianti, took out my phone and made myself comfortable on the sofa. I checked my text messages and was pleased Effie had confirmed a time and place to meet me tomorrow. Once again, I suggested she keep it from her father.

A few minutes later, when Ryan came into view across the playing fields, I switched the phone to video camera mode and turned the mic off. The bifold doors were locked tight and the slight tint would make it harder for him to see inside without getting up close.

When eventually he spotted me, I must have scared him because he jolted backwards, almost falling to the ground.

While anger had brought him to my home, it was pure rage that I needed. One more little push was all it would take. And while I know grunting like a pig was a little childish, it had the desired effect. The phone's mic was turned back on when he began making more threats.

'You fucking bitch!' he yelled. 'Open this door now!'

'Please, leave me alone!' I shouted back. I was sure to make my voice tremble and my camerawork shaky.

'Let me in!'

'Oh God, please just go away! I'm begging you!' I replied, and blew him a silent kiss. 'Whatever you think I've done, it wasn't me.'

'You're a liar!'

Again he banged his fists on the doors with all his strength, making the double layers of glass shudder in their frames. Then he turned to scan the garden as if trying to find something to break the glass with. Eventually he found the brick I used to wedge the garden gate open, drew it back over his shoulder and hurled it. The glass cracked. I backed away nervously as he repeated the action.

The doorbell sounded and I hurried out of the living room towards it.

'Thank God!' I sobbed and yanked it open. 'Please help me!'

Suddenly, the window in the other room shattered and I heard Ryan's footsteps pounding across the wooden floors. But as he turned the corner to find me, he was tackled to the ground by two burly police officers.

I'd dialled 999 the moment the cat jumped from the windowsill, alerting me that someone was approaching the drive. Bieber thought it was Tony but I knew it would be Ryan.

Ryan yelled more expletives as he was restrained. His arms were twisted behind his back and handcuffs clamped around his wrists.

'Thank you, thank you,' I repeated over and over again to the officers. 'I thought he was going to kill me.'

'You should be arresting her!' Ryan spat, squirming and clearly in pain. 'She killed my wife and now she's trying to ruin me!' But the police weren't listening. One read him his rights, while the other called for back-up on a radio.

'Sir, I need you to calm down,' the officer continued, his knee on the base of Ryan's spine, pinning him to the floor.

I shed my crocodile tears as Ryan was pulled to his feet and bundled out of my house, into a police car and driven away.

CHAPTER EIGHTEEN

RYAN

I was handed a transparent plastic bag containing my car keys, mobile phone, belt, some coins and my shoelaces, and asked to sign for them by the duty desk sergeant.

Johnny remained by my side until the paperwork was complete. I'd called him twice in the last two days – once to tell him I'd been arrested and needed a solicitor, and a second time to inform him I was being released on police bail. I begged him not to worry our mum and dad by telling them what I'd done. Judging by his heavy brow and refusal to make eye contact with me, he was furious. He wasn't alone. My enforced timeout made me as angry at myself as he was at me.

We left the grounds of the police station and I skulked several paces behind him as we made our way towards the pay-and-display car park across the road. It wasn't until we entered the car that I spoke.

'I'm ready. Let me have it, both barrels. Tell me what an idiot I am.'

Johnny said nothing. He removed his glasses and wiped them with the sleeve of his hoodie.

'Tell me I've fucked up,' I said. 'Tell me I've put my job at risk. Tell me I could get a criminal record. But just so long as you know, I'm aware of this already.'

'You smell,' he replied.

'So would you if you'd been wearing the same clothes for two days.'

'You told them what she did to you though, didn't you? Charlotte, the baby, stabbing you, the dead pig?'

He flew off the handle when I didn't reply.

'What? Ryan! You have to be kidding me. That was your chance to explain everything, you fucking dick! Otherwise you just look like some nutter who was terrorising her and broke into her house!'

'If I'd have dropped her in it, I'd have dropped myself in it too, about what I did to Effie and stalking her family. And I'm in enough trouble already.'

'Why didn't you give them tape recordings of her telling you how to kill yourself?'

'They're still with Janine, Laura's boss.'

'Well, why hasn't she done anything with them yet?'

'I don't know.' I was wondering the same thing myself, as I'd given them to her weeks earlier. Unless she had, of course, and that had sent Laura over the edge and into my flat. I had this awful feeling that she was really gunning for me now. 'I need you to do me a favour,' I asked.

'Another one?'

'I need you to pick up my car.'

'Why can't you do it yourself?'

'Because it's parked outside Laura's house and my police bail conditions won't allow me anywhere near her.'

'Why, of course – where else would it be other than outside the home of the woman who killed your wife and baby and who tried to murder you.'

'Please don't start, Johnny.'

'Oh, don't worry, I won't. I'm far from starting. I'm done, actually. I'm finished. I'll drive you back to the flat. I'll bring your car back, but then I don't want to see your stupid little face for a while.'

'Come on, that's not fair. I thought I'd drawn a line under this, too. I made amends with Effie and put her grades back up after you made me see what I'd done to her. As far as I was concerned, it was all over.'

'Until you turned up at Laura's house threatening to kill her.'

'I was angry and upset! What would you have done?'

'Called the police and let them handle her.'

'I told you, that's not an option.'

'Because you don't have the balls to man up and admit your part, you've made things a shitload worse for yourself.'

Johnny shook his head as we pulled up outside the flat.

'This has to be the end of it,' he added. 'No matter what she says or what she does from here on, you have to accept the consequences. As much as you hate it, Laura has won. The end. All you can do is hope she sees it that way too.'

CHAPTER NINETEEN

LAURA

Effie and I sat outside her head teacher Mr Atkinson's office, waiting to be called in.

The school secretary was photocopying papers in a room opposite us, and cursed under her breath when the machine jammed. Effie looked anxious and nibbled at the skin around her fingernails. She got that habit from me. I brushed her hand away from her mouth.

'Are you okay?' I asked.

She nodded, but I wasn't convinced. She needed a final pep talk.

'You know how proud of you I am, don't you?' She gave a slight smile. 'I'm so glad you've been able to trust me to help you. It's meant the world to me. We are doing the right thing, so please don't be worried. I'm right here by your side.'

The door to Mr Atkinson's office opened and he ushered us inside. I sat up straight and cleared my throat.

'I'll get straight to the point. One of your teachers has been making sexual advances towards my daughter.' I squeezed Effie's hand and she nodded. 'I'm not sure where to begin,' I continued, making myself sound like I was on the verge of tears. 'Effie's form tutor, Mr Smith, has been behaving inappropriately towards her and has launched a campaign of terror against me.'

'Mr Smith? Ryan Smith?' The poor fool looked utterly bemused.

'I assume the police have informed you he was arrested three days ago for breaking into our house?'

His eyebrows knotted and he shook his head. 'No, they haven't. As far as I was aware, he's been poorly with the flu.'

'I'm a volunteer for the charity End of the Line, and somehow Mr Smith has become convinced that our organisation played a role in the tragic death of his wife. It's quite ludicrous, of course, but it appears that for some reason he has singled me out for blame. And on Saturday he broke into our house and began hurling threats at me. I hate to think what would've happened had the police not arrived.'

'Well, Mrs Morris, um . . . I can't comment on this until I know the full facts—'

'These are the facts, Mr Atkinson,' I interrupted, and passed him my mobile phone so he could see the footage of a raging Ryan for himself. 'I thought he was going to kill me.' I blinked hard and dabbed at the corners of my eyes, as if tears were forming. 'When my daughter arrived home, she was so scared by what had happened that she told me Mr Smith had been behaving inappropriately towards her. She'd been too frightened to say anything before now.'

Mr Atkinson turned to Effie.

'I appreciate this must be difficult, but can you tell me a little about what happened?' He took a pen from a pot and began writing on a pad.

'He's been keeping me behind in class a lot,' Effie said, slowly and quietly.

'Speak up, darling,' I said. 'You're safe now.'

'He takes me into that office at the back of his class where nobody else can see us, and he talks to me like we're friends. It was nice at first. He really seemed to care about me.'

'Right,' said Mr Atkinson. 'He probably shouldn't have been alone with a pupil—'

'Then recently, when he gave me a lift home in his car, he told me he wanted to have sex with me and started rubbing his hand up and down my leg and touching himself. As he started to pull the zip down on his trousers, I managed to open the door and escape.'

I swelled with pride, a little surprised that she'd embellished the story so convincingly. She looked to me for approval and I nodded.

'And this happened in his car, you say?'

Effie nodded. 'I was terrified.' Now she was crying. They looked like real tears, too.

Mr Atkinson scratched his chin, as if trying to recall what to do to set in motion an investigation. He knew he had a duty of care to all his students, even one branded a troublemaker.

'This explains why Effie has been acting out in class,' I added. 'Her marks only started going downhill when Mr Smith returned to school. Look at her records and you'll see how the dates line up. It appears to me that Mr Smith has been – oh, I hate this word – "grooming" my daughter.'

'This is quite an accusation, Mrs Morris, which of course I will be taking seriously. Effie, do you have anything you can give me to back this up? Any eyewitnesses or any evidence at all?'

She nodded. Now it was her turn to remove her mobile phone from her pocket. She opened an app on the screen, and pressed play. A minute later the colour had drained from Mr Atkinson's face.

'Would it be possible get a copy of the recording . . . ?' he said.

I passed him a memory stick. 'I've put the sound file on here for you. So what do you intend to do about this? I wanted to come to you first rather than go to the police or local education authority.'

'No, no,' he replied quickly. 'You did the right thing.'

◆ ◆ ◆

Half an hour later, Effie and I were driving towards her father's house.

'Did I do okay, Mum?' she asked.

'You did brilliantly.'

'How much trouble will Mr Smith be in?'

'I won't lie to you. He'll probably lose his job.'

She paused for a moment to process the magnitude of her accusations. 'But he didn't actually touch me, like I told Mr Atkinson . . .'

'Darling, what Mr Smith did to you was just as bad as what he didn't do. He led you on, he brainwashed you and he left you humiliated, didn't he? He let you believe he was interested in you physically. He might not have said it, but the implication was certainly there. What if he'd gone further with the next girl he picked? What if he'd raped her? How would you feel knowing you could have prevented it if only you'd spoken up? We have bent the rules a little but sometimes that's what needs to be done for the sake of others. I don't expect you to understand just how serious Mr Smith's behaviour is, but when you get older, you'll look back and realise that we have done the right thing.'

'What you told Mr Atkinson about Mr Smith's wife and End of the Line . . . Was that true? Did you ever speak to her?'

'I speak to a lot of people, so possibly, yes. But quite why he singled me out, I don't know. He's also been harassing my manager for weeks now. I don't think you've ever met Janine, have you?'

Effie's eyes fixed on the road ahead. She didn't know whether to tell me Janine was her father's girlfriend or remain silent. For now, I let her off the hook.

'Well, Mr Smith has been bothering her too. She even met with him in the office to explain his wife's death was not our fault.'

I parked close to Effie's new house, but not so close as to be seen. I noted Janine's green Astra parked a little further down the road.

'Okay, well, why don't I talk to your dad in the next few days to see if I can take you and Alice out to Nando's one weekend?'

She nodded. ‘Mum,’ she asked hesitantly, ‘are you, you know, okay now?’

‘In what way?’

‘After Henry.’ She looked away, unsure whether to have brought up the subject.

‘Yes, I’m fine. And Henry’s doing very well. I know he’d love to see you again.’

‘Dad said we aren’t allowed.’

‘You are your mother’s daughter, Effie. When has not being allowed to do something ever stopped you?’

She grinned and gave me a peck on the cheek before leaving the car. When she turned around to wave, I felt my heart skip a beat. I had one child back. Now there were just two more and a husband to go.

CHAPTER TWENTY

RYAN

I locked my car and hitched up my trousers.

I hadn't put the weight back on that I'd lost after Charlotte's death, so my belt was cinched to the tightest hole. The stress of the past few days had nulled my appetite further. I caught my reflection in the car window and I looked drawn. I patted down a stray clump of hair sticking out from my crown that resembled an antenna.

Fake flu or no fake flu, Bruce Atkinson had left me several voicemail messages urging me to return to school for an important meeting as soon as possible. He must have been told about my arrest for threatening a pupil's parent. Whatever he was about to say wasn't going to be good.

I'd left messages for Janine. She had a smoking gun in her hands with my Dictaphone, and I still didn't know for sure if she'd put it to good use yet. If not, what was she waiting for?

I made my way into the school foyer and glanced at my watch. I was a little early but he was already waiting for me in the staffroom. The other teachers watched as he led me into his office, where Bruce's deputy Sadie Marks and Dave Proudlock from Human Resources sat. Both looked as uncomfortable as each other.

'I've asked Sadie and Dave to join us as witnesses,' Bruce began. 'I'll get straight to the point, Ryan. An accusation has been made by a parent and student about inappropriate behaviour.'

'Who?' I asked, but I already knew the answer. Laura had got to him, too.

'Effie Morris and her mother.'

'What have they told you?'

'They accuse you of behaving in an unprofessional manner towards Effie. Mrs Morris used the word "grooming".'

The bitch. So that was her game now – she was trying to brand me a paedophile. She wasn't going to tar me with that brush and get away with it.

'It's rubbish,' I replied. 'I've gone to great effort to try to help Effie and improve her grades, even using my own time to counsel her.'

'Behind closed doors in your office.'

'Yes, but—'

'But you know school rules discourage being alone with any pupil for precisely this reason.'

I nodded. 'But I can categorically say that I never behaved inappropriately with Effie, let alone "groomed" her.'

'Were you ever alone with her in your car?'

'My car? No, of course not.' I hoped my flushed cheeks wouldn't expose my lie.

A moment passed while Bruce looked me dead in the eye. He leaned over his desk and pressed a button on his keyboard. Suddenly I heard a recording of my own voice.

'*About what happened that afternoon. It was completely inappropriate and I want to apologise*,' I heard myself saying.

Shit. Effie had recorded our last conversation.

'*I shouldn't have given you a lift, I shouldn't have said the things I did and I – well, we both took things too far. I'm your teacher and I should have known better. I blame myself for giving you the wrong signals. I won't put either of us in that position again, I promise.'*

Oh shit. Oh shit, oh shit, oh shit.

'*Have you told anyone else?*' my recorded self asked.

'*No.*'

'*So we can keep it between ourselves?*'

There was an awkward gap before I spoke again. '*Have you noticed your grades have improved?*' I asked.

'*Is that your way of shutting me up, Mr Smith?*' Effie replied. '*Giving me better marks so I'll keep quiet about what you did?*'

My silence only added to my guilt.

'*Thought so. Can I go now?*'

My stomach felt as if it had dropped forty floors.

'No, no, no, this has all been taken out of context,' I said. 'This isn't what happened at all!' I looked at Sadie and Dave in the hope of gaining their support, but doubt was written across their faces.

'What were you apologising to her for?' Bruce asked.

'Effie thought I was attracted to her and she tried it on with me, but I turned her down.'

'Where was this?'

'In my car.'

'The car that you told me a few moments ago that she hadn't been inside?'

'Yes,' I muttered.

'I'm sorry to do this, Ryan, but I'm going to have to suspend you and ask you to leave the building with immediate effect.'

'But it's Effie's mum. She has a vendetta against me . . .'

'I note that you failed to tell me you were arrested for breaking into her house and threatening her life on Saturday.'

'If you can just let me explain what happened—'

'I'm sorry, but no. You can explain it to your union representative when I launch an investigation.'

Bruce escorted me through the building and into the car park. I felt many eyes watching me as the children entered the school at the first bell of the morning, wondering what was happening.

'You are forbidden to set foot in the school grounds or school buildings until this matter has been resolved,' Bruce advised quietly. 'I ask that you don't contact me, or any of your colleagues, pupils or their parents. And I suggest you get in touch with your union at the earliest opportunity.'

I remained rooted to the ground, unsure of which way to turn. I opened my mouth to try to defend myself one last time, but I wasn't an entirely innocent party. I had led Effie on, and while I didn't groom her sexually, I had groomed her nonetheless.

'Could you please leave now, Ryan?' Bruce added. 'Let's not make this any worse than it is.'

I climbed into my car, slipped the keys into the ignition and drove away, utterly humiliated. Laura was destroying me and I had no idea how to stop her.

CHAPTER TWENTY-ONE

LAURA

I followed Janine's green Astra from End of the Line's offices into a familiar car park.

She remained seated and held a phone to her ear. Tony eventually appeared from his building and joined her. My stomach did somersaults when, once inside the car, they gave each other lingering kisses. I wanted to run over to them, open the door and drag Janine out by her cheap hair extensions, my fists pummelling that stupid, ugly face of hers. But now wasn't the time to act on impulse. I had a plan I was working towards, and beating her half to death in front of my husband wasn't part of it.

I trailed them as they picked up Effie and Alice from Tony's house, then they drove half an hour to a multiplex cinema in Milton Keynes. There were two similar cinemas in Northampton to choose from, but I assumed they didn't want to be seen by anyone they knew. They were quite content playing happy families, just as long as it was covertly.

I watched from outside as Janine bought the tickets, a family-sized bucket of popcorn, family-sized fizzy drinks and family-sized nachos and cheese. I followed them inside, and from the shadows of a seat fifteen rows behind them, I spent a couple of hours watching them behaving like every other family. They threw their heads back and laughed along to the comedy, and shared their drinks and snacks. But my anger soon made way for resolve. I hoped Janine was making the most of this moment, because it wasn't going to last. Once Tony remembered the woman he'd fallen in love with all those years ago, he'd be on his knees begging me to take him back. I was the girl he loved, not the one he'd read about in my records.

It had been my own fault. I'd removed the lid from Pandora's box. It had all come to a head one day when Tony accused me of not loving the girls. He claimed I devoted all my time to Henry, while his sisters' emotional needs were neglected. Some of what he said was correct, but that was his fault. I'd close my eyes and listen to the close relationship he'd formed with the girls, and there was no room for me. He was doing the same thing to me that my father had done with my sisters – and they'd both left me out in the cold. That made me want to push Effie and Alice further away, or risk being hurt by them like I'd been hurt by my family as a girl.

Our row had been brewing for days; I could smell it in the air like the coming of a storm. Ever since we'd moved into that house and work had commenced renovating it, it had taken over our lives. Everything was always covered in dust or smelling like fresh plaster, and there were workmen constantly traipsing around, speaking in foreign languages. I could see no end to it and I began to hate that place. If we'd stayed in our last home, everything would have been all right.

'Are you even capable of love?' Tony spat out the words as if they were contaminated.

'Of course I am!' I replied. 'I love every one of you equally.'

'Sometimes I look at you when you're with the girls and I don't see anything in your eyes. It's like they aren't even in the same room as you. I think what happened to you as a kid has broken you.'

'Why are you being so cruel?'

'I'm just trying to work out in my head what the hell is going on in yours. I don't even know if *you* know how your mind operates.'

During my first year in foster care, social workers didn't know what to do with me. I'd been appointed therapists who'd tried to break through my shell, but none succeeded. My brain had been prodded and poked at, but nobody had thought to inform me if there was anything wrong with me or offered me treatment. Then, much later, after Nate killed Sylvia while trying to protect me, there'd been no effort to find me another foster carer or family. I'd been downgraded from damaged goods to unsellable. Group children's homes were the best it would get.

Tony's accusations tapped into a long-standing fear that there *was* something very wrong inside me, something deep-rooted that prevented me from loving my daughters as a mother was supposed to. So I made the decision to apply to view my records.

As I'd been in social services care, now, as an adult and through a subject access request, I could obtain a copy of my personal data and they couldn't lawfully deny me access to it. Eight weeks passed before it arrived by post. I waited nervously until after I'd taken the girls to school before I braced myself and tore open the envelope.

To my dismay, I discovered everything written about me was lies. The accusations were horrific in part, and words like 'cold', 'unresponsive', 'lack of empathy' and 'impulsive nature' jumped from the pages. One social worker even suggested I might have been a suicide risk, as my lack of involvement with anyone could mean I didn't value my life. The truth was far from it.

But it was one statement, written shortly before my fourteenth birthday, that left me speechless.

> *Repeated evaluations have failed to determine just one personality disorder in Laura. She has shown traits of Narcissistic Personality Disorder and Self-Deception, amongst*

others. She has a desire to get her own way and is overtly charming but can be covertly hostile towards others. One foster carer noted that she liked to dominate and humiliate an older boy in the same house by making fun of his lack of intellect. Another carer witnessed her stamping on and breaking the leg of the family dog, but Laura refused to accept responsibility. She often appears to believe her own lies and rewrites events in her head so that she becomes a victim. She has repeatedly displayed sociopathic tendencies and we strongly suggest she is not homed with other foster sisters and brothers.

I let the pages rest on my lap and closed my eyes. How could anyone have written something so awful about a little girl? Why had a child who had been through an emotional trauma like mine been branded a 'sociopath'? What chance had I stood at being adopted when I'd been affixed such labels? How many potential families had rejected me because of those words?

Of course every child makes mistakes, but as I became older, I'd learned to mask certain urges – I learned to fit in, I learned to be like everybody else. I rebuilt myself by watching other people's behaviour. Those descriptions weren't an accurate representation of who I was or who I had become.

I knew I could never allow Tony to read my file, so I hid it away in the utility room behind the tumble dryer, next to my cigarettes. But in the weeks that followed, I'd return to it and reread it, torturing myself over and over again until I knew every word off by heart.

Now I was torturing myself again by watching the silhouettes of Janine, Tony and the girls in the cinema. I quietly slipped out of the darkened auditorium and back into the car park. I made for Janine's green Astra, removed my car keys from my bag, and once I was sure there were no CCTV cameras pointed at me, I carved the word 'cunt' into the driver's door.

CHAPTER TWENTY-TWO

RYAN

'I swear to God I am being framed,' I began. 'Please believe me. This woman wants to destroy me.'

'Why don't you just take a moment to compose yourself?' she replied. She slid a box of tissues towards me from her side of the desk.

I wiped my eyes. I'd done nothing but cry since being suspended from my job. Johnny had washed his hands of me and wasn't returning my calls, and Effie's accusations weren't something I could talk to my parents about. I felt completely alone. My solicitor, Tracy Fenton, was on my side, but only because I was paying her to be. She was a masculine-looking woman with greying cropped hair, no make-up, and glasses that hung from a silver chain around her neck. She didn't give me any indication of whether she believed me or not. But she had a job to do and that job was to help me, regardless of my innocence or guilt.

After speaking to my teaching union rep, I'd made an appointment to see her the day after my suspension and explained to her my side of the story from start to finish, omitting nothing. She'd also just received a police update.

'Images of a sexual nature have been found on the hard drive of your school computer, Ryan,' she began. She opened a binder containing photocopied papers.

'What do you mean by "sexual nature"?' I asked, my voice close to breaking again.

'One folder has been found containing one hundred and fifteen images of young females, all wearing school uniforms and in various states of undress.'

I closed my eyes and shook my head. 'How "young" are they?'

'They haven't told us that yet.'

'They're going to look about Effie's age, I just know it. I'm ruined.'

I broke into a sudden sweat. I thought I was going to pass out, so I loosened my tie, undid two buttons on my shirt and moved towards the open window. I hoped the breeze might cool me down.

Tracy flicked through a handful of pages. 'Mrs Morris has made a statement to the police about the break-in but, as far as I'm aware, the police have yet to interview Effie about her allegations. If you are denying all knowledge of these images, then it's likely they were downloaded elsewhere and transferred onto your computer, via something like a disk or a memory stick. The officer I spoke to off the record said they weren't hidden well, in among a folder containing some Word documents, which would suggest they'd been moved there in a hurry. Once I can get a time and date stamp from the files to show when they were created, you and I will need to work out where you were, so that you can provide an alibi. Do other staff members use that computer?'

'Yes, a few.'

'Then although it's in your office, the police need to convince the Crown Prosecution Service that it could only be you who downloaded them, before the CPS makes a decision on whether you're charged and what with.'

'And if I don't have an alibi?'

'We'll cross that bridge if we come to it.'

'And when will that be? I want this sorted out as soon as possible.'

'It could be weeks or even months, Ryan. That's how long these things take.'

'So I'll have this hanging over my head until then?'

'I'm afraid so.'

'I'll never be able to go back to that school, will I?'

Tracy removed her glasses, allowing them to dangle. 'Probably not, no. Should the school and local education authority believe Effie, you will be barred from the National College of Teaching. If Effie makes a statement to the police and it ends up in court and you are found guilty, you'll be put on a sex offenders register. But this is all the worst-case scenario.'

I returned to my chair and held my head in my hands. I shut my eyes tightly. How had I got myself into such a mess? I thought of Charlotte and our baby, and how Daniel would most likely be taking his first steps by now and trying to speak his first few words. The three of us would have been our own little unit, making a life for ourselves in our house. I longed so much for something that had been denied the chance to happen.

'What can I do to help prove my innocence?'

'Nothing, absolutely nothing. Just wait until you hear from me again.'

'I can't just sit around and hope things sort themselves out.'

'That's exactly what you have to do,' Tracy replied firmly. 'I implore you, Ryan. Leave this for me to deal with.'

Only I knew I couldn't.

CHAPTER TWENTY-THREE

LAURA

I once read that if you tell yourself the same thing over and over again, eventually you'll forget where the truth ends and the fantasy begins.

Sometimes when I thought about Nate, I'd close my eyes and picture an alternative world in which he'd returned to his home town of Birmingham. There, in his familiar surroundings, I imagined him starting his life afresh. He'd voluntarily enter into an alcohol detox clinic, like the ones I'd begged him to go to, and then find himself a halfway house to get back on his feet.

I'd help him find some volunteer work in a non-pressured environment. And perhaps eventually he'd find a part-time paid job. He might also meet someone to fall in love with and have an anchor of his very own.

That's what I wanted to believe – not that he was lying in the room next to me, his dead body being prepared for me to view.

According to the police, none of his fellow homeless friends had seen him around in a long, long time. My determination to finish off Ryan meant I'd left very little time for anyone else in my life. I'd neglected Nate, and the guilt of that weighed heavy on my shoulders.

Only now did I realise that Nate had appointed me as his anchor. It's why he'd returned to Northampton from prison, because I'd been here. Through everything he'd suffered as a teenager to his time behind bars and beyond, I had prevented him from being washed away by the tide. Ironically, he'd died in the water, and it was my fault for casting him adrift these last few months.

It turned out Nate's body had not been very far away from me; he'd been tangled up in reeds in the River Nene, waiting for a canal boat's hull to knock against him just hard enough to dislodge him and float him to the algae-covered surface.

He was only identifiable through his DNA, which had been matched to his criminal record. I was his listed emergency contact.

'I still want to see his body,' I told the police officer assigned to his case.

'Like I said on the phone, I don't think that's a good idea, Mrs Morris, because of the time he has spent in the water. He has been what is known as "partially skeletonised" . . .'

'I don't care if it haunts me for the rest of my life. I owe him this.'

Eventually she agreed, and I was led into a small side room to gather myself until the mortuary manager had finished preparing Nate in the body-storage area. I was led into a viewing room and it struck me that it was nothing like the hi-tech, super-modern places you see on television programmes. There were no corpses stored in filing-cabinet-like fridges or neon-lit metal drawers. It was just a plain, inoffensive room with no personality, no special features and no religious artefacts. At its centre, Nate lay under a dark-blue sheet on a wooden trolley. A solitary chair was placed next to it, in case it all became too much for me and I needed to sit, I assumed.

The police officer and mortuary manager remained with me and, at my insistence, the sheet was slowly folded backwards until it reached

Nate's shoulders. There were wisps of hair but no eyes, no lips and barely any facial features left. I'd assumed he'd been picked apart by fish, water rats and bacteria. All that remained were patches of thin flesh and bone.

'How long had he been in the water?' I asked the officer.

'We won't know until the post-mortem results are released, but our best guess is around a year.'

'No, that's not possible,' I replied, and shook my head. 'I was with him five, maybe six months ago, so it definitely hasn't been as long as that.'

'Not according to the coroner's preliminary findings.'

'Could his body have been preserved, perhaps, depending on where in the Nene it was found?'

'The Nene? Who told you he was found there?'

'You did when you called me to say his body had floated to the river's surface.'

The police officer looked at me with a puzzled expression. 'I think there might be some confusion here, Mrs Morris. Your friend's body was found washed up in a cove by the beach in East Sussex.'

CHAPTER TWENTY-FOUR

RYAN

The air inside the leisure centre was humid and smelled of beer and sweat, despite several sets of double doors being propped open.

The packed crowd was made up almost entirely of men cheering, groaning or hurling foul language towards two boxers standing in the centre of the ring, waiting for a man in a short-sleeved white shirt and black bow tie to make his decision.

The white-collar fights had consisted of three two-minute rounds, and were every bit as brutal as professional ones I'd watched on television. It was beyond me how the fighter in the red shorts, vest and headguard had managed to remain on his feet during the continued onslaught from his blue opponent.

Finally, the referee held up the arm of the man in blue shorts as the winner. Tattoos ran the length of the champion's arm, but despite his bloody nose and the perspiration dripping down his face, Tony Morris was still instantly recognisable. A cheer went up when it was announced he'd won his bout. He embraced his opponent, and a pal in the audience helped remove his gloves before he made his way to the changing rooms.

I hovered in the background until he re-emerged wearing casual tracksuit bottoms and a T-shirt. He gravitated towards the bar and sank several vodka and Red Bulls in quick succession before I approached him. I took a deep breath and hoped to God my instinct was right, and that he didn't have any idea what his estranged wife and daughter were up to behind his back. I reasoned that if he had been told, he'd have accompanied them when they'd turned up at Bruce Atkinson's office to accuse me of being a child molester.

'Mr Morris.'

'Yes?' He gave me a polite smile for a second as he tried to place me. He wasn't quite drunk yet, but he wasn't far from it either. 'Mr Smith?' When he smiled, I knew he was in the dark as to the accusations against me.

'Please, call me Ryan. I didn't know you were a boxer.'

'I didn't know you were a fan.'

I hadn't been until that afternoon, when I'd called him at work to be told by his secretary he'd left early as he had a fight that evening. I was glad. I'd rather meet with him in public, where there was less of a chance he'd try to kill me if he knew what his wife and daughter had said I'd done.

'I'm pretty new to the sport,' I replied.

'Think you might fancy having a go at it yourself? We get people from all walks of life here: bankers, solicitors, council workers, even teachers.'

'I think I'd be flat on my back after the first punch. Can I get you a drink?'

'Sure,' he replied, and I ordered us two vodkas. We made conversation for a little longer about why he'd taken up the sport and his IT business, and I quietly hoped he'd bring up Effie and lead me into why I was really there. When he didn't, I knew I'd have to steer the conversation.

'This is a bit awkward, Tony, but I need to talk to you about something.'

'Is everything all right with Effie?'

'Actually, it's about your wife, Laura.'

'My wife?' I'd caught him off guard and he took a step back. 'What has she done?'

His question surprised me. He didn't ask 'what's wrong?' or 'what's happened?' but 'what has she done?', suggesting this wasn't the first time Laura had given him cause for concern. I took a breath and tried to explain it without sounding as if I was the mad one, rather than her.

'While volunteering at End of the Line, I believe Laura talked my wife into committing suicide.'

Tony did not seem surprised. He downed the rest of his drink and picked up his gym bag.

'I don't want any part of this,' he replied, and made his way to the exit, clearly flustered but not outraged. He didn't try to convince me I was being ridiculous and he didn't stare at me as if I were an idiot. He knew that what I'd said was entirely plausible – he just didn't want to face it.

I followed him outside into the car park. 'I just need a few minutes of your time,' I said. 'I don't mean to offend you, but something isn't right with your wife and I need your help to understand what her motives are.'

He stopped and turned. 'Look,' he said, 'I don't know what goes on in Laura's head any more than you do. We've been separated coming up for two years and we don't live together. My daughters live with me. And it's important I make sure their lives are stress-free. That includes keeping them away from Laura and anything she might have done.'

How had I not worked this out from the time I'd spent parked outside Laura's home? It explained why Tony's car was rarely on the driveway, and the animosity between them as they sat together in Bruce's office.

'Please, Tony,' I begged, 'you're the only one who can help me.'

Tony paused and narrowed his eyes as he mulled over my request, then something in him relented. He gave a deep sigh. 'What do you want to know?'

I told him how I'd discovered what Laura had encouraged Charlotte to do. But, as with Janine, I omitted to mention anything about how I'd manipulated his daughter or my house confrontation with his wife. Even in the pale beam from the overhead light, I saw the colour draining from his face.

'Why would Laura want a caller to die?' I asked.

Tony looked at me. 'She is a very complicated woman,' he said, 'with many demons. She has a fixation with death. I can only assume it has extended to trying to assist people to reach that goal. She told me she wanted to volunteer at End of the Line to help others. I had no reason to disbelieve her.'

'And now, after what I've told you?'

He shook his head. He didn't need to vocalise what he was thinking.

'There's more to this,' I continued hesitantly. 'Laura had me arrested recently and is making horrible, career-ending allegations against me. So I need to know exactly who I'm up against.'

'What happened?'

'I stood up for myself, fought back against her.'

Tony shook his head and rubbed the cool night air into his face. He looked as if he was debating whether to tell me what he knew or remain silent. When his eyes returned to mine, he spoke. 'If you knew what she'd done in her past,' he said, 'then you'd be afraid of her too.'

'What could be any worse than talking people into killing themselves?'

Tony looked at me as if he wanted me to work it out for myself.

'Unless,' I continued, 'she's killed someone herself.'

'No, Laura never gets her hands dirty. She manipulates others into doing what she wants them to do.' The alcohol had begun to loosen Tony's lips, and he steadied himself with his hand against the roof of a car. 'I assumed it stemmed from losing her parents when she was a kid and having to stick up for herself when she was put in care.'

He continued by explaining that Laura's father had used her to help him kill himself and her sisters. It went a long way to explaining her obsession with death.

'Three years ago, while we were redeveloping our house, our marriage was going through a rough patch,' he said. 'One afternoon, the tumble dryer stopped working, and wedged behind it I found an envelope Laura had hidden. Inside was a long, detailed psychiatric report about her time in the care of social services. She'd been found a foster home with a woman called Sylvia and her son. Apparently dozens of kids had been in her care over the years and she'd even won a CBE or some such honour for it. Sylvia's boy was a couple of years older than Laura but had some learning difficulties. He was fascinated by her and followed her around like a puppy, doing everything she told him to do, like shoplifting and fighting other kids at school. Sylvia kept Laura there for as long as she could, but she had to put her lad's well-being first and Laura was by all accounts a terrible influence. But when social services arrived to take Laura away, she'd wound Sylvia's son up so much that he attacked his mum. He punched her and pushed her so hard that she fell, hit her head. Died instantly. He was sent to a young offenders institute and then an adult prison. Laura got away with it.'

'Did you tell her what you knew?'

Tony nodded. 'She denied it all. She claimed the report was falsified to hide the local authority's own failings and I really think that's what she believes. You need to know that my wife doesn't recognise her own lies. The psychologists wrote that she rewrites episodes from her history and her recent past if they don't suit her. She will always be the victim, never the guilty one. And she rearranges timelines and locations.

Events that happened weeks ago she'll think happened yesterday, and somewhere completely different.'

'So when you learned all this about her, that's when you left with your children?'

'No, and that's the biggest regret of my life.'

'Why?'

'Because Henry might still be the normal little boy he was when he was born.'

I looked at him and waited for more, but he shook his head and brought our conversation to a close.

'This will be the last time that you and I talk, Mr Smith,' he said, and walked towards a red Audi.

'Can I ask you one last thing?' I said. 'When I first started phoning her at End of the Line, she called me David. Do you know why?'

'That was Sylvia's son,' Tony replied as he clambered into his car, choosing to drink and drive over facing any more questions from me. 'When he came out of prison, he lived rough in Northampton. Laura brought him to the house a few times to clean him up – maybe she'd developed a conscience about what she'd done to him, or perhaps she'd changed their history to something that suited her better. David Nathan, but she called him by his nickname, Nate.'

CHAPTER TWENTY-FIVE

LAURA

Janine eyed me sceptically when I removed two raspberry and white chocolate muffins from a Tupperware box and left them on a plate on her desk.

'They're gluten-free.' I smiled. 'I made them last night.' The first part I was lying about, the second part I wasn't. For once I had baked them myself. 'It seems a shame everyone gets to enjoy my baking but you. Sorry, but I ran out of paper cases.'

'Thank you,' she said and I turned to leave her office, but not before 'accidentally' kicking her vulgar orange handbag.

'Oops,' I said, and smiled as I bent down to straighten it up. She was too engrossed in her muffin to notice me removing her iPad.

Back at my desk, I checked my mobile phone to see if the police had been in touch regarding Ryan's break-in. It'd been six days now and still they hadn't updated me. Likewise, there'd been no contact from Effie's head teacher. What the hell was going on with these people? I didn't want the accusation of Ryan trying to molest Effie to go as far as a court case, because she was not as strong as me – she'd crumble under questioning. I just wanted that accusation and the pornography found on his work computer to be enough to make it impossible for him to return to his post.

They'd eventually learn the images had been placed there by a third party. I'd spent hours trawling the Internet searching for pictures of teenage girls in various states of undress involving school uniforms to show Ryan had a fetish for them. It was impossible to tell if they were underage and it didn't matter – it would add to the mounting pressure I was piling upon him. I'd moved the images to a memory stick and given it to Effie. She'd spent so much time in Ryan's office that she'd seen him input his password into his computer. It didn't take much effort for her to log on, transfer my folder of pictures into his files and leave.

I'd already got what I wanted when Ryan was suspended, but the longer the school and the police took to investigate, the more time they were giving him to plan his next move. I wanted to push him as quickly as possible into whatever he'd do next without thinking it out properly. Then he'd make even bigger mistakes and I could crush him once and for all. And, of course, there would be a next move, because that's what I would do. He and I were a lot more alike than he would care to admit – constantly striving to stay one step ahead of each other.

I took my landline off the hook so I wouldn't be disturbed, put my mobile phone on my lap where nobody could see and went into my media files. It was time to see how far I could go before Ryan cracked. When I had finished, I swapped the phone for Janine's iPad and set to work using it against her.

I watched from my booth as she flicked through the office diary and saw a drop-in caller booked fifteen minutes after my shift finished. I'd asked Mary if she wouldn't mind adding it, as the caller had asked for Janine by name.

'Ryan Smith,' I told her.

'Okily dokily,' Mary had replied chirpily. 'I'll be Big Brother and make sure the cameras are on.'

'Oh, you needn't bother,' I replied. 'I think they're old friends.'

Janine's greed was satisfyingly predictable, and I smiled to myself when she couldn't resist tucking into the second muffin.

Once I'd begun answering calls again, I slipped into autopilot with my responses and questions, all the time keeping an eye on the clock and willing my shift to end. Then I waved goodbye to the other volunteers, grabbed my coat and bag, and made my way downstairs.

When the door to the drop-in office opened a few minutes later, Janine was surprised to find me sitting there, waiting for her.

'Take a seat,' I began. 'I think you and I need to have a long-overdue conversation.'

CHAPTER TWENTY-SIX

RYAN

I had nowhere to go, no friends or family to talk to about the mess I was in, and no way to resolve any of it. From the moment Charlotte threw herself from that clifftop, my life was no longer mine to control.

Alcohol gave me the strength I needed to open the door to the nursery in the flat for the first time since Charlotte and Daniel's deaths. There was a gossamer-thin layer of dust on everything from the changing table to the veneer flooring. I looked up to the ceiling and noticed the missing battery cover from the animal mobile. I'd left it open to remind me to buy batteries the next time I passed a supermarket. By the time I remembered, my family was dead and the mobile never moved. The animal theme continued across a row of cushions scattered on a sofa-bed, emblazoned with textured cartoon giraffes and elephants that would never feel my son's ten tiny fingertips.

I closed the door and took myself to my bedroom. I'd been drinking on an empty stomach, so it hadn't taken much to get me drunk. But now I was tired, so I crawled, fully clothed, under the duvet. I couldn't stop thinking about what Tony had told me about Laura. From the beginning, I hadn't stood a chance against her. She was a survivor who had years more experience of manipulating others and getting away with it than I had. Even her own husband was convinced she had a psychological disorder. She was impossible to predict or outwit.

My biggest mistake had been using Effie to get to her. If I'd just remained in the shadows and called it quits after she'd fled the house, I'd have been okay. Instead, I'd unleashed a whole new vitriolic side to her.

I closed my eyes. I couldn't have slept for long, as it was still light outside when a banging on my front door woke me up, and what sounded like my dad's muffled voice.

I heard the key turn and he entered the hall. I climbed out of bed too fast and my head spun. He was with Mum; she was crying, and immediately I knew they'd learned of my arrest. My heart sank.

'Why haven't you been answering your phone?' Dad demanded. I looked at it – the display was black; the battery must have died.

Mum thrust her iPad into my chest.

'Open it,' she ordered. 'Look at my Facebook page.'

'How long have you had a—'

'Just open it!'

I scanned her timeline and immediately wanted to crawl under a rock and die. Message after message referring to her son as a paedophile and demanding that I should be fired from school or castrated. I felt dizzy and steadied myself against the wall. Dad grabbed the device and swiped through pages from school-related Facebook groups, created by parents to discuss issues that affected their children in different Years.

'Years Seven, Eight, Nine . . . right up to Year Thirteen,' Dad continued, 'all talking about how you've been suspended for molesting a girl and terrorising her mother.'

At the top of each page, and in a post made from an account with no picture but using the name Charlotte Smith, was a photograph of me, an audio file of the recording Effie had made and video footage of me trying to break into Laura's house. I wanted to be sick.

'Mum, this is not what it looks like . . .' I began, but she gave me a look that told me that whatever I had to say wouldn't exonerate me from what she'd read, heard and watched.

'Where's Johnny? He can back me up and tell you this isn't true. Well, not all of it, not in the way they're saying it is. I'm not a child molester. I promise you.'

'Is that your voice on the recording?' Dad asked.

'Yes, but—'

'And who's the girl?'

'Effie Morris, one of my students.'

'And who is that woman whose house you broke into?'

'It's the girl's mother, but she has it in for me. She killed Charlotte.'

'What are you talking about? Charlotte killed herself.'

'Look, I know I'm not making any sense, but it's a long story . . .'

'She's a fourteen-year-old girl, what the hell were you thinking?' Dad asked.

'I didn't touch her!' I yelled in frustration.

'Then what was she doing alone in a car with you? You say you gave her lifts home! I'm not a teacher and even I know that's wrong. And why the hell were you trying to break into someone's house?'

'You're not fucking listening to me!' The speed at which I flew off the handle took even me by surprise. 'You're as bad as everyone on Facebook, believing those lies! You're not letting me give my side of the story.'

'You've had some kind of breakdown,' Mum continued, tears streaming down her face. 'The stress of what happened with Charlotte, you're not dealing with it properly. You've been confused. And those things aren't helping.' She pointed towards a fresh six-pack of lager. 'We can get you help.'

'No, no, no,' I said. The room began swimming faster and faster and the walls and ceiling were closing in on me. I had to get out of there and away from their noise.

I grabbed my car keys from the bedside cabinet and pushed past Mum. However, my shoulder caught hers and knocked her off balance, sending her spinning into the wall and then the floor.

'Shit, I'm sorry,' I said and went to help her up. Dad retaliated by shoving me out of her reach and raising his fist towards me. We remained in stalemate for a moment, before he thought better of it. Instead, he bent down to help Mum up.

There was nothing else I could say or do to pacify them, so I left the flat and staggered towards the car.

I no longer had any choice in what to do next. I knew I had to go and see the only person who could bring an end to all of this, and beg the woman who killed my wife and baby to show me mercy.

CHAPTER TWENTY-SEVEN

LAURA

'I assume you weren't expecting to find me here?' I said.

Janine hovered by the door, debating whether to leave, or stay and face the music. She hesitated, before curiosity got the better of her.

'No, I wasn't,' she replied.

'Take a seat.'

She didn't move. 'I don't answer to you, Laura.'

'But you want to know why I've gone to the trouble of getting you here though, don't you?'

'If it was you who put Ryan Smith's name in my diary, then I'm quite sure I can guess why. You've learned that he and I have met, and now you want to convince me that he's some kind of fantasist who has an obsession with you. Does that about cover it?'

'And what would you say if I said yes?'

'I'd tell you that when he first called asking to see me and gave a brief outline of why, I did think that he was just a troubled soul. Then

I'd tell you that I did a little background research and discovered he was a teacher.'

'Did he mention that he's also taught my daughter Effie?'

'No.'

'Or that he spent months grooming her before making sexual advances towards her? She's fourteen years old. He's currently suspended, pending investigation.'

'No, he didn't. But then I only have your word for that, don't I? And you are hardly the epitome of honesty, are you?'

Janine sank her shapeless frame into the sofa opposite mine, crossed her legs and folded her arms.

'Your body language is quite hostile,' I continued.

'Let's just say that you don't bring out the best in me.'

I leaned forward. 'And why is that?'

'I'm not like the others upstairs who think the sun shines out of your backside. They only like to see the good in people, but I can see what they can't. I'm not blind to how you operate; I've watched you manipulate people with your Mary Poppins act. You can float into the office on an umbrella with your store-bought cakes and the clothes you pretend you've repaired. And you can impersonate a wonderful, devoted-to-her-family mum as much as you like, but I can see through you.'

'I've never claimed to be perfect.'

'You've never tried to dispel the myth either.'

'You made a judgement about me without knowing me. From the day you started, you disliked me.'

'And I was right to, wasn't I? I'm a good judge of character and I've met plenty of people like you over the years. You convince everyone that you're on their side but it's all for show, it's all to hide who you really are.'

'Who am I then? Enlighten me.'

'You're someone who gets her kicks from encouraging vulnerable people to die.' When no expression crossed my face, she continued. 'Ryan was right about what you did to his wife, wasn't he? And she wasn't the first. That's why this branch's suicide statistics are higher than any others, because you are actively encouraging it.'

My eyes flicked towards the security cameras. Their green lights didn't flash, indicating they weren't recording.

Finally, I gave her a condescending smile. 'There is one thing that I like about you, Janine – and believe me, it's only one thing – your self-belief. You really think everything that comes out of your own mouth is the gospel truth.'

'When it comes to you, yes, I do.'

'And just so it's clear, your perception of me has nothing to do with the fact that you're screwing my husband?'

Janine's calm composure faltered ever so slightly before she quickly regained it. 'So it *was* you, then . . . The word scratched into my car door. I told Tony that it was your doing, but he was adamant you didn't know about us.'

I was happy to hear my husband still saw the good in me.

'You try to put me down and make these horrible accusations, when all you really want to do is push me out of End of the Line so you don't have to see my face every day and feel guilty for what you've done to my marriage. You're a homewrecker.'

'I've done nothing wrong, so I don't feel guilty about anything. Tony and me got together long after he walked out on your madness.'

'But you set your sights on him before that, didn't you? I saw your hopeless attempts to flirt with him at Mary's sixtieth birthday dinner.'

'Only they weren't hopeless, were they?' She gave me a sly smile.

'And I suppose you think you know me after everything my husband has told you about me?'

'He's said very little, actually.'

'Do you expect me to believe that?'

'I don't care what you believe. But for some reason, probably only because you're the mother of his children, he still feels a sense of loyalty towards you.'

I was pleased to hear Tony kept secrets from Janine, and I knew just why he hadn't told her about my personal business. Four years earlier, he'd coerced me into 'borrowing' £25,000 of End of the Line's charitable donations to help him when he set up his IT business. I still had the bank account numbers of where the payments had really gone. They were so cleverly squirrelled away that even the charity's auditors had no clue that money meant for them had been directed elsewhere.

Even if it meant dropping myself in it, I'd have gone to the police with them had Tony not allowed me to see Effie the day we met with the head teacher. And, as you don't keep secrets from the one you love, clearly Tony didn't love Janine.

'Did he tell you we spent the night together recently?' I said. 'Several nights, actually.'

'When?'

'After I was attacked.'

'That's right, your "attack".' She used her fingers to mime speech marks. 'Did they ever catch the person responsible?'

I didn't reply.

'I thought not,' she said. 'Funny, that. And Tony was at great pains to point out that he spent the first night on the armchair in your room and the next couple in the spare bedroom.'

'Is that what he told you?'

'It's what I saw. I came to your house when you were asleep to drop a change of clothes off to him the night of your "attack". I love how you've kept the smoke-damaged walls. It's very shabby-chic.' She let out a yawn that seemed to take her by surprise.

She had violated my space. She had been in my house.

I swallowed hard to keep my anger at arm's length.

'No one here likes you,' I said, 'so when I tell them what you've accused me of, they'll all be on my side. And then I'll go to head office and tell them their biggest fundraiser and treasurer is being bullied out of her job by her husband-stealing manager.'

'Go ahead, Laura, be my guest,' she replied, and reached into her ugly orange handbag to remove Ryan's Dictaphone. 'I'd love to know what they'll say when I play this to them.'

CHAPTER TWENTY-EIGHT

RYAN

There was no reply when I knocked on Laura's front door.

The last time I'd been here, I'd not been in control of myself. Her leaving a dead piglet by Charlotte's wedding dress had pushed me over the edge, which is exactly what she'd wanted. Even after all Tony had told me about her, my only hope was that somewhere inside Laura was a scrap of decency I could appeal to.

I knew that by turning up at her home I was breaking my restraining order and risked being arrested again, but that's how desperate I was. She'd left me with no other choice.

I crouched to talk through the letterbox.

'Laura, please answer the door,' I begged. 'I'm not here to cause trouble. I just need to speak to you.' But there was no response. I surveyed each window, but no shadows moved behind them. 'I'll do anything,' I continued. 'Just please withdraw those allegations against me. You've won. I don't have any fight left in me.'

I sank to my knees, then curled up in a ball on the doormat and wept.

Eventually, I clambered back inside the car, found the business card Janine had given me as I'd left our meeting and dialled her direct line again. I was sick of waiting for her to act; I needed her to do something now. I reached her answerphone.

'I'm coming to see you,' I began. I heard my words slur, but couldn't stop them. 'I gave you what you needed and you did nothing. You fucking owe me.'

As I drove in the direction of End of the Line, I still didn't know how to react to my parents' response to the accusations being hurled at me. I wanted to scream, yell, cry, defend myself and hurt them as much as they were hurting me, all at the same time.

Knowing they didn't have faith in their own son wounded me badly. Johnny had already washed his hands of me and now they were doing the same. It was all so unfair.

As I pulled up at a red traffic light, I took a swig from the bottle of vodka I'd left in the glovebox. I didn't care if I was pulled over and breathalysed by the police. Let them arrest me. I was no stranger to it and it'd be the least of my worries. Maybe I should be behind bars anyway? Perhaps I was a danger to myself because I couldn't make rational decisions. If I could, I wouldn't have been caught up in this shitstorm. I'd lost everyone I'd ever loved or relied on, and I had no one to turn to.

I drove through the housing estate where Granddad Pete had once lived, and passed the park where, as a boy, I'd cycled for hours at a time with my mates. I passed the supermarket where we'd hang out, trying to blag cigarettes from the older lads. I saw the bus stop where I'd shared my first kiss with Lucy Jones. My heart ached for the innocent days I'd never get back.

As my past caught up with my present, I realised I had no future. Even if by some miracle this was all cleared up, I'd be forever ruined by the accusations. Laura and Effie's lies were spreading across social media with the speed of a contagious disease and, by now, everyone I worked with and beyond would be aware of what had been written about me. The story would only grow bigger and bigger as each student and parent shared it. My life as I'd known it was over. Mud sticks and I was covered in it.

For the first time since she took her life, I understood how Charlotte had felt when she reached the depths of her despair.

CHAPTER TWENTY-NINE

LAURA

I'd never seen Janine look so self-congratulatory as when she brandished Ryan's Dictaphone in her hand. Her face was so contorted by smugness, it threatened to fold in on itself.

'Do you know what this is?' she asked. 'It's a recording Ryan made of every conversation you and him had. Hour after hour of you going against everything End of the Line believes in, by encouraging him to end his life.'

I let her talk.

'You were supposed to be offering an impartial ear to those people,' she continued. 'No matter what they told you about their intentions, it was your job to listen, not to talk them into dying. You need to be stopped.'

'And I suppose you're the one to do it?'

Janine smiled and then blinked hard.

'Why haven't you done anything with it yet?' I asked. 'I thought you'd have been straight to head office with this little bit of gossip.'

'Let's not underplay this, Laura. It's hardly a "little bit of gossip", is it? It's proof that one of my volunteers has been encouraging and assisting suicide, which, as we both know, is against the law. But after much umming and ahhing, I've decided to give you a choice. I can either pass this to management and report you to the police, or I can give it back to you and you can destroy the evidence.'

'In return for what?'

'That you leave my branch, right now, and never set foot in it again.'

'Is that it? That's all you want from me?'

'Not quite. You've also got to agree not to see your family again. You stay away from Effie, Alice, Henry and Tony.'

'What?' My blood ran cold.

'Tony will be applying to the family court to file for divorce for your unreasonable behaviour. Our bargain is that you don't defend yourself and that you give Tony full custody rights. Once you get your decree nisi, then you can have this Dictaphone and your children can start their new life without you.'

Janine had finally revealed her true colours and they were almost as self-serving as mine.

'You are no better than me,' I said. 'If I'm such a bad person then why are you using those recordings for your own gain?'

'When did I ever claim to be any better than you?' she laughed. 'We all have our own agendas, Laura. Yours is to encourage people to die. Mine is to make a life with your soon-to-be ex-husband.'

'You're fooling yourself if you think that's going to happen. Tony and I are meant to be together, along with our children. Effie is already back in my life.'

'But for how much longer? I'm going to hazard a guess not very. Tony called me just before I came down here. He knows Effie is being molested by her teacher. It's all over the school's Facebook page.

Apparently she's inconsolable. I looked at the profile name that made the first post – Charlotte Smith. Ryan's wife, if I remember rightly? Neither Effie nor Ryan would've benefitted from doing this themselves, so unless Charlotte has risen from the ashes, that only leaves you. I don't think Tony or your daughter will be welcoming you back with open arms any time soon.'

Janine blinked hard again, as if something were distracting her.

'Press play,' I said.

'What?'

'On the Dictaphone. Press play. You can't expect me to agree to your demands without hearing what I'm being accused of.'

'Really?' she replied. I nodded and she shrugged as she pressed a button. She sat back on the sofa as the machine made a hissing sound. A few seconds of silence passed before she looked at the display screen. She pressed a button to fast-forward. She hit play again but still there was silence. Her face went from muddled to anxious and then confused in a moment. She pressed more buttons, played with the volume and checked the batteries. The Dictaphone was blank.

'Well, Janine, it's nice to have met you properly after all this time,' I said, and smiled as I stood up. 'I think I'm going to take my chances and let fate, not you, decide what happens to me.'

'What did you do?' she bellowed, and slowly rose to her feet. However, her legs suddenly gave way and she fell back onto the sofa. She steadied herself before attempting, and failing, to rise up again. I walked towards her as she tried to comprehend what was happening to her body.

'The powdered sedatives I baked into your muffins appear to have kicked in,' I began. She glared at me, bewildered at first, before uneasiness slowly spread across her wrinkled face. 'They're not all "store-bought". Let me take this first,' I continued. I snatched the Dictaphone from her weak grip and dropped it into my pocket.

'Let's set the record straight about a few things, shall we?' I reached into my bag to remove the leather driving gloves Tony had left in the garage at home. 'You and my husband will never get your happy-ever-after. You will never be allowed to expose me and what I have done to anyone. You will never understand why I do it or what it's like to hear a person's last breath, because you don't have the capacity to feel in the way I do. You don't respect the fragility of human life like me. You'll never know how the beauty of death equals the beauty of birth, or how those first and last gasps of air are exactly the same. You don't know any of this because you don't help people. *I* help people. I save them from themselves.'

I pulled the gloves slowly over my fingers and palms, and felt inside my bag again until I found what I was looking for.

'When a person is breathing their last, everything they have done in their life, every success or failure they have ever enjoyed or suffered, no longer matters because we are all equal. Good or bad, saint or sinner, you or me, one day we will all be on a level playing field. I have been fortunate to have been asked many times to be the only person who will ever hear that sound. And while you haven't asked me directly, I can only assume you won't object when I take it upon myself to be here for yours.'

Janine's face was awash with fear. The sedatives made her limbs heavy and her vision blurred. But she could still feel scared. Before she could formulate another word or raise her arm to defend herself, I swung a hammer clean into her windpipe.

The first blow left a dent the size of a ten-pence coin, but the collision of metal and skin and cartilage was more like a soft thud than the crunch I'd expected to hear. Her eyes were open saucer-wide as her nervous system sent pain signals to her brain. The sedatives were affecting her coordination, so when she instinctively tried to move her hands to protect her throat, they hovered hopelessly by her sides instead. She gasped for air through her broken windpipe, slowly suffocating.

I held the hammer above my head again and waited for her eyes to meet mine. I needed her to understand the first blow wasn't a one-off before I directed the second strike to just above her eye socket. This time I heard the crack I'd wanted and the skin split open like a sausage. There was little movement at first, and then her head began to judder involuntarily like she was having a seizure. Her dilated pupils remained focused on mine, and after ten seconds or so, the fit came to an end.

Janine was still conscious when the third blow hit her slap bang on the top of her head, like I was hitting a nail into a floorboard. Her eyes rolled back in their sockets, and I knew that with one more strike it would be over. But I didn't want her dead just yet.

I lowered myself next to her on the sofa and leaned across her, blood from the wound on the top of her head trickling down her face and onto my cheek and neck. There wasn't as much of it as I'd imagined, though.

I rested my ear as close as I could to her lips so that, between the loud palpitations of my heartbeat, I could just about hear her in the last moments of life. It was as if all my senses were being stimulated in unison: everything I saw, heard and felt was magnified, from the scent of metal in her blood to the sound of her fingertips delicately tapping the fabric of the sofa. Janine's breathing, already barely audible, became lighter and lighter until I could no longer feel it against my ear. And then, with one last tiny expiration, her body shut down completely.

At first, I couldn't move. My mind was completely blank and I went into a kind of refractory period. I allowed myself a few moments for my high levels of adrenaline to lower and for my pulse to slow before I continued with the next stage of my plan. There'd be plenty of time for reflection in the future.

I clambered to my feet and indulged myself with one lingering look towards Janine's motionless body. Everything that evil bitch had put me through almost felt worth it in order to steal her last breath.

I needed to act fast. I used the hammer to break the padlock that separated the appointments room from the derelict building next door. I wiped her blood from my face, ear, neck, hair and chin with a packet of wet wipes, then from behind the sofa I removed a bag with an identical set of clothing to that I was wearing and changed. I dropped the soiled clothes, my notebook and Tony's gloves into a bin liner, slipped on a pair of latex gloves and left Janine's body to begin livor mortis and her brain cells to die. I left the door ever so slightly ajar.

Inside the neighbouring building, I affixed a new padlock to the door to delay the inevitable police search. The torch on my phone guided me through the darkened corridors until I reached the rear entrance. With two firm whacks, I broke the lock to the rear door, then dropped the murder weapon on the floor. And, after double-checking I'd missed nothing, I left the building. I removed the pair of man's-size running shoes I'd been wearing to leave impressions on the dusty floor, and slipped my own back on. I screwed up a photograph and tossed it into an overgrown grass verge. Then I slid open a one-way bolt on the gate, put the latex gloves in my bag, clutched the bin liner, checked the alleyway was clear and walked home.

Once there, I threw both sets of clothes I'd worn that day on a hot wash – the first of three cycles I'd put them through – while I showered. Tony's gloves and running shoes had been buried in a shoebox in the field behind the house.

Then I sat at the breakfast bar in my cosy dressing gown and slippers, and poured myself a glass of Rioja. There was still so much to be done, so I started typing a list on my phone. As a company director for Tony's IT firm, I earned a regular monthly wage for doing nothing but remaining quiet about where we'd found the money to fund the business in the early days. So, first I would hire a decorator to repaint and paper the walls scarred by the fire, then I'd have to find a gardener to bring the overgrown rear garden into some semblance of order.

I'd need a glazier to replace the boarded-up bifold doors that Ryan had smashed, then make an insurance claim. I'd probably earn some compensation from him when it went to court. Then once the house was back to how it used to be, it'd be ready for Tony and the girls to move back in.

I put my phone on charge, ready for the influx of calls I was soon to receive about Janine's death. 'Oh my God, no,' I said out loud in many different ways until I found a tone that sounded believable.

I glanced at the clock on the oven; Janine must have been discovered by now. The police were likely already there, and waiting for a forensics team to suit up and search our building along with the premises next door. That's where they'd find the hammer I'd stolen from Ryan's flat when the estate agent wasn't looking. I'd spotted it on a sideboard and was careful to slide it into my bag using only the sleeve of my jacket. Tests would reveal it to be covered in Janine's blood, hair and skin, and Ryan's fingerprints.

In an autopsy, the contents of her stomach would reveal she'd been drugged, but she ate so much and so frequently it'd be hard to tell how they'd got into her system. And as everyone knew, she refused to eat my glutinous pastries. So I'd be safe.

Outside in the yard, they'd find a screwed-up photograph of me that I'd torn from the walls the night I went to 'Steven's' house. In a panic, I'd stuffed some into my pockets before he confronted me. I hoped it might be covered in Ryan's fingerprints and an invisible tracking code linked to the serial number of his printer – or, even better, his prints on the adhesive tape. It wouldn't contain mine, though. I'd worn gloves.

Ryan's vendettas against me, End of the Line and Effie were already on record with the police and the school. Judging by the number of Facebook likes and shares my posts had received, hundreds of people across the community had watched the video of him breaking into my house and witnessed how violent he was. And there was proof in the diary that he'd made an appointment to see Janine this afternoon.

Ryan and Janine. Two birds killed with the same stone. Well, the same hammer.

I became excited when my phone began to vibrate, but it was Effie's name that appeared on the screen.

'Hi, darling, I'm expecting an important call. Can I give you a ring later?'

'How could you, Mum?' she sobbed. 'Everyone at school knows I made that recording. They all hate me and say I had sex with Mr Smith. They're calling me a slag and saying I led him on.'

'Ignore them, darling. In situations like this, it's always the woman who gets the blame.'

'But I am to blame, aren't I?'

'It's not as simple as that, Effie. There are things you're too young to understand, things that he's done that we can't let him get away with.'

'I don't care!' she cried. 'You've ruined my life. I don't ever want to see you again.'

'Effie, please don't be like that. Why don't I meet you for a coffee tomorrow and—'

'No! I'm going to tell Dad what you made me do.'

'Before you do that, remember one thing,' I replied calmly. '*You* started all of this. Your silly schoolgirl crush began this chain of events. Your precious father is already embarrassed by the trouble you've caused him, so I can only imagine what this will do to him. And when the police and the school find out how you lied, you'll have to move schools again and probably face criminal charges for your false accusations. There's not much your dad can do to protect you from that. But you're old enough now to be put into a young offenders institute, aren't you? God knows how you'll survive that. So ahead of telling your father about my involvement, I'd think long and hard about the repercussions first.'

She fell silent. 'You have to remember, Effie – you and I are cut from the same cloth. You are your mother's daughter. There is so much you can learn from me.'

I was so angry with her that I didn't give her the opportunity to reply. Instead, I hung up and knocked back my glass of wine. All this I had done for *her*, for all of us, but she was too self-centred to appreciate it. The more I thought about it, the more my blood boiled.

Whether Effie liked it or not, nothing was going to stop me from getting my whole family back under one roof again. *Nothing.*

CHAPTER THIRTY

RYAN

The wind howled through the slats in the car's grille and under the dented bonnet, making it vibrate. It also blew up and under the wheel arches and along the undercarriage. At times, the car felt as if it was about to be picked up and tossed into the air.

From the early evening onwards, I'd remained in the driver's seat, draining every last drop from the vodka bottle. Now daylight was breaking through the thick veil of night and I was sobering up. But nothing was going to change for me with the dawn of a new day. No amount of alcohol could ever blot out what had become of my life.

I tried to imagine how it could have been, had I not tried to gain a greater understanding of Charlotte's depression; if I'd just accepted that I'd lost my wife to it, then learned to move on.

Every now and again another car appeared in the car park and I'd watch as their drivers exited in running gear or with dogs on leads, all making the most of the early-morning quiet. The wind aside, it was as tranquil a location as I'd imagined it to be.

I'd driven for almost two hours in near silence to reach Birling Gap in East Sussex, the place where Charlotte had killed herself. Several times since her death, I'd mulled over whether I should go and see why she'd chosen that location, but I hadn't been able to bring myself to until now.

And for so long, I'd asked myself what could be so awful about a person's life that they'd feel driven to end it. Now I understood that whether it's a chemical imbalance in your head, a past that haunts you or other people making your world unmanageable, everyone can reach a point where it all becomes too much. It had for me.

Everything I'd once held so close to my heart, I'd lost. There was no coming back from the things I had done, the things I was being accused of doing and the things I was innocent of. I had no wife, no son, no job, no parents, no brother . . . absolutely nothing to live for.

I'd parked in the exact same place Charlotte had, according to the dashboard-cam footage. I opened the car door, grabbed an old coat from the back and slipped it on. I'd looked online at photographs and footage of the area so many times that it felt familiar – comforting, even – despite me never having been there in person.

I took my phone off airplane mode, and message after message flashed across the screen. Missed texts, missed emails, missed calls. Suddenly it started vibrating, and Johnny's picture flashed up on the screen. I hesitated before answering, but I didn't speak.

'Ry?' he asked. 'Ryan? Can you hear me?'

'Yes.'

'Where the hell are you? The police are looking for you.'

'I thought they might.'

'They've been to the flat and then Mum and Dad's. What the hell has happened?'

I didn't reply.

'Ry? What the fuck? They're saying you might have killed some woman?'

'What woman?'

'She volunteered at the End of the Line.'

'Laura?'

'No, Janine Thomson. Was she the one you left the Dictaphone with?'

'Yes.'

'You left her a threatening voicemail saying you were coming to see her and then she was found dead.'

I looked up at the sky, closed my eyes and laughed. She'd beaten me again. Time and time again I had underestimated Laura, and time and time again she had proved me wrong. Whatever she had done now, she had well and truly got me. My name meant nothing, so there was no point in trying to clear it.

'In a moment, I'm going to email you something,' I replied. 'Look after Mum and Dad for me and tell them I'm sorry. I love you, bro.'

'Ry, what are you—'

I hung up, sent Johnny the email I'd spent much of the night composing, turned off my phone and slipped it back inside my jacket.

I'd begun my search for Laura because I'd wanted answers as to why my wife had killed herself. But in my three confrontations with Laura, I'd been too busy trying to get revenge to actually ask her. I made my peace with the fact that I was never going to know.

I walked slowly in the direction of a fence that cordoned off the cliff's edge. I imagined holding Charlotte's hand in one hand and our son Daniel's in the other, and talking with her one last time.

'Did you have second thoughts when you got this far?' I asked.

No. I was sure it was what I wanted.

'Did you think about me?'

Yes, of course I did. I love you.

'Did you talk to the baby?'

Yes, I told him I was sorry and that we would be all right.

'What was the last thing you thought about?'

Our wedding day and when we all went out into the gardens to light the Chinese lanterns. Do you remember? We threw them up into the air and watched as they floated across the fields and into the distance. If I could go back and remain in any one moment forever, it would be right then.

'Why did you leave me?'

It wasn't your fault. It was what I had to do.

Only now, by following in Charlotte's footsteps, could I understand that she wasn't being selfish in taking her own life. No suicidal person is. Like I was now, she truly believed in her heart of hearts that sometimes it is all there is left to do.

And as I climbed over the fence and walked my last few steps towards the cliff's edge, I stared into the horizon and let the wind blow through my hair. I closed my eyes, so that all I could see were the oranges and reds of the sun on my eyelids, and all I could feel were the soft, warm hands of my wife and son.

'I'm sorry, Charlotte. I'm sorry I wasn't able to help you or convince you to stay. I hope before you died that you found a way to forgive me for letting you down, as I forgive you. I love you.'

I love you too, Ryan.

I smiled as we all fell together.

PART THREE

CHAPTER ONE

LAURA – TWO MONTHS AFTER RYAN

The Mayor of Northampton smiled as she pulled the rope cord that opened a small pair of red curtains. The photographer's flash lit up the heavy gold chain of office hanging from her neck as she, myself and the area manager of End of the Line posed for pictures either side of the copper-plated plaque.

Janine Thomson House, it read. *In memory of our friend and colleague.*

A small gathering of staff from our office, and some faces I didn't recognise, representing neighbouring county branches, joined us to mourn our loss as I perched on the steps outside the building. I wasn't sure if I was feeling jittery because I'd been asked to speak in front of a crowd or because Tony was standing just a few metres away from me. It was only the second time I'd seen him since poor Janine's sudden demise.

I'd attempted to make contact by text and I'd left several messages on his phone, but he'd yet to call me back. Seeing him brought my skin out in goosebumps, and just thinking about our future made me want to burst into a broad grin. But I stopped myself; it wasn't the time or the place for that.

I wondered why Effie and Alice weren't with him. I'd watched them a month earlier from my seat way back inside the church at Janine's funeral. The order of service looked nice among the others in my black bag. My girls were sitting in the second row with their father, close to the heart of Janine's family. It was a little excessive – it wasn't as if there had been anything serious between her and Tony. He'd just been using her to get at me: to teach me a lesson . . . showing me that I needed to be a good wife, *a better wife*.

Once Janine's bulk was reduced to a pile of ashes, I'd texted Effie to offer her an olive branch, but she was still wallowing in self-pity. She didn't seem to understand that putting the recording of her and Ryan's conversation online had been a necessary sacrifice. But patching up our relationship wasn't my priority right now – it was Tony. Once we were together, the rest of the fragmented pieces of my family would fall into place.

I guessed he needed to keep up the facade of the grieving boyfriend for now. I wore the copper-coloured earrings and matching necklace he'd bought me for our ninth wedding anniversary, and the black dress I'd worn on our last night out together at his work Christmas party. Back then he couldn't wait to get me out of it as he pushed me up against the filing cabinets in his office and eased his way inside me. His face had been contorted with lust, miles away from how he looked today. Only he and I knew this was an act.

Next it was my turn to speak at Janine's ceremony. I unfolded a piece of paper from my pocket, cleared my throat and began to read aloud.

'Good morning, everyone, and on behalf of End of the Line, thank you for coming.'

I glanced in an appropriately solemn manner at the people around me. Tony was the only one whose stare was cold and intense.

'The horrific death of our dear friend Janine shocked her close friends, co-workers, and the rest of the country, too,' I continued. 'She had dedicated her career to helping others with her generous spirit, kind nature and charity work. And she was repaid for that devotion with a brutal attack that ended her life so very, very prematurely. Unfortunately, we at End of the Line were unable to help the troubled man responsible for her death and, as you will no doubt be aware, he took his own life rather than face the consequences of his actions. But the events of that awful day prove just how necessary a safe haven like our charity is for people who are desperate for someone to listen. That is why we have named this building after Janine Thomson as a reminder to others that we are always here to hear you.'

I dabbed the crocodile tears pooling in the corner of my eye with a tissue, when a polite ripple of applause began. As we made our way inside, a morbid fascination made everyone's heads turn towards the closed door of the room where Janine had breathed her last.

When the police had eventually allowed us access to it, I'd been the one to organise everything from its professional clean-up to the fitting of new locks. I was also the only person to have an extra key, and sometimes, on my way out following a shift, I'd take time to sit in the exact same spot on the sofa where Janine died. I'd close my eyes and relive our confrontation. The thud of the hammer against her head and her last, desperate gasp for air – sometimes I remembered it as clearly as if she were still next to me.

In the conference room at the back of the building, I'd provided the food for the buffet using a little of the money donated in the wake of Janine's death. The story of how the kind-hearted charity worker had been beaten to death with a hammer at her place of work had made national newspaper headlines, and more than £100,000 in donations came flooding in from well-wishers. It irked me at first that she was being held up as a heroine and that I could never take credit for that money, but eventually I made my peace with it. In the end, I'd won.

Also making the news was the man accused of murdering her. Ryan Smith's DNA had been found on the murder weapon and a screwed-up photo of me was discovered in the neighbouring yard. It was assumed I'd been his intended victim until a voicemail from Ryan was discovered on Janine's phone threatening that she 'owed' him.

Ryan's car was later located abandoned in the same place as his wife's, and with the assumption he'd followed in her footsteps over the cliff's edge. I only wish I'd caught his last, desperate breath, as I had his wife's.

Kevin and Zoe approached me to tell me how much Janine would have appreciated my speech, but they knew as well as I did that she'd have hated the fact that I had given it. I looked around the room to see if Mary had changed her mind and joined us, but after finding Janine's body she couldn't bring herself to set foot in our building again.

Suddenly I became aware that Tony wasn't there either. I hurried outside and caught him further up the road, his car keys in his hand.

'Tony!' I shouted. 'Please wait.'

He paused and held his back to me before turning. He seemed angry and I couldn't think why.

'You didn't stay for the drinks.'

'That was a nice speech,' he replied.

'Thank you. I thought it best to keep it brief.'

'It's a shame you didn't mean a word of it.' His directness caught me unawares.

'Can you blame me?' I asked. 'I'd heard the two of you had been dating behind my back. But while Janine and I may not have seen eye to eye, that doesn't matter now. Death is a great leveller and nobody deserves what happened to her.'

'Spare me, Laura. I know how you think. You could barely keep a straight face as you read that script out.'

I didn't want to argue with him, despite his best efforts to pick a fight.

'How are the girls?' I continued. 'It feels like an eternity since I last saw them. I've left them voicemails but they haven't called me back yet.'

'And what does that tell you?'

'I was thinking of popping by the house—'

He moved closer to me. 'You are not coming anywhere near them, do you hear me?' he growled. 'You have done enough to fuck them up already.'

I rolled my eyes. 'Is this still about Effie and her teacher?'

'What else would it be about? She told me everything. How he tried to groom her and how you warned her not to tell me. I'm her bloody father! I had a right to know!'

I bet she hasn't told you everything, I thought. If she was anything like her mum, she'd have remained tight-lipped over being a willing party in setting Ryan up, knowing full well he wasn't a paedophile.

'I dealt with it,' I replied. 'I was trying to show you I'm ready to be a good parent again.'

'A good parent would've told me. A good parent would not have publicly humiliated their daughter by posting the recording on Facebook for the world to hear.'

'The school was taking too long to handle it.'

'Did you know she's now being home-schooled because the bullying became so bad?'

'No. But if you'd answered my messages, perhaps I could've helped her.'

He raised his voice. 'How could you have helped when this is all your fault in the first place? I know what he was accusing you of saying to those callers. So what that bastard did to my daughter and Janine is because of what *you* started.'

Something about his expression told me he had his regrets, too, but quite what they were I couldn't be sure.

'Everything I have ever done is because I love you and our family. All I want is for us to be back together again. Is that too much to ask?'

'No, Laura, everything you do is for your own good and it always has been. Everyone else is just collateral damage in the fight to get what you want.'

'I may have made a few mistakes along the way,' I conceded, 'but this all began because you broke our family up.'

'And it was the best thing I ever did, because the girls and Henry are in a safer environment without you. You are a bad force in all of our lives. Janine was a kind woman and worth a hundred of you. The only good thing to come about from her death is that people will remember her for the wonderful person she was.'

Not for much longer, I thought. In taking her iPad from her handbag the afternoon she died, I had access to the typed list of passwords she'd saved because she was too stupid to remember them. And that included both her bank details and those of End of the Line. Shortly before she met her maker, I'd transferred £40,000 from the charity's account to her own. A further £5,000 had been deposited into her online gambling accounts. It would be a few more weeks before the accountants began their annual audits, and it wouldn't take long to trace the missing money.

I clenched my fists and took a deep breath. 'Tony, this isn't the time or place to have this discussion,' I continued. 'Why don't you come around to the house tonight and we'll talk properly.'

'No, Laura. You're not getting it, are you?' He sounded exasperated. 'I don't ever want to be in that house or anywhere near you again. You are poison.'

'Eight o'clock,' I replied. 'Come round for then and I'll make us something nice to eat.'

He shook his head as he approached his car and drove away.

CHAPTER TWO

LAURA – THREE MONTHS AFTER RYAN

There weren't many mourners at Ryan's funeral – a dozen at best and probably all family, from what I could see, although my view from inside the car wasn't clear. There had been at least twice that number at Chantelle's, and she was a filthy drug addict. But then who would want to be seen in public bidding a final farewell to an accused paedophile and murderer? It wouldn't reflect greatly on anyone.

When the newspapers reported that a body had been found tangled up in fishermen's nets off the East Sussex coast, where Ryan was thought to have stepped off the cliff, I crossed my fingers and prayed it would be him. It was only when he was positively identified through his DNA that I could truly relax.

The date and location of his funeral weren't advertised, and it had taken many calls claiming to be a family member wanting to know where I could send flowers before I discovered the funeral director organising his service and the location.

Ryan's body wasn't driven in a hearse. No family members followed behind in black limousines and there was to be no church service or burial for him. Instead, he'd been taken in the back of an unmarked coroner's van directly to the crematorium in neighbouring Kettering. The only flowers greeting his arrival were my lilies, hand-delivered and left by the door with an anonymous card attached reading *I won.*

Outside the crematorium, photographers from news agencies and a local TV station I'd tipped off took pictures and filmed his coffin being removed from the vehicle and whisked inside. I hadn't only taken Ryan's life away from him, I'd taken his funeral, too.

I decided against joining Ryan's mourners and risk being unmasked, so I remained in my car instead. Although I'll admit to feeling a little frustrated at not being there as the final curtain circled his coffin after all my effort. I wondered what they'd do with his ashes and if they'd be scattered somewhere near Charlotte's. I'd never engineered the deaths of a husband and wife before. I'd find it hard to top that with my next candidates.

As everyone made their way inside, I recalled the last time I'd been to a crematorium was to say goodbye to Nate. There had been even fewer of us there than at Ryan's funeral – myself and six of his vagrant friends, who I'd bribed with enough alcohol to last them a week. I wasn't even sure if they knew who Nate was.

I missed talking to my friend. Even when we weren't in touch, just knowing he was about somewhere had made me feel there was someone on my side. I still couldn't understand how the coroner and policewoman had got when and where he died so wrong. Why did they dismiss my claims so readily? I was sure I was with him at least six months after they reckoned he was dead. Regardless, I was happy not to have shared his last breath.

My house was still empty when I returned home. Immaculate, but empty. Despite the number of open windows, plug-in air-fresheners and reed diffusers I'd placed in each room, the oily smell of fresh paint still hung thickly. The Polish decorators I'd employed had done a wonderful job of papering the walls and repainting the ceilings. Everything from the banisters to the skirting boards and door frames were now coated in a pure, glistening, Arctic white. It was like being inside an igloo.

I'd Pinterested, then replicated examples of rooms I'd seen in online interior design magazines. I used bright accent colours of yellows and greens for my new cushions, curtains and rugs. I had family photographs reprinted and framed to hang on the walls and arranged on the sideboard and windowsills. And I'd brought brand-new bedding and soft furnishings for the girls' and Henry's rooms. I'd done the same with Tony's room, although once we were a family again, it wouldn't be long before he returned to our bed.

The lighter evenings of spring held the darkness at bay, so I pulled open the reglazed bifold doors and sat on a patio chair to enjoy a cigarette. I'd need to give up the habit before Tony and I were reunited, as he loathed the smell of smoke. Around me, the bushes and lawns had been neatly trimmed, the girls' tatty old trampoline dismantled and disposed of at the rubbish tip, the fence repaired, new turf laid and the flowerbeds dug over and replanted. Everything around me was a kaleidoscope of colours and freshness. A new start for everything and everyone.

I couldn't help but smile when I thought about the future. Now there was no Ryan or Janine to interfere in our lives, there was nothing to prevent us from rekindling what we once had, apart from Tony's stubbornness. He hadn't taken me up on my offer to visit the house after the plaque unveiling and talk our problems through. In fact, he'd kept to his word that he didn't want anything to do with me at all.

It was quite disheartening to begin with, but I realised it was my own stupid fault. I had pushed him too far too soon. Maybe a part of him really was grieving Janine's death. I used to pride myself on my patience and there I was, trying to hurry him while he was processing it. And I'm trained to know that people say silly things they don't mean when they're in pain.

My mobile phone rang. I panicked and stubbed out my cigarette like a guilty schoolgirl, flicking the butt behind a watering can. The number was withheld and I hoped it was Effie or Tony calling. They'd recently changed their numbers, so I'd been forced to drive to their house after the legal papers petitioning me for a divorce arrived. However, to my surprise, they'd moved from their rented home. And when I'd visited Alice's school to pick her up one teatime, her teacher told me she'd relocated to a private school in another county, but refused to tell me where. There was no trace of Effie on social media, and Tony had even taken a sabbatical from his own company.

My only means of communication with my husband was by email. I'd tried several times in the last week, informing him that Henry was poorly with a bad chest infection and that he really should visit. When he failed to reply, I wrote again and threw in a few medical terms and threats of a hospital stay for good measure. I also attached a picture of Henry asleep in his bed to lay the guilt on thicker.

'Hello, is that Mrs Morris?' It was a woman's voice.

'Yes. Who's this?'

'It's Belinda from Kingsthorpe Residential Care Home.'

I clutched the phone tighter to my ear. 'Is it Henry? Is he okay?'

'Yes, he's fine. He has a visitor here but I need your permission before I allow them in.'

'Who is it?'

'His father, Tony Morris.'

'Yes!' I replied quickly. 'Yes! And ask him to wait with Henry. I'll be there soon!'

I hung up, flustered and flushed with excitement. I knew Tony couldn't remain angry with me forever, and once he thought our son was ill, of course he'd want to see him.

I was unsure of what to do first. I ran up the stairs two at a time and took a swig of mouthwash to rid myself of my smoky breath. I grabbed a casual outfit – skinny jeans, Converse trainers and a T-shirt that was just tight enough to show off my slim waist. I hurriedly reapplied my make-up and sprayed my neck and wrists with the Issey Miyake perfume that Tony loved.

Can't wait to see you and Henry together, I typed. *On my way now. xx*. Then I grabbed my car keys and rehearsed what I was going to say to him when he learned I hadn't been entirely honest about Henry's poor health. He'd probably be irked at first, but once he saw his son and how devoted I was to him, his animosity towards me would come to an end and he'd forgive my little white lies.

I pulled up in the driveway of Henry's care home, feeling sick to my stomach with nerves. I didn't recognise the girl on reception wearing a 'Trainee' badge.

'My son, Henry Morris, can you tell me where he is, please?' I asked.

'His dad took him out in his chair for a walk in the grounds,' she replied. 'Are you okay?'

I hadn't realised my lips were pursed and my fists balled. I could barely get the word 'yes' out because I desperately wanted to cry happy tears.

It had been more than two and a half years since I'd last seen father and son together, and at times I'd worried if I might ever witness it again. Dusk was approaching, and I didn't want to miss another minute, so I hurried outside and scanned the surroundings, anxious to catch my first glimpse of them together.

The building had been a stately home before the owner fell on hard times and was forced to sell. The extensive grounds were always neatly kept, with flowerbeds, sensory gardens and a play area, all surrounded by lush woodland. Finally, in the distance, I saw Tony kneeling by the side of Henry's wheelchair. Their heads were turned as they looked down a slope and towards the lake below, watching a family of snow-white swans gliding past. I clasped my hand to my mouth and my eyes moistened.

But as I grew closer, something was wrong with the perfect picture before me. I couldn't put my finger on it until I saw Tony's arm. He had a sleeve of tattoos starting at his left shoulder and going all the way down to his wrist, just above the watch strap. The man next to Henry did not.

My stomach flipped one hundred and eighty degrees as I ran hell for leather towards them.

'Get away from my son!' I screamed, and looked around for help but to no avail. 'Leave him alone!' The man turned his head to look at me and I stopped in my tracks.

My son was with a dead man. He was with Ryan.

CHAPTER THREE

JOHNNY

By the look on her face as she approached me, Laura thought she'd seen a ghost. I'd counted on it – I wanted to mess with that mad bitch's head from the moment she first clapped eyes on me.

'Get away from my son!' she cried when she realised I wasn't her husband. 'Leave him alone!' Her head turned quickly, desperately searching for someone to help her. But the area I'd chosen to take Henry to was secluded. The three of us were very much alone.

Her face collapsed when she got a better look at me. I'd cut my hair short like my brother's, and shaved off my beard so I had his uneven stubble. I wore his favourite vintage Nirvana T-shirt and had swapped my glasses for contact lenses.

Her bewildered expression told me she wasn't sure if her eyes were deceiving her. I lifted one hand from Henry's wheelchair and made an action like I was going to let it slide down the slope and into the lake below.

'I don't want to hurt your son,' I said forcefully, 'so I suggest you back up.'

'You're not Ryan.' It was part question and part statement. She hesitated, unsure of her next move. She kept pushing her foot forward, then pulling it back as if doing the hokey-cokey. Her mouth opened and closed, but no more words came from it.

'Feel free to move closer,' I continued, goading her. 'But Henry is strapped into this heavy chair, and when I let go and he ends up in that lake, you're going to have a hell of a job dragging him out by yourself.'

'You're his brother,' she said, the penny having finally dropped. 'I saw you at the fune—' She stopped herself.

'I'm Johnny,' I replied. 'Thank you for your card and flowers. You couldn't even leave him alone after you'd killed him, could you?'

'I didn't kill him. I didn't kill anyone. You have me confused with someone else.'

'Is that how you want to play it, Laura?' I asked. 'Because I have all night.'

Ryan had told me so much in detail about Laura that it felt like I knew her, especially after reading the lengthy email he'd sent me shortly before he died. In it, he'd described what her ex-husband had told him about her and the false accusations Laura and Effie had made against him. Everything that had gone wrong in his life stemmed from something Laura had started. And while Ryan had paid the ultimate price, she'd got away scot-free. But that was about to change.

Henry was becoming restless and squirmed in his chair, perhaps sensing the animosity surrounding him. I hated scaring the boy, but from what I'd learned about Laura he was her Achilles heel and I needed him as leverage for her to take me seriously. I patted his arm gently to calm him, but it had no effect.

'Don't you touch him!' Laura barked, then swiftly changed her tone so it became less aggressive. 'Please, you're scaring him.'

'Why shouldn't I hurt your kid? You didn't give a shit about hurting my family or taking Ryan's son away from him. Charlotte was expecting a boy – did you know that?'

She shook her head, then held her hand up as if she were trying to nip in the bud whatever I was going to say next.

'I don't know what Ryan told you,' she began, 'but he was a very confused man who needed help. Both Janine and I tried, but he was too far gone. Did you know he tried to break into my house and kill me?'

'We all know what he did, because you spread it across social media. He broke in because you pushed him to it. For God's sake, you poured blood on his wife's wedding dress and put a dead pig next to it! What did you expect him to do? Laugh about it? You knew exactly how he would react. You provoked him and he played right into your hands.'

She shook her head. 'No, whatever he said about me isn't true. Look at me. I'm a mum of three young children and I volunteer for a charity that has people's welfare at its heart. How am I a threat to anyone? If you just give me my son back, maybe I can help you to understand your brother.'

I let out an exaggerated laugh. 'Come on, Laura, you can do better than this.'

'The police must have told you they have proof he killed Janine.'

'Yes, and I don't believe it.'

'They found his hammer at the scene.'

'The hammer that was in his flat when you came to look around it. Coincidence, right?'

'Are you accusing me of killing Janine now?'

'Did you? Wasn't Janine in a relationship with your husband?'

She tried to mask a flicker of surprise at my knowledge, before play-acting an eye-roll.

'I know you're only trying to protect Ryan's name,' she said, 'and if I was in your shoes, I wouldn't want to believe the facts either. You grew up with him, you loved him, you don't want to think about the bad things he did. But can't you see? You're making the same terrible decisions he made. Please, I beg of you, for Henry's sake and for your own, don't let Ryan's mistakes ruin your life too.'

If I hadn't known better, I might have thought there was a grain of truth in Laura's words. She made a convincing case and a compelling victim. But I knew my brother.

'Tell me about your son, Laura. Tell me how Henry came to be like this.' My change of tack threw her and she paused for a moment.

'The umbilical cord became caught around his neck during labour and it starved him of oxygen,' she explained.

'Only that didn't happen, did it? That's just a lie you've told yourself because it's easier than admitting the truth. I know exactly what happened to Henry.'

'It was a complicated labour,' she replied firmly.

'Your husband told Ryan that you lie to yourself about your past and re-edit things you've done to paint yourself in a more sympathetic light.'

She tried to mask her surprise. 'I don't know why Tony would've said such a thing but—'

'And I know that Henry's complicated birth is just another one of those lies, isn't it? He was born perfectly healthy.'

'Tony said that?'

'No, Effie did.'

Her eyes narrowed slightly, unable to hide her betrayal.

'When Ryan died and his name was in every newspaper, Effie felt so guilty about the part she played that she came to find me after the funeral,' I continued.

'You can't believe what she says. Effie is a complicated girl.'

'She seemed perfectly okay to me. She told me how you and she made sure her recording of the conversation with my brother was taken completely out of context.'

'But I bet you believed every word of it when you first heard it, didn't you? I'll wager you turned your back on him like everyone else did and that's why he killed himself. That's why you're here tormenting my son and me, because you feel guilty.'

Her words cut deep, but I couldn't show her that.

'Effie told me how Henry was a perfectly normal little boy for the first four and a half years of his life. Then you did this to him.'

'No!' she bellowed, her eyes piercing. 'That's not true! Ryan and Effie have filled your head with lies. I would never hurt my baby.'

I pulled out a photograph that Effie had given me from the back pocket of my jeans and held it up. The wheelchair tugged in my other hand.

'Isn't this him blowing the candles out at his third birthday party? He looks fine to me.'

She stared at the picture of a perfectly normal-looking little Henry surrounded by his friends and his sisters. She closed her eyes and bit her bottom lip.

'Henry was at his friend Megan's house when the girl fell ill,' I continued. 'So her dad dropped him off early while Megan's mum looked after her. But you and Tony were too busy arguing to hear Henry let himself in, and because he got scared by your shouting, he hid himself in his room.'

'That didn't happen.' Her voice sounded small, like that of a child.

'What were you rowing over? That Tony had read the social services report about you and realised he'd married a sociopath? Or was it that Nate – or David, to use his proper name – killed his own mother for you?'

'Shut up! Just shut up!' Laura roared suddenly, and held her hands over her ears. Henry began to shriek with the high-pitched wail of an animal in distress. But I couldn't stop now, so I raised my voice above them both.

'When Tony stormed out, you blamed your new house for your marriage falling apart and not your own actions. Then you poured anything flammable the decorators had left and set fire to it. While you were outside trying to find your husband, your terrified little boy was trapped in his bedroom. Do you ever think about that, Laura? How scared he must have been when the thick black smoke started billowing under his door? Do you think he remembers it? Do you think every night he dreams about choking on those fumes?'

Laura continued to cover her ears, but I knew from the way her face was twisting that she heard me.

'The neighbours called 999 and firefighters rescued Henry,' I continued, 'but by the time paramedics resuscitated him, he'd been starved of oxygen for too long and suffered massive brain damage. Your once happy, healthy kid suddenly had the mental age of a one-year-old and it's all your fault.'

'No, no, no, no!' Laura said, and fell to her knees. I pointed at a still-shrieking Henry.

'I know there was some humanity in you once, because what you did to him fucked you up. They carted you off in an ambulance and kept you in a psychiatric unit before you eventually discharged yourself. But while you were gone, Tony moved him here and the girls out. Even then, you lied to yourself about why you'd been hospitalised. Effie told me that you claimed your mum's cancer as your own, didn't you?'

Laura clambered to her feet and began to pace in a circular motion, like a dog trying to find a comfortable position to curl up and sleep.

'No, that's not what happened. You're wrong,' she muttered. Her fingers pinched at her thighs. She was falling apart before me.

'Your daughters didn't want their dad to tell the police you started the fire, so Tony promised them he wouldn't give you up if they stayed away from you. You thought in time Tony would come round and return, but he didn't, did he? Instead he changed Effie's school to one nearer their new home and he kept the girls away from you. They were all enjoying their new life without you until my naive brother interfered and included you on the email for Effie's school report.'

'Please, be quiet,' Laura begged, her spirit overwhelmed and tears streaming down her cheeks. 'I need you to stop now.'

Then her expression blanked, as if she were reliving the moment she learned Tony had taken her family away from her. Her shoulders hunched like she wanted to fold into herself and vanish. Henry bounced back and forth in his chair and Laura reached towards him as if to offer him comfort. But once again, I took my hand off his chair until she retracted it.

'You know what horrifies me the most about you?' I asked. 'It's that after what you did to this kid, you didn't learn your lesson, because you're still putting yourself before anyone else. In trying to destroy Ryan, you threw Effie under the bus. *Your own daughter*. At least my brother regretted the part he had to play in all this.'

'He only regretted it because he lost,' she replied. Only there was no pride in her victory.

'And what exactly have you won, Laura? Because it sure as hell isn't your husband or your children. You have nothing. Ryan said you rattle around that house on your own. You spend hours locked inside waiting for someone to walk through the door, and I bet nobody ever does. And you know what? They never will. You've lost everyone, even Nate.'

'Why are you bringing him into it?' she sobbed.

'Why not? You brought Charlotte into it when Nate wanted to kill himself.'

'That didn't happen, it was an accident. He slipped into the river and drowned.'

'And you're rewriting the truth again. Nate had tried to die several times over the years, according to the coroner's report. He messed up an overdose and a hanging. I'm putting two and two together and assuming you, the expert in suicide, stepped in to help him get it right, didn't you?'

'I don't know what you mean . . .' She shook her head again, as if old memories she wanted to forget were coming back to life inside her.

'You do, Laura – just tell me the truth.'

'Nate wanted me to be with him when he died, but I couldn't do it, because I couldn't leave Henry,' she wept. 'So I found someone else.'

'Charlotte?'

'Yes.'

'Because she was a vulnerable woman with prenatal depression, and you saw her as ripe for manipulation.'

'Please, Johnny,' Laura begged, clasping her hands together like she was praying. 'Just leave now and I won't tell anyone any of this happened.'

'And then what? You'll have a change of heart and come after me?'

'No, I promise I won't.' She wiped snot from her nose with the back of her hand.

'There's just one thing I need you to do for me before I leave.' I removed my phone from my pocket and switched it to video mode and began recording.

'Because you are so keen on publicly shaming people, and because the Dictaphone my brother gave Janine has disappeared, you are going to look into the lens and admit that you encouraged Charlotte to die. Then you'll confess to what you did to Janine and admit that Ryan was not a child molester and that he is dead because of you.'

Her eyes momentarily left mine and glanced to the distance.

'Hey!' I snapped, and she looked back at me. 'I'm not giving you a choice here. This isn't something you can mull over. Admit it, everything you've done, then I will leave.'

I watched her on the phone's screen as she wiped her eyes and cleared her throat.

'Never,' she replied and, just for a second, she couldn't stop her lips from curling upwards. Then she opened her mouth wide and let out a piercing scream.

I heard hurried footsteps pounding close behind me, and as I turned, something solid hit the side of my head so hard that it pushed me to the ground.

CHAPTER FOUR

LAURA

'Tony, help us!' I pleaded as my husband appeared behind Johnny. 'It's Ryan!'

I could tell from Tony's expression that he thought he was seeing things – that the supposedly dead pervert teacher who'd tried to abuse his daughter was now tormenting his wife and their disabled son. So I didn't give him time to think rationally, only to tap into the instinct he'd learned in the boxing ring – react to a threat by stamping it out quickly.

'He's hurting Henry!'

Tony charged towards us, and before Johnny could defend himself, Tony caught him on the side of the head with a hard punch. It knocked Johnny off balance, sending him sprawling face down onto the path.

Johnny lost grip of his mobile phone and it slid across the gravel, but his grasp also slipped from Henry's wheelchair. I sprinted towards it, grabbing hold of the handles and digging my heels into the ground. Then, using all my strength, I leaned backwards to prevent it from slipping any further down the slope and into the lake. I pulled it towards me until Henry was safe and I could calm his hysteria.

Meanwhile, Tony squatted over Johnny and punched the back of his head and ribs with a ferocity I'd only seen on display in the boxing ring. *Crack, crack, crack*, knuckle against cheekbone, fist against skull . . . A composer couldn't have come up with a musical arrangement that sounded any sweeter to my ears.

'I will kill you for what you've done!' Tony shouted, and I had no reason to doubt him. Johnny's plan to confuse me by mimicking his brother's appearance had backfired spectacularly. But I wasn't going to admit to Tony he'd got the wrong man.

I pulled my son closer to me so he couldn't witness what was happening, not that he'd have been able to make any sense of it.

'Shh, shh, it's okay,' I whispered into his ear, running my hand through his hair, but still he wailed.

However, instead of focusing all my attention on Henry, I couldn't draw my eyes away from the chaos before me. Johnny's arms and hands flailed by his side, making occasional contact with Tony's body, but they were no match for my husband's fury, strength and training. Pinkish-red spit bubbles seeped from Johnny's mouth as he choked on the blood trickling down his throat from his nose and gums. His voice was distorted and unrecognisable.

'I'm not . . .' he croaked, but Tony had no intention of listening to him.

'You lied to me to get to my daughter, you sick fuck! You terrorised my wife and you murdered Janine!'

He called me his wife! A euphoric rush of warmth spread throughout my body.

I could have pleaded with Tony to stop, told him he'd got the wrong man and that we'd let the police deal with it. But I didn't. If Johnny was as tenacious as his brother, this would only continue, and I longed to get my life and my family back. Hatred like his would not disappear any time soon.

Meanwhile, the passion and the energy spilling from my husband's rage was infectious and arousing. An unceasing tingling began around my pelvis, and the more animalistic Tony became, the more primal I felt. I craved him, I lusted after him, I wanted him inside me.

'He told me he was going to drown Henry,' I said, clutching our son tighter.

'I wouldn't . . .' Johnny began, but again, he didn't get to finish. Tony had hold of the back of Johnny's hair, yanked his head upwards and slammed it back onto the path. Despite the dimming light, I could still make out his irises as they fluttered towards the back of his head, leaving milky white orbs in their place.

My stomach felt as if it was riding a rollercoaster, rising quickly and anxiously anticipating the descent. Tony had someone's life in his hands and he was about to make the single most important decision that could alter everything. I clenched my fists into tight balls and with all my might I willed him to take that next, crucial step.

I'd never felt closer to – or more in love with – my husband as I was in the moment when he killed Johnny.

CHAPTER FIVE

LAURA – TWO MONTHS AFTER JOHNNY

I sat in my office hunched over a keyboard, glaring at a spreadsheet on the monitor, trying to make sense of next month's work rota. With ninety-four volunteers all requesting hours that didn't include the middle of the night, it was no mean feat trying to accommodate everyone's wishes.

I glanced out from the open door of my office and across the room at the afternoon team. Kevin, Sanjay, Zoe and Joella sat in their booths, half of them on calls and the rest filling their downtime reading Kindles and magazines.

It had been more than a week since I'd last found time to join them in the trenches, and I was badly missing the anticipation of the next call. I'd been so busy and much more cautious since the whole Ryan and Johnny debacles, but now I was itching to find a new candidate. However, since the powers that be in our head office had offered me Janine's job as branch manager, much of my time was taken up by tiresome administrative tasks.

My lips curled into a smile as I sat in Janine's former seat, my elbows on her desk, distracting myself from rotas by picking out stubborn crumbs of gluten-free biscuits from her keyboard with eyebrow tweezers. If she could see me now, she'd be turning in the grave I'd sent her to.

The spotlight had been shining upon my branch brighter than it ever had before, and none of it for positive reasons. First came Janine's murder on the premises, and then head office's humiliation at discovering she'd shifted money from the charity's accounts into her own and to an account she held for a gambling website. When the internal investigation began, the theft became public knowledge thanks to an 'anonymous' whistleblower. And soon, the eponymous plaque erected in her name was quietly unscrewed from the wall outside. With her reputation tarnished, I'd disposed of it myself.

End of the Line had lost the public's trust and so calls to it fell sharply, along with local donations. So it was the sensible decision to ask me to take charge. I was the brave volunteer who'd survived two attacks from unhinged brothers who'd also targeted my daughter and disabled son. And in publicly forgiving them, my selflessness had made me the face of the charity and garnered it positive press.

The rest of the team were elated by my promotion, including Mary, our oldest volunteer and my former mentor. I'd informed her by phone, as she'd yet to return to the office following the shock of finding Janine's body. She still blamed herself for failing to prevent the murder and for not monitoring Ryan's fateful visit from the video room, even though it was me who'd told her he was Janine's friend. I was quite happy to let her carry the burden of guilt for as long as she required.

The alarm sounded on my phone to remind me that my day there was coming to an end. An hour and a half later and I was walking up the street towards the house, recycling bags crammed with groceries and the handles digging into the palms of my hands.

Sometimes I'd catch myself absent-mindedly looking around the street, hoping to see Nate. He'd always felt intimidated by Tony, so rather than ring the doorbell, he'd hover for hours, waiting for me to enter or leave the house. I missed him, but Johnny's words continued to haunt me.

I had been so sure that Nate and David were two completely different people – until now, because when I gave it more thought, their voices were the same and their circumstances similar. David had lost all hope when his wife had been killed by three men who broke into their house; Nate's mum had died at his hands while three men she'd sold our bodies to hovered at the doorway. Or was that a lie, too? Had I remembered my life under Sylvia's roof as different to the way it had actually been?

Perhaps my memory had been playing tricks on me lately again, creating mixed-up images and snapshots of what I thought to be true. I suddenly recalled a buried memory from a year and a half earlier, of a conversation I'd had with Nate. He'd had enough, he told me, he had no fight left in him, and while he'd said the same thing many times before, I knew this time he meant it. He wanted my help to die but he was afraid and didn't want to go alone, which is when Charlotte came into the picture.

Then I remembered the last day I ever saw him, when Nate came to the house to bathe and I helped to clean him up. I'd put him in an old suit and shirt of Tony's, handed him a pay-as-you-go mobile phone and gave him enough cash to get a train ticket to East Sussex and a taxi. He looked so handsome.

Then I saw myself standing alone by a bus stop outside Chantelle's funeral and then outside a hospital ward arguing with a doctor about a patient who hadn't been admitted. That was why I hadn't been to David's funeral. It wasn't because I was too sad to face it, it was because he had never existed.

A moped's horn brought me back to reality and I found myself standing still in the middle of the road. A cold sweat rushed across my body and I hurried to the safety of my house.

'Hello?' I shouted, taking deep, calming breaths as I pushed open the front door and pulled the key from the lock. 'Is anyone around to give me a hand unpacking the shopping?'

The mention of shopping bags wasn't the best way to lure two children and a husband into the porch. Nevertheless, Alice appeared, carrying that bloody cat under her arm like a furry clutch bag. The anticipation of being reunited with Bieber had been one of the reasons why she couldn't wait to move back in. Neither of Tony's two rental houses had allowed pets and she'd missed him.

'Where's your sister?' I asked as we carried the bags to the kitchen.

'She's still upstairs with Mrs Hopkinson. I won't have to be home-schooled when I'm her age, will I?' She dropped the cat to the floor and it hissed at me before strutting out of the room. One day, a canal and a bag of bricks would wipe that entitled look from its face.

'I don't think so, darling. If you don't make stupid decisions like Effie then there'll be no reason for us to take you out of school and hire a private tutor.'

Reassured by my answer, she began stacking the shelves with cans of vegetables and soups with military precision.

'Labels showing,' I reminded her. 'Is your dad home yet?'

'Uh-huh.' She pointed towards the garden. 'Why does he look so sad all the time?'

I spotted Tony, his arms outstretched and his palms flat upon the waist-high garden fence posts. He was staring into the distance across the playing fields. It was a common sight since my family had returned, as if he were wishing himself a million miles away from where he was now. I told myself he wouldn't be like this forever, but as time marched on, my doubts began.

I'd hoped that ending another person's life might have given us a common thread to bind us together, but we'd yet to reconnect. He remained repulsed by killing Johnny, while I'd never been prouder of him for protecting Henry and me. He'd shown me that, deep down, he would do anything for the people he loved.

I called to mind an image of Tony, two months earlier, standing over Johnny's lifeless body and rolling him over so he was face up. I remembered how Tony's expression had changed from pure rage to confusion when he realised the cut, bleeding, battered man wasn't who he'd thought it was. Panic spread through him and he looked to me for an explanation.

'You said it was Ryan,' he began, eyebrows arched and forehead wrinkled.

'It doesn't matter who it is,' I replied bluntly. 'He was threatening to hurt us.'

'But I've killed him! What did you let me do?'

'It was self-defence. You were saving your family.'

Tony's adrenaline was dissolving, leaving his arms weak and unsteady. I held them firm in my hands. His shirtsleeves and cuffs were smeared with Johnny's blood.

'Look at me, Tony. I will tell the police what Ryan's brother was trying to do before you came. I'll stand up for you. I'm your wife. I won't let anything happen to you for trying to protect us.'

I helped him to a nearby bench, where he sat and held his head in his shaking hands as I called the police. Soon after, Johnny's body was driven away in an ambulance and Tony was arrested on suspicion of murder and taken to the police station to be questioned. After being treated for shock, which I feigned, I accompanied a still-terrified Henry back to his room where he was calmed by staff and put to bed.

Then it was my turn to face a police grilling. Twice I left the interview to be sick as I recounted the horrors of the evening. By the time I was allowed to leave, there could be little doubt in their minds that Johnny had been threatening me and Henry in revenge for the death of his brother. It was Tony's and my word against the actions of a dead man.

Alone in the interview room, I thanked God that I'd sent my husband an email before I'd left the house saying that I couldn't wait to see him with Henry. The message, plus the others I'd sent that week claiming Henry was ill, had concerned and confused him enough to turn up at the care home. If he hadn't found me, I hate to think what evidence Johnny might have recorded to use against me. I made a mental note to take flowers to his funeral like I had to Ryan's, only this time the card would read *I won again.*

As Tony remained in custody overnight, the police brought our scared and perplexed daughters back to the family home for the first time in almost two and a half years. I gently explained the abridged version of what had happened and how brave their father had been.

Alice bought into it immediately and sought my reassurance our family was now safe. Effie knew when something didn't add up. However, she was wise enough not to question me. She hadn't admitted to seeking out Johnny after his brother's funeral and spilling my secrets to him, and I wasn't going to reveal that I knew. I let her wind herself up wondering instead. But if she ever brought up her gut-wrenching betrayal, I'd make it clear that along with her teacher's blood, she now had his brother's on her hands.

On Tony's release the next evening, his explanation mirrored mine and I watched with quiet delight as the high regard Effie held him in crumbled. For the first time in her life, she knew he'd lied to her. Now Tony and I shared a level playing field where our daughters were concerned.

'What did you tell the police?' I asked him when the girls had gone to their newly decorated bedrooms, leaving us alone. He'd become a shadow, sitting in the near darkness of the dining room.

'What you told me to say, that I was trying to protect you.'

'And did they believe you?'

'My solicitor says they'll probably accept it wasn't murder, but they're investigating whether I used unreasonable force. I could still face a manslaughter charge.'

I regarded my broken husband and wondered how long it might take before I could repair him. He turned his head to look at me, but I couldn't see his eyes. His voice was emotionless and detached.

'Why did you want me to kill an innocent man?'

I shook my head. 'I don't know what—'

'No,' Tony interrupted. 'Don't do that. Treat me with respect.'

'How much respect did you show me when you told Ryan about that social services psychiatric report?' He didn't reply. 'Johnny was by no means innocent,' I continued, 'and he was trying to make me admit to things I didn't do. He was as hateful as his brother.'

'What did he want you to admit to?'

'It doesn't matter now.'

'You made me a murderer. I have the right to know why.'

I considered unspooling like a reel of cotton until I was laid bare across the floor, admitting everything he wanted to know and more. I contemplated telling him how I'd encouraged Charlotte and many others to die, how I'd set up Ryan with the help of Effie, and even that I'd killed Janine. But the thought vanished as quickly as it appeared.

I turned towards the kitchen and flicked on the spotlights to illuminate the worktops. 'Right, you must be hungry. Let's see what I can rustle up, shall we?'

I removed a shrink-wrapped sirloin steak from the fridge and put some microwaveable potato wedges into a bowl.

'Do you know why I think I was confused about you moving out?' I continued. 'Because you kept coming back to the house when I wasn't here. I'd find a coffee mug I hadn't used in the dishwasher, a pile of mail that I'd left in order of size that had been shifted around, and the bedroom doors closed. If you didn't love me or want our life anymore, then you wouldn't have kept returning. So I think I must have told myself you and the girls weren't really gone. It's funny how the brain can play tricks on you, isn't it?'

'I was returning to find the evidence you have of the End of the Line donations that we used to set up the business. I didn't want you holding that over me anymore. You know I paid it back in donations of my own once we started making money.'

'Well, that doesn't matter now, does it, because we're all back together.'

Behind me, the legs of Tony's chair slid backwards. His tone was deliberate and measured.

'If you think I'm going to spend a second longer under this roof with you, then you are deluded, Laura. I'm taking the girls and we're leaving.'

I shook my head. 'No, you're not, Tony. We're back together now as a family – as we should be – and none of you are leaving this house.'

He gave a forced laugh. 'And what would ever make me want to stay here?'

'How about this? Because when you beat the wrong man to death, he was trying to video-record a confession from me. And when his phone fell to the ground, it continued to record until after you ended his life and I pressed stop. I now have that phone in my possession with footage that proves you weren't just trying to protect us, you'd lost control and thought you were getting revenge on a man who molested our daughter and duped you into spilling my secrets. When you heard that recording of Effie and him online, you were angry and ashamed of yourself. So if you leave me again or try to take the girls away from me – I will hate myself for it, but I will hand that phone to the police. There will be no doubt in their minds that you used unreasonable force and you will go to prison. And even if your daughters still want anything to do with you, they'll only be able to visit for an hour every two weeks – provided I give them permission, which I doubt I'll do. The rest of the time, they'll spend here with me. Just me. Effie is already ruined, and the same will happen to Alice once her friends find out their father is a murderer. Is that what you want, Tony? Because I don't think it is. So I am asking you not to make me do this.'

He paled and blinked hard as his brain registered my words. Suddenly he lurched towards me from across the room; my arms covered my face and chest to protect myself and he pinned me to the fridge. He wrapped his hands around my throat and pushed into my windpipe. I struggled to breathe, like Janine when I'd hit her in the throat. At that moment, she'd been terrified of me, only I wasn't terrified of Tony. They say you only hurt the ones you love, so he must still have feelings for me. I didn't put up any fight.

'Go on then,' I urged, my voice a rasp. 'Kill me with your daughters upstairs. You've seen what being in care did to me, and that's just what'll happen to them.'

I could feel the heat of his breath on my cheeks, but despite what he wanted to do to me, he couldn't bring himself to carry it out. His satisfaction at the thought of killing me wasn't as great as his love for his girls.

I gritted my teeth and my heart was racing. He let go and stepped backwards while I clutched my neck and pulled myself together.

'So,' I continued eventually, 'is steak and chips okay? I've got a packet of peppercorn sauce somewhere.'

He shrank back to his chair in the dining room, a beaten man.

Later, I decided to give Tony a grace period of a couple of weeks before suggesting it might be in his best interests to move out of the spare room and back into my bed. But even sleeping next to each other didn't bring us closer.

Over the next two months I did everything in my power to make our transition into a proper family a successful one. Fortunately, Alice wasn't old enough to know the sort of person her mother really was, and appeared oblivious to the hostility Effie was showing towards me. I sensed Effie's frustration at not being able to admit the truth to her sister or her dad without dropping herself in it. Likewise, Tony couldn't admit to anyone that he'd murdered a man in a blind rage. I was the keeper of all their secrets. I had plenty of my own, including the spot in the field behind the house where I'd buried a sealed Tupperware box containing Johnny's phone and Tony's gloves and running shoes, the ones I'd worn when I'd bludgeoned Janine. I hoped never to need them, but an insurance policy did no harm.

In the search for a new normality, I instigated Sunday as 'family day'. We'd begin by visiting Henry in the morning, followed by a drive to a countryside pub for a roast beef and Yorkshire pudding lunch. The afternoon would be spent sprawled out across the sofas watching a DVD.

At first it didn't matter that Alice and I were the only ones outwardly enjoying this time, but gradually it began to grate on me. My husband was still far from being the Tony of old I loved. The Crown Prosecution Service had yet to decide whether to press any charges against Tony and it played heavily on his mind. He no longer worked overtime or went to the gym, and when he returned home from work each night, he barely let the girls out of his sight. It was as if he feared something – or someone – might influence them in a way he didn't approve of if they weren't under his supervision.

'You can trust me,' I told him. 'You know I'd never do anything to hurt them.' He responded with silence.

Now, as Alice unpacked groceries in the kitchen, I watched Tony in the garden alone, a haunted man pinching his eyes and shaking his head. I observed for the first time how much weight he'd lost. His once-broad shoulders were rounded and his muscular frame more angular. Seeing my strong, energetic husband so weak and unattractive frustrated me. I'd been waiting so long for his return, but my patience wasn't infinite. He was becoming as meaningless as my father after my mother's death.

If things aren't going to get any better for him, I might need to reassess our situation.

The thought came out of the blue. I wanted to dismiss it, even told myself off for thinking it. But then, like thoughts do, it expanded to another until it spiralled into a full-on conversation in my head.

There is always a way out of his suffering. Who better to help him than you?

Tony was the last thing I wanted to lose from my life, but he wasn't the man I'd married.

Don't rush into a decision yet. Just know that the next candidate might be closer to you than you thought.

I was beginning to wonder if I'd always be the one to suffer, so other people didn't have to.

I was about to join Tony in the garden when my phone vibrated. An email icon appeared on the screen. There was nothing in the subject line, but the address gave me a chill. JanineThomson@gmail.com

I hurried into the garage for privacy and opened the message. Only three words had been typed.

More to follow, it said.

'More to follow?' I said out loud. What did that even mean? I was about to delete it when I noticed the email had an attachment, a sound file.

The fluorescent lightbulb above me began to flicker like a Morse-code light show. I waited anxiously for the file to download, wondering what on earth it could be. Nothing could have prepared me for the answer.

'*I'll do it*,' I heard a recording of my voice say. '*If you are serious about wanting to end your life, then I will be with you in person when you do it. I will be on your side from the beginning to the end of this process, but this is a business relationship. We both have our parts to play, Steven. Yours is to tell me who you are and mine is to ensure your transition is a smooth one.*'

The phone slipped from my grasp and fell to the floor. The protective plastic case prevented the screen from cracking, and I scrambled to pick it up and listen to it again. Were my ears playing tricks on me? Was I imagining this? I pressed play again. No, it was for real.

Blood filled my head and made me woozy. I felt as if I were rocking back and forth, but my body wasn't moving. I feared I might collapse, so I grabbed hold of a shelf too hard, pulling it from its wall brackets and sending it crashing to the floor. Paint spilled across the concrete like lava, splashing my shoes and bare legs. I needed to calm myself, but I couldn't. This clip had the potential to destroy everything I had spent so long working towards.

I had deleted every file from that Dictaphone, so where in God's name had this come from? And why today, five months later?

Think, Laura, think. There must be a way out of this.

Only there wasn't.

In the blink of an eye, somebody else had taken control of me.

What do you want? I replied, and pressed the send button. Ten anxious minutes passed and still there was no response. I struggled to breathe, as if I were having a panic attack.

Anchor, Laura, I told myself. *Think of your anchor.*

I closed my eyes as tightly as I could and pictured Henry's face, but not even he could keep me tethered this time. I held my hands over my mouth, bent double and screamed until my throat was raw.

EPILOGUE

EFFIE

I watched upstairs from behind the blind in my bedroom window as Dad stood at the end of the garden, alone and lost in thought.

Once again, he was staring aimlessly across the playing fields, like he wanted to be anywhere but trapped in this prison we were supposed to accept as our home. I couldn't remember the last time he'd given us one of his big beaming smiles that made everyone around him feel warm and fuzzy. Nowadays he looked as miserable as I felt. Mum had done this to him. She had turned him into a ghost I scarcely recognised.

I couldn't bear to see him like this any longer. It was time to set the wheels in motion and put an end to this, before she killed him. I attached the file stored in my Cloud to the email and hit the send button.

I lay back on my bed, slipped my noise-cancelling headphones on and picked a Best of R & B playlist on Spotify to listen to. What I really wanted to do was creep downstairs and watch Mum completely freak out over why a dead woman was emailing her clips of a conversation she'd had months ago with a dead man. I wanted to see how long she could hold it together before she cracked. It had happened before, when she went schiz over Henry. I hoped she wouldn't fall apart immediately, though – I wanted her to suffer. I wanted to make her life as hellish as mine and Dad's.

I missed living with just Dad and Alice. Everything had been so much easier without Mum in the picture. It hadn't always been that way. In fact, at the start, it had been hard to accept, especially for Alice. Before Mum's sudden reappearance, the last we'd seen of her was Dad holding her back as two paramedics resuscitated my unconscious brother on a trolley. Mum was hysterical, screaming and with spit flying from her mouth like little white bullets.

'I've killed him! I've killed my baby!' she kept repeating, and made deep, horrible moaning noises I'd never heard anyone make before. I guess that's the kind of shit that happens when you almost burn your son alive. Anyway, in the end she was sedated and driven away in an ambulance.

Alice and I stayed the night with an elderly couple across the road. They kept offering us drinks and snacks, as if that would make everything okay. They put up two camp beds in their spare room, but at some point during the night, Alice crept under my covers and welded herself to me.

'Are we going to die in a fire, too?' she asked, but I couldn't truthfully tell her that we weren't.

Over the next few days, Dad's eyes became redder and redder, and while Mum remained in a psychiatric evaluation unit, Henry came out of his coma and we were told it was unlikely he'd ever be the brother we remembered. At Dad's suggestion, Alice and I didn't visit Henry or Mum.

To give him credit, Dad treated us like adults and levelled with us about what Mum had done. He explained that she'd confessed to starting the fire because she blamed the house for all the arguments they'd been having. But she didn't know Henry was upstairs and Dad had yet to tell the police.

I was much more of a daddy's girl than a mummy's girl, but I still hated the thought of Mum going to prison for what had been an accident – albeit a pretty fucking major one. Eventually we agreed it was best if Dad lied to the police and said Henry had a fascination with matches. In return, Dad didn't want us to go anywhere near Mum, and we agreed not to have anything to do with her until we were older.

Everything changed after that. We moved house and I moved schools. We changed phone numbers and left behind everything and everyone that was smoke-damaged.

I think I missed the idea of having a mum more than her actual presence. She was never one of those hands-on parents like Dad was, so Alice and I learned pretty early on not to expect a lot from her. Sometimes she looked at us as if she wasn't quite sure how we'd landed in her world. Not Henry, though. She worshipped him. I loved him, too. He was sweet and funny and he was always trying to make me and Alice laugh with a silly dance or funny face. Now, by all accounts, he was little more than a vegetable.

We adapted from being a family of five to a family of three fairly well. In my last school, I'd seen how Farzana Singh had been relentlessly picked on when her mum came off her bipolar meds and started dancing Bollywood-style during parents' evening. I wasn't going to let that happen to me in my new school. So from day one I went in there all guns blazing, cocky and confident, and I surrounded myself with like-minded bitches. I told them Mum had remarried and moved to Australia, but all the time that I ruled those corridors, I was just waiting to be unmasked.

I wasn't sure about Janine when Dad started seeing her. I'd heard so many horror stories from my friends about how their parents' new partners totally messed with the family dynamic, and I didn't want Janine doing that to us. But she didn't try to fill Mum's shoes and she actually wanted to spend time with us, which is more than Mum ever did. I knew Janine volunteered with Mum at End of the Line, but not once did Alice or I ask how she was. We rarely even spoke of her between ourselves. Janine tried to bring her up a few times, but she changed the subject when it became obvious we weren't comfortable with the conversation. I overheard Dad talking to Janine about Mum a couple of times, and a small part of me was curious whether Mum was better or had gone full-on Looney Tunes. But in the end, it was easier not to think about her than to remember what she'd done to Henry.

Then, after a two-year absence, Mum came crashing back into our lives without warning. I'll give her credit, she timed it well. I'd fallen pretty hard for my English teacher, Mr Smith, and I was sure the feeling was mutual, but then he did a one-eighty and totally blew me off. I was gutted and had no one to talk to – I'd lost so many friends when Matt spread it around I'd sent his naked selfie to his family and boss and he'd lost his job because of it. Then my grades suddenly turned to crap and I stopped caring.

I was cautious at first, because the mum I remembered wouldn't really have cared about what had happened with Mr Smith and me. But this all-improved, brand-new version of Mum was desperate to know everything that was going on in my life. I figured I should be able to trust her with anything.

I took a chance and told her what a fool I'd made of myself over my teacher. I thought she might tell me I'd probably got the wrong end of the stick and imagined he was interested in me, but she believed every word I said. She was convinced he was a paedo and had been grooming me. I didn't think he was, but I was so angry with him I played along and started exaggerating what had happened. I thought it was what she wanted to hear.

It surprised me how much I enjoyed having a mum in my life again and on my side, so when she came up with a plan to get back at Mr Smith, I was more than willing to go along with it. Then, gradually, I saw her change. It was as if, rather than just teaching Mr Smith a lesson, she got a thrill out of ruining his life. It was like revenge mattered more than I did. That didn't stop me from doing what she asked. I didn't even question her when she told me to steal a dead piglet from the school science freezer.

Then she gave me a memory stick and told me to transfer its files onto Mr Smith's work computer. That's when I started to get scared. Mum had told me not to open it, but curiosity got the better of me. There were dozens of pictures of young girls in school uniform on it, some with their tops off and others showing everything else. I knew in my gut that Mum had taken it to extremes and I should end it, there and then. But I didn't. I didn't want to disappoint her.

When Mum told me Mr Smith had been arrested for breaking into her house and threatening to kill her, I had a sick feeling in my stomach. Then, after we played Mr Atkinson the recording of Mr Smith apologising to me and he was kicked out, I knew this had all gone way too far. Mr Smith became the talk of the school, but nobody knew why he'd gone until the police turned up and took away his computer. Then the rumours started that he was a paedophile.

Had he molested someone at school? That's what everyone wanted to know. My name came up a few times. It was known I'd had one-on-one meetings with him about my falling marks. I denied it and, because of my reputation for taking no shit, they knew not to push me too far and left me alone.

Meanwhile, after their initial meeting, Dad agreed to let Alice stay in touch with Mum. At first just by text, and then finally he allowed them to spend an afternoon together. That was the day when, early in the evening, I caught Alice going through Janine's handbag while Janine was in the bath.

'Are you stealing?' I asked.

Alice glared at me, red-faced. 'No.'

'Then what are you doing?'

'I can't tell anyone. It's a secret.'

'Well, you'd better tell me or I'm telling Dad.'

'Mummy wants to borrow something from Janine,' Alice said reluctantly. 'This recording thing.'

She held up a Dictaphone.

'What does she want with it?'

'I don't know. I think she wants to play a trick on Janine. I'm going to give it to her at school in the morning, then she's going to give it back to me at lunchtime. I can put it back when I get home. Am I in trouble?'

'Not if you give it to me first.'

In my bedroom, I pressed play on the Dictaphone. I couldn't see why someone had recorded Mum talking on the phone at End of the Line. Then I realised who she was speaking to – it was Mr Smith, although he was calling himself Steven. I looked at the display: it had been recorded about ten months ago. And then I understood why Mum wanted to get her hands on it.

She was trying to talk him into dying.

I listened, part fascinated and part horrified by the things she said. Conversation after conversation: she agreed to watch him die, then began listing the best ways to do it . . . It was sickening. She was totally fucked up. I gradually understood that there'd been some kind of game between Mum and Mr Smith and they had both used me to get at each other.

I Bluetoothed all the files onto my laptop then handed Alice the Dictaphone to give to Mum. I told her not to listen to it and not to tell Mum I'd found her going through Janine's handbag. She promised. She's a good girl. An honest girl. My innocent little sister had no idea how important this recording was.

At first, I didn't know what to do with these recorded conversations now they were in my possession. I could only guess that Mr Smith had given them to Janine. She obviously knew what was on them, so maybe Dad did, too. I couldn't be sure.

But before I got the chance to ask him, Mum hung me out to dry: she posted all over social media my recording of Mr Smith apologising to me. By lunchtime, every kid at school thought I'd had sex with my English teacher. They started yelling words like 'slag', 'slut' and 'teacher's whore' at me in the corridor. I did my best to ignore it. Then, on the way home, a gang of boys from Year 11 cornered me in the park. They started grabbing my breasts and bum, saying I was 'easy'. I was terrified they were going to rape me. I broke free and ran home. I called Mum, screaming at her down the phone and crying, but she didn't even apologise. In fact, when I threatened to tell Dad what we'd done to Mr Smith, she warned me what would happen if I did. I nearly told her about the Dictaphone, but I bit my tongue. I was going to fight fire with fire. I vowed to ruin her like she'd ruined me.

Then, just when I thought that day couldn't get any worse, Dad came home early from work, tears streaming down his face. He was sobbing and it was a while before he could tell me what had happened. Janine had been killed at End of the Line and the police were hunting for Mr Smith.

I immediately had a horrible, gut-twisting feeling that Mum had played a role in this. And if she had, then so had I. I ran to the bathroom and couldn't stop being sick in the toilet. A day later, when Mr Smith killed himself, I had another death on my conscience.

I couldn't live with the guilt. I lost my appetite, I barely slept, I locked myself in my bedroom and wouldn't speak to anyone but Alice and Dad – certainly not to my bitch of a mother. I had no one to confide in. Mum and Mr Smith had used me, but I didn't think he was capable of murder. Mum, on the other hand, was capable of anything. I had to tell someone what I knew.

I remembered Mr Smith had a brother. I'd seen his photo on his phone when he gave me a lift home. So, after his funeral, I approached

Johnny Smith on Facebook and a few days later we met. Mr Smith had told him what he'd done to me, so Johnny wasn't as angry as I thought he'd be when I admitted, shamefully, the part I'd played in his brother's death. He asked me loads of questions about Mum and I told him everything, apart from about the Dictaphone conversations. I might need those myself. Once I'd given him enough background information on her and what she'd done to our family, I sat back and waited. Only I never heard from him again.

As time went on, I mellowed out a little and even thought about putting it all behind me. Mum was back out of our lives again, we'd moved house once more, I had a private tutor and Alice changed schools. We were no longer living in Mum's shadow.

But it all changed when the police arrived to tell us her and Dad had been involved in an incident at Henry's care home and someone had died. They were being questioned. The police let Mum go first, so she took us to our old house to stay with her.

Mum told us what had happened. Dad had been protecting her and Henry from Mr Smith's brother. She said Johnny had threatened to hurt Henry. It had all got out of hand, and in self-defence Dad had killed Johnny. Mum kept telling us Dad was a hero, but I knew there was more to her story than she was letting on. There always is.

Poor Alice couldn't get her head around what was happening and I held her hand as she cried. I swallowed hard to stop myself showing Mum any emotion and waited until Dad was released on police bail. I knew he would tell us the truth. Only he lied to us as well. I could tell, because he couldn't look either of us in the eye when he spoke, and his version was virtually word for word what Mum had said.

Later that night I sat on the landing at the top of the stairs, listening to them argue. Dad wanted to take Alice and me home, but Mum wouldn't let him. And she had video evidence that would ensure he'd end up in prison for what he'd done, even though she'd manipulated him into doing it. From the sound of it, he went to attack her, and I willed him with all my heart to kill her. But he wasn't like her. He had no choice but to stay and protect us from her.

Mum and Alice seemed happy we were all living back under one roof, but we were far from being a family. She was more maternal towards Alice than she'd ever been with me, but I wasn't stupid. She was only sinking her claws into my sister to get to me.

◆ ◆ ◆

Over the weeks, I watched as Dad slowly disintegrated before my eyes, and it was all because of Mum. I fucking hated her. For a long time I believed Mr Smith, Johnny and Janine were dead because of me. But eventually I realised it wasn't my fault – it was the woman who called herself my mother who was to blame. She manipulated us all, but she wasn't the only one who could make someone's life hell. Today was as good a day as any to start wiping that smug, satisfied look from her face.

I slipped off my headphones and checked the inbox of the email account I'd created. Mum had already replied to Janine Thomson's email asking what she wanted. The fun had only just begun.

I thought about replying, but hesitated. Instead, it would be more entertaining to drag this out for as long as possible. I was going to play with her like those killer whales you see in YouTube clips, tossing a seal into the air, catching it in its jaws, then spitting it out and doing it all over again before finally going in for the kill.

I'd send her another clip a few days from now, then another in a week or so. Maybe I'd start withholding my phone number and calling her, playing excerpts of her conversation with Ryan down the line.

I hoped her sanity would be the first thing to go, because then maybe she'd be locked up in that loony bin again and we'd be able to get out of this house. But if that didn't work, I'd make the recordings public and ruin her.

'You have to remember, Effie, you and I are cut from the same cloth,' she told me once. 'You are your mother's daughter. There is so much you can learn from me.'

She was right. I had learned from her.

And now it was time to start putting all those lessons into practice.

ACKNOWLEDGMENTS

First and foremost, thank you to John Russell for all your support during the writing of this and my other books. Your understanding and patience make this book business so much easier! And thank you for sitting guard outside the office to prevent me from being distracted too often. Thanks also to my mum, Pamela Marrs, for your constant encouragement.

I'd like to offer my appreciation to Chris James, who gave me the seed of an idea that became this book. Thank you for allowing me to pick your brains about what it means to be a helpline volunteer. Your input was invaluable.

Thanks to my early readers, Jim Ryan and Andrew Webber, and to the Queen of Grammar Kath Middleton for preventing me from making a fool of myself with draft one! Thanks to Rhian Molloy for your help with school-related formalities and to Rachael Molloy for preventing me from sounding like an old man when I was trying to write like a teenager. Also to Nicole Carmichael for your advice and support.

Thank you to Carole Watson for making me aware of the point at which this story could begin. I hope you enjoy what I did with the rest of it.

Thank you to Tracy Fenton for your support – and for your name – and all the thousand members of Facebook's THE Book Club. Your ongoing support continues to amaze and delight me and I look forward to continuing this journey with you all.

My gratitude also goes towards Jane Snelgrove at Thomas & Mercer for bringing me into the fold, to Jack Butler for his support and to Ian Pindar for his invaluable assistance in making Laura that little bit nastier.

Thanks to Margaret McCulloch-Keeble for assisting me in my journey around a mortuary, and Karen-Lee Roberts for her assistance with police procedural work. And also to my friend Lyndsay Wiles for helping me to understand how it feels being a parent to a child with special needs. You have no idea how much I admire you.

Laura is a work of fiction. But this book is dedicated to the millions of kind-hearted, good, good people around the world who dedicate their spare time to helping others – be it in person, via a telephone conversation or through an online messageboard. You are unsung heroes.

Finally, thank you to whoever you are, for purchasing this book. Whether you've been with me from the start or have only just found me, you have my utmost appreciation.

AUTHOR'S NOTE

There are more than 400 organisations across the world made up of voluntary members who offer their time to talk to people with suicidal feelings. For details of your nearest organisation, please visit www.befrienders.org.

ABOUT THE AUTHOR

Photo © 2017 Robert Gershinson

John Marrs is a freelance journalist based in London and Northampton. He has spent the past twenty-five years interviewing celebrities from the worlds of television, film and music for numerous national newspapers and magazines. *The Good Samaritan* is his fourth novel. Follow him on Twitter @johnmarrs1, on Instagram @johnmarrs.author and on Facebook at www.facebook.com/johnmarrsauthor.